A male Variant with a crooked back galloped down the sidewalk. It leaped over bloated corpses, flying through the air. Beckham shot it in the face with a movement so smooth it surprised him.

Five rounds left.

"Eyes! Who's got eyes on?" Beckham yelled frantically.

A smaller Variant charged him from the right and Beckham turned to fire. He jerked the barrel aside at the last second when he realized it was a child. The shot went wide, whistling past the creature's head. Beckham knew the thing racing toward him wasn't a boy. It was a monster. He took aim again and shot it between the eyes. The tiny Variant crashed to the ground, skidding across the pavement until it came to a rest in front of Beckham. He jumped over the corpse and pushed on.

Three rounds left.

"Jinx!" Beckham shouted.

Gunfire erupted from his six. Jensen and Chow took turns holding the Variants off their tail with short bursts.

"Come on!" Beckham stormed through the clogged street toward Eighth Avenue, where they had last seen Jinx.

Books by Nicholas Sansbury Smith

THE EXTINCTION CYCLE

Extinction Horizon
Extinction Edge
Extinction Age
Extinction Evolution
Extinction End
Extinction Aftermath
"Extinction Lost" (An Extinction Cycle Short Story)
Extinction War (Fall 2017)

TRACKERS: A POST-APOCALYPTIC EMP SERIES

Trackers
Trackers 2: The Hunted (Spring 2017)
Trackers 3: The Storm (Winter 2017)

THE HELL DIVERS TRILOGY

Hell Divers
Hell Divers 2: Ghosts
Hell Divers 3: Deliverance (Summer 2018)

THE ORBS SERIES

"Solar Storms" (An Orbs Prequel)
"White Sands" (An Orbs Prequel)
"Red Sands" (An Orbs Prequel)
Orbs
Orbs 2: Stranded
Orbs 3: Redemption

EXTINCTION AGE

The Extinction Cycle
Book Three

NICHOLAS SANSBURY SMITH

www.orbitbooks.net

Copyright © 2015 by Nicholas Sansbury Smith
Excerpt from *Extinction Evolution* copyright © 2015 by Nicholas Sansbury Smith
Excerpt from *The Remaining* copyright © 2012 by D. J. Molles

Cover design by Lisa Marie Pompilio
Cover art by Blake Morrow
Cover copyright © 2017 by Hachette Book Group, Inc.

Orbit
Hachette Book Group
1290 Avenue of the Americas
New York, NY 10104
orbitbooks.net

Previously self-published in 2015
Published in ebook by Orbit in February 2017
First Mass Market Edition: July 2017

Orbit is an imprint of Hachette Book Group.
The Orbit name and logo are trademarks of Little, Brown Book Group Limited.

The publisher is not responsible for websites (or their content) that are not owned by the publisher.

The Hachette Speakers Bureau provides a wide range of authors for speaking events. To find out more, go to www.hachettespeakersbureau.com or call (866) 376-6591.

ISBNs: 978-0-316-55805-1 (mass market), 978-0-316-55804-4 (ebook)

Printed in the United States of America

OPM

10 9 8 7 6 5 4 3 2

For Mom and Dad. Thank you for showing me what hard work is and for teaching me to never give up on my dreams.

"The world had seen so many Ages: the Age of Enlightenment; of Reformation; of Reason. Now, at last, the Age of Desire. And after this, an end to Ages; an end, perhaps, to everything."

—Clive Barker, *The Inhuman Condition*

1

The tunnels below Manhattan reeked of death, but Master Sergeant Reed Beckham blocked it out. Injured, rattled, and down to only his Beretta M9, his focus was on keeping his men alive.

He pulled his shemagh scarf up to cover his nose and burst around another corner, following the sound of clanking gear and labored breathing through the underground sewer system. Light danced across the green-hued view of his night-vision goggles and bent eerily in the darkness. The graffiti-covered walls seemed to narrow as he ran, the artwork distorting as if he were in some sort of carnival fun house.

Breathe, Beckham ordered himself. *Breathe.*

He ignored the burn in his lungs and concentrated on the six helmets that bobbed up and down ahead. The loyal soldiers had followed him into the tunnels to escape the firebombs and the Variants, but Beckham feared he had only delayed the inevitable for these brave men.

"Keep moving!" Staff Sergeant Jay Chow shouted. The Delta Force operator turned and waved Beckham forward.

An inhuman shriek answered, echoing in the enclosed space. The rapid clicking of joints followed as the Variants homed in on Team Ghost's location.

Beckham brushed against a wall and threw a glance over his shoulder. The creatures clung to the shadows, their diseased flesh glowing in the moonlight streaming through partially open manhole covers. They skittered across the walls just close enough to keep his team in view.

The monsters had transformed into perfect predators that could see in dim lighting, heal remarkably quickly, and move like insects. Dr. Kate Lovato called it evolution. Beckham called it natural selection. And with every passing second, the Variants grew stronger while the human population dwindled. Nature had selected the Variants.

Beckham had been there from day one, back in Building 8 when the virus that turned men into monsters first escaped. But even now, the sight of the Variants flooded him with raw fear. Adrenaline emptied into his system like a fast-release pill as he ran.

The creatures were testing him. Seeing how far they could approach before Team Ghost opened fire. He responded with a shot from his M9. Rock and dust exploded from a wall. The warning would only buy them a precious minute or two.

A sudden tremor rumbled through the tunnel. Fragments of concrete poured from the ceiling, showering the team with debris. The jets were making a second pass on Manhattan, firebombing Midtown.

Beckham thought of his brothers-in-arms and of Timothy and Jake, hoping to God they were all out of the kill zone. He shook the thought away as he bolted through a cloud of dust and ash, one hand shielding his face. He slopped through ankle-deep sewage and turned every hundred feet to fire off another shot.

A frantic voice broke through the chaos.

"Which way?"

"Left!" came a second voice.

"Right!" shouted another a second later.

Beckham could barely see the junction ahead. None of them had any idea where they were or where they were going. Entering the tunnels had been a last resort. Now, deep beneath the streets, Beckham's only plan was to keep moving.

"Left! Go left!" he yelled just as a second torrent of dull thuds hit the streets above. These explosions were closer, and the aftershock sent Beckham crashing into a wall. He braced himself with an elbow and whirled to fire at a trio of Variants darting across the ceiling. Two of them melted into the darkness, squawking in anger, but the third and largest creature dropped to all fours, its muscular limbs tearing through the water.

Beckham fired another shot and took off running. By the time he passed the next corner, his team was fifty feet ahead. Brad "Timbo" Timmins's bulky frame loomed in the darkness.

"Come on!" the Ranger huffed.

"I'm with you!" Beckham replied between raspy breaths. His earpiece crackled with static as he made up lost ground.

"You got a *plan*?" Lieutenant Colonel Ray Jensen asked.

Beckham couldn't lie. He was still trying to come up with a plan B. So far, running around in the maze of tunnels wasn't working.

"We're going to need to make a stand! Get these Variants off our ass!" Beckham finally shouted. "Ammo count!"

The replies trickled over the comm channel. Between the seven of them, they had a handful of mags for their primary weapons and only a couple of frag grenades. Several of his men were also down to sidearms.

Beckham searched the green oblivion of the tunnel

as he considered their options. This wasn't the first time he'd had his back to a wall. At Fort Bragg, Beckham and Horn had been down to their knives before Chow had showed up with the cavalry. But this time no one was going to ride in and save him. Team Ghost was on their own.

A croak echoed through the passage. Two more answered the call. The evil cries rattled his senses. He examined his vest for something useful, anything that might buy them some more time to escape. Two smoke bombs hung next to his remaining M67 grenade.

Out of desperation, he plucked one off and tossed it as far as he could. It landed in the water about a hundred feet away with a plop. Smoke hissed out of it a moment later.

"I'm right behind you," Beckham said into his mini-mic. The ceiling rumbled as jets swooped overhead for a third pass, drowning out his voice.

Command was hitting the Variants hard. After 1st Platoon had drawn them out of their lairs, General Kennor had likely ordered every available pilot in range to mount up. The flyboys were showering New York with hellfire and death. Beckham clenched his jaw—Kennor had used him, his men, and thousands of other soldiers as bait.

A shard of concrete slashed Beckham's arm, tearing him from his thoughts. A second piece clanked off his helmet so hard it threw him off balance. He dropped to a knee and raised his pistol toward the smoke. Moonlight from an open manhole bathed him in light. He flipped up his NVGs and squinted at the smoke.

"Move!" Timbo shouted.

"I'll catch up!" Beckham yelled back. He held his position and continued searching for the monsters. The swirling cloud quickly spread over the corridor. His heart thumped as he waited. Seconds ticked by. Five. Ten. The footsteps of his team splashed through the water, gradually fading.

A flash of motion broke through the curtain of smoke. A colossal Variant lingered at the edge of the barrier. It tilted its head, yellow eyes blinking as it searched for Beckham.

He fired on reflex, his trigger finger responding to the stab of fear with three shots. The rounds punched into the thick Variant's sweaty chest, jerking it from side to side. It let out a roar and leaped to the wall.

Beckham fired off two more shots. One clipped the Variant's cranium, blowing off an ear and a piece of skull. That only enraged the monster. It clambered across the bricks, closing the gap between it and Beckham. He could smell it now. The sour stench of rotting fruit carried over the putrid sewage.

"What the hell are you—" Chow started to say over the comm when Beckham's gunfire silenced him. He fired again and again, but the monster's thick muscles seemed to absorb the bullets. The high-pitched screeches and the popping joints of other Variants echoed through the tunnel in between gunshots.

Beckham knew what came next.

Fatigue had screwed with his senses. He should have known the smoke wouldn't cover their escape—should have known his bullets wouldn't stop them. Without thinking, he reached for his last grenade, bit off the pin, and tossed it at the beast of a Variant that was now only fifty feet away.

"Frag out!" Beckham shouted.

He turned to run when something knocked him onto his back in the water. There was no time to react, no time to call for help or curse the fact he hadn't seen the other Variant stalking him through the manhole above.

There was only a fraction of a second to whip his head away from the Variant's open maw.

The beast pushed against Beckham's chest, forcing him below the rancid water. Stars broke across his vision as he battled his way to the surface. A realization hit him then. He had four, maybe five seconds before the grenade exploded. The timer counted down in his mind as he fought.

Five seconds.

Beckham clamped a hand around the creature's thick neck while flailing for his pistol with the other. He came up empty, the weapon lost in the muck.

Another second passed. He panicked, knowing he was well within the kill radius of the grenade. In a final desperate attempt to escape the monster, he reached for his knife. He jammed the blade into the open mouth of the Variant. Teeth shattered as he plunged the tip into its brain with a wet *thunk*.

A gurgling croak escaped the monster's swollen lips before it went limp. The deadweight pushed Beckham down, forcing him beneath the water again. He heard a muddled voice as he struggled back to the surface.

"Beckham! Hold on! I'm com—"

The words vanished in an explosion. Shrapnel whistled through the tunnel, tearing into the flesh of the corpse on top of him. A piece bit into Beckham's exposed right shoulder. He winced from the raw heat and felt his right arm turn numb. Pinned down, he was forced to watch helplessly as fissures broke across the ceiling. Chunks fell from the network of cracks into the foul water.

He squirmed under the dead Variant as it pushed him back under the surface, but his right arm was out of commission. The corpse had saved him from the blast only to suffocate him beneath the water.

Red flooded his vision and a memory of the night he

spent with Kate floated into his mind. It disappeared into a flashback of Building 8 and the members of Team Ghost who had never made it out.

The memories gnawed at his mind as his lungs groped for oxygen. Darkness slowly replaced the red. His body was numb now. So numb he could hardly feel the weight of the Variant roll off him. His eyes snapped open as someone grabbed his flak jacket and hauled him from the water.

A voice, distorted by the dull ringing in Beckham's ears, called out for him.

"Beckham! You with me, man?"

"Yeah," Beckham managed to say. He was still alive, but he knew he was in bad shape. His shoulder burned like someone had dumped battery acid on it, and his lungs felt like they'd been crushed. He squinted to focus on the face hovering over him.

Fingers snapped in front of Beckham's eyes. His vision slowly cleared to the sight of Chow looking him up and down for injuries.

Beckham took in deep breaths and coughed up lungs full of sewage water. The burn of stomach acid ate at his throat. He ran his tongue over slimy teeth and spat into the muck.

"You okay?" someone else asked.

Beckham could hardly hear anything over the rush of blood singing in his ears. He sat there for a few minutes as the world slowly returned to normal.

"We need to get moving," another voice said.

Beckham flipped his NVGs back into position. Smoke and dust whirled through the tunnel behind Chow, Jensen, and Timbo. He twisted to see Staff Sergeant Drew "Jinx" Abbas, Corporal Gerard Ryan, and Platoon Sergeant Vince Valdez holding security on their rear guard.

"You good, man?" Chow asked.

"Everything but my right shoulder," Beckham said. "Got nicked by some shrapnel."

"Help him up," Chow ordered. "And be careful."

Beckham grimaced as Timbo bent down, grabbed him under the armpits, and hoisted him to his feet. The other men formed a perimeter around him, like a legion of knights protecting a fallen warrior.

"You're one crazy son of a bitch," Jensen said as he stared at the destruction.

"Had to hold them," Beckham said.

"Yeah," Jensen said. "Looks like you did."

"For now," Beckham added. He applied pressure to his wound and scanned the dissipating smoke one more time for movement. Nothing stirred. The Variants had been reduced to scattered chunks of gore.

"Let's move out," Beckham said. He was light-headed, but they had to keep moving.

"Hold up, man. Let me look at your shoulder," Chow said.

"It can wait," Beckham said. "Someone give me a gun. I lost mine in the blast."

Jensen handed him a revolver. Beckham flipped open the cylinder of the Colt .45 and counted the six hollow-tipped cartridges.

"That's my girl," Jensen said. "She ain't no peacemaker, and I want her back."

Beckham knew the lieutenant colonel was sizing him up, seeing if he was fit to fight. If he were in Jensen's shoes, he would be doing the same thing.

"On me," Beckham said. He didn't give his men a chance to protest. He strode through the group and led them away from the carnage, blood still dripping from his shoulder.

Ringing followed him through the tunnels, singing in

his ears. He lost track of time in the rancid, damp network of storm drains and sewers.

The next corridor widened and curved into a larger passage with brick platforms on both sides. Beckham jumped onto the right ledge and hugged the wall, happy to be out of the shit. Jensen and Jinx hurried across the platform on the left, Timbo close on their six.

Beckham pressed down on his wound. If he made it out of this, he was going to need stitches and some powerful antibiotics to combat sepsis. The injury blazed bright red from the bacteria that had already entered his system.

"You got eyes?" Chow asked.

"Looks clear," Beckham replied.

There was no sign of Variants or other threats in the tunnel. For the first time in hours, Beckham could make out the trickle of water. The ringing from the grenade was still fading, but the air force had finally finished its bombardment.

As the team worked forward, the trickle intensified into a steady stream. Falls cascaded in the distance. The shades of green folded into darkness, the end of the tunnel transforming into a cavernous room that seemed to be set lower than the tunnel they were in. Beckham slowed as he approached a waterfall of sewage spilling over the edge into the massive room.

He formed a fist with his hand and then pointed to his eyes and then at the drop-off. Jensen and Timbo acknowledged with nods and eased into a stealthy formation on the left platform.

"Let me bandage you up," Chow whispered. He squeezed by Beckham and crouched in front of him. "How you feeling, man?"

"Dizzy," Beckham replied. A random star floated across his vision.

"You've lost some blood," Chow said. He reached into his pack and pulled out a small medical box. Then he leaned in and flipped his NVGs, using what little light the tunnel behind them provided for a better view.

"Looks deep," Chow said.

"Feels..." Beckham shook his head. He caught a glimpse of Timbo walking closer to the ledge.

Chow cut away a piece of Beckham's shirt and dressed the wound with antiseptic. The cold gel burned its way into his shoulder, and Beckham gritted his teeth. He closed his eyes and waited for the agony to pass. Chow applied a bandage over the injury.

"Should stop the bleeding," Chow said. "But we need—"

Timbo's voice flickered over the comm, cutting Chow off.

"Holy...Holy FUCK!"

Beckham's eyes flipped open. The Ranger was crouched at the end of the left platform, peering over the side. In a blink of an eye, he stumbled away and fell on his ass, scrambling backward.

"Contacts?" Beckham said, his heart kicking. He pulled away from Chow and walked slowly to the edge of the tunnel.

Timbo didn't immediately reply. His gasps crackled across the comm channel as he scrambled away.

"What the fuck did you see?" Beckham asked.

"I...I..." The shock in Timbo's voice gave Beckham pause. He'd never heard the man so terrified.

Beckham inched closer to the ledge with Chow as a shadow. Together they crouched and looked over the side. The image his eyes relayed to his brain went unprocessed. It had to be a trick of the light, a mirage. An illusion fired off by his overtired brain. Or at least, that's what he wanted it to be. A moment passed like a year.

This was no illusion.

This was real.

A half dozen other tunnels dumped into a central chamber, feeding a pool of sewage below. The walls and ceiling of the massive room were covered with hundreds of human prisoners, their bodies plastered to the walls with thick vines of webbing that crisscrossed their flesh like bloated veins. Some were mutilated beyond recognition. Others were missing limbs.

Variants crawled across the walls, their backs hunched, clinging to the bricks with talons and the hairlike fibers Kate's team had discovered. One of them clawed its way through the sticky film covering an unconscious man. His eyes shot open when the creature clamped down on his stomach and ripped into his flesh. He screamed, but his voice was quickly lost in the roar of the waterfall.

"Let's go," Chow whispered.

Beckham swallowed, unable to formulate a response. He backed away from the ledge only to see a woman attached to the wall on his right. Her eyes met his and she reached out with a trembling hand.

"Please. Please help me," she whispered, her lips trembling.

Beckham brought a finger to his mouth, but it was already too late. Their whispers had attracted the nearest creature. It let out a high-pitched scream that made Beckham's heart kick. The clicking of joints and the scratching of claws followed as the sleeping Variants stirred and searched the darkness.

"We need to move," Chow said. "Now, man."

Footsteps pounded the platforms as the team retreated, but Beckham hesitated. His eyes shifted from the prisoner to the Variants racing across the ceiling.

"Please," the woman cried. "Please don't leave me."

Beckham threw a glance over his shoulder. The other men were halfway down the hall. Only Chow remained.

"Come on," he said, waving frantically.

"No," Beckham said. "Help me." He wasn't going to leave someone behind. Not when she was in arm's reach.

Chow hustled over without further hesitation. "You're fucking crazy."

"Hold my belt," Beckham said. He drew his knife and crouched, using the blade to cut away the sticky vines across the woman's feet and legs. When those were free, he slit through the webbing across her stomach and chest. Her body sagged forward, but Chow grabbed her before she plummeted into the water below. He pulled her to safety and she collapsed to the ground in a CBRN suit. Beckham bent down to help her when he saw the deep gashes on her legs beneath the torn suit.

"You're going to be okay," Beckham assured her, hoping it wasn't a lie. He caught a glimpse of the Variants charging across the ceiling and walls. They were close now. Seconds away.

"Beckham, Chow, where the hell are you?" Jensen said over the comm.

"On our way," Beckham replied. He grabbed the two grenades off Chow's vest and considered what he was about to do. The decision took only a split second. If he couldn't save the mutilated captives, he was going to make sure they didn't suffer any longer.

"Get her out of here," Beckham said. "I'm right behind you."

Chow looked at him and nodded. The woman moaned in agony as he bent down and scooped her up.

Beckham cradled the grenades in one arm and fired off a flurry of well-aimed shots with the Colt .45 to buy him a few seconds. When the Variants scattered, he jammed the pistol into his belt and plucked the pin off one of the grenades with his teeth. He launched it into the air with his good arm and watched it stick to the webbing of a prisoner. Then he pulled the pin off the second grenade and tossed it over his shoulder as he ran.

Steam surrounded Dr. Kate Lovato in the shower stall.

"It's hot," Jenny whimpered in the adjacent stall.

"Do you girls need help?" Kate asked.

"No," Tasha, Jenny's protective older sister, said. "We're okay."

Kate took in a breath and stepped under the showerhead. Bringing a hand to her face, she wiped away the sticky blood caked on her skin. For a moment the water turned scarlet at her feet as it swirled around the shower drain.

The horror of the past three weeks surfaced under the warm flow of water. Everything she'd lost. Every*one* she'd lost. It all came crashing down. Guilt ate at her as she stood there—yet deep down she was also relieved. She was still breathing, still alive. And a part of her believed Beckham was still alive too.

Kate had to believe it. Hope was the only thing that would keep her working. The survivors of Plum Island thought she was a miracle worker, but Kate knew better, especially now. After an hour of listening to radio transmissions trickling in from around the world, she knew that nothing short of a real miracle would save the human race.

Her first bioweapon had eradicated all but a small percentage of those infected with the hemorrhage virus. Convinced that the surviving Variants couldn't be treated, her focus was now on designing another weapon that would exterminate them all before it was too late. Millions more would surely die before it was all over. In the end, she could only hope that humans came out on top.

Kate twisted the faucet off, grabbed a towel, and stepped out of the shower. Tasha and Jenny were already sitting on a bench, wrapped in towels. She reached for the duffel bag she'd retrieved from her quarters. Kate pulled out a clean set of clothes for each of them and turned away to slip on her own clothes.

"We need to hurry," she said once she was dressed. "Your dad is on his way back."

Both girls' eyes lit up. Even after all the horrors they'd seen, there was still joy there. Like Kate, they still had hope.

She grabbed the girls by the hand and led them into the hallway. The stink of fresh death hung in the air. Crimson stains covered the carpet where so many of her colleagues had died. Kate froze, remembering her fellow researcher Cindy's final moments. They had never liked each other much, and in the end Cindy had chosen to hide instead of coming with Kate and the others. The decision had cost the woman her life.

Kate swallowed and continued on, navigating around a pair of bloody shoes and a small pile of bullet casings.

"Just keep walking," she said to the girls. "Don't look down, okay?"

"Doctor," said a Medical Corps guard waiting for her at the end of the hallway. For a moment his youthful features reminded her of Jackson, the marine who had saved their lives just a few hours ago—and lost his in the process.

"Wait up!" said another voice from behind them.

Ellis hurried down the corridor, his jet-black hair slicked back and glistening under the LEDs. "You weren't going to leave without me, were you?"

Kate shook her head. "No, but we need to hurry."

"Let's go," the soldier said. He opened the door with

one hand and raised his rifle with the other, sliding the muzzle into moonlight. "Stay close," he ordered.

"I thought the island was cleared," Kate said, gripping the girls' hands a bit tighter.

"It was, ma'am, but Major Smith isn't taking any chances."

Silhouetted guards manned a heavy-caliber machine gun, and an industrial spotlight was set up behind a wall of sandbags in the center of the hexagon-shaped base. The beam swept across the path and then arched over the horizon, illuminating plumes of smoke rising from the smoldering wreckage of the Chinook helicopter on the tarmac. Kate stared at the flayed metal carcass as they walked, wondering exactly how the Variants it had been carrying had escaped. She'd been against bringing live test subjects to the island, but she took no pleasure in being proved right.

For weeks Plum Island had been spared from the horrors surging across the globe. Now the base looked like a war zone. Overhead, two blinking red dots crisscrossed the darkness, and Kate heard the distant thump of helicopter blades.

Static broke from the radio on the vest of their soldier escort. "Echo Two and Three incoming. All medical crews report to tarmac," said a female operator.

The guard continued on as if he hadn't heard the transmission at all, but Kate paused. She crouched in front of the girls and pointed at the sky.

"You ready to see your dad?" she asked.

"Is Daddy in one of those?" Jenny said, her voice hardly a whisper.

"Yup, he's coming home."

"Is Reed coming home too?" Tasha asked.

Kate fought the growing dread rising inside her and said, "Not yet, honey. Not yet."

2

General Richard Kennor hustled through an underground tunnel on his way to Central Command. The sun wouldn't rise for hours, but most of his staff was already awake. Judging by their exhausted looks, some of them hadn't slept at all. The same was true of him, and it showed. His movements were sluggish and his eyes were swollen with fatigue. The caffeine had worn off hours ago, and he was operating on pure adrenaline. Sleep during wartime was like sleep during the first months of having a child: It came in short intervals, if at all.

An entourage trailed the four-star general as he continued down the crowded hallway. The bunker, buried deep beneath Offutt Air Force Base, was the same location former president George W. Bush had been taken after the September 11, 2001, attacks. Now it was the temporary home of more than two hundred people from every corner of the nation, ranging from congressmen to Navy SEALs. There was even an anchor from CNN who had managed to sneak in with a senator's political staff. When the evacuations began weeks ago, chaos and pure luck had ensured that these few had lived.

Kennor watched the flow of human traffic as he walked. In most cases these were important people—people the government had believed should survive an apocalyptic event. Kennor, however, could have done without two-thirds of them. He needed military personnel, men and women who knew how to fight a war. Fortunately, President Mitchell had given him a blank check to wage the war against the Variants as soon as he had been sworn into office.

He didn't like the new POTUS, and not just because of his political affiliation. The former president pro tempore of the Senate was weak. That was the biggest flaw in a leader, to Kennor's mind. The chaotic first few weeks of the outbreak had proven Mitchell's time in Congress hadn't qualified him to lead a country, especially during a time of war. His only redeeming quality was the fact he stayed inside his bunker at Cheyenne Mountain and kept his mouth shut while Kennor handled the heavy lifting.

"Sir," came a voice that distracted Kennor from his thoughts.

A pair of guards opened the double doors to the command center and Kennor hurried inside. He took the first left into a small conference room. His personal staff—his three closest confidants—were already inside. They rose from their seats around the war table and stood at attention as he entered. Their grave looks served as a powerful reminder that the human race was losing the war. Operation Liberty had failed on a massive level.

"At ease," Kennor said as he took a seat. Most of them had been with him the better part of a decade fighting the War on Terror. To his left was Colonel Harris, a man with slicked-back white hair and a mustache to match. Across the table sat Marsha Kramer, a middle-aged lieutenant colonel with crimson hair and a pair of dimples that rarely got any use. Kennor's oldest friend, General George Johnson, was on the right, his bald head shining under the bank of lights overhead.

His hand shook as he reached for the folder marked CONFIDENTIAL. Breaking the seal, he pulled out a briefing and took a moment to scan his staff.

"Let's get started. Harris," Kennor said.

The colonel stood, back ramrod straight. "In front of you, General, is the initial report from Operation Liberty. We suffered heavy losses in every major city. The Variants overran almost every single FOB established. New York is lost. So is Chicago. Minneapolis. St. Louis. Nashville. Atlanta. It's a mess, sir."

Kennor shook his head. He'd been caught with his pants down. Thousands of soldiers from every branch of the military were dead because he had ignored the advice of Lieutenant Colonel Jensen and Dr. Kate Lovato. The cities he had so desperately wanted to protect were now in ruins because he'd made the wrong call.

"The good news is that the air force pounded the Variants hard with firebombs. The troops drew them out of their holes, and the flyboys turned them to ash. Preliminary reports indicate we killed a significant number."

"Do we have any idea how many are left?"

"Several recon teams have been deployed, and satellite imagery is being monitored as we speak," Harris said.

"I want numbers," Kennor snapped. "*Solid* numbers."

"Yes, sir," Harris said and made a note on his pad.

"How about survivors? Do we know how many people are left out there?" Kramer asked.

Harris's slight hesitation was all Kennor needed to know it wasn't good.

"I'm afraid we don't have solid numbers there either," Harris said.

"Then give me your best guess," Kennor replied.

Harris raised a brow and matter-of-factly said, "Extinction, sir. We're looking at the eventual near annihilation of the human race if we don't stop the Variants in the next month."

"You mean to tell me the Variants have killed the majority of the world's population in less than a month?" Kennor said.

"That's precisely what he's saying," Kramer said. "With all due respect, sir, those things aren't mindless zombies. We have underestimated them every step of the way. If we are going to win this war, we need to change our tactics."

Kennor shook his head. "NYC proves these things can be killed. Draw them out and bomb them to kingdom come."

"Draw them out with what, sir? More marines?" Kramer said. There was a challenge in her questions. Under normal circumstances, he'd have called her out for insubordination, but things had changed.

As the Pit Bull of the American Military—a nickname he'd always hated—he had overseen countless missions during the War on Terror. The Variants had proved much harder to kill. Now the jihadists were fighting the same enemy he was, and the irony was hard to swallow. The world had changed practically overnight and circumstance had turned enemies into allies.

A moment of tension lingered and then passed. Kennor wasn't ready to admit defeat or retreat, but he was toeing a fine line. The frustration of his staff went beyond fatigue. They were all losing their confidence in his ability to lead. He'd seen other commanders fall victim to the same thing, but he was not going to be one of them. He'd made mistakes, but it wasn't too late to turn this war around.

Kennor looked to an uncharacteristically quiet Johnson. The man had always been a voice of reason. He needed that voice now more than ever.

"What do you think, General?" Kennor asked.

Johnson exchanged a glance with Kramer and Harris. After a pause he said, "I think we need to carefully consider our next moves. With so much hanging in the balance, we can't afford another Operation Liberty."

Johnson cleared his throat as if he wanted to say more. Kennor scrutinized him, knowing Johnson wasn't finished. He could see the wheels turning in the general's head by his mannerisms. Johnson crossed his thick arms across his chest and clenched his jaw. Kennor wasn't prepared for what he said next.

"It's time to retreat," Johnson said sternly. "We need to pull our troops out of the cities completely. Leave only a few recon teams behind."

"I agree," Kramer added. "It's time to give science another chance. Perhaps we need to give Doctor Lovato and her team another opportunity to destroy the Variants."

Kennor massaged his wrinkled forehead. "Retreat," he muttered. "I never thought I would hear anyone on my team say that word."

"Sir, our military isn't just fractured. It's been shattered," Harris said. "We're strained in every area. I'm not sure—"

A rap on the door interrupted him. The door swung open and a young corporal named Jimmy Van strode into the room. A bead of sweat trickled from his receding hairline.

"General Kennor, sir. We just received some urgent news," he said. Van hesitated, looking at the general's staff.

"Go ahead, son," Kennor said.

"Raven Rock Mountain Complex." The corporal paused for a second and then said, "It's... It's been overrun."

Kennor shifted in his chair to give Van a better look.

"What do you mean, overrun? That's one of the most secure locations in the country. Hell, it's the alternate joint command and backup for the Pentagon. There are a couple hundred people hunkered down there, including the UN ambassador and the secretary of state."

"I'm sorry, sir," Van said. "The Variants found a way into the tunnel system and overwhelmed the forces there."

"My God," Kramer gasped.

Silence crowded the small briefing room. The loss of Raven Rock was another nail in the coffin; no location on the planet was safe. Kennor scanned his team. Fatigued and strained, they wore identical looks of defeat.

"Van, I want you to arrange a search-and-rescue mission. If anyone is alive in there, get them the hell out."

Van nodded. "Yes, sir."

Kennor stood, pushed his chair under the table, and looked to Harris. He suddenly felt as weak as President Mitchell, but at least Kennor wasn't stupid. His staff had convinced him there was only one option left on the table, and the fall of Raven Rock proved they were right.

"I want a coordinated tactical withdrawal," Kennor said.

"Are you telling us to retreat?" Harris asked.

Kennor paused, the words burning in his throat. "Yes. Order a full retreat from every city," he said. "Get our men and women out of there. We're falling back to our strongholds."

With nothing else to say, he turned away from his staff and hurried out of the room. In a sudden fit of rage he slammed the door behind him as he retreated for the first time in his career.

Beckham had just enough time to dart around the next corner before the second grenade went off. The deafening explosion rattled the tunnel, and fragments of rock fell from the ceiling. He closed his eyes and ran through the storm of debris, saying a mental prayer for the innocent lives that had been lost in the lair. In his heart he knew he'd done the right thing. No one should have to suffer like that.

At least they had saved someone. At a time where every life counted, he considered that a victory. Chow carried the woman around the next corner and disappeared from sight. Beckham halted and turned to check the entrance to the tomb. A thick cloud of smoke lingered where the grenade had gone off. Chunks of stone filled the tunnel. He raised his Colt .45 and waited for the smoke to clear.

Beyond the perpetual ringing, he heard a howl. As the haze dissipated, he saw the source—a single clawed hand protruded from the pile. It curled and went limp after a final twitch.

Beckham waited another second, just to make sure, and then ran. His team was waiting at a T-intersection. Timbo was bent over, his hands on his knees, panting heavily. Jinx stood guard in the corridor. He moved his Beretta M9 in a slow sweep as he searched the other tunnels for hostiles.

"Valdez, you hold security with Jinx," Beckham said. "The rest of you, take five." He crouched next to Chow, who was busy dressing the injuries on the woman's legs.

"How is she?" Beckham asked.

"Weak. But she'll live."

He applied another bandage and looked up. "What are we doing, man? We can't just run around down here forever."

Before Beckham could respond, the woman let out a long moan.

"It's okay," Chow said. "You're going to be all right."

She blinked, trying to focus on Chow and then Beckham.

"Where am . . ." she began to say, then her eyes widened with realization. She scrambled away from the two operators, dragging her legs across the platform until her back hit the wall.

"Don't be scared," Chow said. "We're here to help."

"What's your name?" Beckham asked.

The woman reached for the curtain of hair covering her filthy face and pulled it to the side.

"Meg," she whispered.

"I'm Master Sergeant Beckham, and this is Staff Sergeant Chow. We're Delta Force, and our team is going to get you out of here."

She glanced over at the other men. "How many are you?"

"Seven," Beckham replied.

Meg let out a sad laugh. "You can't save me. We'll never make it out of the city."

Beckham exchanged a glance with Chow. Both of them knew she was probably right, but they were soldiers and admitting defeat wasn't in their nature. Surrendering was death. They had to keep fighting.

"We need to get back up top," Beckham said as Jensen approached. "If we can find that marine convoy we passed on West Fiftieth and Seventh Avenue, we can load up on ammo and pile into one of the Humvees."

Jensen nodded. "I was thinking the same thing, but I have no idea where the hell we are. Could be blocks away or could be miles."

"Any plan is better than running around in this maze," Chow said.

"I don't like the idea of moving in the dark. Maybe we should wait for sunup when the Variants are less active," Jensen said.

"Not sure we're going to last that long down here, sir," Beckham replied. "We're low on ammo and low on fuel."

Jensen looked over his shoulder and nodded. "I definitely don't want to get cornered again without ammo."

"Then it's settled. We go topside as soon as everyone has a chance to take in some nutrition and water," Beckham said. He looked toward Chow. "Redistribute ammo. Make sure everyone has a mag for their primary weapon."

Chow nodded. "I'll take care of it."

The operator hurried away with Jensen, leaving Beckham alone with Meg. He reached for his water bottle and gave it a quick shake. It was almost empty. He was just about to take a swig when Meg moaned.

Beckham handed her the bottle. "Here, drink." He helped her bring it to her lips and held it there as she finished it off.

"Bet you're hungry too," Beckham said. He pulled an energy bar from his pocket and peeled back the wrapper.

"No," she said, waving it away. "I feel sick."

"You have to eat. You'll need energy."

She studied the bar in the dim lighting like it was poison. Beckham pushed it closer.

"You really think you can get me out of the city?" Meg asked.

"I'll do everything I can to get you out of here. I promise you that."

A pained grin broke across her face. "Guess not every man left in this city is a yellow-bellied coward after all."

Two Black Hawks hovered overhead. The sound of the blades whipped through the early morning silence as the smoke from the smoldering Chinook swirled across the tarmac.

"Daddy!" Tasha shouted as the choppers descended. Kate grabbed the girl's hand and held her back.

"Doctor," the Medical Corps guard said. "My orders are to escort you back to Building Five. Major Smith has requested your presence at the command center."

She shot him a glare. "Can't he wait a few minutes? Their father is on one of those choppers."

The young man frowned and flicked his headset on. "Command, this is Sinclair. Holding position on eastern edge of tarmac."

Kate couldn't hear the response over the whirring of the Black Hawks' rotors, but the man's eyes told her she could stay.

"Thank you," Kate mouthed.

The beam from a spotlight centered on the wall of smoke creeping over the concrete. The soldiers roved the light from side to side, penetrating the thick haze. In the glow Kate saw two dozen men trudging across the tarmac.

Kate squeezed the girls' hands tighter as the men emerged with their helmets bowed in defeat. Their uniforms were soiled with dried blood and ash.

One of them stood taller than the others. She knew right away it was Horn. He jogged ahead when he saw them standing behind the concrete barriers.

"Tasha! Jenny!" he yelled, picking up speed.

"Daddy!" the girls yelled. Kate loosened her grip and let them run to their father. He scooped them up in his arms and held them tight. Hot tears blurred her vision as she watched. Tragedy had opened the door for a miracle, and once again a father was reunited with his daughters. But Kate wasn't sure how many more miracles were left.

3

Meg ignored the rancid smell of sewage. She was more concerned with her shredded legs. When she had finished her first Ironman triathlon, she'd endured the pain from the thousands upon thousands of steps, bicycle rotations, and swimming strokes that went into the 140-mile race. That day, her muscles had been stretched like too-tight guitar strings. She had thought they were going to snap before she crossed the finish line.

The agony she felt now was worse. She still hadn't gotten a good look at the damage the creatures had inflicted on her body. The tunnels were too dark for that, but she knew from the pain that it had to be bad.

"Give me a weapon," Meg said.

The two soldiers carrying her down the tunnel hesitated for a moment. Beckham, the man on her right, shook his head.

"No way in hell you can fight like this," he said.

"A weapon," Meg repeated. "Please give me something. A knife or a gun."

"I'll give you my knife before we go up top," Beckham replied.

It wouldn't replace her axe, but a blade would do. Steel always made her feel better—even if it wouldn't do much against the monsters. Ahead, the other soldiers had stopped. They clustered around a skeletal ladder that led to a manhole.

"Jinx, check it out. See if you can get eyes on the street," Beckham said. "Chow, help me with her."

Meg groaned as the two soldiers helped position her back against the wall. Chow kept a hand on her shoulder to keep her from falling over. Her head felt foggy. The cloud was so thick she could hardly think. She could only seem to focus on one thing: the blade Beckham had promised her.

"I'm going to check these dressings," Chow said. He crouched down in front of her. "This might hurt."

Meg gritted her teeth in anticipation. The faint scraping of metal sounded somewhere in the distance. For a second, Meg's heart caught in her throat as she remembered Jed and Rex dropping the manhole cover into place, sealing her into this mazelike grave. Then she felt the presence of the soldiers who had come to help her, not abandon her. Meg's breathing slowed and she relaxed while Chow examined the bandages he'd put on her injuries.

Overhead, the man they had called Jinx climbed the ladder. His feet disappeared and moonlight flooded the tunnel, casting an eerie glow over the team that had saved her. Covered in ash, the soldiers looked like ghosts.

The sight reminded her of one of her first days on the job. In the aftermath of the September 11 attacks, she and all the other rescue workers had looked a lot like these soldiers. That awful day had prepared her mentally for everything she'd seen since then—everything except the monsters.

Meg cursed as Chow pulled away one of the bandages. She cursed again when she saw her injuries.

Chow pushed his NVGs up and caught her gaze. "Don't look," he said.

It was too late. Meg couldn't pull her eyes away from

the exposed muscle on her right calf. She wouldn't be completing any triathlons again. Not that it really mattered—the only race she was likely to run was away from the zombies, or whatever they were.

"Hey, lady," came a voice.

A soldier with an unmistakably Italian nose stood behind Chow. He stared at Meg with broken eyes. "Hey," he said again.

Meg managed a weak response. "What?"

"How many made it out of the city?" he asked. "Before things got really bad?"

She understood his sadness. He was from New York. Probably Queens or the Bronx, judging by his accent.

"I don't know," Meg replied solemnly, her heart hurting for the man. "Not many. When the virus started spreading, things got bad really fast. The air force took out the bridges first."

The soldier bowed his head. Before he could reply Beckham said, "Jinx, you got eyes?"

Meg couldn't hear the response but saw Beckham's features tense.

"Went too far. That convoy is two blocks away," Beckham said. "In the other direction." He peered into the darkness of the eastern tunnel.

An African American man with the build of a career soldier spat and wiped a sleeve across his mustache.

"What do you think, sir?" Beckham asked the man.

"Two blocks, ain't far," he replied. He stepped out of the moonlight and said, "I'll leave this one up to you. You've gotten us this far."

"You boys ready for a quick jog?" Beckham asked his men.

The other soldiers nodded and approached the ladder. Beckham crouched back down next to Meg. "When we get up top, Timbo's gonna carry you."

His voice sounded so confident that for a moment she actually believed he would get her out of the city. She held out a shaky hand. "Fine with me. Long as you give me that," she said, pointing at his knife.

Beckham reluctantly unbuttoned the sheath and extended the handle to her. "Hopefully you won't need it."

Instead of grabbing the handle, she put her hand over his. "Just promise me one thing," Meg said, searching his eyes.

The strength there told her she could trust him. He was not Jed or Rex. He'd proved that when he'd stayed behind to save her from the zombies' lair, and she could see by the way he interacted with his men that he wouldn't abandon them either.

"If those things come—don't let them take me again. You put a bullet in my head before that happens." Meg coughed into her shoulder and then squeezed his hand harder.

The man nodded once and she let go of his hand, taking the knife. Chow helped her up, but she kept her eyes on Beckham as he walked away. Like the rest of this band of soldiers, she had already started looking to him for leadership—for hope.

"Looks clear up here," Jinx said.

Beckham stopped under the manhole, tilting his helmet into the light. "You take point, Jinx. Valdez, you're on rear guard. Timbo, you think you can carry Meg up this?" He placed a hand on the ladder.

"Yeah, no problem," Timbo grumbled. He threw the strap of his rifle over a shoulder and approached her. "Hang on tight. Okay, ma'am?"

She nodded and tensed her muscles as Chow handed her off to Timbo. He picked her up and draped her over his back with the grace of someone who had carried wounded comrades before. Despite his care, her legs hurt so bad she let out an uncontrolled whimper.

The other soldiers were already moving up the ladder in single file. They disappeared one after the other into the night. Meg's arms dangled over Timbo's back. She gripped the handle of the blade tighter.

Footfalls pounded the concrete above and a soldier said, "Go, go, go!"

Timbo's labored breathing reverberated through the narrow passage. Meg could feel each breath, his chest moving her up and down. Panic set in as he climbed. Sweat dropped from her forehead and plummeted into the stream of sewage flowing below.

"Almost there," Timbo grunted. "You just hang on tight."

The cool night air. The numbness. The radiant moonlight. It all washed over her as Timbo emerged from the manhole, forming a sensation that bordered on an out-of-body experience. She felt detached. Not safe exactly, not yet, but close enough.

The soldiers fanned out across the street, setting up positions behind a cluster of vehicles covered in soot. Everything about their actions radiated experience. Timbo stopped behind a pickup truck as Jinx wedged his body through a narrow gap between bumpers. He slowly strode out into the intersection, scoping Ninth Avenue as he moved.

Nothing moved in the derelict streets or the empty windows of the skyscrapers towering overhead. The quiet city was a concrete and metal graveyard—a crumbling museum showcasing how things used to be.

No one else seemed to hear the faint clicking of joints in the silence. Not in time, at least. Meg should have known not to trust the deceiving sense of security. It vanished in a heartbeat as a shadowy figure crashed into Jinx and a pair of claws dragged him screaming into the darkness.

For ten years, Kate had dedicated her life to the rarest and deadliest diseases. In college, when her friends were choosing paths in fields like pediatrics, dentistry, or optometry, she had picked virology. Years later, when they were swabbing the throats of kids with colds or fitting them for braces, Kate was holding the hands of children who were dying of malaria in third-world countries. Through all of it she'd been resilient, praying that her work would help those who needed it the most in some small way.

Kate never thought for a moment she would be sitting in a room with the survivors of the worst virus the human race had ever seen. The fact that it had been engineered as a weapon made her feel so much worse. The very scientific discipline that was supposed to eradicate disease had wiped out most of the people on the planet.

She fidgeted at the thought, still unable to completely grasp the nightmare she was living in. Ellis's head slumped onto her shoulder as he fell asleep with his back to the wall.

"Sorry," he mumbled, rubbing his eyes.

Tasha and Jenny were curled up on the floor next to Riley. The young Delta Force operator slept with his head propped up on a fist, his broken body cradled by a wheelchair.

The lobby of Building 5 was crowded. The old and young. Men and women of all races and abilities. There was no discrimination here. The only conversations were hushed. Hands were held, prayers were whispered, and tears were shed.

This was the new world.

In some ways it wasn't all bad. Now that the Variants had

effectively ended all human wars everywhere in the world, Kate supposed it didn't matter what anybody believed anymore. Humans had finally set apart their differences and come together. Unfortunately, it had taken the imminent threat of extinction to bring them to this point.

Shouting from the command center echoed down the hallway. Tasha pulled on Kate's sleeve.

"Are they yelling at my daddy?" she asked.

Kate crouched down. "No, honey. They're just talking. He's going to be back in a few minutes."

Jenny trembled and sniffled. Sweat glistened under her auburn bangs.

"Are you feeling okay?" Kate asked. She held the back of her hand to the girl's forehead.

Unblinking, the girl nodded and said, "I'm tired."

"I'm sorry, sweetie. You lie back down and try to get some sleep," Kate said. It was just shy of 4 a.m. and the adrenaline from the attack was finally starting to wear off. Kate felt the memory of the attack like a phantom weight on her chest. Beckham was trapped or dead in New York, and a third of Plum Island's population had been killed. The truth hurt so bad she could hardly move.

She snapped alert at the hoarse voice of the Medical Corps guard.

"Doctors, Major Smith is ready for you," he said.

"I'll watch 'em," Riley said. He straightened his back with a wince and rolled his chair closer to the girls.

Kate nodded and followed Ellis into the sweltering command center. The stink of battle filled the air, reminding her of the medical tents from missions overseas. She could almost taste the sour tang of blood and sweat. Horn and the other survivors of Operation Liberty sat around the war table, oblivious to her presence.

"Have you heard from the others?" Kate called from the doorway.

Horn, Peters, Rodriguez, Smith, and a handful of men she didn't know turned in her direction but didn't reply. Horn put his elbows on the table. She could see his face fall from where she stood.

"We lost contact with them shortly after the bombs dropped," Horn finally said.

"Well, try again!" Kate snapped without thinking. Her eyes involuntarily roved from the new female radio operator sitting at the terminal across the room, to the soldiers, and back to the radio operator. The middle-aged woman stared back defiantly. Silver hair fell over the shoulders of her surprisingly neat navy uniform. She felt the stab of embarrassment at her own appearance. They were all looking at Kate like she was crazy.

Kate turned back to the table, her cheeks hot and flushed. Several soldiers bowed their heads but Horn held her gaze. "We have, Kate. Multiple times."

"Send a chopper and search for them. You can't leave him there…"

Major Smith rose to his feet. "We have a chopper on standby, Doctor. But we can't deploy one without extraction coordinates."

"Kate, calm down," Ellis whispered.

It was then she realized she was shaking. "I'm…I'm sorry."

Smith gave her a silent but meaningful look and gestured for her and Ellis to join them at the table.

"We received a message from Central Command a few minutes ago," Smith said. "They have ordered a full retreat from every city. General Kennor has requested a call with you later this morning, Doctor Lovato."

"Me?" Kate asked.

"Yes," Smith replied patiently. "Central is putting forth a new strategy, and they want your help."

Before Kate could respond, the radio operator twirled

her chair away from her terminal. She cupped her hand over her headset and said, "Sir, I'm getting a transmission from New York."

Smith hurried over to the equipment. "Put it on the speakers."

"Yes, sir," the woman said. She twisted a dial and static coughed from the PA system.

"Plum Island, this is Beckham. Does anyone copy?" There was a pause and then, "Team Ghost is on the run. I repeat, we're on the run and need extraction, ASAP."

The crack of gunfire surged from the speakers. Kate flinched, her heart leaping at every sound. Beckham was alive—for now. She rushed over to Smith's side as the other soldiers crowded around.

There was a break in gunfire. "We're at Fiftieth and Eighth, going to try and make it back to Pier Eighty-Six in a—"

Smith flicked his mini-mic to his mouth and said, "Echo Three, Smith. Warm up the bird. Ghost Team is on their way to Pier Eighty-Six."

The other men were already hurrying out of the room by the time Smith gave the order. Horn touched Kate's hand on his way out. "Don't worry. I'm going to bring him back."

Beckham bolted toward the sounds of Jinx's screams with his Colt .45 out in front, scanning for a target. Muzzle flashes lit up the dark streets as Variants charged their position. He looked past them, yelling, "Jinx! Jinx, where are you?"

Chow was shouting now too. "Tell us where the fuck you are!"

Beckham hesitated once he saw the numbers they were facing. The creatures charged toward Team Ghost from every direction. They spilled out of manholes and came crashing through the glass doors of nearby buildings. A dozen scampered across the walls of a bombed-out skyscraper.

Ghost's gunfire drew them in like moths to a flame. Beckham felt every shot, counting them in his head, hoping they had enough ammunition—but knowing they didn't.

Beckham slowed to aim his revolver at a female perched on a scorched Toyota Corolla a hundred feet away. An MK11 sounded behind him before he could pull the trigger, and her skull exploded in a cloud of mist from the 7.62 mm round, saving Beckham from using one of his precious cartridges. She tumbled to the ground, blood gushing from the gaping hole where her face had been.

"On me!" Beckham yelled.

He jumped onto the hood for a better vantage. Ryan and Valdez acted as flankers, setting up firing positions to cover the east and the west. Beckham would have ordered Timbo with Ryan instead of Valdez, but the Ranger was busy carrying Meg, and Valdez had proven to be an expert marksman. The marine sergeant from 1st Platoon had killed more Variants in New York than Beckham had.

Chow and Jensen covered the rear, while Timbo struggled forward with Meg bouncing on his wide shoulders. He was falling behind despite her frantic pleas to go faster.

The entire team was running on fumes. They were all morning-after-leave tired, but the current threat was far worse than a bad hangover. As Beckham scanned the streets, he realized what a terrible mistake he'd made. He had broken every fucking rule in the book by giving chase to the Variant that had Jinx, and his order to open fire had only drawn more of the things from their lairs. He could blame it on the fatigue, but he knew better. The wound still hadn't healed from the massacre of Team Ghost at Building 8 a month earlier. Seeing Jinx pulled away into the darkness had torn the scab off that wound. Now he'd put the lives of every person on his team in jeopardy by giving chase.

And still Ghost worked their way forward, muzzle flashes forming a fiery barrier around the group. Beckham searched the terrain desperately for any sign of the fallen operator.

A male Variant with a crooked back galloped down the sidewalk. It leaped over bloated corpses, flying through the air. Beckham shot it in the face with a movement so smooth it surprised him.

Five rounds left.

"Eyes! Who's got eyes on?" Beckham yelled frantically.

A smaller Variant charged him from the right and Beckham turned to fire. He jerked the barrel aside at the last second when he realized it was a child. The shot went wide, whistling past the creature's head. Beckham knew the thing racing toward him wasn't a boy. It was a monster. He took aim again and shot it between the eyes. The tiny Variant crashed to the ground, skidding across the pavement until it came to a rest in front of Beckham. He jumped over the corpse and pushed on.

Three rounds left.

"Jinx!" Beckham shouted.

Gunfire erupted from his six. Jensen and Chow took turns holding the Variants off their tail with short bursts.

"Come on!" Beckham stormed through the clogged street toward Eighth Avenue, where they had last seen Jinx.

"We have to get out of here!" Valdez yelled.

"Not without Jinx," Beckham said.

"I'm down to my last mag!" Valdez snarled.

"We're not leaving him!" Chow shouted back. "I don't care if we have to use our knives."

Even if Beckham wanted to, it was too late to turn back and retreat. The entire city block was swarming with monsters, hemming them in on all sides. Several rogue Variants made dashes for Team Ghost. Each was cut down by controlled fire. Jensen and Ryan halted to shoot at a pack that had broken off from the horde trailing them. They took turns, stopping every hundred feet to thin the horde.

It was obvious that the Variants were continuing to evolve, growing smarter and more cautious. Their actions both in the tunnels and out here on the streets were similar to those of predatory animals hunting in packs. They were testing Beckham's men, figuring out who was weak. They'd started by grabbing Jinx and now they would do the same with the rest, picking them off one by one rather than risk a suicidal charge with their main force.

"Jinx! Say something!" Beckham said into the comm. The response was faint, more of a croak than a word. He couldn't tell if it was static or the operator struggling to reply.

A flash of motion at the intersection with Seventh Avenue commanded his gaze. Beckham jumped onto another hood just in time to see two Variants dragging Jinx past several abandoned Humvees.

"Twelve o'clock!" Beckham shouted. "Ryan, hurry!"

The Ranger crouched behind a vehicle and scoped the street with his rifle while the rest of the team covered the perimeter.

"Why have we stopped?" Meg yelled.

"Ryan, take them out!" Beckham shouted.

Two cracks sounded and Beckham watched the Variants' heads disappear in a satisfying spray of red. He ordered the team forward with a hand signal before the bodies had slumped to the ground.

"Jinx…Hold on…We're coming!" Beckham wheezed.

His response was lost to a torrent of gunshots. Beckham gritted his teeth and sprinted toward the convoy. When he reached the edge, he slowed to raise his Colt .45 and moved the barrel from side to side over the motionless street. Pounding boots and frantic voices followed him into the intersection. He darted through the street and collapsed at Jinx's side.

The operator held his neck with glistening hands. Blood gushed out from between his fingers. His wild eyes searched Beckham's face in the moonlight. Beckham gripped Jinx's wrist and whispered, "It's okay, man, it's okay." They locked eyes as Jinx struggled for air, blood gurgling in his mouth.

By the time the team caught up, Jinx was gone. Beckham bowed his head and closed Jinx's eyelids as more gunshots broke over the screeches of the Variants.

Chow dropped to his knees and shook Jinx's body. "Jinx! Jinx! We're going to get you out of here." He felt for a pulse, knocking Jinx's limp hands away from his throat and revealing a deep gash that stretched across his neck.

Beckham pulled Chow away. "He's gone. We've got to move!"

"I got us a Humvee!" shouted Valdez over the comm. The cough of a diesel engine confirmed it.

"Help me with him," Beckham said.

Together, Chow and Beckham carried Jinx's body to the truck. As soon as the team was inside, Valdez pounded the gas, the tires squealing as they left the army of Variants in a cloud of dust and ash.

4

Ten minutes had passed since Kate had watched Horn kneel next to his girls and tell them he was going back to Manhattan to pick up Beckham. They had begged him not to go, but Kate had known by the look of fury in his eyes that he wasn't going to leave his best friend in the field again. Horn had hugged his daughters good-bye, knocked fists with Riley, and followed the other soldiers through the crowded lobby, shouting, "Move, move!"

"He's going to be okay. I promise," Kate reassured the girls after their father had bolted out of the building. She wanted more than anything to follow the men onto the tarmac and watch the chopper fly into the darkness. For a moment she considered it, but then a voice echoed down the hallway behind her, calling her name.

"Doctors, there's something I need you to see." Major Sean Smith was standing in the corridor with his arms crossed.

"Just a minute," Kate said. She strained to see outside the windows of the crowded atrium one last time and then glanced down at Tasha and Jenny. Both girls were sobbing uncontrollably. She didn't want to leave them.

"I'll take 'em," Riley said. He offered a reassuring nod and leaned over his wheelchair to snag Jenny in his arms. He placed her gently on his lap. She wrapped her arms around his neck and buried her face in his chest. Kate waved good-bye to the girls and followed Ellis down the hall.

Smith sat at the head of the war table, typing his credentials into the main computer. "One of the Variants survived the attack," Smith said without looking up.

Kate joined Ellis and the major at the table. The monitor flickered on and Kate saw a female Variant on the floor of a holding cell, hands and feet bound by chains. The bone on her right leg was exposed under a flap of skin and muscle. Bright ribbons of flesh hung loosely from her left arm, and her face was a mess. One of her eye sockets was caved in, the eyeball missing. Kate couldn't stop staring at the monster squirming in a puddle of its own blood.

"Awful," Kate whispered.

Smith scratched his chin. "I've ordered one of my technicians to try and keep it alive."

"What... Why? We already have two others," Kate said.

The door to the holding cell slowly opened and a man in riot gear took a careful step inside. He glanced up at the camera, his eyes hidden by a mirrored visor. After flashing a thumbs-up, he crouched down with a box of medical supplies.

"Neither of the other specimens is injured," Ellis said as they watched. "If this one survives, it could prove to be very useful in our research. Just think about how much it could tell us about their healing abilities."

"That's precisely what I was thinking," Smith said.

The Variant jerked toward the technician, snarling through broken teeth as he bent down to tighten the chains. Staggering backward, he hit the wall and held out an armored arm like he was about to fend off a rabid dog. The creature pushed itself to its feet and used its good leg to spring toward him. He batted it away with an arm and reached for the Taser on his belt. Before he could grab it, the Variant was on him again. This time it clamped onto his armored wrist with swollen sucker lips. He hit the creature with his free hand, pummeling its broken eye socket with his fist.

"My God," Ellis said. "It's like it feels no pain."

The technician hit the monster again and again, his fist striking harder each time. He finally knocked it away. Instead of pulling his Taser, he scrambled back to the door, grabbed a tranquilizer gun from his supplies, and shot the creature in the neck.

Smith crossed his arms and shook his head. "I hope you can find a way to kill these things."

"We will," Kate said, staring at the screen. The female Variant collapsed face first onto the concrete. Her body twitched several times before finally going limp.

"I need a guarantee the Variants won't get out again," Kate said. She realized how insane she sounded. Each time the Variants had been brought to the island, they had escaped. Too many innocent lives had already been lost, but Smith was right—they had to continue their research. Kate knew what she had to do, and what she had to ask for. It meant putting humanity's dwindling survivors in jeopardy, but without a live specimen, her research would be limited to observations from other facilities.

"I want a third of your remaining forces posted at Building Four. The Variants need to be sedated and monitored at all times," Kate said.

The major seemed to consider her words and said, "Okay, Doctor."

Kate nodded and brushed away a strand of hair that had fallen over her face as she focused on the monitor. The technician was working on the unconscious Variant. He dressed its wounds and then injected something into its chest.

"Why don't you snag a few hours of sleep before you begin?" Smith said. "Report back here at 0900 for the call with Central."

"No time for sleep," Kate said. "And tell General Kennor I don't have anything to say to him."

Smith raised a brow. "He requested to talk to you specifically."

"And *I* requested that he reconsider his tactics for Operation Liberty. How many died because of his stubbornness? The man is clearly too egotistical to listen to reason. I'm not wasting another minute with men like Gibson or Kennor."

"Gibson's dead," Smith said coldly.

The memory of shutting the doors to the ICU and sealing Gibson and the others inside sprang to Kate's mind. The past few hours had been so chaotic she'd almost forgotten about the colonel's fate. Hearing it now brought her a perverse sense of satisfaction that she couldn't suppress. She was glad Gibson had perished at the hands of one of the monsters he had created.

Kate didn't reply. There was too much on her mind, too many things she could say. She turned to stare out the observation window, imagining the burned Variant that had ended Gibson's life, plunging its talons into the man's soft flesh. It was odd, taking pleasure in death, especially now that every human life was so precious. A month ago she would never have felt anything other than horror. But the apocalypse had changed her. Hardened her. She was no longer the same woman she'd been before the hemorrhage virus emerged.

The whine of the M240 from the Humvee's turret and the cries of the Variants seemed so far off, like they were in a part of Beckham's mind that he couldn't completely access. He was hardly paying attention to Valdez's erratic driving as the Humvee sped down West Fiftieth. The only thing he seemed to be fully aware of was Jinx's blood soaking into his uniform.

A sharp jerk to the right sent Beckham crashing into the side door. The pain snapped him out of his shell shock. His senses activated like he'd taken a shot of adrenaline. He could hear and feel everything.

"They're fucking everywhere!" Timbo yelled over the comm.

The Humvee tore through the intersection, giving Beckham a glimpse of Ninth Avenue. Every inch of asphalt was packed with the creatures. The horde surged over burned-out cars and flowed across the surface of every building, moving so fast they seemed to blend together in a sea of pale flesh.

He turned away from the view to check on Meg. She was in shock, her catatonic gaze locked on the windshield. She shared a seat with Chow, both of them jammed between the door and the console that separated them from Beckham. Jinx lay across their laps.

Up front, Jensen and Ryan shared the passenger seat, while Valdez leaned to the side of the steering wheel to see through the filthy window. The sunrise bled through the glass. At first Beckham couldn't quite believe what he was seeing. Hours before, he would have bet against ever seeing the sun again.

A voice crackled in his ear at the same moment a Variant careened into Beckham's window. The creature's skull hit the glass with a smack, leaving behind a smear of blood.

"Holy shit!" Chow said.

Beckham hardly flinched. He was more focused on hearing the incoming transmission.

"Ghost, this is Echo Three. En route to Pier Eighty-Six, ETA five minutes. What's your location? Over."

"Echo Three. Ghost." Beckham paused and smacked the front passenger seat. "Where the fuck are we?"

Valdez leaned farther to the side for a better view out the driver window. "About to hit Tenth Ave. Shouldn't be more than a few—"

"Watch out!" Jensen screamed.

There was a flash of white, then the unmistakable crunch of metal on bones. The windshield cracked in every direction as the naked body of a Variant rolled off.

"Hold on!" Valdez yelled. He swerved to avoid two more of the creatures. The overcorrection sent the Humvee fishtailing, and the rubber screamed as they spun out of control.

They hit something else a moment later that made a wet *thunk*. A second and then a third body crunched under the tires, causing the truck to jolt violently.

Chow held on to Meg to keep her from sliding out of their seat and Beckham grabbed Jinx's body. He closed his eyes as Valdez clipped the back of a car. The windshield disappeared in an explosion of glass and the turret grew silent.

When Beckham opened his eyes, Jensen was already kicking out the final shards. Valdez twisted the steering wheel, put the truck in reverse, and yelled, "Somebody get those things off our ass!"

Beckham whirled to see a pack of Variants that were almost on them. They charged forward into the morning light. Every muscle beneath their almost translucent, thin skin seemed to flex. He locked eyes with a hairless female, her yellow eyes smoldering with rage.

"Timbo! You okay up there?" Chow yelled, patting the man's legs.

The bulky Ranger's response came in the crack

of heavy gunfire. The rounds shredded the Variants behind them as Valdez backed the Humvee away from a snarl of vehicles.

Ryan fired one of the rifles he'd picked up off the street from the front passenger window, and Jensen unloaded a magazine of his own out the now-absent windshield while Valdez shifted back into drive. The truck lurched forward and continued down Fiftieth.

"Meg, you okay?" Beckham asked.

She nodded and groaned.

"Echo Three, Ghost. We have an army trailing us," Beckham said into his mini-mic.

"Roger that, Ghost. We're flying hot."

The distant rumble of a jet broke over the city. Were they coming in for another bombing run? Had Horn and the survivors of 1st Platoon made it out of the blast zone? Beckham's mind hammered with questions he'd forgotten in the chaotic violence.

"Echo Three, did First Platoon get out?" Beckham asked. White noised surged over the comm long enough for his heart to skip.

"Roger that, Ghost. Got several of 'em with me now. Came to save your ass."

"Almost to Twelfth," Valdez said. "Just one more block."

Ryan changed magazines and jammed his M16 out the window as they passed through the intersection. He mowed down three Variants making a run for their position.

"Hold on," Valdez shouted. He took a left at Twelfth Avenue, turning so hard the Humvee almost tipped on its side. The change in direction gave Beckham a view of the Hudson River, its banks littered with the dead, and the distorted shapes of Variants coming down from the north to join the chase.

The crimson sunrise flickered over the water and flooded the city streets with light. Typically bright light hurt the Variants' photosensitive eyes and scared them off. But it wasn't enough to stop them this time. They were too focused on food.

Beckham caught sight of a sailboat drifting toward the shore. It disappeared behind the clogged vehicles on the opposite side of the street, and Beckham shifted his gaze toward the sky, searching for Echo 3.

"I'm out!" Timbo yelled. "Someone give me a rifle." He reached down and Ryan handed back one of the extra M16s he'd picked up.

"There have to be thousands of them!" Timbo yelled as he pulled himself back into the turret. The crack from his rifle came a beat later.

Beckham continued to scan the sky. There, through the gleaming sunlight, he could make out the shape of a chopper. He imagined what the scene would look like from above: a single vehicle moving at a breakneck speed through the ashes of a burned-out city with an army of enraged monsters chasing it. The sight was like something out of the movies.

He gripped one of Jinx's limp hands, wishing desperately that he could fire on the Variants that had killed his brother-in-arms. Sitting there and doing nothing felt like a betrayal.

The truck swerved to the left before taking a hard right. When he looked up, the Humvee was on the pier. Both Bradleys and the other Humvees were there as well, abandoned where 1st Platoon had left them. Echo 3 hovered over the end of the platform. Valdez navigated around the vehicles and raced toward the chopper.

The high-pitched roar of the M240 machine gun sounded as soon as their Humvee was clear. The door gunner unloaded a barrage of 7.62 mm rounds that whizzed overhead. Beckham twisted and watched the projectiles pound the concrete and slam into flesh. A geyser of limbs, rock, and bone exploded into the air.

Beckham felt a moment of relief that quickly turned into panic as he looked back out the windshield. They were heading full speed toward a concrete barrier. Valdez slammed on the brakes and the truck ground to a halt just inches from the blocks. Beckham was jerked forward, Jinx's body nearly rolling off his lap.

"Everybody out!" Valdez shouted.

"Chow, Timbo. You carry Jinx. I'll get Meg," Beckham said as he opened the door. "Valdez, Ryan, Jensen, you lay down covering fire."

He staggered out onto the dock. The Variant horde streamed down Twelfth in both directions. They were changing their tactics again. With thousands joining the chase, the Variants seemed to realize that their individual chances of getting hit by a bullet were slim.

The army of monsters surged forward.

Beckham forced himself to look away. He bolted around the side of the vehicle to help Meg, nearly crashing into Valdez and Ryan. The two men took a step away from the truck to give him space and began to lay down covering fire. Jensen was already shooting from the other side of the truck.

"Help me," Chow said. He struggled to drag Jinx's body to the edge of the seat and Timbo helped pull him from the vehicle.

"Chow, you help Beckham with Meg," Timbo said, jerking his head toward the woman. "I'll carry Jinx."

Beckham leaned down, and with Chow's help they hoisted Meg to her feet. She glanced up at Beckham, still clutching the blade he'd given her.

"We're really leaving?" Meg said as if she didn't believe it.

"Yeah," Chow said. "Come on, we have to move."

They squeezed through the gap in the barriers and hustled toward Echo 3. Meg muttered a response Beckham couldn't make out. He tightened his grip on her and focused on the bulky outline of the soldier behind the M240. The man raked the weapon back and forth, battling for every inch of the pier.

Whipping wind from the rotors hit them as they got closer, and Beckham squinted to see Rodriguez and Peters jump from the chopper.

"Get inside!" Rodriguez yelled as he raced past.

The ground trembled from the hammering of thousands of feet. The otherworldly screeches from all those gaping mouths reverberated through the city. Reality seemed distant.

Meg went limp in his arms when they were one hundred feet from the Black Hawk. The knife slipped from her hand, hitting the concrete with a faint clank. Beckham put everything he had left into hoisting her up, his injured shoulder blazing. Working with Chow, they carried her toward the bird. Timbo beat them there. He placed Jinx inside and then grabbed Meg with his massive hands.

Beckham's eyes flicked to the door gunner. He saw then it was Horn, his features raw with pain in the flash of gunfire. It was the look that only seeing a fallen brother could produce.

The whine of high-caliber rounds intensified as Horn channeled his rage into the assault. Beckham turned back to the battle and cupped his hands over his mouth.

"Fall back!" he shouted. Despite Horn's efforts, the pier was already being overrun. Hundreds of Variants flowed onto the dock. Some spilled over the side to avoid the gunfire, splashing into the Hudson River. Others climbed onto the vehicles and through the spray of bullets.

A wave ten thousand strong crashed down Twelfth Avenue, fighting, clawing, and biting its way to the pier, hungry mouths starving for human flesh. The monstrous army stretched across Beckham's entire field of vision.

"Beckham, gun!" Chow shouted. He grabbed an M16 from the chopper and tossed it. Valdez and Ryan were already retreating by the time Beckham loaded and shouldered the rifle. Peters and Rodriguez had taken up position halfway between the bird and the concrete barriers. Jensen, unyielding, was still firing from the side of the truck.

"Fall back!" Beckham shouted. "FALL THE FUCK BACK!" His voice cracked, the countless screams finally taking their toll on his psyche.

Chow and Beckham joined Peters and Rodriguez. There was no need to aim when they got there. Everywhere Beckham lined up the iron sights, he found a target.

Jensen backpedaled with his rifle shouldered, squeezing off burst after burst. Tracer rounds from the M240 whistled overhead, thumping into the wall of Variants that had reached the abandoned Humvee. The rounds cut through the creatures and peppered the vehicle with holes, punching through metal. Air hissed out of the shredded tires.

"Move your asses!" Beckham screamed.

"Let's move!" Chow shouted. He pulled Beckham away. "Come on!"

A flash of motion behind the chopper stopped Beckham's heart midbeat. The Variants had jumped into the water to flank the team.

"Behind you!" Beckham shouted.

A half dozen of the creatures pulled themselves onto the dock, water dripping off their veiny, muscular flesh. The pilots lifted off just as two of the Variants launched into the air. One of them crashed back to the ground but the other grabbed on to the left landing wheel. The chopper jerked to the right, the creature swinging with only one hand still gripped to the wheel.

Jensen crouched next to Chow while Beckham aimed for the Variant's long arm. He held in a breath and squeezed off a shot that cut through the wrist, leaving its clawed hand still attached to the wheel while the rest of its body fell into the water.

The chopper rotated in a circle, giving Horn a clear shot at the remaining Variants. He opened up again, his gunfire marking out a perimeter around Beckham and the other men, the large-caliber bullets kicking concrete into the air. The rounds punched through flesh and shattered bones, splattering the dock with pink chunks of gore.

"Let's go!" Horn yelled, waving them forward with one hand.

The chopper lowered again, and the three men piled inside next to Timbo, who had been firing from the doorway beside Horn. Rodriguez and Peters jumped in a moment later, but Ryan and Valdez were still retreating.

"Out of the way!" Beckham shouted. He pointed his rifle out the door as soon as the men were clear and squeezed off covering fire for Ryan and Valdez.

They were only fifty feet away from the chopper. So close it seemed like Beckham could reach out and touch them. Five seconds. Maybe ten. That's all they needed. To most people, that amount of time would go unnoticed, but for Valdez and Ryan, every second was a matter of life and death. Both of them had abandoned firing and ran like madmen, their arms pumping and their helmets bobbing up and down.

Beckham pulled a dry magazine from his M16 and reached to Chow for another when he saw more Variants jumping from the water along the side of the pier. They climbed onto the dock. The pilots saw them too, and he pulled up before Beckham could react, knocking him against a wall.

"NO!" Beckham shouted. He watched helplessly as Ryan was taken down in a blur of motion, the monsters tackling him from two directions. Beckham glimpsed the terror in his eyes and the bloody mist exploding from arteries as they tore him apart. And then he was gone.

Beckham sucked in a long, stunned breath. He scrambled back to the edge of the open chopper door. Horn was firing madly in an effort to save Valdez, but it was too late. The rounds shredded the first wave, but another pack that had emerged from the river circled the marine. Valdez spun with his rifle blazing, dropping several of the monsters. The others reached out with talons as long as knives. They cut into him, tearing gaping wounds across his body. He spun as they slashed him, his eyes falling on the chopper, a defiant look still on his face. The man was as tough as a bag of bricks. It took five of them to finally bring him down.

Beckham forced himself to watch. Valdez had given his life for Beckham's men. He'd fought valiantly to the end so that his brothers would live. Looking away would dishonor him.

Halfway down the pier, the main mass of Variants surged over the concrete barricades. Thousands of talons reached toward the sky. The creatures climbed over one another in an effort to reach the helicopter. What was left of Ryan and Valdez was quickly consumed, buried in the heart of the diseased flesh.

The pilots maneuvered over the river and pulled away from the city. Beckham said a prayer, scanned the ruined New York skyline one more time, and collapsed next to Jinx's limp body. The nightmare that was Operation Liberty was finally over. A handful of heroes were dead and New York was lost, but he had a feeling the war had only just begun.

5

The monsters were gone, but signs of the nightmare they had unleashed on Plum Island were everywhere. Bloodstains crisscrossed the concrete. Bullet casings littered the ground. A single helmet remained on the tarmac.

Kate stood at the front of a group of civilians, waiting again for Team Ghost to return. She was only a hundred yards away from the charred skeleton of the Chinook. It sat there like a brooding beast, the blackened metal still steaming. Above it all, the Black Hawk sparkled in the sunlight. Kate squeezed Jenny's and Tasha's hands as they watched the helicopter approach.

"Clear a path!" someone shouted. Four medics in Medical Corps uniforms pushed through the group. They broke off into pairs and hurried across the tarmac carrying stretchers.

"What are they doing?" Tasha asked.

"They're going to help the soldiers," Kate replied.

"Is Daddy hurt?" Jenny asked.

"No, honey."

Tasha looked up with glossy eyes. "Is Reed?"

"He's going to be just fine."

Riley wheeled his chair after the medics. Fitz followed close behind, ignoring the orders from a Medical

Corps guard posted at the edge of the tarmac. Kate was still amazed at how fast the young marine sharpshooter could run on his prosthetic blades.

Kate watched anxiously as the chopper set down and disgorged over a half dozen men. The medics rushed forward beneath the blades. They pulled two people from the craft a moment later, a soldier and a woman in a CBRN suit. Team Ghost huddled around the medics and helped place the injured onto the stretchers.

She scanned the group, counting the survivors. Timbo, Peters, and Rodriguez were the first to come into view. Next she saw Chow and Jensen. Horn and Beckham took up the rear, jogging alongside the medics. A pale, limp hand hung from the stretcher on the right. There was no question then that another life had been lost.

The woman on the other stretcher reached up slowly, and Beckham grabbed her hand. Kate's heart lurched at the compassionate gesture. After everything he'd been through, the fact that the hardened soldier could still be so gentle and kind was the thing she admired most about him.

Ellis stepped up beside Kate. She hadn't heard him approach. He stooped down to pick up Jenny and then held her so she could see the approaching team.

"They found another survivor out there?" he asked.

"I...I don't know," Kate replied. "I overheard First Platoon had a couple of survivors, but they were taken to one of the destroyers off the coast."

"Maybe Beckham's team found someone else," Ellis said.

"I guess so," Kate said. She stepped back as the Medical Corps soldier in front yelled, "Make room!"

Jensen was the first to reach the end of the tarmac. He stopped to stare at the downed Chinook.

"He doesn't know," Kate whispered more to herself than anyone.

The commander took off his helmet and ran a hand over his head. Kate could only imagine what he was feeling. He'd returned from war to a home that had been ravaged by monsters.

Major Smith pushed through the crowd and met Jensen and the others on the tarmac. Riley and Fitz were already there. The kid swiveled his wheelchair to watch the medics continue past, his blue eyes locked on the stretcher. He wheeled after it and then stopped, his hands falling to the sides of his chair.

Kate's heart shattered at the sight. She saw Jinx's face then—and the gaping wound that stretched across his neck. He was gone a moment later, the medics rushing him and the woman away.

When she turned back to the tarmac, Beckham was staring at her. Every inch of his uniform was covered in blood and grime. She could smell the raw sewage on him from where he stood.

Kate didn't care. Horn ran to his girls, and she ran to Beckham. He wrapped his arms around her and squeezed her so hard she could hardly breathe. When he finally let up, she tilted her head up and searched his eyes. They were still strong and confident, even now, after so much had been lost.

"Are you okay?" they asked each other at the same time.

They shared a sad, companionable chuckle that lasted only a fraction of a second. He pulled her in tight again and said, "What happened here?"

"Horn didn't tell you?"

Beckham looked toward the medics and said, "There wasn't much talking on the ride back."

Kate wasn't surprised. The last thing the men had

needed to hear when they were in New York was that their home was under fire.

"That Chinook," Kate said, pointing. "It was carrying a load of Variants for medical research. Eighteen of them. One of them got out. It killed the crew and the chopper crashed. The creatures escaped and...murdered over a third of the island's population."

"Christ," Beckham said. "Riley, Fitz, you, and the girls. You're all okay?"

"We're okay," Kate said. "We have Fitz to thank for that. If it weren't for him, we wouldn't be talking right now. None of us would be."

Beckham's features softened, his jaw relaxing. "Thank God for that." When he turned to the Chinook, all trace of emotion disappeared from his features. He had hardened back into an operator right before her eyes.

"How bad is it out there?" Kate asked in a voice shy of a whisper.

Beckham bowed his head. "It's gone, Kate."

"What's gone?"

He caught her gaze and said, "The whole damn world."

Jensen walked into a quiet command center wondering if he should have stayed behind instead of going to the front with Team Ghost and 1st Platoon. There had to have been something he could have done to prevent the massacre on Plum Island. Maybe if he had sat Operation Liberty out, the Variants would never have escaped the Chinook. Maybe he would have ordered the bird shot down before it made land.

No, you can't think like that.

The domino effect of decisions could drive a man

mad. If he had stayed behind at Plum Island, then he'd be kicking himself over Jinx, Ryan, Valdez, and the countless marines who had died.

Regret was a part of war. Every single decision stayed with a soldier for the rest of his life. There were no take backs, no time machines. You had to believe that everything went down the way it was supposed to, or else you'd go crazy.

Jensen strolled over to the observation window. All of this could have been avoided—the virus, the war. He couldn't wrap his mind around the numbers. Even if he tried, he couldn't picture what a billion people looked like, let alone six.

Major Smith walked into the room and looked Jensen up and down twice. "Shit, sir. You look like you've been through the grinder."

The major eased the door shut and stood there, twisting his wedding ring around his finger. His eyes were ripe with exhaustion. Despite that, he seemed relatively alert.

"Talk to me. How bad is it?"

Smith stiffened and said, "Bad, sir. We lost sixty-five people—eleven scientists, thirty-four soldiers, and twenty civilians."

Jensen shook his head. "I thought we were safe here," he said grimly.

"And Colonel Gibson is dead," Smith added.

Jensen clenched a fist. "How'd he die?"

"A Variant, sir. It breached the secure medical wing where Gibson was being held. I was told there wasn't much left when it got done with him."

"A fitting end," Jensen replied in a dark voice that sounded like it could have come from a stranger. He felt no trace of compassion for the colonel. Dying of a heart attack would have been the easy way out, but Gibson didn't deserve the easy way. His fate felt like retribution.

"Base is on lockdown, sir," Smith said. "Guard posts are set up at multiple locations. The towers are all manned, and I've repositioned the remaining guards to patrol the fences. Even if those things can swim, they won't make it past the beach."

"I wouldn't be so sure about that," Jensen said, remembering the Variants back in the Hudson. He could still see them swimming alongside the pier to flank Echo 3. The last thing he was going to do now was underestimate the creatures.

"I want every available man on security detail," he said. "I'll give the strike teams a few hours of bunk time to recover from Operation Liberty. At 1500, I want them back on patrol."

"Understood, sir. We have a call with Central at 0900. General Kennor has requested to speak with Doctor Lovato."

Jensen checked his watch, raising a sleeve smeared with shit and blood. The stink assaulted his nostrils. He needed a long bath in hot bleach.

"That gives us about five minutes," Jensen said. "Where is she?" He looked around the empty room. "Where the hell is everyone?"

"Doctor Lovato's not coming, sir."

"What do you mean she isn't coming?"

"She refuses to speak to the general. Said she has nothing to say to him and that he won't listen anyway."

The words hung in the air for an uncomfortable second. Jensen dug in his pocket for the tobacco he'd picked up from a marine in New York. He tucked a chunk into his mouth as he spoke, his words coming out muffled. "Where's Hickman and Benzing?"

Smith hesitated and shook his head.

Jensen swallowed hard. The juices burned as they trickled down his throat. "Goddamn son of a..."

"I'm sorry, sir," Smith said, his features tense and his eyes watery. If Jensen didn't know better, he would have thought the man was holding back tears. He wasn't used to seeing the major show any emotion.

"They were good soldiers," Jensen said. "Loyal soldiers."

Smith nodded and glanced at the radio equipment along the wall.

Jensen decided against asking him how they died. All that mattered now was moving forward. He would hold a proper service for those they had lost, but for now he needed to work on salvaging what he could.

"Smith," Jensen said sternly. "You need to get it together. Lots of people are counting on us."

"Yes, sir," Smith replied and straightened his posture. "I have a fill-in for now, but she's not an experienced radio operator."

"I'll take whomever I can get. We need the intel now more than ever," Jensen said. He paused in an effort to manage his thoughts. "Anything I should know before our call with General Kennor?"

Smith sat down at the war table and turned on the computer. His hand shook as he moused over to the video feed.

"Smith, what aren't you telling me?"

The major looked up. "I was going to let the general tell you, sir."

Jensen crossed his arms and waited.

Smith drew in a deep breath and let it out in a huff. "General Kennor has issued a full retreat. We've lost the cities, sir. The military is pulling back."

The door creaked open, distracting Jensen from his churning stomach. A woman with shoulder-length gray hair and eyes as sharp as an eagle's stood in the doorway. She threw up a tight salute and said, "Corporal Hook, reporting for duty, sir."

Jensen returned the salute halfheartedly. Pointing at the radio equipment, he said, "Put together a sitrep based on whatever you're hearing over the Net. I want a report by 1600."

"Yes, sir," Hook said. She hurried over to the wall of monitors, grabbed a headset, and took a seat without asking questions or making small talk. He liked her already.

"Connecting to the call with Central," Smith said from the table.

Jensen spat a wad of chew into the trash and took a seat next to the major. "Anything else I should know?"

"We're running low on supplies—both ammo and food," Smith said, shaking his head. "Just when you think shit can't get worse."

Jensen frowned. "Things can always get worse, Smith. At least we're still breathing. Supplies can be restocked...humans can't."

"Yes, sir. I'll put in a request at the end of the call."

The computer beeped at them and a live feed of the ops room at Central Command emerged on the screen. Insignias of the army, navy, air force, and marines decorated the concrete wall of the Command bunker. The chair behind a mahogany table with maps and papers draped across it sat empty.

Jensen heard a door open and shut. A man with white hair strolled in and tossed a folder on the table. He took a seat and stared into the camera with eyes accentuated by purple bags that looked a lot like bruises. At first, Jensen could hardly believe it was Kennor. If it weren't for his wrinkled face, he would have thought the man sitting in front of them was a boxer who had just taken a few too many punches to the face. Jensen wished he could add a bruise for not listening to Kate in the first place.

The general opened his folder and licked a finger before thumbing through the pages, scanning the words so quickly it made Jensen sick. Did he even understand how bad things were?

Kennor paused at the last page, raised his bushy gray brows, and then frowned. A curse followed.

"Jensen, Smith," he said, looking at them in turn.

"General," Jensen said.

"Heard Plum Island was attacked in a freak accident last night."

"Yes, sir, we had sixty-five casualties. Colonel Gibson was one of them."

Kennor didn't even flinch. "How many injured?"

Jensen did flinch at that. *How many injured? Is Kennor that clueless?*

"Zero, sir," Jensen replied through clenched teeth. "The Variants don't leave behind injured."

Kennor's forehead tightened, and he grumbled, "Where's Doctor Lovato?"

"Not here," Jensen said.

Kennor glared at him, letting his eyes do the talking.

"She's in the lab, sir," Smith said. "Cooking up a new weapon."

"Good," Kennor said. "I want a sitrep at 0700 every day from here out. If she makes a breakthrough, I'm the first person you tell."

Jensen nodded. "Certainly, sir." He wanted to reach through the screen and strangle the old bastard. But he kept his calm for the sake of those under his command. The general was still in charge, and Jensen had to respect that. Kennor was stubborn, but he wasn't a madman. He wasn't Colonel Gibson.

"As you two probably already know, Operation Liberty has failed. I've issued a full retreat to outposts, bases, and strongholds," Kennor said. "That means it's even more important that Doctor Lovato develop something as soon as possible."

"Understood, sir," Jensen said. After a pause, he added, "How will we deploy this weapon? Aren't we strained for resources?"

"We'll figure that out when she creates one," Kennor said. He looked away from the camera and held up a finger to someone Jensen couldn't see.

"I'm needed in ops, but there's one last thing you two need to know. This is confidential. You are to share it with no one," Kennor said. His forehead became a canyon of wrinkles, so many that it looked like it hurt. "Raven Rock has fallen."

Jensen fidgeted in his chair. Surely the general was mistaken. There was no way the alternate command center could have been overrun.

"The Variants got into the tunnels beneath the base," Kennor said. "I deployed a search-and-rescue team, but we lost contact with them shortly after they arrived."

Jensen didn't know what to say. The implications were startling. First New York, then Plum Island, now the retreat from the cities and the loss of Raven Rock.

Kennor stood and straightened his uniform. "Actually, you can share this intel with Doctor Lovato. Tell her we are losing this war."

"She understands perfectly, sir," Jensen said. He didn't think he sounded condescending, but Kennor responded with a glare.

"Sir, we have a request," Smith said.

"What is it?"

"We're running low on munitions and our food supply is dangerously low too. Requesting a resupply of both."

Kennor shook his head. "I can't authorize that."

The response came so fast Jensen wondered if the general had even heard the question. When Smith started to protest, Kennor raised his hand as if he were about to scold a private.

"We have requests coming in from every remaining military asset across the country. You'll have to wait your turn," Kennor said.

"Sir, Plum Island could help bring an end to this war. If it weren't for Doctor Lovato's first bioweapon—"

"I realize that, Lieutenant Colonel, but President Mitchell has authorized resupplies based on priority level, and as of now Plum Island isn't at the top of the list."

"General," Jensen said, "if you want a scientific solution to this war, you need to get me the tools."

"Don't take this the wrong way, Jensen, but we have other teams working on solutions." He folded his hands and caught Jensen's gaze. "You're a soldier. You'll have to make do."

Jensen nodded, threw up a salute, and waited for Kennor to shut off the feed. As soon as the general signed off, Jensen stood and walked to the observation window, barking orders. "Smith, I want you to count every gun, every round, every can of Campbell's Chunky Soup. We need to know exactly how long we can stretch our rations. Hook, I want to know what's going on in the rest of the country."

The corporal swiveled her chair away from the monitors. "Sir, I've been scanning the channels and I'm not picking up much."

"What do you mean?" Jensen asked.

"I mean I'm not hearing much chatter at all," she said. "I don't think there are many people left out there."

6

By midmorning, a blanket of calm had settled over Plum Island. The only sounds were the sporadic chirp of a bird and the faint rap of footsteps. Beckham heard everything, his senses still on full alert. He hadn't slept for thirty-six hours but couldn't seem to shut off his mind. After everything he had been through, it wasn't going to be easy to let his guard down enough to get some shut-eye.

He sat with Kate on the steps of Building 1, watching the cleanup crews carry bodies draped with white sheets into the medical building. Neither of them spoke. Being next to each other was enough for now.

Beckham wondered how long the quiet would last. He wanted to reach out and put his arm around Kate, to pull her tight, but he feared her soft touch could break him, so he pretended he didn't need it. He tried to feel something—wanted to feel something—but beyond the lingering pain of losing so many of his brothers, there wasn't much that seemed safe to feel besides anger.

Anger was a dangerous emotion. Like wind through a house of cards, the rage threatened to blow everything away. He'd gotten pummeled by a Variant at Bragg and taken shrapnel to the shoulder in New York, but it was always the mental wounds that hurt the worst. They went deeper than the bruises and cuts that tattooed his skin. He was a Delta operator, yes, but no amount of training or experience could prepare him for the anguish that came with the loss.

"Will you stay now?" Kate asked, breaking the long silence.

"I hope so," he said. "Need to heal."

Kate scooted closer, just inches away from him. He almost flinched. She read his body language with a single, critical look.

Seeing her expression, Beckham said, "Sorry."

"No, *don't* do that. You don't apologize. You're a hero, Reed."

Beckham shrugged; he didn't feel like a hero. Before he could react, Kate brushed up next to him, placing her head on his shoulder. The fresh stitches screamed at him, but instead of pulling away, he leaned closer.

"I'm sorry about Jinx and the others," Kate said. She stared ahead now, her eyes following another white-draped body on its way to the medical building.

"He died fighting. Can't ask for anything more than a soldier's death," Beckham said. He looked to the north, toward New York City, and thought of Jake and Timothy. The cop and his son they'd rescued from Manhattan during Operation Liberty were safe on a destroyer now, sailing somewhere away from the monsters. He took solace in knowing that Jinx's death hadn't been for nothing. In the end, they had saved a few precious lives.

Kate let out a sigh and said, "What comes next?"

"Was about to ask you the same thing."

"Back to the lab."

Beckham shifted, trying to relieve the pressure on his wounded shoulder.

"I'm going to design another weapon," she continued. "Something that will kill every last one of the Variants."

"That's what we should have done a week ago," Beckham said. His anger and frustration bubbled over now. "That son of a bitch, Kennor. In some ways he's no better than Gibson. If he would have just *listened* before Operation Liberty. And don't get me started on Lieutenant Gates, that piece of shit. Called in an air strike and left us out there to fight an army of Variants numbering in the hundreds of thousands."

Kate placed her hand over his and gently squeezed his battered knuckles. Then she kissed him on the cheek. "You're a good man, Reed."

Hearing those words drained the anger from him. It flowed out with a breath and was gone. He pulled Kate toward him and kissed her with a soft ferocity.

Their lips parted and Beckham bowed his forehead against hers. "You get to the lab. I'm going to go check on Riley and then sleep for a day or two, if I can."

Kate smiled, flashing the dimples that made his heart race. She gave him another kiss that kindled an emotion he had spent most of his life trying to bury. Now, after all hope seemed lost, it had arisen from the grave. He decided then to embrace it. To stop hiding behind his armor and weapons. He could be more than just a soldier.

Beckham gave Kate a meaningful look and reached down to help her up.

"Where'd you find her?" Kate asked as they walked up the stairs. "The woman you brought back."

Beckham stopped midstride, remembering the nightmarish lair beneath New York.

"Reed?"

He shook his head and turned partially toward her.

"If you'd rather not talk about it, I understand," Kate said.

"It's okay," he said. "We found her in the sewers.

There were hundreds of survivors down there. Maybe more. I don't know."

Kate squinted, her features tensing. "What do you mean there were survivors?"

Beckham could see she was trying to understand, but nothing he said could describe the true horrors his team had stumbled upon beneath the streets. There was no simple way to explain what he'd seen, and the thought of admitting to her that he'd killed the human prisoners made him feel queasy.

"Reed, you can tell me. I can handle it." Kate swept a strand of brown hair behind an ear. "I need to know."

Beckham didn't want her to feel responsible. The burden she carried was already heavy enough to send a normal person over the edge. She'd blamed herself for the Variants since the deployment of her bioweapon. If she knew what they were doing and what he had tried to stop...

"If I'm going to design another weapon, I need to know everything you do. I'm assuming what you saw is no different than in other cities. I already know they are going underground to avoid sunlight."

"That's not the only reason," Beckham replied, a bit too fast. He closed his eyes, sucked in a breath, and exhaled. "They store their food down there, Kate."

When he opened his eyes, Kate had taken a step back. "Store their food?" Her blue eyes widened as she realized what he meant.

"We discovered a storeroom of human prisoners. There were hundreds of mutilated survivors that the Variants were feeding on. We saved Meg, but...I was forced to kill the others."

Kate cupped a hand over her mouth. She whimpered into her palm and then peeled it away. "I'm so sorry."

Beckham wrapped his arms around her. "It's not your fault. The blame rests solely on that bastard Gibson."

"No," Kate said, pulling away. She sobbed and wiped away a tear. "If VariantX9H9 had killed all of the Variants, this would never have happened. There wouldn't be any lairs. You wouldn't have had to kill *anyone*."

Meg jerked awake and reached for her axe that wasn't there. The movement sent the most awful pain of her life searing through her legs. She gritted her teeth. Behind blurred eyes, she saw a bank of lights. Her mind went blank a moment later, the agony shutting off her brain.

When she woke again, she felt nothing. If it weren't for the nurse staring down at her, she would have thought she was dead. A warm, reassuring smile touched the sides of the young woman's face.

"This might sting," the nurse said. She reached forward with a large needle that looked more like a small knife.

Meg didn't bother protesting. She couldn't even if she wanted to. She watched as the nurse inserted the tip into her arm. It hurt as bad as she thought it would. Her muscles knotted, tensing around the needle. She blinked, a tear falling from her eye, and then there was darkness.

The third time she woke, she was alone. Her body felt strange, like it wasn't hers anymore. She knew it was the drugs. In the past she would have refused them. She was an all-natural kind of a gal, but a lot had changed in the last month. Her husband was dead, and the world was full of monsters. She drew a deep breath in an attempt to calm her nerves. The door squeaked open a moment later and a bearded man with neatly parted brown hair entered her room.

"Hi, Meg, I'm Doctor Hill," he said. He approached her bedside with his eyes locked on a clipboard.

She tried to sit up, but that hurt worse than the needle. She grimaced as the pain passed.

"Probably want to sit still," Hill said gingerly. "Your legs are pretty torn up. I stitched them back together, but honestly, I'm not a surgeon." He flipped a page over the clipboard and continued, "I was a physical therapist working at Fort Bragg. Got lucky and was rescued about a week ago."

She glared at him incredulously. A physical therapist had stitched her up? She didn't want to see what was beneath the white covers.

"Thanks," she murmured.

"Good news is you're going to be fine. Will take some time for your legs to heal, but once we get you hydrated you'll start feeling better."

Meg craned her neck to the left and looked out the window. A patrol of armed soldiers walked down a concrete pathway.

"Where am I?"

"Plum Island," Hill replied. "You're safe now."

Meg let out a weak laugh and closed her eyes again, drifting back into the perpetual nightmare inside her head.

Fitz scoped the beach with his new MK11. It was midafternoon and he was still on edge from the attack the night before but the semiautomatic sniper rifle eased his anxiety. The weapon was his favorite. It operated like other rifles but was highly accurate and durable.

He played the crosshairs over the water, half expecting to see the pale skin of a swimming Variant. After an hour of pacing back and forth, he finally took a seat on a stool and rested his aching body. He was fighting to keep his eyelids open, and his thigh muscles burned like he'd just finished a marathon. He desperately needed sleep, a deep-tissue massage, and a shot of whiskey.

Scratch that. He needed a *bottle* of whiskey.

Just when he was starting to relax, his earpiece crackled.

"Tower Four, Command. We have a report of an unidentified ship drifting south in Gardiners Bay. You got eyes on?"

"Stand by," Fitz said.

He walked to the edge of the box. This wasn't the first report of a derelict ship. Vessels dotted the horizon like shells on a beach. Their crews had either abandoned them or were dead.

Hoisting his rifle onto the ledge, he set the bipod and pointed the sleek black muzzle toward the bay. The horizon warned of a midafternoon storm. Swollen gray clouds rolled across the sky, a sharp contrast to the teal waves. Fitz squared his shoulders and then roved his aim slowly to the right until he saw metal.

"Got eyes," Fitz said. "Definitely a ship. Stand by for identification."

He zoomed in, expecting to see a freighter, or perhaps a yacht out of Martha's Vineyard. Instead of a luxury cruiser, he saw a navy destroyer. And it wasn't anchored either. A powerful wake trailed the boat as she split the waves.

"Command, Tower Four. I have eyes on a navy destroyer with the markings USS *Truxtun*, one zero three. She's coming in pretty fast."

A long pause followed his report, long enough to tell Fitz that Command was already planning how to blow the boat out of the water if it got too close. Unless Lieutenant Colonel Jensen had some secret Hellfire missiles, that wasn't going to happen.

The electronic wail of a siren sounded from the public address system before Fitz could get his thoughts straight. He brought his eye back to the scope. The ship appeared to be on a collision course with the island.

Fitz chambered a round and centered his sight on the bow—as if a shot from his gun would do anything. Still, the cold steel in his hands made him feel better. He scanned the deck of the boat for contacts as it came into focus, but there wasn't a single person in sight.

A ghost ship.

He imagined a Variant at the helm, crazed and starving, its yellow eyes focused on the island. His heart rate increased as the whine of the emergency sirens blared louder.

"Command, Tower Four. No hostiles. Please advise. Over," Fitz said.

The whoosh of helicopter blades pulled Fitz's gaze to the north. Strike teams raced across the tarmac and piled into the trio of grounded Black Hawks. By the time he moved back to the other side of his tower, the birds were airborne. The mechanical chatter of their rotors masked his labored breaths. He watched them race across the sky toward the *Truxtun*.

"Tower Four, stand by for orders," the operator finally replied.

Fitz brought the scope back to his eye. The ship plowed through the water at full speed, whitecaps bursting across the bow. Echo 1 intercepted it first. The crew chief didn't hesitate. They opened up with the M240 and sprayed projectiles across the ship's path. Echo 2 and Echo 3 flanked the destroyer as it flew by, circling and giving chase.

Fitz followed the ship's progress with his scope. It looked like it was going to hit the eastern peninsula of the island. "Come on," he murmured. "Stop, you son of a bitch."

He watched, astonished, as the new threat continued barreling toward the island. That was the thing about the apocalypse; you never knew what would happen next.

The mechanical whine of gas-powered turbines pulled Fitz from his thoughts. Echo 1 had opened fire on the bow of the *Truxtun*. Whoever was steering the ship didn't change course. The destroyer charged right through the hail of gunfire. Echo 2 and Echo 3 unleashed a barrage on the port and starboard sides of the ship.

Why would a navy ship ram the fucking island?

If they wanted resources, all they had to do was point their Tomahawk missiles and Lieutenant Colonel Jensen would wave a white flag.

Nothing made sense . . . until the ship shot past the beach and continued on a straight course toward the Connecticut shoreline. The Black Hawks seemed just as surprised as Fitz. They hovered over the water like oversized bees, their blades buzzing as they waited for orders.

Then Fitz understood. The ship had never been on a collision course at all—there was no one at the helm. The *Truxtun* was truly just a ghost ship.

Fitz watched the destroyer continue toward mainland as the choppers returned to base. When the ship was only a speck on the horizon, he collapsed on the stool, took in a long breath, and exhaled.

"Command, Tower Four. Anyone got any whiskey?"

7

Kate held out her arms as Ellis zipped up the back of her suit. Five minutes had passed since the alarms had stopped screaming, but the sound was still reverberating in her ears.

"A destroyer?" Ellis asked. "With no one behind the wheel? How the hell does that make any sense?"

Kate frowned. "Does anything make sense anymore?" Mentally, she was beyond exhausted, but she needed her wits for what came next.

Kate was beginning to hate the lab. It was yet another reminder of what she'd created. The other labs were dark. There were no scientists in CBRN suits huddling around computer monitors on the other levels or robotic arms retrieving samples in the centrifuge. They'd lost most of their support staff in the attack, and the survivors had been given time to regroup. Kate and Ellis were the only ones determined—or crazy—enough to be here today.

"Not going to lie," Ellis said, waving his badge over the security terminal. "I'm excited to get back to it. I've been thinking about another bioweapon and I have an idea."

The glass doors whispered apart and Kate strolled

past the empty lab stations. Banks of LED lights clicked on simultaneously and the room lit up with a clean, white glow that made it feel lonelier than it already was.

"I have an idea too," Kate said after a long pause.

"You first," Ellis said. He pulled a stool across the floor to her station.

Kate sat, keyed in her credentials, and moused over to a research paper she'd read earlier.

"What do we know about the Variants' weaknesses?" Kate asked.

Ellis glanced up at her, his brow furrowed. "Is that a rhetorical question?"

"No. I'm being serious."

He shrugged. "We know they're sensitive to light. That's about it."

"That's why I've been reading about optogenetics," Kate said. She scooted her stool over and pointed at the PDF on-screen. "Know anything about it?"

"Only what Wikipedia taught me," he chuckled. "One of my old classmates worked in the field, and I didn't want to sound like an idiot the last time we had dinner."

Kate would have laughed a month ago, but she didn't feel much like laughing now. She forced a smile he probably couldn't even see.

"I'm not an expert on it either, but I know that light has been used to control neural activity through genetic targeting. Before everything that's happened, researchers made breakthroughs in controlling the behavior of animals—"

Ellis interrupted her by shaking his helmet. "You're not thinking what I think you're thinking, are you? You were the one who said the Variants aren't animals we can control."

"I'm not talking about controlling them. I'm talking about killing them," Kate said, her voice cutting. She shifted her gaze from the computer to his eyes. "You don't need to remind me of what I've said in the past."

He shied away, slouching half a degree in his chair. "Sorry."

Kate was silent for a moment. There was so much going on in her head she was having a hard time keeping it straight. She pawed her visor in a futile attempt to rub her tired eyes, forgetting she even had her helmet on.

"The main problem is weaponizing it. Most of the applications require light-sensitive probes to be implanted in the brains of subjects," she said.

"That's not exactly an option."

"No, but what if we could use the same concept to kill them? To exploit their weakness to light."

Ellis frowned and said, "What's the difference between shooting them with bullets or shooting them with some sort of light gun? Both require soldiers, and last I checked the world was running very short on those."

Kate thought of Beckham. No matter what she designed, someone would have to test the weapon in the field. The idea of him risking his life out there again made her heart ache.

"What's your idea?" Kate asked. She turned away from her monitor, crossed her arms, and waited.

"I've been so focused on the epigenetic changes the Variants are going through, I've neglected the obvious," Ellis said, talking quickly and waving his hands. "I can't believe I didn't think of this weeks ago. I was just so stuck on the—"

"Slow down," Kate said.

"Right, sorry," he replied after a pause. "Remember how the stem cells are proliferating at a rapid rate?"

"I do. They're responsible for their healing capabilities, immune system health, and rapid transformation." Kate tried to guess where he was going with this, but she was too exhausted to speculate. He didn't wait for her questions anyway.

"Well, what if we isolate a sample of bone marrow stem cells from one of the Variants? We could run it through the HTS system and look for a protein that's only expressed in the infected. Then we could develop antibodies that would target their stem cells and deliver something to knock them out," he said. His voice carried a sense of awe. "It would only work on Variants, since the protein would be specific to them."

Kate considered the idea. It wasn't much different from what she had created with VariantX9H9. The bioweapon had worked on only those infected with the hemorrhage virus. But this time whatever they ended up developing would need to kill every one of the creatures. There was no margin for error.

Ellis studied Kate for a reaction, his eyes bright behind his visor.

"So you think we should use a technology like targeted drug delivery?" Kate asked.

"Precisely," Ellis said, nodding. "Think it might work?"

"Not sure," Kate said. "But I like the idea."

A childish grin broke across Ellis's face that reminded Kate of her brother, Javier. It was the same smile he'd used to get out of countless scrapes when they were growing up. "First things first," she said, forcing herself to focus on the present. "We need to start with the bone marrow stem cells."

Kate turned to the exit of the lab.

"Where are you going?"

"To take a sample from a Variant," she said. "Are you just going to sit there, or are you coming with me?"

Beckham awoke with a violent jerk. His breathing was heavy, his back drenched with sweat. The distant memory of a nightmare clung to his mind. He had been in the tunnels, plastered to a wall, unable to shoot the Variants crawling toward him. For a moment he was paralyzed by the powerful dream.

"Jesus, boss. Are you okay?" Horn sat on the adjacent bunk, his daughters on each side. Riley was in his wheelchair at the end of his bed.

"'Bout time you got your ass up," Riley said with the hint of a grin.

Beckham ran a hand through hair that needed trimming and looked at his watch. The slight movement of his shoulder sent pain racing across his battered chest.

"Fuck, I've been out awhile," he said, trying to hide the pain.

"Hey, little ears on deck here," Horn said with a pointed look toward his daughters.

"Right. Sorry, Big Horn. And sorry, Tasha and Jenny," Beckham said, nodding at each girl in turn.

"You've been out five hours," Riley said. "If you don't count the weirdness with the boat and the alarms. That woke us all up, but you fell right back asleep."

Beckham scooted to the edge of his bed and scanned the mostly empty room. The other soldiers were on patrol, and the majority of the civilians had been issued rooms in Building 1. Horn and his girls had one of those, but they'd stuck around to sit with Beckham. Kate had offered him her bed, but he wanted to be with his men for now.

"Big Horn, you should take the girls to Building One. Get settled in your new quarters," Beckham said. He couldn't mask the reluctance in his tone. Selfishly, he wanted them to stay. It felt too good to have them by his side. He wasn't sure how long it would last, but for now they were a family again.

"Nah, we're staying here for a while," Horn said.

"Yeah," Riley added. "Fu—I mean, the heck with that. I miss the barracks."

At the far end of the room, Chow stood staring out the window, chewing on a toothpick like he always did when deep in thought. Beckham made a note to talk to the man later. Jinx had been Chow's best friend. They had fought together for years, weathering the toughest of times in remote locations around the world. And now he was gone, another victim to Colonel Gibson's dream of saving young GIs. The irony continued to sicken Beckham.

The double doors to the barracks swung open and Lieutenant Colonel Jensen strode inside, flanked by Major Smith.

"We have a situation," Jensen said. As he stood in the doorway, he seemed taller, his shoulders broader. The officer had earned Beckham's trust and respect. He no longer felt like he was looking at Gibson's shadow—he was looking at an ethical leader. When the time came Beckham wouldn't hesitate to order Team Ghost to follow Jensen back into battle and he had a feeling they would have the opportunity sooner rather than later.

Beckham stood and rubbed his shoulder as Jensen approached. He bit back the urge to ask questions. Jensen was all military right now, clearly on a mission. He stopped in the aisle separating the rows of bunks and looked at Beckham. They exchanged a short nod, and the look told Beckham that his respect was mutual.

"As you know, the USS *Truxtun* shot by the island at 1400. Normally I wouldn't care since it didn't run aground here. But…" Jensen glanced at Major Smith, who took over.

"The ship has crashed into the shore at Niantic, Connecticut," he said, clapping his hands together on the word *crash*. Tasha and Jenny giggled. Horn pulled them closer, wrapping his arms around their shoulders.

"I sent Echo One out for recon. Weird thing is, doesn't look like anyone's home. We haven't seen a single body either. All attempts to hail the crew have failed," Smith continued.

"Not sure I understand the problem, sir," Horn said. "What do we care?"

Jensen's nostrils flared so wide Beckham could see the inside of his nose. "Supplies," Jensen said, resting his hands on his hips and taking a deep breath. "We're running low. Ammunition, food—it's all dwindling. The survivors from Bragg—and the attack on the island last night—put a dent in both stockpiles. Unfortunately, Command is stretched just as thin and General Kennor denied my request this morning for a resupply."

Riley moved his chair, the wheels squeaking and drawing the attention of the entire team. "The attack also put a dent in the human supply count," he said grimly.

"You're right," Jensen replied. He took a step forward, crossed his arms, and shifted the chew in his mouth to the other side. "But that doesn't change our current supply situation. And I'm not sure we can count on Command for much longer. I'm thinking long term here, gentlemen, and it's time to start accepting the obvious. We're going to be on our own eventually."

Jensen let the words hang in the air. Beckham could read the man like a book. He was doing what any leader would do in a crisis situation—he was preparing his men for the worst and hoping for the best. Beckham had done the same thing countless times.

"I'm considering a mission to see what we can salvage from the ship. It's safer than an expedition into the cities," Jensen said. "The ship has run aground next to a sparsely populated area, and recon flights haven't seen a single Variant."

"I don't like it," Beckham said. He assumed the man had come to Ghost for volunteers. Beckham wasn't going to hold back his opinion when his team's lives were on the line.

"Me either," Horn added. "Even if there aren't any Variants onshore, there could be some on board. Maybe an entire ship of 'em."

"Or other hostiles," Riley said.

Jensen regarded each man in turn. "You're absolutely right. I've considered this, but I think the reward is worth the risk. I'm not going to order anyone to come with me. This is a strictly volunteer mission, but I was hoping you'd be in. I need two others. Peters, Rodriguez, and Timbo have already agreed."

"I'm in," came a determined voice.

Beckham didn't need to turn to see it was Chow. The operator had turned away from the windows. Losing Jinx had been hard on everyone, but Chow seemed to have been hit worst of all, making him restless and angry. It was clear that he didn't want to do recon. He wanted revenge, and that kind of attitude got men killed. Beckham had seen it many times. The worst had been on a mission in Fallujah. An insurgent sniper had taken out a marine walking alongside a Humvee. The poor kid was dead before the medic could pull him off the road. Instead of taking cover, two of his buddies had run into the open, guns blazing, bloodlust taking over. Three marines were dead a minute later. By the time it was all over, the sniper had picked off half a fucking platoon.

He wasn't going to let the same happen to Chow.

"You sit this one out," Beckham said.

Chow flicked the toothpick to the other side of his mouth, glaring. "Hell no, man. I'm going."

"No. You sit this out," Beckham repeated. "You too,

Horn." He rubbed his shoulder again and then cracked his neck from side to side. "I'll go," he said. "I'll bring Fitz too, if he's game. We could use him on this one."

Beckham knew Jensen wanted another operator, but Fitz was good with a rifle. Damn good. He had saved Kate and countless others. He didn't want to know what she would say about him leaving again, but this was a short mission. Hopefully she would understand.

"That good enough?" Beckham asked. He locked eyes with Jensen and the officer nodded.

"Can I go?" Riley asked. His features were hard, and Beckham wondered if he was serious. Then he winked and cracked a half grin. Despite the Kid's good humor, the sight of Riley confined to the chair made Beckham want to punch a wall.

"Thanks," Jensen said. "You guys get some rest. Master Sergeant Beckham, report to Command at 1700."

"Yes, sir," Beckham replied.

Jensen and Smith left Team Ghost and Horn's daughters in a companionable silence. The quiet was broken a few moments later by a brittle voice.

"You can't save us all," Chow said. "World doesn't work like that, man. You don't get to make decisions like this for me." He hurried out of the room and slammed the door shut behind him.

"Give him time," Horn said. "He just lost his best friend."

Beckham nodded and took a seat on his bunk, the energy draining out of him. Chow was right. He couldn't control a situation that had spiraled completely out of control. Panda, Tenor, Edwards, Jinx, Ryan, Valdez— Beckham hadn't been able to save any of them. And by the time this war was over, Beckham had a feeling he was going to bury more of his brothers.

Or maybe they'd be the ones burying him.

Meg maneuvered her wheelchair through the doorway, using her palm to keep the door open. A soldier wheeling his own chair down the hall stopped to gawk at her. He ran a hand over his mop of wild hair as she struggled with the door.

"What the hell are you staring at?" she asked.

He shrugged. "Wondering when you'd ask for some help."

She turned the wheel with her left hand and elbowed the door with her other arm. The metal swung open and then came back and hit her on the elbow before she could react. She bit back a cry and glared at the soldier.

"You going to help me or what?" she said.

The man laughed and wheeled over. He held the door open so she could finally move into the hallway.

"Thanks," she said.

He sat there, continuing to stare. Up close, she could see that his eyes were bright blue.

"Dude, what the fuck?" Meg asked. "Do I have something on my face, or what?"

He shook his head, grinned, and held out his hand. "I'm Staff Sergeant Alex Riley, but you can call me Riley. Or 'Kid' is fine too. That's what my brothers call me."

She regarded him with a raised brow, giving him a once-over. His legs were both in casts, and his face was covered with the soft yellow of healing bruises.

"Meg," she said, grabbing his hand reluctantly.

"Welcome to Plum Island. How'd you get here, if you don't mind me asking?"

Meg licked her dry lips. "Look, I've been bedridden all day. I'm tired, my legs are killing me, and I just want some fresh air. Can we skip my life story?"

"Sure," Riley said. His eyes darted away to the window to the room behind her. "I'm here for a checkup, just thought I'd say hi." He started wheeling away and said, "Nice to meet you, Meg."

She sighed and watched him go. When he was halfway down the hall, she said, "I was rescued from New York."

He twisted around and looked at her for a moment. "Beckham found you, didn't he?"

Meg remembered the name. "Yeah," Meg said, wheeling after Riley. "Yeah, he did. Do you know him? I want to thank him."

Riley smiled so wide his dimples nearly went all the way to his ears. "He's my team leader."

"Can you take me to him?"

"You aren't going anywhere!" a woman shouted.

Meg looked over Riley's shoulder to see the hospital's only nurse running down the hall. Doctor Hill was right behind her.

"What on earth are you doing?" the doctor asked.

"I was about to get some fresh air…" Meg began to say.

"You need to rest, Meg. Rest and heal," Hill said.

She glanced back at Riley and he winked at her.

"You can't see Beckham right now anyway," Riley said.

"Why not?"

"Because he's about to leave for another mission."

"He just got back," Meg said, shocked.

"He's Delta Force—and even if he wasn't, that's just how he is," Riley said. "He won't rest until there are no more missions."

8

The clouds vanished as afternoon turned into evening. A carpet of blue stretched across the seemingly infinite sky. Warm rays of sunlight sparkled over the waves below. The view was hypnotizing, and Fitz had a hard time leaving his guard post when his shift was up. If it weren't for Lieutenant Colonel Jensen's sharp voice barking in his headset, he would have kept staring.

"Fitz, report to Command, ASAP," Jensen said.

"Roger that, sir," Fitz replied. He scoped the north with his MK11 one last time, hoping to catch a glimpse of the *Truxtun*, but saw only the vast blue of calm waters.

Fitz thought he heard a distant scream come from across the sea, but he saw nothing. Imagined or real, it was time to get moving. He gritted his teeth and climbed the skeletal ladder to the beach. Each rung put pressure on his thighs, the muscles burning with every step. When he reached the bottom, he bent down to rub them and check his prosthetics. As he examined the carbon fiber blades, the voices of his fellow amputees back at Bragg came up from memory. They'd called each other *Flex-Foot Cheetah* and *Blade Runner*. Both were nicknames he'd never liked much. His legs didn't define him; they only helped him get from point A to B, like a car. And he didn't label his friends by what they drove.

He wiped the sweat from his forehead with a swipe of his palm and crouched down for a better look. There was a small dent on the right blade just above the curve. He reckoned it was the result of his fall the night before. A dark speck of blood had settled in the indentation, and he couldn't seem to wash it off.

Fitz threw the strap of his rifle over his back. He stretched for several minutes by reaching down to his blades. When his muscles felt better, he took off running toward Building 1. Four soldiers were jogging across the concrete path ahead. He couldn't help but wonder if Jensen was cooking something up. When he saw Beckham, Fitz knew the answer. Something was definitely happening.

So much for a nap, shower, and a shit.

"Master Sergeant!" he yelled.

Beckham halted at the base of the stairway to the Command building while the other men continued inside. The operator's face lit up the moment he laid eyes on Fitz.

"Fitz, good to see you," Beckham said. He looked him up and down. "You look like hell, Marine."

"Clearly you haven't looked in a mirror lately," Fitz replied with a chuckle.

They shook hands and fell quiet, the somber mood of the day taking over. Beckham looked away for a moment. Fitz could see the pain of a memory surfacing on his friend's mind.

"Sorry to hear about Jinx," Fitz said.

"He was a good man," Beckham replied.

Fitz didn't know what to say, so he simply nodded and tried to stand as tall as he could despite the pain in his thighs and knees.

"Glad I caught you before going inside," Beckham said. "I haven't had a chance to thank you yet for saving the day here."

Fitz grimaced and shook his head. "Man, you don't need to thank me. I did what anyone else would have done."

"No," Beckham said sternly. "Most men would have run the other way in your situation."

Fitz considered that as he glanced at the blue sky. He was a marine, which meant he was trained to run toward a fight, not away from it. But Beckham was still right; Fitz had known men who cowered in the face of evil. The Variants were more awful than any enemy he'd faced in Iraq—that was for damn sure.

"Just doing my duty," Fitz finally said. He bowed his head slightly like he was tipping his hat. Beckham grinned and patted him on the shoulder.

"Anyway, thanks. Your reward is a new mission that I volunteered you for. Hope you don't mind," Beckham said.

Fitz adjusted the strap of his rifle on his shoulder. "Depends on what it is," he said.

"We're about to find out."

Fitz looked up at the double doors and then back at Beckham. "Let's get on with it then."

The command center was packed by the time they got there. Jensen and Smith stood at the head of the war table. Rodriguez, a short Hispanic marine, sat across the other side, his wide shoulders bent over a map. To his right was Timbo, his dark, muscular arms crossed as he waited. Peters, another marine with the build of a long-distance runner, sat across from Timbo. The thin man was staring out the window with an absent look on his face. Peters was a bit of a space cadet, and Fitz wasn't sure if he liked him or not.

Jensen looked up from the maps when the door closed behind Fitz.

"Beckham, Fitz, take a seat," he said.

Fitz plopped down on one of the cushioned chairs. His body greedily accepted the respite. He worked a knot in his thigh with the tip of his thumb, keeping one eye on Jensen.

"Gentlemen, I know you're all tired from New York. I'd love to let you sleep for a few days. Problem is, I spoke with General Kennor this morning and our request for a resupply was denied. We lost more than bodies last night. We lost precious ammunition, and our food reserves are dangerously low. Fortunately, the biggest treasure chest of food, gasoline, ammo, and gear just showed up practically on our doorstep," Jensen said.

Fitz wanted to shake his head when he saw where the conversation was going.

"As of 1600, the shoreline and adjacent area was Variant-free. I'm not sure how long we can count on that," Jensen continued. "If we're going to make a move, we need to do it tonight."

"We haven't even buried our dead yet," Timbo said.

"Unfortunately, we don't have time to mourn right now...or rest," Smith said. "We need to think of the living."

"He's right," Beckham added. "We've all seen how bad things are in NYC. The cities have fallen. Outposts like this island are the end of the line. We need to build something here. Something sustainable. And that's going to require taking risks."

"Boarding that destroyer is one hell of a risk," Fitz said. "We don't know anything about it. Have we heard anything from them at all?"

Major Smith frowned and tapped his pen on the table. "We've been flying recon for several hours. They haven't seen any movement. All hails have gone unanswered. Doesn't look like anyone's on board. I checked with Central, and the ship went dark several days ago."

"And it just happened to shoot right by the island?" Timbo grumbled.

"Do you know how many ships are drifting out there?" Jensen said, his tone growing frustrated. "Thousands."

Fitz raised a brow. "I don't like it. I don't like it at all. There could be a hundred Variants belowdecks."

"That's why I'm sending in our best," Jensen said. "We'll proceed with caution. We see any sign of the creatures, we get the hell out of Dodge."

Fitz shook his head this time. Jensen ignored him and said, "I'll take strike team Alpha with Timbo and Rodriguez. Beckham, you've got Bravo with Fitz and Peters."

"I'm going!" shouted a voice from the doorway.

The soldiers all spun. Chow was standing in the door, decked out with a flak jacket bulging with extra magazines. He held a helmet with "four-eye" night-vision optics under his left arm. Strands of jet-black hair hung over his forehead, partially covering his right eye. Jensen was pitching the mission as a salvage op, but Chow looked like he was heading to war.

"Give us a moment," Beckham said to Jensen.

Beckham jogged over to Chow and they exchanged a few hushed words that Fitz couldn't make out. Chow took a step back, glared at Beckham like he was about to punch him, and then finally nodded. They walked back to the table in silence.

"Chow's with me," was all Beckham said.

Fitz could almost smell the tension in the room. It was the stink of sweat, blood, and fear. Everyone in the tiny command center had been through so much. Hell, Fitz still hadn't taken a proper shower, and he'd hardly slept a wink for nearly twenty-four hours. He was having a hard time holding back his reservations about the proposed salvage mission.

Jensen broke the silence. "Echo One will drop Alpha on the bow. Bravo will be dropped on the stern. Alpha will clear the CIC first while Bravo works on clearing the compartments belowdecks. Any questions?"

No one replied and Jensen looked at his wristwatch. "All right. You have two hours to snag some shut-eye. We meet on the tarmac at 2100." He took a minute to scan every face and then stood. "That's all. Dismissed."

Fitz groaned as he got up and followed the others out of the room. When he got outside, Beckham had already pulled Chow aside.

"Fitz, hold up," Beckham said. "You too, Peters."

The marines stopped and waited. Fitz filled his lungs with the crisp, cool air as Beckham massaged his shoulder.

"Are you up for this? If not, tell me. There's no shame in sitting this out," he said, shooting a glance at Chow. "If you're in, you're in for the mission as Lieutenant Colonel Jensen described it. That means no going rogue and trying to be a hero if we meet the enemy."

"I'm good," Peters said casually.

Beckham held the man's eye for a beat before turning to Chow.

"I'll be fine," Chow said. "Just want to get this over with and give Jinx a proper burial."

Fitz was up next. He forced a half smile. "I'm with you."

Beckham kept his eyes level with Chow's gaze.

"Like I said, Beckham. I'm fine. You don't have to worry about me," Chow added.

Beckham clapped a hand on Chow's shoulder. "All right, brother," he said and then looked toward the tarmac. Sunlight flickered off the idle Black Hawks, the metal shimmering in the final moments of the day's heat.

"Get some rest, if you can," Beckham said. He pivoted away from the view and began the walk back to the barracks. That's when Fitz saw the bloodstain on the operator's upper back. Nobody had questioned whether Beckham was fit to go on this mission. Fitz was starting to wonder if someone should.

"Have you ever done this before?" Kate asked.

Ellis shook his helmet. "Can't say that I have. Never been in a situation where I needed riot gear."

Kate paused to scan her partner. Black armor bulwarked his chest and neck. He pulled on his leg and arm guards and then donned a helmet with a metal grill.

"I meant have you ever taken a bone marrow biopsy?"

Ellis bent down to lace up his boots. "Nope. Never done that either."

Kate finished putting on her own gear and considered the task ahead. The definition of insanity was doing the same thing over and over and hoping for a different result. Every time they entered the facility where they kept the Variants was a risk. Flying them to the island had been a risk. But in order to save lives, they would need to continue to take risks. This time there was no one else to do it but Kate and Ellis.

She slipped the chest armor over her shirt just as the door to the small locker area in the armory opened. A tall Medical Corps soldier with olive skin and green eyes strolled inside.

"Doctors," the man said with the dip of his helmet. "I'm Sergeant Lombardi. Lieutenant Colonel Jensen requested that I help you with the test. Which one are we going to put down?"

"The injured female Variant in Cell Three," Kate

said. "I want one that's healing. The stem cells will be proliferating at an extraordinary rate."

Lombardi continued across the room to a locker and inserted a key, nodding like he knew what she was saying. "Can't put that one under though, Doc. The tranquilizer almost killed it the last time. Too damn weak right now. We were lucky to save it." He opened the locker and pulled out a metal rod. Holding it firmly in his hand he said, "Not to worry. It will already be restrained by metal chains, and I'll be bringing this."

Ellis backed away from the oversized Taser. "Looks like it would just piss one of 'em off to me."

The sergeant shook his head and reached back into his locker. He removed his riot suit and began changing right in front of them.

Kate caught herself staring at the man's tanned, well-muscled physique. Ellis was doing the exact same thing. He quickly glanced over to Kate and then at the ceiling as if he didn't know what to look at. She could see the color rising in his face. She felt the heat of embarrassment in her own cheeks, but when Ellis's nervous eyes darted back to Kate, she smiled. She'd always wondered why Ellis had never mentioned a girlfriend, and now she knew.

"Here's the plan. I'll go in first and zap the fucker in the face," Lombardi said with one of his legs halfway into the padded suit. "Doctor Ellis and I will then tighten the chains so it won't be able to move. That should give Doctor Lovato a chance to take a bone marrow sample."

"Sounds like a pretty shitty plan to me, Sergeant," Kate said. "No offense. We were watching last time you tried to restrain it."

"Either of you got a better idea?"

Ellis looked at the Taser with narrowed eyes. "Not really. But I will take one of those."

Lombardi grinned, revealing a bottom row of crooked white teeth. "I can arrange that." He reached down and tossed the Taser to Ellis. Then he grabbed his armored vest and continued suiting up. He finished by pulling on an armored wrist piece that had teeth marks from an earlier attack.

There was something about Lombardi that made Kate nervous. He seemed sloppy. Inexperienced. Beckham would never have joked in such a situation. As the thought went through her mind, Kate realized that working with Beckham and his team had spoiled her. Not everyone was a Delta Force operator after all. Anxious to get started, she decided to let it slide.

Kate readied the biopsy needle and took in a breath. *Nothing to it,* she told herself. Insert the needle in the patient's bone, remove the center of the needle, and move the hollowed needle deeper into the bone.

Only this wasn't a normal patient. This was a monster.

Kate shivered inside her suit. "Let's get this over with."

"Follow me," Lombardi said. He led them out of the armory and down the steps to the adjacent building. A patrol of soldiers passed, their tired eyes scanning the underbrush. They moved sluggishly, fatigue weighing them down with every step. They seemed to barely notice the three medical personnel in riot gear.

Lombardi opened the door when they got to Building 4 and gestured for her and Ellis to go inside. Kate's skin prickled as soon as she entered the facility. She could almost hear the claws scratching across the ceiling and the popping joints of Patient 12—the Variant that had nearly killed her. The armored suit suddenly felt paper thin. She hesitated inside the lobby, peering down the hallway. Two soldiers patrolled the wing with assault rifles.

"Well, come on," Lombardi said, waving them forward.

Ellis stopped and walked back to her. "You don't have to do this, Kate. I'm sure Sergeant Lombardi and I can take care of it."

She shook her head slowly. "No, I'm fine. You need me."

"You sure?"

Kate brushed past Ellis, their armor scraping. "Okay then," she heard him say as she walked toward Lombardi. The sergeant was already at Cell 3.

"Stay right outside this door," Lombardi told the two guards. "If anything happens, you have permission to take the patient down." He took a peek through the glass and then turned back to Kate and Ellis.

"Okay, remember the plan?" he asked.

"You Taser it in the face," Ellis said. "Then we tighten the restraints and Kate gets our sample."

Lombardi gave a thumbs-up and crouched next to his bag. He pulled a second Taser and unfolded it with a slap to the side of his leg. It extended into a two-foot-long weapon.

"Follow me," he said.

Kate fell into line behind the men. The sooner they got the sample, the sooner she could start working on another bioweapon.

Lombardi unlocked the door and pulled it open. The naked female Variant lay on its back on the floor. It twisted viciously against its restraints, rattling its chains. The monster's lean muscles stretched and lines of blue veins stretched with them. Bandages on its shredded right leg leaked a puslike yellow jelly, and the wound on its left arm bled freely.

A screech followed as the creature homed in on the team with its only remaining eye. It wiggled from side to side, moaning in pain.

Kate followed the men inside the room with one hand

on Ellis's shoulder and the other holding the syringe. Lombardi circled the monster, the tip of his Taser sliding across the floor.

The Variant twisted its head, whipping thin strands of blond hair over pale, translucent skin. It snarled and snapped at Lombardi's foot. He parried the attack with his Taser and shocked it in the forehead.

A high-pitched howl erupted from the monster's mouth. The sound intensified until it was so loud it hurt Kate's ears. She dropped the syringe and cupped her hands over her helmet in reflex.

Lombardi hesitated as the creature jerked on the ground. Then he bolted forward and shocked the Variant again. This time he hit it between its breasts. Saliva and blood exploded from its mouth, peppering his visor. The Variant sucked in several deep breaths, gasping to fill its lungs.

Now was their chance. Kate scooped up the needle and patted Ellis on the back. He was already moving to the right. Lombardi crouched down and tightened the chain on the Variant's left arm and then its left leg. Ellis followed suit, and in a matter of seconds they had the monster stretched across the floor in an X shape. Both men prepared to strike with their Tasers.

"Come on!" Lombardi shouted.

Kate approached with a guarded half step. The creature snapped at her with jagged, broken teeth as she grabbed for its left arm.

Kate jerked backward. She felt her heart pounding so hard it threatened to jump out of her chest. The monster was studying her, and for a moment Kate saw a hint of fear, a fragment of humanity. It vanished when the thing chomped again, the fear giving way to rage.

"Move it, Doc!" Lombardi shouted.

Kate pulled off the plastic tip of the needle and

grabbed the Variant's arm again. This time she didn't flinch as it gnashed its teeth.

She inserted the needle into the bone, removed the center, and moved the hollow needle deeper. The monster let out a low whine, the tone almost melancholy. Kate withdrew the needle, retreated to the wall, and placed the sample in a secure plastic box.

The Variant thrashed and screeched as Kate darted through the open door, past the soldiers, and down the hallway until she was back at the entrance to the building. She didn't even glance over her shoulder to see if Ellis and Lombardi were following. When she got outside, she placed the box carefully on the ground, pulled off her helmet, and took in a long breath of fresh evening air.

"Is that you, Kate?" said a voice below.

Kate brushed a curtain of hair from her face. Beckham stood on the walkway, looking up with a furrowed brow. He was decked out in combat armor, a rifle slung over his back.

"What the hell are you wearing that suit for?" Beckham asked.

She took a second to catch her breath and said, "I could ask you the same thing."

He glanced down at himself and then looked away. "I have to go back out there."

Kate followed his gaze to the north, where the *Truxtun* had last been seen. It only took a second to realize where he was going.

"You said you were staying for a while. You said you weren't going on any missions for—"

"I have to go, Kate." His eyes flitted to the box on the concrete landing. "What exactly were you doing in there?"

Kate huffed. She wanted to hear something from him:

an apology, an explanation, some display of emotion—anything but questions.

"Were you inside one of those cells? With a Variant?" Beckham asked.

"Does it matter?"

"Yes it matters. Those things are extremely dangerous and you put your life in jeopardy every time you're around one of them, Kate. You went in there without even telling me."

"When were you going to tell me about your mission?"

"What do you think I was on my way to do right now?" He straightened his helmet with a tap of his hand. "How about you do your job, and I'll do mine. Things will work better for us that way."

Kate's heart ached. He was right, she should have told him. But she had been independent for so long she wasn't used to running her actions by a partner.

"I'm sorry," she said. "I shouldn't have gone in there without talking to you first. But please don't go back out there."

She walked down a step.

"I can't let my men go without me. I *won't*," Beckham corrected. "I won't abandon them."

"What about..." Her voice trailed off and she searched his eyes for an answer. It wasn't that Beckham didn't care, Kate realized. The problem was that he cared too much.

"I'm sorry, Kate. I'll be back in a few hours," Beckham said. He offered a short nod and then hurried away.

9

Darkness shrouded Plum Island. Another day had passed and countless more lives had been lost. The scars from the previous night still lingered. Beckham noticed every single sign of battle as he strode across the tarmac with Fitz, Jensen, and the others: the metal frame of the Chinook, the dried blood painting the ground, the bullet casings.

After two hours of downtime and a fight with Kate, he was having second thoughts about the mission. Maybe he needed to sit this one out and let someone else take his place. He was injured and exhausted.

A sidelong glance at his team reminded him they were all in the same boat. Every man wore the same solemn, tired look. Beckham was just doing a better job of hiding it than they were.

There was no one else to take his place, and he wasn't about to let Chow go out there on his own. The memory of the mission to Bragg was still fresh in Beckham's mind. In the search for his family, Horn had broken a cardinal rule—he'd let his emotions get the best of him. Beckham had done the same thing by giving chase in New York when Jinx was taken. Chow was liable to make the same mistake on the *Truxtun*. Beckham couldn't stop him from going now, but he could monitor his actions. Just like he'd monitored Horn's at Bragg.

To add to the stress, Beckham didn't like the way he'd left things with Kate. She deserved better. He'd been a prick, but he would make it up to her when he got back.

The distant chirp of crickets followed the teams across the tarmac to the choppers. As soon as they arrived, Beckham and his squad began their final preparations. This time they all carried suppressed weapons even though it wouldn't make much of a difference if they ran into Variants. The creatures could hear a pin drop on the floor.

Beckham screwed a suppressor on his M9 and then tightened the strap of his helmet and checked his optics.

"Listen up," Jensen said. He licked his lips and waited.

All around Beckham, the other men stopped what they were doing and faced the lieutenant colonel.

"Situation is still the same. Ops has been hailing the *Truxtun* all day—still no answer. Recon hasn't found anything. Guess they heard a dog barking, but that's about it," Jensen said.

"A dog?" Fitz asked.

"Yeah, a dog. Four legs and a tail," Jensen said.

Fitz blushed and Beckham grimaced. Tensions were too high. The knot in his gut tightened. Maybe the mission wasn't a good idea after all.

"You know the drill. Once we clear the ship, I'll call in Echo One and Two. We'll load up on all the weapons and supplies we can manage to jam into the birds. Got it?" Jensen said.

Beckham locked eyes with Jensen, ready to protest, but he backed down at the last second. Now wasn't the time to question the mission. He should have done that hours before, during the briefing. His job now was to follow orders and achieve their objective.

"Yes, sir," Beckham said after a brief pause.

"All right, men, let's mount up," Jensen said, his voice filled with a dangerous enthusiasm. He grabbed his weapon and jumped into Echo 1.

The rotors on both choppers made their first pass, whooshing overhead. Beckham jogged after the others to Echo 2. He took a seat next to Fitz and immediately traced a finger over his vest pocket. Inside was the tattered picture of his mom. He patted the pocket carefully, worried that he would damage his last copy.

Chow took the seat, closed his eyes, whispered something under his breath, and then exhaled.

Good, Beckham thought. Maybe the operator had his emotions under control after all. He bumped his friend on the arm with a friendly fist. "In and out. Easy as shit," Beckham said. "Get some ammo and grub and get back safe. Then we honor Jinx and the others. Give them the funerals they deserve."

Chow nodded slowly as the chopper rose into the air. Beckham leaned back, resting his helmet on the metal wall, praying the *Truxtun* was an unguarded treasure chest free of Variants.

The domed buildings shrank as the chopper pulled away from the island. Somewhere down there, Kate was working on another weapon that was supposed to save the world. She'd put her life in jeopardy to get a sample from a Variant, and although the thought of her getting hurt made him furious, he wasn't mad at Kate for doing her job. Neither of them was good at delegating dangerous work, especially when that work involved protecting the lives of others.

As the facilities vanished from view, he feared that what made them alike would also be what drove them apart.

"I don't want to talk about it," Kate snapped.

Ellis held up his hands defensively. "I'm sorry. Jeez."

"I can't believe he's going back out there," Kate said. "He hasn't even been back for twenty-four hours yet. And I can't believe Jensen is attempting the salvage run."

Ellis pursed his lips as if he was unsure of what to say. He took a step toward the entrance to the lab, but hesitated.

"Don't you think the mission is ludicrous?" Kate asked.

"I thought you didn't want to talk about it." Ellis put his hands on the hips of his CBRN suit.

"Well, now I'm asking," Kate said.

"Yeah, I think it's stupid, but I get why they're doing it. We need supplies, and there's no telling how long that ship's going to be there before the Variants or someone else raids it."

Kate pulled her key card and waved it at the entrance to the lab. The security panel beeped at them, and the glass doors whispered open. She was still boiling mad. Her conversation with Beckham had struck a nerve, but deep down it was more than that. Her heart truly hurt. She'd known him for just over a month. He'd saved her life and she'd spent the most passionate night of her life with him, but she was starting to realize that he would always put his men first. She wasn't sure she could live with that.

"Let's get started," she said. She crossed the lab carrying the box containing the biopsy of bone marrow from the Variant.

"I'll prep the culture dishes and prime them," Ellis said.

Kate buried her thoughts of Reed and focused on the task at hand. She met Ellis at the center lab station and opened the box containing the sample of bone marrow. Before she knew it, she'd lost herself in her work.

After the dishes were primed for the mesenchymal

stem cells, they fed them into a high-throughput screening system. The robotic system would deposit the cells into plastic dishes with tiny wells. The cells would then incubate and run automatically. The machine's plate reader would determine whether a reaction had taken place in each well. If there was a unique protein in the Variant's stem cell surface, the machine would tell them.

"You think this is really going to work?" Kate asked.

"I sure hope so. If we can identify a unique protein, then I think I can come up with some antibodies that will target the cells."

Kate finished loading the isolated stem cells into the HTS machine. She activated the system manually and took a step away from the controls.

"Even if we can identify this protein and the antibodies to target the cells, how are we going to deploy it as a weapon? When I designed VariantX9H9, we still had pilots and a working military. That was weeks ago. I'm not sure General Kennor could even—"

"Let's not get ahead of ourselves," Ellis said. "First we need to find the protein. Then we're going to have to make antibodies, and then we're going to need to test it on the Variants. Plus we've got to come up with a payload for the antibodies—some way to deliver the antibodies that will kill the Variants' stem cells. After we accomplish all of that, we can worry about who will deploy it. If worse comes to worst, maybe the military could use it on individual cities, one at a time. Taking them back from the Variants without having to send in troops."

Kate didn't find Ellis's plan all that reassuring. A lot of people were going to die in the days or even weeks that it would take. But he did have a point—they could only do one thing at a time, in sequence. Until they found the protein, there was no sense in worrying about anything beyond that.

"Looks like we're all set here," Kate said.

Ellis crossed his arms. "Now we sit back and wait for the results."

Beckham had been on plenty of warships before, but he'd never seen one run aground. The five-hundred-foot long, nine-thousand-ton ship looked like a beached whale. A mountain of sand and rocks ran along both sides of the hull where it had carved a path.

"Area clear of hostiles," one of the pilots said over the comm. "Prepare for insertion."

Beckham scanned the LZ to double-check. "You got eyes on anything?"

"Negative," Fitz replied.

"Looks dead down there," Chow said.

Peters crouch-walked over to the fast rope and grabbed hold as the chopper descended into position over the stern. Echo 1 was already hovering over the bow. Beckham watched Jensen's team drop onto the deck and disappear from view.

"Peters, you got point. Chow, you're on rear guard. Fitz, you're with me," Beckham said. He quickly fell into line behind Peters, tapping him on the shoulder. The marine slid down the rope and moved into a covering fire position as soon as his boots hit the deck.

Beckham paused to touch his vest pocket one last time and then grabbed the rope. Once on deck he squared his shoulders and swept the stern for contacts while he waited for the others.

Fitz came next, his metal blades landing with a click.

"Eyes up," Beckham said, flashing a hand signal toward a door—also called a hatch—leading into the ship. Peters was already running for it.

"Slow your ass down," Beckham said when he caught up. He glanced back at Chow and then Fitz. He didn't want either of them on point.

"I'll take lead," Beckham said. Peters scowled. The kid had an attitude problem—kind of like Riley, but without the humorous side.

Beckham slowly led the team across the deck. When they reached the hatch, he grabbed the handwheel. He twisted it a hair to ensure it was unlocked.

"Bow is clear," Beckham heard over the comm. "Alpha proceeding to bridge."

"Roger that," Beckham replied. "Bravo entering ship."

He stepped to the side as Chow took his place at the handwheel.

"Execute," Beckham said.

Chow rapidly turned the handwheel and opened the hatch to allow Beckham inside. He flipped on his night vision and moved into an empty passageway. There was no sign of a struggle and no bodies. Beckham knew better than to see it as a good sign. The three hundred sailors were somewhere on board, and someone had cut the power. He took in a breath, smelling for Variants, but the distinct sour fruit smell was absent.

"Clear," he said as he cautiously advanced. "Alpha, you got eyes?"

"Negative so far, 'bout to enter the bridge," came Jensen's reply.

"Copy that." Beckham continued working his way forward with his weapon aimed at each closed hatch. Halfway down the passage, he stopped to check one of the handles. This one was locked, so he continued past it.

Labored breathing and the click of Fitz's blades reverberated off the bulkheads as Bravo advanced. Beckham stopped at a T-intersection and balled his hand into a fist. He edged around the corner, eyeing the passage to the left. Sensing it was clear, he pivoted into the center and swept his rifle to the right and then down in an arc as he spun to the left again. Both sides were empty.

The left passage led to the galley and mess hall. A sign for the berthing area hung to the right with an arrow pointing down the passageway. Beckham turned back to his men, assessing them. Chow was doing okay so far. He still didn't trust Peters, though. Not yet. He hated doing it, but he decided to split the team up.

"Peters, on me. We'll take the right," Beckham said. "We're Bravo One and Two on the comms. Chow and Fitz are Three and Four. Clear the galley and mess hall."

Chow nodded and patted his helmet in confirmation. Beckham tightened his grip around the handle of his M4 and slipped into the right passage with Peters behind him. The hatches to the berths were wide open. The sight made him pause. Each room was a potential hiding place for hostiles. They would need to clear each one.

He directed Peters to take the right side with a hand signal. Beckham took the left. He entered the first room and swept his rifle from bunk to bunk. One of them was sealed off with a blue drape. He approached it with his rifle in one hand and pulled back the curtain with the other.

Empty.

Where the fuck was everyone?

He continued into the next room and then the next. Each revealed the same thing. Empty bunks.

"Bravo Two, you got anything?"

"Negative," Peters replied.

"Alpha, you got eyes on?" Beckham asked.

The response was quick. "Bridge is clear. No sign of struggle."

"Copy that," Beckham said. His mind raced as he continued to the head where the toilets and showers would be. Peters was already there, kneeling in the entrance and tracing a gloved finger over the floor.

"No bodies in here," he said.

"Blood?" Beckham asked.

"Yup," Peters replied. "Lots of it. It wraps around the corner that way too." He pointed down the passage.

Beckham shouldered his rifle and continued to the next junction. He hugged the bulkhead and peered around the side. The trail of blood continued down the passage to the left and ended at a hatch that went belowdecks.

"Alpha, you copy? Over," Beckham said into his headset.

"Roger, Bravo. Loud and clear," Jensen replied.

"I think I found our missing crew."

"What's your location?"

"Just outside the berthing area."

"Alpha on the way."

"Roger," Beckham said, moving back to the head. He squeezed past Peters and double-checked it. Maroon streaks crisscrossed the ground, pooling as if someone had dumped buckets of blood on the floor. Overhead, the ceiling was splattered with the same dark blots.

Beckham continued on, planting his boot firmly with every step, careful not to slip. He checked each stall but didn't find a single body. Whatever had happened had likely started here. His gut dropped as he remembered their mission to Building 8, where the hemorrhage virus had started. Ghost had cleared those first few levels, expecting to find scientists waiting to be rescued. Instead they'd found the first infected—and the dead bodies they'd hoarded for food. The memory of that first gruesome discovery in the mess hall made his heart pound.

Chow's voice flickered in his ear. "Bravo One, Bravo Three. Something you need to see in the galley."

Beckham caught the small break in the man's voice, and he knew exactly what it meant. Chow was spooked.

"Alpha, meet us in the galley," Beckham said. He motioned for Peters to follow. Beckham's boots made squishing noises as he ran into the passageway, the blood sticking with every stride.

It took only a few seconds to reach the galley. Fitz was waiting outside the entrance. It was hard to read his features with the NVGs hanging over his head. Beckham held his questions and entered the room.

Chow was standing next to an oversized food locker that wasn't very different from the one Ghost had found the scientists in at Building 8. The operator pointed down as Beckham approached. He already saw the dark path leading to the walk-in fridge. He checked the temperature gauge. It was 42 degrees inside. With the engines offline, the freezer was starting to warm.

"I don't like this, man," Chow said.

"Fitz, hold security at the hatch," Beckham said. "Peters, get over here."

Chow grabbed the handle and waited for orders. Raising his M4, Beckham held a breath inside his chest and nodded.

A cloud of cold air rushed out of the room as soon as Chow yanked the door open. Beckham moved his weapon in an arc, stopping on something hanging to one side of the room. At first glance it looked like a slab of meat, but then Beckham saw the human head attached to it and he caught the smell of rot.

Chow followed Beckham inside and stopped abruptly. He lowered his rifle but said nothing, staring at the corpse. A shredded pair of trousers covered its crotch and the stubs where its legs had been. Its arms were gone, torn from their sockets.

"Jesus," Beckham whispered. He forced himself to get closer and crouch next to the body. He flipped his night vision up, using the soft red glow from an emergency light to examine the remains. The man's features were warped by horror. Beckham tried to close the man's eyelids, but they were frozen open.

A low growl came from behind one of the shelves in the right corner of the room. Beckham swept his gun toward the noise. Chow heard it too and raised his rifle. They exchanged a look and walked toward the metal rack stacked with food. He couldn't see anything on the other side. Another weaker growl responded to their footsteps.

Beckham's breath came out in icy puffs as he walked. When he got to the final shelf, he pointed to his eyes, then to Chow, and then to the right side of the shelf. The operator moved into position. They burst around the corners simultaneously, Beckham anxious to put a bullet in whatever was making the sound. He almost pulled the trigger before he saw the German shepherd. It was curled up on the lap of a navy officer's corpse. The man's chin rested limply against his chest. Everything below his waist was covered in blood.

The dog snarled as they approached. Beckham waved Chow off with his other hand and took a knee.

"It's okay, boy," Beckham said. "I'm not going to hurt you."

The dog cowered, trying to back away. Beckham reached out to let the animal sniff his hand when the man's head shot up and his eyes snapped open. The officer gasped for air and batted icy eyelids. The red glow illuminated his wide, frightened eyes.

"Help me," he said. "Please, help me."

Beckham didn't have time to reply. Gunfire rang out in the distance, and a voice crackled over his headset.

It was Jensen, and he was screaming. "Contacts! We got multiple contacts!"

10

Riley was furious. The state-of-the-art post had been built without ADA access. Everywhere he went, he needed help. He wheeled down the hallway of Building 1, where Kate and the other scientists lived. Smith had redistributed the rooms after the attack had killed most of the former residents. Horn and his girls got one, and so did Riley. He was glad to be out of the medical ward, but he would have rather been assigned a bunk in the barracks. Now everything was a challenge. Especially taking a shit, which he'd been holding off on doing for hours.

Horn nursed a bottle of Jameson they'd manage to barter off one of the newer Medical Corps guards while his girls slept soundly next door. He sat on the small couch in Riley's room, his gaze locked on the window.

"I hate waiting like this," Horn said. He wiped his mouth with a tattooed arm.

"Beckham can take care of himself. He'll be fine," Riley said, in a less than convincing tone.

"He's been lucky, Kid. You know that, and I know that," Horn said. "Doesn't matter how good he is. Eventually that luck will catch up to him."

A moment of silence passed over them. He wanted to

reassure Horn everything would be fine, that Beckham and the others would find nothing but food and ammunition, but he had the sinking suspicion they were probably walking into a boatful of bodies or worse.

"I don't like sitting on the sidelines either," Horn said.

Riley looked down at his casts and let out a sad chuckle. "Man, I've been the fucking water boy for weeks now. I want back in the game."

"Fuck it, I should have gone," Horn grumbled. He took a long gulp and then punched the cushion next to him. "Beckham needs me out there."

"Your girls need you here."

Horn bowed his head and ran a hand through his thin, strawberry hair. "I still can't believe Sheila's gone. It's finally starting to sink in. The girls are going to grow up without their mother."

"I'm sorry," Riley said. "But that's another reason you need to be here for them. And I'm pretty sure that's why Beckham wanted you to sit this out. They need their father."

Horn wiped his eyes and sat up straight. "Yeah," was all he managed to say.

Goose bumps rose on Riley's arms. "I gotta go to the can. You mind getting the door for me, Big Horn?"

"Sure, I need to check on the girls anyway. Make sure they're sleeping."

As they made their way to the door, Riley said in what he hoped was a casual voice, "So, what do you think of that Meg chick? A real firecracker, huh?"

Horn held the door open and glanced down at him, his freckled forehead lined. "You serious, man? You're really thinking about a woman right now?"

"Bro, I'm always thinking about women."

Horn jerked his chin toward the hallway. "Go take your dump."

Riley wheeled into the hall. Before he could get out of the way, Major Smith came bolting out of nowhere.

"Riley, Horn! We've got a problem. It's the *Truxtun*."

"We got multiple contacts! Something's wrong with them. They're bleeding from their eyes and ears," Jensen said. His panicked voice vanished under the crack of suppressed gunfire amplified by the enclosed passages.

"Come again, Jensen. Did you say bleeding?"

Another flurry of suppressed shots sounded and then Jensen's reply.

"Yes! These hostiles are bleeding from multiple orifices!"

Beckham couldn't believe what he was hearing over his headset. "Where are you?" he shouted back.

The crackle of static was the only reply.

"What do we do?" Fitz asked. "Go to them or wait?"

Beckham glanced back at the freezer where Chow stood waiting for orders. "Seal that guy inside with the dog. We can't bring them with us right now," Beckham said. "We'll come back for him."

Chow slammed the door shut and locked it from the outside. If something happened to Beckham and his men, the officer wouldn't have any way to get out. Then again, if something happened to them, the Variants would kill the officer anyway. His fate was tied to Bravo team now.

"Let's go," Beckham said. He ran toward the sound of suppressed gunfire, but the close quarters made it hard to locate the source.

"Jensen, relay your position," Beckham said over the comms.

"Upper deck, just outside the CIC!"

Beckham opened the hatch that led from the mess to the stairwell and the sound of gunfire echoing through the bowels of the ship immediately grew louder. He looked up the dark stairs—what the navy referred to as ladders—that led to the next deck and said, "Eyes up, on me."

The hatch at the top of the ladder was already open. As soon as he approached, a volley of gunshots tore through the passage. An angry shriek followed...Someone had found a target.

Beckham stumbled away from the entrance and slammed his back against the bulkhead for cover. "Hold your fucking fire!" he called out.

Whoever was shooting didn't let up. Another torrent of rounds hit the bulkhead. One of the bullets ricocheted, pinging through the open hatch and whistling past Beckham's leg.

"Jensen, hold your fucking fire!" Beckham shouted, his voice raw with anger.

"Fall back!" Jensen yelled back.

The gunshots seemed to move farther away. Beckham counted the seconds, listening to the impacts. When he was sure they were clear, he poked his head into the passage.

A pile of bodies lay at the opposite end. Something moved in the shadows beyond the graveyard. It was a Variant, hunched, coiled, and gripping a gushing wound. More of the creatures rushed into the passage, crawling across the bulkhead and overhead.

Beckham glanced to the right, where the gunshots had come from. Jensen, or whoever had fired, was gone. He retreated through the hatch before the creatures could see him and used his fingers to tell the story to the rest of Bravo, holding up four of them and then pointing.

His team nodded in unison. Beckham raised his

suppressed M4 and jumped back into the passageway, firing at a beast that moved into his crosshairs. The round took off the top of a skull, a flap of skin, and flesh forming a skirt around the exit wound. The other Variants dodged around the falling body, each of them roaring with anger.

The click of Fitz's blades came from Beckham's right and the crack of his rifle sounded a second later. Peters and Chow fell into line behind them to guard the rear.

Even with the suppressors, the muzzle flashes lit up the dim passage as Variants charged for their position. Beckham centered his rifle on the closest creature's head and squeezed the trigger. The bullets pinged off the ceiling where the monster had been only a second before. It dropped to the floor and galloped forward, using its back legs to spring into the air.

This time his shots found a home in the Variant's chin. Another creature took its place, but Fitz nailed it with a head shot before it got close to them.

A second wave of Variants pumped into the passageway like blood through a vein. Beckham's senses were on full alert, his brain and body in sync. He fired efficiently, conscious of his ammo at first but quickly giving up on firing discipline. The creatures were fast, even in the narrow space. Their motions were blurred by their speed, making it difficult to find vital targets.

"Fall back!" Beckham shouted.

"Changing!" Fitz said. He moved out of the way and Chow took his place.

The pile of dead grew with every shot. Bullet casings clanked off the deck as the team emptied magazines into the mass of veiny flesh. Beckham backpedaled, his boots crunching over the casings.

He almost stumbled when he saw the face of the nearest Variant. Blood trickled from its eyes and nose, and

Beckham remembered Jensen's panicked words. A chill spiked up his back when he realized what was happening. Somehow, these bastards were still infected with the hemorrhage virus. That meant they would have all the abilities of a Variant but also the symptoms of the Ebola virus.

"Run!" Beckham screamed. "Don't get any blood on you!"

Beckham grabbed a protesting Chow by his flak jacket and pulled him down the passageway. Fitz and Peters were already moving, their weapons probing the darkness for more contacts.

"They're contagious!" Beckham yelled.

Chow risked a glance over his shoulder and then ran faster. "How is that possible?"

Beckham didn't have an exact answer but knew it wouldn't take much for the virus to have worked through the *Truxtun*. If a single person had been infected, it would have spread throughout the ship with lightning speed.

Peters ran into the next passage. "Fuck this!" he shouted, pulling ahead of the rest of Team Bravo. Beckham watched helplessly as the marine ran full tilt into an ambush.

"Watch out!" Beckham shouted. Peters was gone in an instant, a trio of infected dragging him away screaming. Beckham grabbed the back of Fitz's armor and yanked him away from the junction just as a group of the creatures came clambering over the bulkheads.

Bravo was cornered.

Without thinking, Beckham pushed Fitz through an open hatch and into another stairwell. Chow followed, and Beckham slammed it shut behind them. He braced his uninjured arm against the metal, hoping it would be enough to keep the monsters back.

"Check the ladders, above and below!" Beckham shouted without turning. The door vibrated as one of the monsters slammed against the other side. The pounding that followed made Beckham think the monsters were using a battering ram of some kind...but that was impossible. The infected weren't that smart.

He stepped backward and aimed his rifle, his hand trembling. Peters was gone—dead in the blink of an eye. Alpha was on the run, and now Bravo was trapped.

Fitz and Chow joined Beckham at the door after they had cleared the ladders. They centered the rifles at the hatch and planted their boots.

"What do we do?" Fitz asked.

Beckham pulled the magazine from his gun to check his ammo. "What we have to," he said as he slammed the mag home. "We fight our way out of here."

"Infected? What do you mean *infected*?" Kate shouted.

Major Smith twisted the wedding ring on his finger. "Jensen reported that the crew is displaying symptoms of the hemorrhage virus."

Kate suddenly felt light-headed. A wave of nausea hit her and she took a breath to calm her nerves.

"It's possible they had a sample of the virus in a lab on board. Maybe someone was accidentally infected. The military was working on a cure in multiple undisclosed locations," Ellis said.

"Someone must have been infected after VariantX9H9 was deployed," Kate said. "That's the only explanation that makes sense."

Smith grunted. "What the hell does this all mean?"

"It means the crew will experience all of the epigenetic changes from the VX-99 chemicals, but they're also infected with Ebola. Think back to the first days of the outbreak, before VariantX9H9 was dropped."

"The crewmen on the *Truxtun* are essentially Variants with Ebola," Ellis added.

"Great. That's just fucking great," Smith said. He shook his head and looked at Kate. "So what do we do, Doctor?"

She glanced over at Riley and then at Horn, who held Jenny in his arms with Tasha by his side. Both operators wore the same helpless looks. They'd fought the creatures since day one, and they knew that the added threat of the hemorrhage virus raised the stakes tenfold. Even if Beckham and his men could fight their way through the ship, the risk of infection made the odds of escape even worse. She wanted to cry. Instead she clenched her jaw and looked Smith square in the eye.

"Get the extra CBRN suits and prep a chopper," she said.

Smith took a step back, hesitating.

"If you want to save your men, Major, you'll do exactly what I say."

Beckham flinched as the door shook from another impact. The creatures continued their assault. Each strike sent a vibration that echoed off the bulkheads and overhead. The cacophony rattled his senses, and he tightened his grip on his rifle as he prepared for them to come crashing through. Chow and Fitz fidgeted next to him, sweat bleeding down their faces.

"Jensen, do you copy? Over," Beckham said for the tenth time.

Static crackled over the comm channel. The headsets were either pooched or Alpha team was gone. Beckham had a feeling it was the latter, but he wasn't ready to give up hope. What he needed was a plan.

"We need to get to the bridge. If we can make our way to the bow, then maybe we have a chance of getting out of here," Fitz said.

"What about the guy and his dog back in the freezer?" Chow said. "We can't just leave him in there."

Beckham felt all eyes on him. There were three options: attempt to rescue the officer and his dog and make their way to the bridge, abandon them and go straight to the bridge, or save their own asses and jump ship. He threw the third out as soon as it crossed his mind, but he didn't like the other two either.

"Bravo, do you copy?" came a voice in Beckham's earpiece. It was Jensen, and he sounded shaky. "We made it to the bridge. Rodriguez is gone. It's just me and Timbo now. We're locked in the CIC."

"Stay put," Beckham said. "We'll be there as soon as we can."

"We're not going anywhere," Jensen said. "Good luck."

Jensen signed off, the regret in his voice audible over the comm. Beckham didn't have time for regrets now. The infected were howling at the door, slamming into the metal relentlessly.

"We can't go back out the way we came in," Beckham said. "Even if we could fight our way past those things, the risk of infection is too high."

The pounding on the door increased as they spoke, the monsters on the other side growing more desperate.

"We can't just sit here," Chow said.

"I know," Beckham said. "I think we need to try for the galley. The officer may be our best shot at getting back to the bridge."

"Was afraid you were going to say that," Fitz said.

"But hey, we did lock him in a fucking freezer. I wouldn't be able to sleep at night if we just left him there."

Beckham looked first up and then down the ladder. Perhaps there was a way to get back to the galley undetected. It was worth a shot, but they needed to move fast.

"On me," Beckham said. He aimed his M4 into the green-hued darkness and continued down to the lower deck. He paused by a closed hatch and waited for several beats, listening with an ear to the metal. Silence. The banging was still only coming from above.

Beckham pointed at Chow and then the door. Chow nodded back, twisted the handle of the door, and swung it open. Beckham shouldered his rifle and strode into the empty passageway.

After a quick sweep confirmed it was clear, he waved his men forward. They worked their way back to the galley quietly. Beckham could hardly hear the click of Fitz's blades.

The door to the galley was still open when they arrived. Beckham flashed a hand signal to Chow and followed him inside. They cleared the room and hurried to the freezer door. The officer was waiting just inside, his teeth chattering. The dog let out a soft growl and leaned its head against the man's blood-soaked shirt.

"We're going to get you out of here," Beckham said.

The man shook, his crossed arms trembling. He managed a nod and tried to move.

"Did anyone else make it?" Beckham asked. He didn't have much time but needed to know.

The man shook his head, twitching. "I think we're it. There were others, but they're all dead now. I tried to escape with Apollo here. He's a bomb-sniffing dog." He paused, closing his eyes. "We heard the choppers earlier. Apollo barked up a damn storm. That's when we hid in here."

Beckham patted the dog on the head. This time it didn't make a sound and accepted the scratch of his fingers greedily.

"Name's Beckham," he said.

"Scottie," the man replied.

Beckham helped him to his feet. "You're hurt pretty bad," he said, eyeing the man's stomach.

"I'll be fine."

"Can you walk?"

Scottie nodded. "I think so."

"Good," Beckham said. "Because I need you to take us to the bridge."

11

"Doctor Lovato, you can't board the *Truxtun*. You're too important," Major Smith said. "If something happens to you—"

Kate cut him off. "You're getting me a ride to that ship." She glared at the major, her eyes burning. Reed had saved her multiple times, but now it was her turn to save him. She'd requested a case of CBRN suits, a helicopter, and an armed escort, but Smith was determined not to let her go.

She felt a powerful grip on her shoulder and turned to see Horn. "Kate, Major Smith's right. Besides, what the hell are you going to do?"

"Take a fire team to the ship, fight our way to Beckham and the others, and give them CBRN suits. Then we fight our way out," Kate said.

Horn loosened his hold on Kate's shoulder and put Tasha on the ground.

"Sounds like a good way to get killed," Ellis said. "I suppose I'm coming with you, right?"

"No one is going," Smith said. "Lieutenant Colonel Jensen wouldn't want you to risk your lives for him. You are way too important."

"Is Reed going to be okay?" Tasha asked.

"Yes," Kate said firmly. "He's going to be just fine."

Horn massaged his forehead. "This is messed up, really messed up. I didn't think we would have to worry about the infected ever again!"

Jenny whimpered, burying her head in his side. Horn pulled her close and stroked her hair.

"Jesus Christ," Smith said, shaking his head. "We're going to have to light the beach up with bombs. There's no salvaging anything now."

"What did you say?" Kate asked sharply.

Smith looked at her like she was trying to trick him.

"Light the beach up with bombs," Kate said, more to herself than anyone. She scratched at her cheek as an idea formed in her head. "Get General Kennor on the line."

Smith looked even more confused now. "Doctor, I'm not following."

"Listen very carefully," Kate said. "Give him the coordinates of the *Truxtun* and ask him to order an air strike."

Horn grabbed Kate's arm as soon as the words left her mouth. His chest heaved as he waited for an explanation.

"An air strike of VariantX9H9," Kate continued. "We don't have to rescue them after all. The bioweapon will do that for us. If they can find a place to hunker down and give the weapon a chance to work, maybe they can ride this out."

A grin broke across Horn's face. He slowly let go of her sleeve and faced Smith. "Do it, Major. Do it right now."

Scottie stumbled beside Beckham as they moved down the passageway. Wounded and probably half-blind by the darkness, the officer could hardly walk. Beckham kept to his side, one hand on his rifle and the other steadying Scottie.

"The infected are on the third deck," Beckham said. "We need to find a way past them to get to the bridge."

The dog brushed up against Scottie's leg. "There's one way. A direct route," Scottie said. "It's not far." His teeth had stopped chattering, but he still trembled from the cold. Beckham wondered how long the man had been in the freezer. If it weren't for the warmth of Apollo's body, he would have likely frozen to death before the engines had shut off.

"Show me," Beckham said.

Scottie continued to a hatch they had passed earlier. "Through here."

"I'll lead," Beckham said. "Fitz, you take rear guard. Chow, keep close to Scottie." He placed his ear against the metal and listened. The distant shriek of an infected reverberated through the ship. Beckham wasn't sure if it had come from above, below, or beyond the hatch. The enclosed space muffled every noise.

He cursed their luck and prepared to fire as he opened the hatch. Instead of pale, distorted flesh, he saw only another ladder well on the other side. He continued up to the next landing and waited for the rest of his team to join him at the hatch.

"The bridge is at the end of this passage," Scottie whispered.

Beckham nodded and opened the hatch. He pulled it back slowly, trying desperately not to make a sound. He cleared the right side first but froze when a shrill screech caught his ear. The horrifying sound was so loud there was no question where it had come from. The infected were here.

"MOVE!" Beckham yelled, squeezing off a burst before he even had eyes on the targets. He planted his boots and steadied his wild shots. His heart pulsed with the rhythm of the rounds. The infected raced forward, springing to the bulkheads and overhead.

The crack of suppressed gunfire broke out all around him as all hell broke loose. His ears rang from the close combat, but he didn't take his eyes off the monsters. Tracers lit up the passage, and in the glow he saw the bloodshot eyes of the contagious Variants. Some of them disappeared in chunks of bone and flesh as bullets ripped into their bodies. Others kept coming, their swollen lips widening as they charged forward like sharks preparing to swallow his team whole.

Apollo barked furiously from the hatchway, jaws snapping. Beckham could see the dog in his peripheral vision. Scottie stood his ground and so did Beckham. Surrounded by Fitz and Chow, his senses snapped to attention, activated by his need to protect his brothers.

He centered his sights on an infected male who had broken off from the front of the pack and he fired off a three-round burst. The creature was fast—lightning fast. It darted around the spray, taking only one of the shots to its side.

Beckham dropped to a knee, ejecting his magazine in the same motion. The monster charged, its swollen lips aimed at Beckham's face. He pulled a magazine from his vest, slammed it inside, and raised his rifle just as the creature leaped into the air. A millisecond was all that separated him from the infected's jaws.

Before he could pull the trigger, the monster's head disintegrated. Beckham felt a tug on the back of his flak jacket and he fell on his ass, blood splattering the floor where he had knelt a moment before.

He scrambled to his feet and emptied his new magazine into the pack. Two of them dropped from the bulkhead, clawing at their gaping wounds, leaving four of the creatures hurtling toward Beckham. One of them halted, confused, like it knew it was suddenly fucked. The other three rushed into the line of fire. They jerked as the rounds tore into their flesh, plastering the area with arterial blood.

Injured monsters struggled across the floor toward Beckham, long and bloodied limbs reaching up. He fired on those that were still strong enough to crawl but didn't waste bullets on the ones he knew were taking their final breaths.

Apollo's steady growl suddenly turned into a bark. Beckham glanced back at Scottie just in time to see the man disappear down the ladder as a creature pulled him into the darkness.

General Kennor paced his office, impatiently waiting for updated numbers. The numbers were all that mattered now. They represented bodies. Soldiers. His staff wanted him to believe that American soldiers could no longer win the war, so he'd agreed to the unthinkable: a retreat. But now, in the late hours of the evening, he was regretting his decision. He was a control freak. Always had been. By giving up control, he felt like he was raising the white flag. His old muscles and bones longed for the chance to fight again. He was no coward. He'd fought in Vietnam and Korea, and he wore the scars from both wars proudly. They were as much a part of him as his uniform.

But the Variants were unlike any enemy he had ever faced. Colonel Gibson had inadvertently created billions of supersoldiers. Now those monsters were bringing the human race to its knees. He needed someone who knew how to fight them. Someone who understood how the creatures operated.

A rap on the door pulled Kennor from his thoughts. He turned anxiously to see Colonel Harris standing in the open doorway to his small office.

"Talk to me, Harris. How bad is it?"

The colonel kept his face stern, but the twitch of his right eye said it all. He handed Kennor a piece of paper with a list of military bases across the country.

"Things are still chaotic, sir. But here is what we know," Harris said.

Kennor carried the paper over to his desk and sat. He slipped on a pair of glasses and clicked on his lamp. The light spread over a list of military bases and dozens of red Xs. It wasn't a formal briefing, but he didn't need to ask what the red marks meant.

Edwards Air Force Base, McConnell, Moody, Dover, and countless other bases were gone. Fort Knox, Fort Hood, and Fort Jackson had marks next to them. Barstow, the logistical base for the Marine Corps, did too. The list went on and on.

"How?" Kennor asked, his voice shallow.

"The Variants have penetrated every installation and overwhelmed the forces inside. At this rate, we're losing a base almost every twenty-four hours."

"Jesus. I..." Kennor dropped the paper on the table and stood. "What about civilians? Do we have a current count?"

"Only estimates, sir. The best guess from lead ops is that there are less than seven million survivors left worldwide, and that number drops significantly every day. Most of the civilians are on military bases or in bunkers. There may be some in the cities, but we simply have no way of knowing how many. Like I said, these are estimates—"

Kennor pounded the table with a fist and watched Harris flinch. "There's only *one* percent of the population left world fucking wide?" he roared. "How is that possible? A week ago there was just one Variant for every three human survivors."

"With all due respect, General, there are over five hundred million Variants. They hunt in packs and swarm like a cross between insects and predatory animals. They are taking over every inch of the country, one stronghold at a time. They kill, feed, and bring the rest back to their lairs," Harris said.

The radio on Colonel Harris's belt crackled. He glanced down at the device and moved to shut it off when a voice said, "Colonel, do you copy? Over."

"Sir, I should probably see what this is about," Harris said.

Kennor nodded and sat back down in his chair, suddenly light-headed. He looked at the ceiling and tried to understand the enormity of the situation. The numbers were all that mattered, but he couldn't wrap his brain around the scale of the devastation. *Only seven million people left, and dropping every day.*

"Colonel, we have a request from Plum Island," said the voice on the radio. "Major Smith wants an air strike on the USS *Truxtun*."

Harris's face twisted with confusion. "An air strike?"

"Yes, sir. They are requesting VariantX9H9. They claim the vessel has been overrun by Variants infected with the hemorrhage virus. Lieutenant Colonel Jensen and two fire teams are on board."

Kennor pounded the table a second time when he connected the dots. "That dumb son of a bitch," he growled. "Jensen must have ordered a salvage op after I denied the resupply request."

Harris nodded. "Probably, sir. I'm told he also went to New York for Operation Liberty when he was told to stay behind."

"The man can't follow goddamn orders," Kennor said. He shook his head and stared Harris in the eye. "Approve the request. Have our birds from Langley make the drop."

Harris hesitated, holding the radio away from his mouth. "I'm sorry, sir, but..."

"No," Kennor said, a cold wave of horror washing over him. He grabbed the paper off his desk and scanned the names, stopping on a red X next to Langley.

"Fall back!" Beckham shouted. Scottie was already gone. The man's screams were distant, growing fainter as the monsters pulled him belowdecks. The sounds seemed to enrage Apollo even more.

Beckham grabbed the dog by the collar with his left hand and tugged him away from the door. Apollo resisted, struggling in his grip as another infected leaped up the ladder. Beckham raised his rifle with his right hand and shot it in the chest. The monster tumbled head over heels. Two more quickly emerged from the shadows. He squeezed off another burst that sent them spinning into the darkness.

"Come on, Apollo!" Beckham shouted, yanking the dog's collar. He retreated toward the sound of Chow's and Fitz's footfalls, keeping his eyes on the open hatch as he pulled Apollo down the passage.

"Down here, Beckham!" shouted a voice.

Beckham flung a glance over his shoulder. The door to the CIC was wide open. Chow and Jensen stood out front, waving frantically. Fitz and Timbo were inside. A pile of bodies—contagious bodies—separated what was left of the two strike teams.

Apollo fought to get free, growling and squirming.

Beckham tightened his grip and then fired at two infected crewmen who burst through the open hatch. The first shots were wild but the second volley found targets, two skulls detonating. Both bodies slumped to the ground with meaty *thunk*s, life draining from them in an instant. A few days ago—hell, maybe even less— these men had been human. Two more creatures burst from the open hatch and Beckham dispatched them without hesitation.

He flung the strap of his rifle over his back and worked on pulling the frantic dog the final stretch. Bullets streaked past him on both sides as the other men opened fire from the CIC.

"Leave the goddamn dog!" Jensen yelled.

A sudden wave of Variants crashed through the open hatch into the area. One of them tripped and somersaulted. It leaped to its feet and jumped onto the bulkhead so fast it made Beckham queasy. Shots lanced down the passage, shattering bone and spraying the bulkhead with infected blood.

Apollo suddenly jerked from Beckham's grip. He grabbed the dog under the belly, picked him up, and then took off running toward the CIC. Apollo's weight made every step excruciating, Beckham's injured shoulder burning with every stride.

The sound of scratching claws and shrill shrieks followed them as he ran. Chow and Jensen fired off another volley of carefully aimed shots.

"Come on!" Chow shouted.

Beckham leaped over another body and almost lost Apollo in the process. They were close now, only about fifty feet from salvation. He navigated around another three corpses and gripped Apollo tighter against his chest. Something reached up and grabbed one of his ankles when he was ten feet away from the door. He stumbled and crashed to the floor. Apollo jumped from his arms and landed just outside the CIC. The frightened dog darted inside.

The hand around Beckham's ankle tightened and pulled him backward. He reached out for something to hold on to but came up empty. He dragged his gloved fingers across the floor, screaming, "Shoot it!"

"I can't get a shot!" Chow screamed back.

Beckham pulled his sidearm, twisted onto his back, and blasted the infected crewman that had his ankle. He shielded his eyes from the bloody mist and turned away just as another pair of hands grabbed his shoulders and pulled him toward the CIC.

Pain blurred Beckham's vision as he waited for the hallucinations to set in—for the infection to rip through his body. He flinched as the hatch slammed shut. When he managed to open his eyes, he was on his back inside the CIC. Timbo, Jensen, Chow, and Fitz were hovering over him.

"Get away from me!" Beckham shouted, crawling backward. "I could be infected." His back hit a bulkhead and he wiped his face clean with an arm. His heart skipped at the sight of blood smeared on his sleeve.

The other men stood their ground, their weapons lowered toward the deck. Apollo made a sad whine and approached Beckham cautiously. The dog sniffed him and then sat by his side.

12

Kate rubbed her temples. She was hardly listening to the chatter coming from the wall of radio equipment. Horn, Riley, and Smith were there, huddled around Hook as she twisted a knob with exaggerated care.

"Try and get Jensen back on the line," Smith said.

"Yes, sir," Hook replied.

Kate closed her eyes for a moment to calm her nerves. When she looked back over the water, it was still. Not a single whitecap in sight.

A voice pulled her away from the view.

"Alpha Team Leader, this is Plum Island. Do you copy? Over," Hook said.

A strained voice, weakened by static, came from the wall-mounted speakers.

"Kate, you better get over here," Riley said.

She was already moving across the room. Her heart hammered in sync with her feet. She squeezed past Horn and Riley to stand next to Hook. Smith paced behind them.

"Plum Island...do you..." Static surged. "We're locked in the CIC. Bravo Team Leader is..."

Kate held a breath in her chest, aching for news.

"He's got blood all over him," Jensen said.

No. Please God, no.

Smith faced her and said, "What do they do?"

"Let me talk to Reed," Kate said.

Hook handed her the headset and Kate took a seat. "Jensen, this is Kate. Put Reed on. Now, please!"

White noise coughed out of the speakers, like there was a heavy wind in the background. There was a sharp crackle and then a voice.

"Kate..."

It was Beckham, and despite the digital interference she could hear the fear in his voice.

"I'm here," Kate replied. "Are you..."

"I have blood on me, Kate. It's...It's everywhere."

Kate could hardly form a response.

Focus. FOCUS!

She had to set aside her feelings. He needed a doctor, not a panicked woman.

"How do you feel? Are you experiencing any hallucinations?" she asked, her voice sharp. She remembered her brother's final words, the terror in his voice, his shrill screams as the virus ripped through him.

"I don't know," Beckham said. "My head hurts, but I don't know if that's from infection or—"

"Listen to me, Reed," Kate said. It pained her to say it, but she had no choice. "You need to stay away from the others right now. We've called in an air strike of VariantX9H9. It will kill virtually every contagious Variant in the area."

"Your bioweapon?"

"Yes," she said, trying to keep her voice calm, clinical.

"And how long will it take?"

"The jets are already airborne."

There was a pause and then, "Peters. Rodriguez. They're dead, Kate."

"But you aren't," Kate said.

The observation window suddenly rattled. She cupped her headset and strained to hear over the rumble of the incoming jets. Barking sounded across the channel and then pounding.

"Reed, what is that?" Kate shouted.

"We found a dog," Beckham said. "And the infected are trying to get inside."

There was shouting in the background. She recognized Timbo's deep voice and Fitz's southern accent. The roar of the jets grew louder, the walls trembling in their wake.

"They're almost there, Reed. Just hold on!"

"Kate?" he said.

"I'm here," she said, her voice shaky.

"I'm sorry for earlier—"

The noise from the jets drowned out Beckham's voice as they tore through the sky. She spun back to the window just as three F22s roared over the island.

A wave of panic gripped her as she watched. If Beckham was infected, her bioweapon would kill him. The realization hit her like a missile from one of the jets, and her heart felt like it was going to explode. If Beckham died on that ship, she wasn't sure if she would be able to keep going.

Beckham sat with his back to one of the stations in the CIC, sucking in breaths tainted with the pungent scent of rotten fruit and infected wounds. The creatures slammed their diseased flesh into the hatch a few feet away, ringing the bell on the bridge with each strike.

"Will that hold?" Timbo shouted.

"Should," Jensen said.

"What about that one?" Chow pointed to the only other exit to the room, which led to the bow. Beckham glimpsed the brilliant moon through the small porthole and wondered if it was the last time he'd ever see it.

"Keep an eye on that hatch," Jensen ordered.

The infected beat harder at the entrance. Each impact vibrated through the CIC. Apollo's barking grew louder, vicious and guttural. The sounds amplified until the scream that only an F22 Raptor could make broke through the wall of sound. Timbo and Jensen moved to the lookout windows, searching for the jets.

Fitz and Chow flanked Beckham, their weapons shouldered and their frightened eyes flicking from Beckham to the hatches. Beckham studied the end of Fitz's M27 and imagined it aimed at him. Would his men hesitate if he was infected? Would he hesitate if he were in their shoes?

No. I wouldn't.

"If I turn, you put a bullet right here," Beckham said, tapping his throbbing forehead. His mind burned with worry. Every ache, every hint of pain became a sign that he was infected.

"Incoming!" Timbo yelled from the lookout. The Ranger backed away from the glass, motioning Jensen to follow. They retreated to the center of the bridge next to a navigation station.

Beckham heard whispering in his mind, a soft voice he could hardly place at first.

It's okay, Reed. Get up. You need to get up.

Was he losing it? Was this the trickery of the virus?

Hollow thuds rang out, followed by explosions and the thunder of jets. They had dropped their payloads, and Kate's bioweapon was airborne.

Beckham heard his mother's voice a second time.

You have to get up, sweetie.

It was a hallucination, but he didn't feel the bloodlust associated with the hemorrhage virus. Instead, despite the depth of his panic, her soft, reassuring voice put him at ease. Beckham pushed himself to his feet.

"Stay down," Chow said. He shifted his rifle away

from the hatch, the suppressed muzzle coming danger-ously close to Beckham. He didn't blame Chow; he was an operator, and right now Beckham was a threat.

"It's okay," Beckham said.

The hatch rattled in response, their voices infuriat-ing the infected on the other side. Chow trained his rifle back on the steel.

"Those Raptors dropped VariantX9H9. In a few hours, anything infected with the hemorrhage virus will be dead," Beckham said. "Including me."

Fitz's eyes softened. "You're going to be fine. If you were infected, you would already know."

"Doesn't always work like that," Chow said. "I've seen people turn in seconds, but I've also seen it take longer."

"He's right," Beckham said. "You need to stay back."

Chow reached down and picked up Beckham's M4. "Sorry, man, it's just a precaution."

Beckham offered a nod and then reached out to Apollo. The dog glanced in his direction, baring white canines. It let out a low growl, fur trembling.

"It's okay, boy," Beckham said. He saw then Apollo's dark eyes weren't on him. They were locked on the port-hole where bulging lips had smacked against the glass.

"Contact!" Timbo yelled. He rushed to the hatch just as an infected crashed through one of the lookout windows behind him. Shattered glass exploded into the air and an infected Variant rolled across the ground. It jumped into a catlike crouch, tilting its bony face in Beckham's direction and blinking bloodshot eyes. Timbo fired a burst that erased the beast's features.

Before the body hit the ground, two more frail-looking creatures dove through other windows. Both skittered across the floor on all fours, arching their naked backs, vertebrae protruding. Their joints clicked with every motion as they darted for cover.

Chow and Fitz worked their way around the stations for better vantages while Beckham pulled on Apollo's collar to hold the dog back.

"Watch your fire zones!" Jensen yelled as he squeezed off a shot. The round hit one of them in the back and sent it twirling toward Timbo. With no time to fire, the Ranger reached up and snapped its neck in one swift motion. He tossed the limp body aside just as the other emaciated creature lunged at him, clamping its lips onto his muscular forearm.

Timbo let out a roar and tore the thing off his arm in a spray of blood. He took the back of its head in his other hand and slammed it into the helm over and over until its face had caved in like a smashed pumpkin.

Beckham glimpsed motion through the lookout windows behind Timbo as three more of the infected came barreling across the bow. They charged the windows in full stride, blood dripping down their pale, sunken faces. Chow and Fitz cut the first two down, but the third lunged through the shattered glass, shredding flesh and muscle in the process. It dropped to the floor and crouched, ready to spring.

Jensen pulled his Colt .45, took two steps forward, and shot the creature twice in the heart before it could strike. Chunks of gore and blood exploded from the exit round, peppering an oval radar station.

The body slumped to the ground and Jensen quickly holstered his pistol and changed the magazine in his rifle.

"Looks like that's all of them," Chow said, panting. He backpedaled from the broken lookout windows, his M4 still shouldered and involuntarily roving for contacts.

Jensen and Fitz crowded around Timbo. The Ranger collapsed in a chair, cupping his arm and shaking his bowed helmet from side to side. "It fucking got me, man!"

Beckham pulled back on Apollo's collar again as the

dog growled at the corpse next to Timbo's feet. Bloody tears streaked down the monster's collapsed face. There was no question it was infected with the hemorrhage virus.

Closing his eyes, Beckham sucked in a breath of air. Instead of his men watching him turn, he might be forced to endure the pain of witnessing one of his own brothers transform into a monster. His eyes snapped back open just as Timbo jolted in the chair.

Chow, Fitz, and Jensen slowly raised their guns. Timbo's hand slipped away from his injured arm. He glanced down at the exposed muscle and then back up at his team.

"Do it!" Timbo roared.

"Maybe you won't turn," Fitz said, looking over at Jensen for support. The lieutenant colonel kept his gaze on the Ranger.

"He already is," Chow whispered. "Look at him."

"Wait!" Beckham shouted.

Timbo looked over at him and snorted. "It's okay, man. I had a good run. Time to go home now." He squirmed in his chair, fighting the biological weapon raging through his system. But even the big man couldn't hold back the hemorrhage virus. His eyes rolled up into his head and a stream of blood trickled from his nose. He reached up to claw at his eyes, letting out a scream that reverberated through the CIC.

Before anyone could react, Timbo jumped from the chair, batted Chow's rifle away, and shoved him into a wall. Chow crumpled to the ground, his weapon sliding across the deck.

"Timbo, stop!" Beckham yelled a second too late.

Jensen was already firing at the bulky Ranger's back. The barrage of rounds cut through Timbo's flak jacket and Timbo turned to face him, a confused look on his face as if he didn't recognize his commander. The Ranger, Beckham's friend, was already gone.

Chow jumped to his feet and karate-kicked Timbo in the chest with such force it sent them both sprawling backward. Timbo crashed into an ops station. Blood gushed from his flak jacket, saturating his fatigues.

Jensen centered his weapon on Timbo but paused. The Ranger tilted his head and narrowed bloodshot eyes at his brothers in turn, stopping on Beckham. Past the crazed look, there was a flicker of sadness that vanished just as Jensen fired a round into the center of Timbo's forehead. The crack echoed through the room as Timbo stumbled backward into a station and then crashed to the deck.

"I'm sorry," Jensen said, lowering his rifle. "God, I'm so sorry." He dropped to his knees and sobbed.

The hatch continued rattling, but none of the men were paying attention. In a few hours, the noise would fade away and the infected crewmen would join Timbo, Peters, Rodriguez, and Scottie in death.

The mechanical whir of chopper blades pulled Kate toward the tarmac. She ran after Major Smith as fast as she could in her bulky CBRN suit. Ellis trailed her, yelling for her to wait.

"You know what to do if something happens to me!" Kate shouted back. Ellis was a gifted scientist and could continue their work without her if something were to happen. His footfalls faded away and she pushed on, battling the fierce wind from the rotors.

Horn was already at the chopper, decked out in a white CBRN suit that fit snugly around his muscles. He manned a viscerally terrifying machine gun that looked more like a cannon. He reached down and offered a gloved hand to help her inside. She took a seat next to Sergeant Lombardi.

"You sure you want to come?" Horn asked.

Kate simply nodded.

"You're clear to go!" Smith yelled from the tarmac. He flashed a thumbs-up and ran back to the concrete barriers where Riley and Ellis waited with Horn's girls. Kate didn't wave good-bye as the Black Hawk lifted into the sky.

"He's going to be okay," Horn said. "Try not to worry."

Three hours had passed since the aircraft had dropped their payloads. She had assured Smith that most of the people infected with the virus would have bled out by now. He'd reluctantly allowed her to go on the mission, but it had taken some convincing.

And now she was in the air, the water below sparkling in the moonlight. She watched the island become a dot on the horizon and then she turned away, searching the approaching Connecticut shoreline for the *Truxtun*.

Kate's earpiece crackled. "ETA two minutes," the lead pilot said.

Horn rotated the machine gun and Lombardi moved to the door with his rifle. Both men were prepared for a fight that Kate hoped they would avoid.

"There she is," Lombardi said, pointing toward the coast.

Kate followed his finger to the outline of the destroyer.

"Alpha, Echo One, do you copy, over?" one of the pilots said.

Jensen responded a moment later. "Copy that, Echo One. We're on the bow, waiting for evac." He sounded defeated, his voice brittle.

The chopper pulled to the left as the pilots prepared to circle the ship. Kate looked over the side as the beach vanished and a road clogged with abandoned vehicles came into focus. Corpses littered the asphalt between the cars. Kate hardly felt anything at all and realized in that moment she'd grown immune to the sight of carnage, something she had never thought could happen.

Then she saw two smaller shapes sprawled on the road. Children, she realized. Their clothing flapped in the wind as the chopper passed overhead. A stab of despair ached in Kate's gut then, reminding her that she was still human after all. She hoped Horn hadn't seen them but knew he had. Since meeting Beckham and his team, she'd learned these men saw everything.

Kate shifted to the other side of the troop hold. They passed over a ridgeline thick with trees as the pilots circled the *Truxtun*. Branches whipped back and forth, only partially obscuring a Variant perched on a stump. It watched them pass, tilting its head at an unnatural angle. Horn saw it at the same moment Kate did. "Contact!" he yelled.

Lombardi scoped the trees. "We got more than one!"

Kate's heart pounded as she saw the Variant bolt across the ridge and jump to the road below. Two dozen of the creatures burst from the thick canopy and pursued the leader, their naked bodies clambering toward several figures on the bow of the ship. They must have spotted Beckham and the others, Kate realized.

"Get me into position!" Horn shouted at the pilots.

The Black Hawk changed course quickly. The high-pitched whine of the heavy machine gun came a second later as Horn fired. Tracer rounds lanced through the darkness and slammed into concrete and cars. The barrage of projectiles splattered the road with body parts. Half of the pack of Variants fanned out for cover.

The pilots circled for another pass to finish the job. Two injured Variants crawled across the road, dragging stumps where their legs had been. Horn picked them off and then focused his fire on the more elusive creatures. He mowed down another four on the second pass. A third of the original pack continued toward the *Truxtun* in a mad dash.

Kate glimpsed four figures and a dog waiting on the deck of the destroyer. As they flew closer, she saw Fitz's metal blades glistening in the moonlight. Jensen stood to his right and Chow to his left. They all had their weapons pointed toward the bow of the ship. Behind them another man stood watching, his hand holding the collar of a German shepherd.

"Reed," Kate whispered. The chopper pulled away and she spied a large body covered in blood lying on the ground behind him. It was Timbo and the soldiers were trying to bring him back to the island.

The chopper maneuvered for a third pass. The remaining Variants were almost to the destroyer now.

"Kill them, Horn! Hurry!" she yelled.

Horn worked the gun back and forth, sending more of the monsters spinning into the darkness. Two made it through the gunfire. One leaped onto the roof of a mini-van and looked up at the chopper, swiping with its claws. Horn centered the gun on the van and fired.

The Variant disappeared in a cloud of red as the rounds ripped through it. The windows shattered and the tires exploded.

The remaining creature galloped across the sand and leaped onto the side of the ship. It skittered up the metal, using its flexible joints and microscopic hairs to climb up the hull.

"Stop it!" Kate shouted.

Horn trained his machine gun on the ship just as the crack of Lombardi's rifle sounded. Red mist exploded from the monster's back. It skidded down the metal and fell to the ground.

Kate worked her way back to the edge of the open door as the chopper descended over the ship. Chow and

Jensen were dragging Timbo by his boots across the deck, leaving a trail of blood.

"You can't bring him!" Kate yelled.

"He's coming with us!" Jensen shouted.

"He's infected!" she shouted back. "His blood puts us all at risk!"

Chow dropped one of Timbo's boots, but Jensen held on and stared at the Ranger for a few more seconds. Fitz stopped to whisper something and patted Jensen on the shoulder before continuing to the chopper with Chow.

"Help them, Lombardi!" Horn shouted.

The sergeant pulled Kate out of the way and reached out to grab Fitz. The marine clambered inside and collapsed onto the floor. Chow and Jensen followed, but Beckham hesitated.

"Come on!" Fitz shouted.

Kate reached out to him. "Now, Reed!"

Beckham glanced down at his uniform and then back at Kate. "I have infected blood on me too!"

"But we don't know if you're infected," Kate insisted.

"Move your ass, Beckham!" Horn shouted.

Beckham finally grabbed the dog and carried it toward the chopper. It squirmed in his arms, fighting to get free. The other men took seats at the opposite end of the compartment as Beckham set the dog inside and climbed aboard.

The pilots pulled the bird away from the ship and Kate scooted across the floor to Beckham. He held up a hand and said, "Stay back."

"No," Kate said, batting his arm away and sitting next to him. "No more pushing me away. You're going to be fine, Reed. We're going to get through this together."

He offered a weak nod and turned to look out over the *Truxtun*. Fitz, Chow, and Jensen were all staring at Timbo's body as the chopper ascended into the sky.

13

Fitz wasn't sure what time it was. Five in the morning? Six? His internal clock had ceased operating after two days of virtually no sleep. That's all he wanted now—a few wonderful hours of shut-eye. The bank of LEDs in his isolation room was far too bright for that. He tried closing his eyes, but the light penetrated his eyelids and every time he came close to sleep, he jerked alert.

"Is this really necessary?" Fitz shouted.

"Yes," came the muffled voice of Dr. Hill through a speaker. "We have to keep you quarantined until we're sure you aren't infected."

Fitz squirmed against his restraints to see if he could spy Beckham in the adjacent room. The blinding light of the LEDs made it impossible to see through the glass panels. He felt like a rat in a cage.

But that was fine. He knew the blood running through his veins wasn't infected, and soon enough they'd let him out. It was Beckham he was worried about. The tough son of a bitch had been through the wringer, and it would be a tragedy to lose him now.

"How's Beckham?" Fitz asked.

"He's doing just fine," Hill replied. "So are Jensen and Chow. This is just temporary. I'm sure you guys will be out of here in no time at all. Until then, you should try and get some sleep."

"Maybe if you turn off the lights," Fitz said.

"I'm sorry," Hill replied. "We need the lights in order to monitor potential infection. If you start developing a sensitivity, that's an important sign."

Fitz was wiggling to get comfortable when he heard the chatter of approaching voices from the hallway. A moment later, the speaker buzzed.

"Fitz, this is Kate. I just got your blood test back. You're all clear. Hold on one minute and we'll get you out of there."

The door creaked open, and relief flooded over Fitz at the confirmation of what he had already known: He wasn't going to turn into one of those things.

The doctors walked into the room and undid his restraints.

"Is Beckham clear too?" Fitz asked, rubbing his left wrist while Kate worked on unstrapping the belts holding down his blades.

The sudden appearance of her dimples answered his question.

"His tests came back negative. So did Jensen's and Chow's," Kate replied. She offered him a hand as he slung his legs over the side of the bed.

Fitz exhaled and grabbed her hand. Good news wasn't something he was used to, but it still did little to relieve the overwhelming weight of the losses on the *Truxtun*. Timbo, Peters, and Rodriguez—Fitz added their names to the growing pile of dead that was already stacked high with those of his fallen brothers. He hadn't known Peters or Rodriguez well, but he'd fought with Timbo back at Fort Bragg. Now they were all gone, and there wasn't even anything left to bury.

"You okay?" Kate whispered.

"Tired as all hell, but I'm fine," Fitz said. He let out

a sad sigh as Kate helped him off the table. He followed the doctors into the hallway, and they gathered outside of Beckham's room.

"Reed," Kate said into the comm, "I'm coming in." She unlocked the door and walked over to his bedside.

Fitz held back and grabbed Hill's arm when he went to follow Kate.

"Give 'em a minute, Doc," Fitz said.

Hill nodded and crossed his arms. Fitz turned to the side, trying to be somewhat discreet as he watched from the other side of the glass. Even in the darkest of moments, seeing them together reminded him of what he was fighting for.

Kate unbuckled Beckham's straps and helped him sit up. He rubbed his forehead and then cracked his neck from side to side. The white shirt they had given him after decon was stained scarlet over his right collarbone, and his face still showed the yellowish tint of dying bruises and small red cuts. Like so many other warriors, Beckham hadn't had a chance to heal since the outbreak started.

Fitz couldn't hear what they were saying, but he didn't need to. Their body language said it all. Kate brushed a strand of hair from Beckham's eyes, and he reached out and wrapped his arms around her. Beckham locked eyes with Fitz over Kate's shoulder.

Fitz smiled at Beckham and said, "Let's give 'em some privacy." He continued down the hall with Hill to Chow's room. The operator didn't mutter a single word as they entered.

"You're clear," Hill said. "The test came back negative."

Chow remained silent. He closed his eyes and jerked them open again like he had just woken from a nightmare.

Fitz stopped at Chow's bedside and reached to unbuckle one of his restraints. "You okay, man?"

"Yeah," Chow murmured. "I just want to get the hell

out of here." He sat up and ran a hand through his long black hair. "What time is it?"

"Almost 0600," Hill said. "Just in time for breakfast."

"Do me a favor, Doc," Fitz said. "Go inform Jensen he's okay."

Hill nodded and left them alone. Chow scooted off the bed and stood. "I'm fine," he repeated.

Fitz scratched an itch on his ear. "You shouldn't be. I'm not. How many more of us have to die before it's over?"

"However many it takes," Chow said grimly. "You've done good. During the attack the other night, on the *Truxtun*, at Bragg. I'm glad you're with us, man."

"Thanks," was all Fitz could manage to choke out.

"Let's get out of here," Chow said. He patted Fitz on the back and strode out into the hallway, where Hill was waiting outside Jensen's door.

"Hold up!" a voice shouted from the other end of the hall. Major Smith jogged down the passage with a pair of Medical Corps guards trailing him. Their footfalls echoed with urgency.

"Major, their tests came back negative," Hill said.

Smith didn't respond. He held up a hand, motioning for the guards to stop. Fitz took a step back, his heart racing. Something was about to go down, he could feel it.

"Give me the key," Smith said. He glanced over at Fitz and gave him a quick up and down. Then he snatched the ring of keys from Hill and unlocked the door.

"About damn time," Jensen snarled as Smith entered the room. "I need to get back to ops—"

Smith slammed the door shut and approached the lieutenant colonel slowly. Fitz could see the major's lips moving but still couldn't hear a damn word. Jensen struggled in his restraints before Smith was done. The major held up a hand to calm him.

"What's going on?" Beckham asked when he and

Kate joined Chow and Fitz outside. Hill had retreated to the other side of the hall, watching curiously.

"Not sure," Chow said. "But doesn't look good."

They watched in silence as Smith finally unbuckled Jensen. Fitz could hear raised voices through the thick glass. A few minutes later, Smith opened the door and Jensen stormed into the hallway.

"Let's go," he snapped.

Fitz exchanged an unsure glance with Beckham and then followed. They rushed down the halls of Building 3 in tense silence.

When they got to the lobby, Jensen finally turned and said, "Beckham, Chow, Fitz, get some rest. Kate, I want you back in the lab as soon as possible. General Kennor has decided to take charge of the island. We'll have a service for the dead at sunset." With that he swung the doors open and staggered out onto the steps.

Fitz wasn't sure what to think. Kennor was the four-star general behind Operation Liberty, the man who had ignored Kate's advice and sacrificed thousands of his brothers and sisters. Fitz trailed Kate and the others onto the stairs outside. They stood there in the quiet of the morning, all of them likely thinking the same thing: Things were about to change drastically on Plum Island.

The chatter of voices sounded outside Kate's room. The familiar sound of Riley and Horn with Horn's daughters put Kate at ease. She relaxed her head on Beckham's chest and closed her eyes.

Neither of them had said much since they returned to Building 1. They didn't discuss Operation Liberty, the *Truxtun*, or General Kennor's new orders. They simply lay there, taking solace in each other's company.

The minutes passed by and Kate let them. She would join Ellis in the lab shortly, but for now all that mattered was this.

"I'm sorry, Kate," Beckham finally whispered. "I was an asshole. You didn't deserve that."

Kate pulled her head away from his chest and rolled herself up onto her elbow.

"I'm sorry too," she said. Her hair fell over her face, and Beckham reached over and brushed it away.

Kate searched Beckham's brown eyes. She touched his lips with a fingertip and leaned in to kiss him lightly. The kiss wasn't an invitation but a reassurance that she was there, that they could just be.

"Is Apollo okay?" Beckham asked. Kate felt his chest muscles tense as he lifted his head off the pillow.

"He's still undergoing tests. The hemorrhage virus isn't communicable across most species," Kate said. "There have been some animals, however, where that isn't the case—primates, for example—so we're taking precautions. We should know more by tonight."

Beckham nodded and relaxed his head. "You better get to the lab."

"Will you be able to sleep?"

He let out a sigh. "Yeah, I think so."

"I'll be back around dinnertime. We can go to the service together. Okay?"

Beckham nodded and pulled his arm away from Kate, using it to prop up his head. He gave her a meaningful look.

Kate leaned in to kiss him one more time and then left him there. She clicked off the light on the way out but didn't turn around, fearing she wouldn't be able to leave if she did.

She walked to the lab in silence, her mind a mess of worry. Ellis was already busy at his station. She quickly suited up and hovered her key card over the security panel. The door chirped at her and Ellis turned. A shit-eating grin broke across his face when he saw her.

"Kate, we did it!"

"Did what?"

"The results from the HTS system just came back. We discovered a protein only expressed by the Variants."

"You're certain?" She went to his station and stared incredulously at the protein's tertiary structure on his monitor.

"I'm more than certain," Ellis said. "I've run the results through a sequencing database and compared spectra results with the database of known human proteins. There isn't a single match. Nothing even comes close."

Kate took a seat at the station and went over the notes.

"I've already started mass spectrometry along with a peptide mass fingerprint to characterize and sequence the protein," Ellis continued.

"Do we know the function?" Kate asked before he could finish.

Ellis shook his head. "I'm still working on it."

"Good," Kate said without taking her gaze from the screen. "But for now let's focus on developing an antibody to target the protein."

Ellis grinned even wider. "I'm already one step ahead of you."

Raised voices pulled Beckham from the grips of a deep sleep. He reached for his sidearm, forgetting at first where he was. Moonlight streamed through the shades covering the window. In its glow, he saw a picture of Kate and her brother on the bedside table next to the sleek outline of his new Beretta M9.

He sat up and rubbed his shoulder with a fingertip.

Crusted blood came off under his nails. He swung his legs over the side of the bed and then made his way to the small sink and mirror in the corner of the room. Four days' worth of facial hair could almost be considered a beard. He snorted at the sight. Between the bags under his eyes, the jaundice circles of old bruises, and the cuts on his face, he looked worse than ever.

Beckham gripped the sink with both hands and leaned in to stare at his reflection. His gaze shifted to Kate's grooming products, and without further thought he grabbed a small pair of scissors and went to work. He trimmed his overgrown mop of dark hair as best he could and took a razor to his chin. A rap on the door came just as he finished shaving. He'd had to use one of her razors and some pink shaving foam that smelled like strawberries, but it had gotten the job done. He turned to see Kate peeking inside.

"Reed, people are starting to gather outside. Are you ..."

"Yeah, I'm ready," Beckham said. He ran a hand over his shortly cropped hair and faced her.

"Wow, you look a little bit different. But I like ..."

Beckham stopped her midsentence by striding over and pulling her to his chest.

"We're going to get through this. And when it's all over, there's going to be a place for us," he said.

She leaned her head back and found his eyes. "You have no idea how good it feels to hear you say that, Reed." Kate leaned in to kiss him and then made a face. "Why do you smell like a daiquiri?"

Beckham felt a smile starting. He didn't let it finish. Now was time to honor his brothers. He turned one more time to look at the mirror. The fresh haircut and shave certainly helped his appearance, but the man staring back still looked like he was ready to go to war, not stand in a ceremony.

14

Clouds had drifted across the moon, but the sky was alive with stars. Beckham and Kate stood on the steps outside Building 1, hand in hand. The perpetual glow of city lights that had polluted the sky just a month ago was gone. The once-great metropolis of New York in the distance was now home only to Variants.

Beckham pulled Kate away from the door to make room for Horn and his girls. Both operators wore the uniforms they had been issued when they arrived at the island. Missing were the medals they had earned in distant lands at a time when Beckham's biggest fear had been terrorists. He never thought he'd feel nostalgic for his time in Iraq and Afghanistan.

He shook the thoughts from his head as Horn led his girls onto the landing. Beckham's heart ached when he saw Jenny and Tasha in clean white dresses they must have gotten from another family on the island. Their curly red hair was neatly braided, and their small faces were solemn.

"Ready?" Horn asked. He grabbed Tasha's and Jenny's hands and helped them down the steps. The hems of their dresses rippled in the soft breeze.

Halfway down the path, Beckham saw the only other remaining original member of Team Ghost waiting outside the barracks. Fitz and Chow flanked Riley on both sides, their arms crossed.

Beckham squeezed Kate's hand tighter.

Their group grew in size as Fitz, Riley, and Chow fell into line behind Beckham and the others. He walked alongside Kate, his pace slow but purposeful. It felt a lot like marching. Beckham considered saying something but decided to save his words for the service.

The garish glow of a bonfire flickered over Building 3, urging Beckham and the others onward. Besides a few patrols, the base looked deserted. The remaining population had gathered on the beach.

"Girls, you wanna help push?" Riley asked, cutting through the silence. "I'm not going to be in this thing much longer. Might be your last chance." He twisted in his chair and gestured to Tasha and Jenny with a hand.

The girls looked up for their father's approval. He offered it with a nod, and Jenny grabbed the back of Riley's chair.

"Not too fast!" Riley said, as Tasha gripped the other handle. The girls put all of their strength into pushing Riley, giggling. The kid had always been one of the bright spirits that helped Team Ghost through the darkest of times.

Beckham checked the guard towers as they walked. Each had two soldiers inside. The long muzzles of their rifles looked out over the island.

"Better let me, girls," Chow said when they reached the gravel path that wrapped around Building 3. He took over and guided Riley's chair, rocks crunching under the wheels.

The leaves of trees rustled softly overhead. Beckham squeezed his way out in front and pulled Kate ahead. He halted at the edge of the shoreline, his breath stripped away by the sight of the white crosses in the dirt separating the beach from the trees.

"Daddy, is Mommy buried over there?" Tasha asked.

Horn bent down and scooped her up. His features

tensed in the glow from the bonfire raging on the beach below.

"No, sweetie," Horn said, cupping the back of her head with a large, gentle hand.

Beckham said a mental prayer for those civilians and soldiers buried in the fresh graves. Jinx was the only soldier they'd managed to recover during their missions outside of the island. The rest of Team Ghost and the Rangers and marines from Fort Bragg were all lost. Building 8, New York City, and the *Truxtun* had claimed them. He still hated himself for leaving Timbo behind, but he understood the reason. At least they had retrieved his dog tags. Beckham would bury those in the spot ahead marked for Timbo.

Kate squeezed his hand as they continued walking. Beckham's heart swelled in his chest when he saw Jinx's body resting on a cot draped with a US flag not far from Timbo's grave. A shovel marked the spot where they would lay Jinx to rest, but they would not erect a tombstone or lay flowers at his grave. It was Islamic tradition, one Jinx—who was a Muslim—had asked them to honor long ago when they'd shared their plans for how they wanted to be buried.

Drew "Jinx" Abbas had been a jokester on the outside and had kept his faith a secret to most, but beneath that he had also been a deeply spiritual man. Beckham had always respected him for that. Team Ghost had been the only people who knew their brother was Muslim, but it hadn't mattered to them, even in a time when the War on Terror had brought a wave of anti-Islamic sentiment. He was their brother, in life and in death.

Jensen met them on the sand and said, "I'll give you a few minutes to honor the fallen."

"Thank you, sir," Beckham said. He appreciated Jensen's display of respect and nodded. He could see the strain in the commander's features. After all, he had been the one to end Timbo's life.

Beckham dropped Kate's hand and felt a little tug on his sleeve. He looked down and saw Jenny's questioning face turned up to him.

"Is that Mr. Jinx?"

"Yes," Beckham replied. He leaned down and gave her a hug, glancing up at Kate as he embraced Jenny. "Stay with them, please."

"Come here, girls," Kate said, her arms outstretched.

"Let's go, Team Ghost," Beckham said, jerking his chin toward the graves. Chow, Riley, and Horn followed him, but Fitz hesitated as if he was unsure if he was welcome.

Beckham waved the marine onward, a small gesture to tell him he had earned the right. He was their brother now, just as much as Jinx and Timbo had been.

Fitz trudged through the sand, his blades sinking with every step. Chow struggled too, grunting as he pushed Riley's chair.

"Help me up," Riley said. "I'm not sitting down for this."

"You sure, Kid?" Horn asked.

"Yeah, Big Horn," Riley said. He grabbed the arm guards to hoist himself up.

Horn shrugged and looked at Chow. Together, the two operators pulled Riley from his chair and carried him between them to the grave site.

"Fitz," Beckham said, "can you help Riley keep his feet?"

The marine nodded and took Riley's weight from Chow, who joined Beckham beside the cot. Together they lifted the flag, revealing Jinx's body wrapped in the traditional funeral shroud of his faith.

Beckham and Chow stepped to the side and folded the flag in silence. When they'd finished, Chow carried the banner and handed it to Horn, who cradled it with one hand against his stomach. Beckham took a knee next to Jinx's body.

"Rest in peace, brother," he whispered.

"Hope you're in a better place, bro," Chow said. He crouched down and placed a hand on Jinx's chest.

"Help me with him," Beckham said. He grabbed Jinx under the arms and Chow picked up his feet. They gently hoisted his body off the cot.

"Careful," Chow said.

They lowered him into the wooden box already in the grave with exaggerated care. Chow bowed his head and whispered a prayer under his breath. He let out a deep sigh, tore the shovel from the dirt, and began filling in his best friend's grave. Beckham and the other men watched in silence, the crimson glow from the fire flickering over Chow's silhouette as he worked.

No color guard stood ready to offer a volley of shots. They didn't have ammo to spare. Jinx wasn't receiving a burial at Arlington, just an unmarked grave on the beach, surrounded by what was left of his brothers-in-arms.

When Chow finished, he pulled his sleeve over his forehead and jammed the shovel back into the dirt. The breeze rippled their uniforms as they stood and paid their final respects to their fallen friends. After a long silence, Horn held out the folded flag to Chow, who took it and held it over his heart.

The sound of a barking dog came across the wind as Beckham led his men back down the beach. Several figures were making their way through the trees behind Building 3. Apollo darted toward Beckham the moment he saw him.

"Apollo," Beckham said. "Come here, boy."

The dog stopped and sat a few feet away, looking up with obsidian eyes and wagging his tail. Beckham patted his head and then snapped his fingers. Apollo quickly followed him down the beach toward the bonfire.

A crowd was gathered around the flames, watching embers shoot into the night sky. Jensen met Beckham at the edge of the beach.

"I'm not much for speeches," Jensen said. "But I need to inform everyone about the change in command. Hate to do it now, but I'm not sure when General Kennor will send my replacement."

"Best to do it when everyone is here," Beckham said.

Jensen offered a rueful nod that told Beckham the officer was doing his best to keep it together. After the massacre in New York and the horror on the *Truxtun,* he looked like he'd aged fifteen years.

"Mind if I say a few words after you?" Beckham asked.

"I was hoping you would," Jensen said. He patted Beckham on the back and they joined the crowd. Horn stood with his girls. Beside them was a woman on crutches whom Beckham didn't recognize at first until Riley called out, "Hey, Meg!"

It was no wonder he hadn't recognized her. Meg was still covered in bruises and cuts, but her dark eyes were lively instead of haunted and her hair was neatly swept into a ponytail. She cracked a smile and waved with a crutch. The smile widened when she saw Beckham.

"Master Sergeant," she said, "I've been wanting to thank you for what you did in New York. You risked your life to save mine."

Beckham didn't mean to frown, but felt his brow forming one anyway. "You don't need to thank me."

"Yes. Yes, I do. If it weren't for you, I would have died in that awful place."

Jensen cleared his throat across the bonfire, interrupting their conversation.

"Thank you for coming," he said. "Tonight we pay our respects to those that we've lost in this war. Mothers, fathers. Sisters and brothers. Children . . ." He paused and bowed his head. "I want to take a few minutes for those of us who believe in a higher power to pray."

Beckham grabbed Kate's hand. Apollo leaned against his legs and whined softly. The fire crackled and popped as the crowd paid their silent respects.

"Thank you," Jensen said after a moment of quiet. "I also want to inform you of some changes. General Kennor has revoked my command. He's sending his own men to take over this post."

A few whispered conversations broke out, civilians turning to one another in confusion and alarm.

"I hope you will all show our new commander the respect you have shown me, and I thank you for your support during my tenure. There are difficult days ahead, but together, we can—we will—get through them," Jensen said. He spotted Beckham in the crowd and waved him over.

"Sit," Beckham said to Apollo.

Beckham tugged on the sides of his uniform to straighten it. He walked over to Jensen, saluted, and waited for Jensen to return the salute. The formalities done, Beckham shook the officer's hand.

"Thank you, sir," Beckham said. He faced the crowd and exhaled. He wasn't a man of many words, but tonight he had a few to share. He shifted his gaze from face to face, stopping on Horn's.

"Sheila Horn was a good mother and wife to Staff Sergeant Parker Horn. We lost her at Fort Bragg, along with so many of our Delta brothers. We lost even more in New York and then on the *Truxtun*." Beckham paused, his voice cracking. As he scanned those in front of him, he knew that they'd all lost brothers and sisters in the war. He didn't want to single out his own men. "Tonight we remember everyone who has fallen."

"Amen," said someone in the crowd.

"I know you're all scared. You have every right to be. I'm scared too. But I'm also certain that the human race will overcome," Beckham continued.

He looked at Kate, her face bathed in the orange light of the bonfire. She smiled back at him.

"I promise you that my men and I will do everything in our power to keep you safe while Doctor Lovato develops a new weapon," Beckham said. "Our future begins here, and together we *will* defeat the Variants and we *will* retake our cities."

The clapping and cheering of the small crowd was drowned out by the sound of an approaching helicopter. Several of the civilians pointed at the sky, and Beckham threw a glance over his shoulder. The outline of a Chinook emerged from the clouds. It circled the island and then disappeared over the trees to land on the tarmac beyond.

Jensen stepped up to Beckham's side. "General Kennor moves fast."

"Yes, he sure does, sir," Beckham replied.

"Thank you all!" Jensen shouted. "If you'll follow Major Smith to the grave sites, we will continue the service."

The crowd had started to disperse when raised voices sounded from the main campus. Half a dozen men decked out in black fatigues and body armor emerged from the trees. They jogged onto the beach carrying scoped SCAR rifles.

"Lieutenant Colonel Jensen!" one of the men shouted.

"You didn't waste any time," Jensen said.

Beckham stood his ground next to Jensen as the team approached. The officer leading the group halted and balled his hand into a fist. Then he pushed his black helmet up, revealing a face pockmarked with acne scars and a pair of striking blue eyes.

"Colonel Zach Wood. It's been a while," Jensen said.

"I haven't seen you since, what? That joint project with Colonel Gibson?" He placed careful emphasis on the words, as if wanting to make sure that Beckham heard them.

"Sounds right," Wood replied dryly. "Wish I was here to give you good news, but as you know I'm here to relieve you of your command. If you would please come with us, we have a lot to discuss." He stretched out an arm, fingers pointed back toward the buildings.

Jensen hesitated. "Sir, we are having a service for our—"

"Now, Lieutenant Colonel," Wood said. He turned away and flashed a signal to his men. They circled around and waited for Jensen to fall into line.

It took everything in Beckham to watch quietly while Colonel Wood and his team escorted Jensen away.

"Reed," Kate said. She placed a hand on his back, helping calm the anger that threatened to boil in his gut.

"He didn't deserve that," she said.

"No," Beckham said. "He didn't." They walked over to the graves in silence and found a spot at the back of the crowd. Beckham saw the fresh dirt of an unmarked grave he'd missed before. It was on the north end of the others, about ten feet from the white crosses.

"Who's buried there?" Beckham asked.

"Gibson," Kate replied. "I guess they figured it was better that way."

Beckham scratched Apollo behind his ears and stared at Gibson's grave. The chapter on Gibson was closed, but Wood had worked with the man. Somehow Beckham had a hard time believing that a high-ranking officer like him hadn't known about the work going on in Building 8. Then again, he'd mistrusted Jensen because of his association with Gibson, and Beckham had been wrong.

But while Jensen had proved himself as a man Beckham could trust, he had little—if any—faith left in Central Command or the colonel they had sent to take over. Not now, after they'd all sacrificed so much. Beckham silently vowed that if Wood turned out to be another traitor like Gibson, he'd take the colonel out himself.

General Kennor sat in his office with the lights off and his eyes closed. It was a guilty pleasure he'd developed over the years. No one ever seemed to knock when the lights were off. Not unless there was a war.

A rap on his door came a few minutes after he'd closed his eyes. He recognized the brisk, efficient knock.

"Flip the lights, will you, Colonel Harris?" Kennor said. "I was trying to get some sleep."

The glow from a bank of lights over his desk spilled over the room.

"Sorry, sir. Thought you would like to know that Colonel Wood has touched down at Plum Island. He's relieved Lieutenant Colonel Jensen of his command and has taken over the post."

"Good," Kennor said. "Jensen's a damn fool. I should have known I couldn't trust him after New York."

Kennor cursed himself for giving up so much control. He was already retreating from the cities. He would not allow himself to lose places like Plum Island. It had a vital part to play in his plan to win the war.

Kennor repositioned a picture of his grandkids on his desk. It was the only personal item he'd managed to take with him before he had been evacuated from the Pentagon. But no armed entourage had taken his family to an underground bunker. They had been lost in the madness of the outbreak.

"Sir, is there anything else?" Harris asked. He clasped his hands behind his back.

"Yes," Kennor said. He ran a finger over the picture and then leaned back in his chair.

"Tell Colonel Wood I want him to oversee Doctor Lovato's work. Everything goes through him. If she wants a goddamn test tube, she needs to get it approved."

"Understood, sir." He pivoted away from the desk and walked to the door.

"Oh, and Harris?" Kennor said, stopping him in midstride. "Tell him to monitor Jensen's men. After that stunt they pulled on the *Truxtun*, I have questions about their loyalties."

The next morning Beckham and his team gathered on the lawn outside Building 1. Fitz, Horn, Chow, and even Riley trailed him across the grass. Colonel Wood and an entourage of his soldiers waited for all of the enlisted men and women to report for a briefing. More troops had arrived under the cover of darkness. Beckham counted a dozen of them, all wearing the same black fatigues inscribed with the Medical Corps insignia. There were more on the towers and more patrolling the shoreline and wooded area around the buildings.

With a square meal and a decent night of sleep under his belt, Beckham felt the most refreshed he'd been since the outbreak. Alert and on edge, he was ready to hear what Wood had in store for the island.

Jensen and Smith stood behind the colonel. Neither of them showed any emotion. Beckham suspected Jensen was doing the exact same thing he had done when they met Lieutenant Gates back in NYC—he was waiting for Wood to lay the cards on the table and then act accordingly. Beckham would do the same damn thing in his position.

"I'll keep this short as we have a lot of work to do," Wood said. He shielded his face from the bright morning sun with a hand. "As many of you already know, I'm Colonel Wood with USAMRIID. Under orders from General Kennor, I have officially taken over this post. I will be splitting my time between this facility and several other top-secret locations as we pursue a weapon to destroy the Variants. You will all be assigned a new CO during this time. I don't care what branch you are from or what you did before. You will report to your CO at 1000 hours to receive your new orders. Some of you will be deployed to other locations. Make no mistake: This is war, and as soldiers we will do what we have to."

Beckham clenched his jaw as if he were bracing himself for a blow to the face, but Wood stopped there. He turned to Jensen and Smith, exchanging a few words Beckham couldn't hear.

"That is all, dismissed!" Major Smith shouted.

Jensen caught Beckham on his way out. He waited for most of the men to disperse and then said, "You better steel yourself, Beckham. Things are gonna get fucked."

"Figured as much," Beckham said. "Wood talks a big game, but—"

He felt a nudge on his shoulder. "Boss, shut up," Horn whispered.

Beckham turned to see Wood standing there.

"Master Sergeant, I'd like to have a word with you," he said.

"Yes, sir," Beckham replied, trying to conceal his surprise.

Wood waved off the two soldiers flanking him and continued across the grass. "I'm told you're the best soldier we have on the island."

"I don't know about that," Beckham said as he

followed Wood. "But I have seen what the Variants are capable of. In fact, I saw where this all started."

Wood stopped, keeping his back to Beckham. "Building Eight, I presume?"

"Yes, sir."

"The hemorrhage virus should never have escaped the facility."

The top-secret building was no longer a secret, but Beckham still found it interesting that the colonel would bring it up. It confirmed his suspicions that Wood might have known what Gibson was doing all along.

"I'm flying out to one of our other locations in the next couple of hours," Wood said. "But I wanted to talk to you before I leave. I've assembled a strategy that puts Plum Island on the offensive. That requires recon missions. I've done my best to keep you and your men together. Horn and Chow will be assigned to your team, but I'm keeping Fitz on the towers. Your CO is Lieutenant Colonel Jensen."

Beckham considered protesting but stiffened instead. "Understood, sir."

Wood nodded and let out a low whistle. His entourage followed him toward the Command building. Beckham watched them go and then glanced at the blue sky framed by swollen storm clouds. There was no question in his mind that this was Wood's attempt to keep a tight leash on Team Ghost and Jensen. The colonel didn't trust them, but that was fine because Beckham didn't trust Wood either. He would keep his head down for now, like he always did, and wait until the truth revealed itself.

With the wind picking up, Beckham turned back to his team to give them the news. The storm on the horizon wasn't the only one coming, and he was going to be damned if he let anyone—human or Variant—destroy everything he had worked so hard to build here.

15

Kate was doing her best not to think about anything but work. By midafternoon she'd already logged seven hours in the lab. She'd spent most of the time studying the new glycoprotein expressed by the Variants.

"We're really calling it the Superman protein?" Kate said, glancing skeptically at Ellis. "How'd you come up with that?"

"Take a look," Ellis said. He swiveled his monitor in her direction and pointed. "The beta sheets in its tertiary structure look like a cape."

"So?"

Rolling his eyes, Ellis said, "The Variant Superman protein is attached to oligosaccharide chains. Remember? The sugars?"

Kate nodded, leaning closer.

"The protein enables better, quicker interactions with the biochemical cascade associated with wound healing. It's why the Variants heal so quickly. Get it?"

She cracked a half smile. Ellis was a nerd, and a brilliant one at that. In the past she'd heard of scientists naming proteins Sonic Hedgehog and Pikachurin. She also vaguely remembered one called Superman. She asked just to be sure.

"Isn't there already a protein called Superman?"

"Yeah, but that's just for plants," Ellis said. "I'm calling this one the Variant Superman protein, but we can still call it Superman for short."

"It's settled then," Kate said. "Let's start the sequencing."

"On it," Ellis said.

They spent the next few hours sequencing the peptides corresponding to various sections of the protein. When they were finished, Ellis synthesized a string of peptides for immunizing the animal subjects Kate was prepping. With the extermination of the rhesus population, she was forced to use mice.

"I'll be back in a few," Kate said. "Gotta get the rodents."

"No problem. I'll have this completed in fifteen minutes."

Kate left Ellis to his work and crossed the lab, weaving her way through the compartments. Motion-activated lights flickered on as she entered the empty labs. The only other scientists at the facility were all on call now, waiting in case Kate needed them, but the labs were deserted.

She hesitated outside of the observation window to the animal testing room, remembering the rhesus monkeys she'd infected with the hemorrhage virus weeks earlier. She could still imagine their crimson eyes and their clawed hands rattling the cages.

The door beeped as she waved her key card over the security panel. She pulled the door open and continued inside. Shelves stacked with the remaining rodent populations stretched across the room. There were rats, mice, a few guinea pigs, and even a ferret. Most of them were frail from lack of proper nutrition. Others were missing large patches of hair from stress and the constant tests the technicians had performed. Only a few were in decent testing condition.

Kate picked the plumpest mice she could find and put their cages on a cart. She pushed them quickly back to her lab, trying not to look at the animals. Their suffering would be over soon.

"Almost set," Ellis said when she returned. "Got our specimens?"

"A dozen," Kate said. She positioned the cart near a clear lab station and waited for Ellis to finish prepping the adjuvant solution. It contained the peptide sequences that would be used to incite an immune response from the mice. In turn this would create antibodies targeting the Superman protein in the Variants.

When he had finished with the prep, he swabbed the base of each mouse's tail with sterilizing solution and then injected the solution into their veins.

"All done," Ellis said, taking a step back and standing by Kate's side.

"How long should it take before we can perform a bleed?" she asked.

"Normally ten to fourteen days. There's no way to speed up the animals' immune system to make antibodies faster, but we could always perform a bleed earlier. That would just mean we get a lower concentration of antibodies."

"We'll have to start in the next day or two," Kate said. "General Kennor is going to want this done as quickly as possible."

Ellis let out a sigh. "I think I can make that work. Question is, what do we do while we wait?"

"We think long term."

"Right," Ellis said. "We still haven't determined a way to deliver the weapon."

"I've been trying not to think about this, but we may

not have enough time to manufacture a weapon that we can use on a worldwide level before..."

Ellis nudged the bottom of the station with his boot. "Before the Variants wipe every last man, woman, and child off the face of the planet?"

Kate nodded grimly. "I read a study on endangered species in undergrad. Scientists found that in order for the human race to survive, they would need a minimum healthy population of two hundred and fifty adults in a single location."

"Like the two hundred and fifty at Central Command?" Ellis said.

"In theory," Kate said. "There are other places too. China, North Korea, Russia, Austria, and a host of other countries built these underground cities during World War II and the Cold War. Places where humans could survive in case there was ever an apocalyptic event."

"Austria was supposedly the most prepared country a few years ago. They drilled into the mountains and built bunkers that were stocked with enough supplies to last years," Ellis said. His eyes suddenly brightened under the lights. "The cities may be gone, but there still have to be pockets of resistance, right? Places like these underground cities."

Kate nodded uneasily. She wanted to believe that, but everything Beckham had told her said otherwise. Most of the human race had been forced into shelters underground, but the disease had infiltrated isolated locations before—places like the *Truxtun*—and like the caged mice in front of her, they were trapped.

"We can still stop the Variants, Kate," Ellis said. "We have to stop them."

"I know," Kate said. She watched the rodents hopefully. Inside these tiny creatures, the antibodies she needed to build her new weapon would soon begin to seed.

Lieutenant Colonel Jensen had done some things in his career that he regretted, but never in all of those years had he done anything that kept him up at night. Not until the *Truxtun*. Nothing he could do would bring his men back or relieve the pain he felt for taking Timbo's life. He could only pray that God would forgive his sins and give him strength to continue fighting. He doubted, however, that God would forgive Colonel Gibson or Colonel Wood.

Jensen's gut told him that Wood had known what was going on at Building 8. Gibson and Wood were like brothers and had worked together since Vietnam. Though Jensen knew better, you could at least make the argument that Gibson possessed a moral compass. He had designed VX-99 in hopes that other parents wouldn't have to lose their sons and daughters on foreign battlefields. The result was disastrous, but a part of Jensen understood why Gibson had done what he did.

A very small part.

Wood, on the other hand, had no sense of morality. He didn't even understand the concept. Referred to as "the Snake" by his fellow officers, he was known for his cutthroat tactics. There were rumors that Building 8 wasn't the only top-secret biological warfare program Wood had worked on. Some of Jensen's colleagues had hinted that Wood had his own hidden facility focused on weapons of mass destruction.

As much as Jensen wanted to bury Wood next to Gibson, he had to carry on with his duty. The military still had rules and protocols, even at the end of the world. Jensen had sworn an oath and he still believed in his country—although he was starting to lose faith in those that protected her, especially after the disaster that was Operation Liberty.

Jensen buried any thoughts of mutiny as he jogged toward the tarmac. He had new orders—a recon mission to Connecticut to observe the Variant migration patterns. Command had sent word through all channels that the creatures were leaving their lairs and traveling farther afield for human prey. His job was to document their behavior and look for anything that could help win the war, but he doubted a flyover would tell them anything they didn't already know.

When he passed Building 1, he glimpsed Kate and Beckham embracing on the steps. Jensen slowed, hoping to catch the operator's ear before they departed for Connecticut.

"It's just a recon mission, Kate. I won't even leave the chopper," Beckham was saying. He caught sight of Jensen, kissed Kate on the cheek, and then ran down the stairs. "Good evening, sir," he said.

"Is it?" Jensen said. He waved to Kate and added, "Let's take a stroll."

Jensen led Beckham away from the building in silence. He checked the path for any of Wood's men. The last thing he wanted was for any of the soldiers to eavesdrop on their conversation.

Ahead, a patrol marched in the opposite direction. When Jensen rounded the corner, the crackling of leaves and snapping of branches commanded his gaze to the trees behind Building 1. A trio of soldiers in black fatigues had just emerged from the thick canopy.

"How's Kate doing?" Jensen asked casually in case the soldiers were listening. He continued forward, using the glow from the industrial lights to guide them toward the tarmac.

"She's hanging in there. Sounds like they're making

some headway with their experiments. She says they identified a protein only expressed in Variants, but I don't really understand all the science mumbo jumbo."

"Don't know what that means either, but it sounds promising. My first CO told me that if you don't know what someone's talking about, you just nod and grin."

"Mine said the exact opposite," Beckham said. "Told me not to react at all."

They shared a laugh as they reached the concrete barriers on the edge of the tarmac. The black silhouettes of Echo 1, 2, and 3 rested ahead. The pilots were starting to warm the birds up.

A dozen soldiers flocked around the Black Hawks, stacking gear and loading weapons. Half wore the black fatigues of Wood's men. The other half sported tan camo and body armor. Amongst them were a few marines and Rangers from Fort Bragg and the last members of Delta.

Just a recon mission.

After everything they'd been through, Jensen wasn't going to underestimate a mission ever again.

"Beckham," Jensen said quietly, "we've got to watch our backs now more than ever."

"Always do," Beckham replied.

"I'm not talking about the Variants."

Beckham halted and gave him a cockeyed glance. "Wood?"

"He's connected to Gibson's work. I'm not sure how deep their ties go or what Wood knew about VX-99, but we shouldn't trust him."

Beckham's face tensed like he was suffering from a massive migraine. "You think he could have been involved with Building Eight?"

"Can't confirm or deny that," Jensen said. "But I would guess he was, in some capacity."

"Roger that. He seemed suspicious to me as well."

Jensen nodded. "Figured as much."

They continued the rest of the walk in silence. Jensen dropped his rucksack on the ground beside Echo 2 and waved his new team over. Chow, Horn, Beckham, and a sergeant from Wood's staff gathered around.

"Everyone, this is Sergeant Valentine. He'll be accompanying us on our flyover of Niantic," Jensen said.

Valentine stepped forward. He was built like a turtle, with a bulky midsection and a short neck. "Command wants us to chart enemy movement. We are not to engage. I repeat: We are not to engage any hostiles." There was aggression in his voice that seemed unnecessary given that they were supposed to be on the same team.

"Thank you, Sergeant," Jensen said. "We understand our orders from brass. And this here silver oak leaf means you need to understand *my* orders." He tapped the pin. "But I expect you already know that." He didn't care if he sounded condescending. Valentine clearly suffered from little man syndrome, and given how uncomfortable he looked in his gear, chances were he'd never seen combat at all. Jensen made a mental note of that. The last thing he was going to do was let some green-ass sergeant pull any stunts like Lieutenant Gates had during Operation Liberty.

"Yes, sir," Valentine said. "Understood, sir."

Jensen looked Valentine up and down, shifted the chew in his mouth, and then pulled a map in a waterproof sleeve from his vest.

"Beckham, you know this area the best. I'd like you to direct the birds. Give the pilots a heads-up about where to look for the enemy."

"Yes, sir," Beckham replied. He accepted the map from Jensen's hand and took a few minutes to study it. A gentle drop of rain fell on the paper, beading on the acetate. The sky opened up just as Beckham folded the map and put it into a pocket.

Anxious to get in the air, Jensen said, "Let's mount up."

Horn climbed inside the craft and manned the M240. Chow and Beckham flung their scoped M4s over their shoulders and piled in. Jensen waited for Valentine before jumping inside.

The heavy thump of blades sounded as the pilots fired up the birds. Each man took his seat and began his pre-mission routine. Chow chewed on a toothpick, Beckham traced a finger over his vest pocket, and Horn pulled up his skull bandanna and flexed his right fist in and out. Valentine sat stiffly, his gaze shifting from face to face. He stopped on Jensen's and they locked eyes for several seconds.

Valentine looked away first. He settled his back against the compartment wall and grabbed his helmet as the bird ascended into the sky. Jensen let his lips curl into a brief smile.

That's right. Back in your shell, you little bastard.

The other two Black Hawks peeled off in opposite directions. Movement at the opposite end of the tarmac caught Jensen's attention as they pulled away. He grabbed the handle by the door and worked his way to the side. A cluster of troops were moving across the tarmac toward the last remaining aircraft. He didn't need his scope to see Wood and his entourage boarding the Chinook.

Jensen secretly hoped it was the last time he saw the man. He even let himself wish that Wood somehow found himself up to his neck in Variants wherever the bird was taking him. But deep down Jensen knew that if Wood died, Kennor would just send another watchdog his way.

Fitz took in a breath of salty air and looked over the side of guard Tower 9. The building had been erected at Pine

Point, on the southern tip of Plum Island. Unlike the other towers, this one didn't have a vantage of the entire island. It looked out over Gardiners Bay to the south and Orient, New York, to the west. He could hardly see the six white domes of the Plum Island compound.

Overhead, thin clouds lit up as they rolled past a brilliant moon. Below, the black water sparkled. The tower wasn't the worst in terms of the view, but it was the most isolated. A Humvee had dropped him and Apollo off at the end of the dirt road before returning to the post. Other than the dog, he was completely alone. From where Fitz stood, he could only see the silhouetted figures of the snipers in Towers 7 and 8. The towers had been built on the beach to the northwest and northeast. If something happened, he was far from help, but that's why he had his MK11 and Apollo. He trusted his shooting skills enough not to worry, and the dog had survived for who knew how long amongst the infected on the *Truxtun*, so having Beckham's new friend watching his back was an added relief.

His main concern tonight wasn't Variants. It was Colonel Wood. The son of a bitch hadn't believed in him enough to place him under Jensen's command. The man had actually looked at him with a pitying glance when Fitz had volunteered to go on tonight's recon mission.

Fitz hated that. He wasn't useless. He didn't need the colonel's pity—he needed a chance. The same chance Beckham had given him at Fort Bragg. He was a marine, and he could still fight. He was determined to prove the colonel wrong and make his way back onto Team Ghost.

Breathing heavily, he gripped the stock of his MK11 in one hand and mounted the bipod onto the wooden ledge. A soft rain had begun to fall. The drops fell at an angle, pinging off his helmet and cooling his flushed cheeks as he glassed the ocean. He channeled what was left of his anger into his current mission—his duty to protect the island.

He spent the next few minutes scoping the dark waves. The lonely shapes of derelict ships drifted in the distance. It was the same sight he'd seen every night since he'd been posted to the towers. But when he moved the scope back toward the shore, he saw something odd at one thousand feet out.

What in the hell?

He chambered a round and zoomed in on a trio of shapes. They bobbed up and down in the dark water. The tide carried them toward the shoreline. It was probably plastic cartons or something dumped into the sea, but he made a mental note to check on them in a few minutes when he had a better view.

Maneuvering to his right, he started his first sweep of the sloped shoreline to the northwest. The surf slurped against the beach, white foam forming at its edges. Despite the beach, Plum Island was no paradise—the sand was littered with plastic bottles and other trash, and rows of electric fences lined the shelf of the beach and the short ridgeline beyond.

Variants would have to climb the ten-foot-tall fences, clear the razor wire, and survive the twenty 7.62 mm round box magazine in his MK11 if they wanted to get on the island.

Fitz moved his twenty-inch barrel to Tower 8, sighted the sniper, and then glassed the woods to the northeast. Beams from the fire team patrolling the area backlit the trees as the soldiers searched for threats.

He checked on Apollo next. The dog glanced up from the sand and wagged his tail. Fitz had tried carrying him up the ladder, but apparently Apollo didn't like heights, so Fitz had left him on the beach to stand watch.

Apollo's ears perked as a female voice crackled over the comm. "Tower Nine, Command. Please report."

Fitz didn't bother checking his watch. He knew he was late on his sitrep.

"Sorry, Command. All looks clear out here," Fitz replied.

He returned to his rifle and searched for the floating objects he'd seen earlier. They had drifted another two or maybe three hundred yards closer to the island. The sky had cleared enough to allow moonlight through, and Fitz zoomed in for a better look.

With a few twists of his scope, he identified the curved bottom of a capsized yacht about halfway between Plum Island and Orient. He swept the crosshairs back to the floating lumps and saw this wasn't plastic after all. These were bodies.

He checked for any flicker of movement, any sign they were still alive. Each wore a life jacket, but that hadn't saved them. They were all facedown in the water. There was no question—the poor souls were dead.

"Command, Tower Nine, I have eyes on three casualties," Fitz said into his comm.

"Copy that, Tower Nine. No sign of survivors?"

"Negative so far," Fitz said. "Stand by."

Fitz wiped away the cold drops of rain running down his forehead and did another quick sweep of the area. A flash of underwater motion broke across his crosshairs as he slowly moved the rifle.

"What the hell was—" Fitz began to say. He jerked his rifle back and searched for the contact. The long, narrow body of a sea creature blurred past his crosshairs like an arrow under the waves. Whatever kind of fish this was, it was moving fast.

He pulled the bipod off the ledge and shouldered the rifle to scan the waves with naked eyes. There, six hundred feet out, he saw the creature again. It might have been a dolphin or even a shark, something sleek and pale in the water.

Fitz brought his rifle up again and zoomed in. The contact was gliding just beneath the surface. He slowly roved the rifle to the left, where he spotted more of them, all closing in on the floating corpses.

"Tower Nine, standing by for report."

Fitz didn't reply. He let out a breath and focused on the school of monster-sized fish surging under the waves. They had to be sharks. Variants couldn't hold their breath that long, could they?

He flinched as one of the life jackets disappeared under the water. The other two vanished a moment later and the shimmering black water turned a frothy red.

"Tower Nine—" the operator began to say.

"Stand by," Fitz muttered, his irritated voice cutting her off.

He pressed his eye back to the scope just as a shiny skull crested the water, steam rising off the hairless scalp. Even from five hundred yards out, he could recognize the yellow eyes of a Variant.

"Command, I have eyes on a hostile. I repeat…" His voice trailed off as a dozen heads emerged from the water.

Fitz's heart spiked with anxiety when he saw a blur of pale bodies two hundred yards to the northwest. It was a second wave of Variants.

"My God," Fitz whispered.

"Repeat your last, Tower Nine."

"Command, I…uh…I have eyes on multiple hostiles."

There was a short pause and then, "Tower Nine, how many hostiles do—"

Fitz fired off a shot. It was a bull's-eye; the head of one of the monsters burst into shards of bone and brain.

The others dove below the surface of the water before he could squeeze off another round.

"Command, I have a dozen contacts. Requesting support at Tower Nine!" Fitz said, his voice rising to a shout.

Steady, Fitz, steady...

He waited for the creatures to get closer. When they were in his sights he fired calculated shots that zipped through the water and found flesh. The Variants swam using the breaststroke, gliding effortlessly, using their legs to propel them forward like frogs. Their flexible joints and muscular bodies made them perfect swimmers, and Fitz now suspected they had also evolved to hold their breath longer than humans.

The chatter of gunfire from Tower 8 sounded as Fitz changed his first magazine. Apollo was barking, his howls echoing up into the boxy tower. Fitz ignored the dog and concentrated on the water. The Variants were picking up speed. At this rate they would reach the shore in a few minutes.

There were hundreds of the monsters now, all coming from New York. Fitz imagined they had exhausted their resources there and had taken to the water to find food. Plum Island, unfortunately, was right in their path.

Fitz fired as quickly as he could line up his shots. Injured Variants struggled above the surface, bleeding from gaping wounds, while others swam for the shore. Concentrating on those that continued toward him, he aimed for their glistening heads.

He finished off another magazine and reached for a replacement. After palming it home, he picked up the rifle and leaned over the ledge, firing at the first creatures that leaped from the surf. Their naked, hairless bodies glimmered in the moonlight, revealing frail, starving physiques. Bulging veins crisscrossed their bony rib cages, the skin so tight it looked like plastic wrap.

Some of them dropped to all fours, their joints snapping and clicking over the gunfire.

Fitz counted thirty Variants, and thirty quickly turned into fifty. He cut them down as fast he could, but they continued to emerge from the water like frogs, leaping onto the beach. The night filled with the shrieks of enraged monsters and Fitz's own uncontrolled shouting. The blood rushed in his ears, his heart threatening to break through his chest.

"Command! Where are my reinforcements?" Fitz yelled into his comm as a pair of Variants collided with the electrical fence. The metal rattled with the current frying both of the monsters. They tumbled back onto the sand, their bodies smoldering. Instead of deterring the others, a tall male jumped on the first fallen corpse and leaped to the top of the fence. Others followed, leaping and throwing themselves on the chain-link mesh and razor wire. They wrapped their claws around the metal even as they were jolted with electricity. Most of them died right there, their bony bodies going limp, but their sacrifice allowed others to climb the ladder of Variant corpses.

Within minutes, the fence was crumpling and the breeze reeked of burned flesh. Fitz watched with a sense of awe as he fired, amazed at the intelligence of the creatures. They were starving and desperate, but most of them were still smart enough to make it over the fence using the bodies of the fallen.

An air-raid siren screamed in the distance. As he changed magazines, Fitz threw a glance over his shoulder to see a pair of Humvees squeal to a stop on the road behind the tower. Two fire teams piled out and ran to the fences. The automatic crack from their M4s was only a short relief that vanished when he looked back over the beach.

The mass of monsters swarming over the sand

prompted a fear in him that reached deeper than any he'd felt during his time in Iraq. It was more powerful than what he'd felt during the escape from Fort Bragg—more powerful than what he'd felt on the *Truxtun* or during the first attack on the island.

This time it wasn't a Chinook that had brought the monsters to the post. The Variants had finally found the island on their own. They'd brought the battle to Plum Island, and Fitz feared this time he couldn't stop them.

16

Rain pelted the side of the Black Hawk as it passed over the *Truxtun*. Beckham fought to keep his emotions under control at the sight of the ship. Seeing it again plunged his mind back into the horrors of that night. At least this was no rescue op or salvage mission. Pure recon.

"Take us over Niantic," Beckham said into his comm.

"Roger that," one of the pilots replied.

The chopper banked hard to the right and pulled them over the highway still littered with the remains of Variants that Horn had turned to mulch two nights ago when he'd rescued them all from the grounded destroyer. Despite the carrion field of flesh, there was no movement, or activity of any kind.

Beckham flipped on his four-eyes and scanned the desolate landscape. The green-hued darkness revealed only more abandoned vehicles and rotting corpses.

"Anyone got eyes on?" Beckham asked.

"Nothin' at nine o'clock," Chow said.

The M240 clicked as Horn searched the road for contacts. "Negative, boss. I don't see shit."

The rooftops of Niantic came into view a moment later. Beckham raised his M4 and glassed the streets. Valentine leaned over his shoulder for a better vantage, his breath hitting Beckham's neck. It reeked of stale coffee.

"Where the fuck are they?" the sergeant asked.

"Just wait," Chow said. "It's still early. They hunt mostly in the darkness."

The pilots circled the city again, this time taking the bird over the boatyard where Beckham's team had been ambushed in an attempt to catch their first live specimen. A flashback to the Variant boy with the shredded legs made Beckham shudder.

He shook the thought away and scooted away from Valentine. As soon as he got to the open door, the comm came to life.

"We got movement," Horn said. "Three o'clock. What the hell is that?"

When Beckham glanced to the shoreline, he saw why Horn sounded so confused. An F150 pickup was hauling ass down the street, zigzagging between gridlocked vehicles.

Beckham followed the truck in his scope, noting a male driver and a female passenger. Tucked between them was a smaller figure—a child.

"Found your Variants too, Valentine!" Horn shouted.

Beckham swept his scope to the horde of Variants thirty deep behind the pickup. The creatures leaped from car to car. From above it looked like an army of ants swarming after an injured beetle.

"Get us into position," Beckham said into the comm. "Horn, you take out the pack."

"Roger that," one of the pilots replied.

"NO!" Valentine yelled. He scrambled to the cockpit. "Ignore that order. We are not to engage."

Beckham twisted and flipped up his NVGs. He locked eyes with Jensen, who nodded.

"Stand down, Sergeant," Jensen said.

"But, sir. Our orders are only to observe," Valentine argued.

"You got a family, Sergeant?"

"Yes, sir, I do."

"If that was them down there, would you still refuse to *engage?*"

"Sir, our orders are—"

Jensen shouldered his rifle and worked his way to the side of the chopper next to Beckham. "Those orders have changed!"

The Variants were gaining on the truck, flowing through the streets and lunging from vehicle to vehicle. The driver must have seen that the creatures were closing the gap. He clipped a minivan in an attempt to maneuver into the other lane.

The truck fishtailed and the bed crashed into a sedan. The passenger window shattered. The driver slammed on the gas pedal, and smoke boiled off the burning tires as the vehicle lurched forward. A long-limbed, muscular Variant threw its body onto the roof of the minivan and then jumped into the bed of the truck. Beckham steadied his breathing, waiting for a clear shot as the creature clambered to the back window of the truck and slammed its head into the glass, shattering it.

"Take that one down, Beckham!" Jensen shouted, pointing. "The rest of you, open fire on the pack!"

The M240 coughed to life, the whine of the machine gun filling the troop. The rounds smashed into vehicles and the Variants behind the pickup, punching through metal and flesh.

Beckham centered his crosshairs on the Variant in the back of the truck. He waited for the perfect window and squeezed the trigger. The first shot pinged off the side of the bed, but the second hit the creature in the shoulder. It spun and almost tumbled over the back tailgate. Before

Beckham could fire a third time, the Variant had recovered and jumped on top of the cab.

"Fuck," Beckham muttered. The shot was nearly impossible now. If he fired, he risked hitting the driver or passengers. He zoomed in just as three bullets tore through the roof of the truck. Someone was firing from inside.

The bullets found their target. A spray of blood burst from the Variant's exit wounds, and the force of the blasts launched it into the air. The creature landed back on the roof a second later, still miraculously alive. It clawed frantically for something to hold on to. The driver jerked the truck to the right, and the monster flew over the side and smashed against a car door. It slumped down the side, leaving a streak of blood across the metal.

Horn's bullets cut through the meat of the pack still pursuing the truck. The high-pitched howls of the monsters reverberated through the night as the rounds shredded their bodies and sent torn limbs rolling across the scarlet asphalt. The driver of the truck didn't waste the opportunity to escape. He pounded the gas and sped away from the massacre.

Once the Variants saw their quarry had escaped, the majority of the pack fled. Only two persisted, staggering through the smoke after the truck. Beckham focused on the one holding a bloody stump where its arm had been. In the past, he would have saved his ammunition, but the Variant was still dangerous, even with one arm. He took it down with a shot to its head.

Less than a minute was all it had taken to paint the street with a fresh coat of blood. The last Variant dashed into the night, evading the gunshots and leaping into the bay. The pickup continued down the main street until it was clear of the massacre and then slowed to a stop.

"Take us down over the beach!" Jensen shouted.

Beckham changed his magazine as he scanned the LZ for contacts. It was close to the extraction point during Team Ghost's first mission to Niantic. The bullet-riddled, rotting bodies of the Variants they'd killed would still be there.

"Chow, on me!" Beckham shouted as soon as the chopper was hovering over the site. After a quick sweep for hostiles, Beckham jumped out and landed in the wet sand with a plop. Raindrops smacked his face as he made his way to the road. His headset crackled when he was halfway there, and a message that stopped him mid-stride sounded in his ear.

"Echo Two, Command. We are under attack. I repeat, we are under attack. All birds return home, ASAP," a female voice said.

Beckham whirled back to the chopper. Jensen was standing at the door, his hand cupping an ear.

"What do you mean, attack?" Jensen said over the comm.

"Variants are storming the shore," the radio operator said. "There are hundreds of them. We need support!"

Beckham's heart fluttered as he turned back to the truck. It was stopped at the road and a man wearing green camo and a baseball cap was pulling a boy no older than six out. A woman darted from around the other side of the vehicle.

"Get back here!" Valentine shouted from the chopper. "We have to go!"

Chow had halted a few feet in front of Beckham. They exchanged a glance. Would the few extra minutes it took to extract the family cost lives on Plum Island?

Beckham had to take that chance. He couldn't leave these people behind. Especially when they were so close.

"Come on!" Beckham shouted. "Hurry!" He sprinted to the street and met the family at the guardrail by the side of the road. Holding out his hand, he helped the woman over the top.

"God bless you," she said, her voice shaky.

The man didn't utter a word as he pulled the boy over the railing. He simply nodded at Beckham. The boy's mile-long stare seemed like a symptom of shock, and his parents both looked like they had been through the wringer. Their faces were covered in grime and their clothes were soiled with blood and dirt.

"Let's go," Beckham said.

The family didn't need to be told twice. They started down the beach and ran for the chopper. Chow and Beckham hung back to cover their escape and then darted after them.

There was something about the way the man carried himself that seemed military. It made sense—if they had survived out here this long, the man likely had training. At the Black Hawk, Jensen helped the woman and the boy inside. The man climbed aboard and Chow and Beckham jumped in after him.

"Get us out of here!" Beckham said. As soon as they were in the air, he half crouched over to the family.

"What's your name?" Beckham shouted over the chop of the blades.

"Red," the man said. He scratched at his beard and glanced up. "This is my wife, Donna, and our son, Bo."

"Where are you taking us?" Donna asked.

Jensen hovered over Beckham's shoulder. "Somewhere safe..." Jensen said, his words trailing off like he didn't believe it.

Bo glanced up. "Where?"

"Place called Plum Island," Beckham said, looking at Red. "Where were you coming from?"

Red's eyes hardened and he hugged Bo closer to his chest. "Hell," he said.

Beckham moved back to the door just as the crack of gunfire broke out in the distance. He raised his rifle and scoped the island. Tracers lanced across the southern shoreline.

"Thought you said this place was safe!" Red shouted over the rotors.

Meg yelled for the third time, "What the hell is going on?" And for the third time there was no response, her voice lost in the whine of the emergency sirens.

Red light swirled in the hallway outside her room. She grabbed the handrail of her bed frame and then leaned over to reach for the crutches propped against a nearby chair. Her fingers found one of the grips, but when she wrapped them around it, the tip spun away. The crutch clanked on the floor, half under the bed.

"Damn it!" Meg shouted. With no small amount of effort, she scooted her back against the headboard until she was sitting up. The limited movement sparked a streak of pain that took her breath away. She hadn't taken any pain pills for a couple of hours, and without them the wounds hurt like they'd been cooked over an open flame.

She sucked in a deep breath, released it, and screamed at the top of her lungs, "Somebody help!"

After waiting several beats, she came to terms with the fact she was alone. No one was coming to help her. She collapsed against the handrail, gritted her teeth, and swung her bandaged legs over the side of the bed.

You can do this, Meg. You're a damn Ironman.

She held in a breath and prepared to move as the door swung open and Riley rolled inside.

"Post is under attack, let's go!" he said. He scooped up her crutches and handed them to her.

"We're under attack?"

"No time to explain. We've got to get to the shelter."

Meg nodded and put her left foot down first. It hurt like hell, but at least it would hold her weight. She hopped over to Riley. The burn wasn't as bad as she thought it would be, or perhaps she just wasn't thinking about the pain. A slew of questions rushed across her mind but she stayed silent, determined to get somewhere safe before interrogating her rescuer.

"Follow me," Riley said.

"Wait."

Riley glanced up, his blue eyes searching hers.

"You carrying? I feel naked without my axe."

"Here, you can have this," he said, plucking the sheathed knife from where he'd tucked it beside his hip. "Be careful with it."

Meg balanced herself on the crutches and carefully reached out to take the sheath. She tucked it into her pants and nodded.

"Now let's move!" Riley said. He maneuvered his chair through the door and took a right down the hallway. The glow of emergency lights bathed the two in an ominous red as they struggled down the empty corridor.

"Where are we going?" Meg shouted over the wail of the sirens.

"Building Five!"

"Which one is that?"

Riley pulled around another corner, the wheels on his chair squeaking. "It's just next door. Don't worry, there are two guards waiting for us outside. They escorted me here to find you."

"You came here for me?"

Riley glanced over his shoulder and cracked a half grin. "Wasn't gonna leave a lady in distress."

Meg would have smiled back, but her lips twisted into a scowl from the pain. She hoped Riley didn't see it.

"Where's Doctor Hill and the rest of the medical staff?" Meg asked. If they had left her here, so help her, she was going to...

"Already evacuated!"

"Without me?"

Riley turned again and said, "Shut up and move!"

He pushed open the final set of doors to the lobby and worked his way across the threshold with several powerful rotations of his wheels. She still couldn't get over the fact that Beckham and his men had done so much for her. Jed's cowardice in New York had ruined her faith in the military, but Team Ghost had restored it.

The crack of gunfire sounded over the sirens as soon as they moved into the lobby. The shots seemed to be coming from all directions. She resisted the urge to pull the knife from its sheath—mostly because she'd have to limp along with the blade between her teeth.

Riley stopped at the doors leading outside and pulled a pistol from a holster tucked down by his waist. He pulled back the slide to chamber a round and said, "Can you see anything out there?"

Meg moved cautiously to the glass doors and peered through. Two soldiers waited on the steps, their rifles aimed into the darkness.

"Looks clear," she said.

Riley pushed the doors open and wheeled onto the landing just as a helicopter roared overhead. Meg hopped out after him and spied several men inside the troop bay above. The one crouched to the side of an oversized machine gun looked familiar. Meg felt the hint of a smile coming on when she realized it was Beckham. He always seemed to be showing up just in the nick of time to save the day. He glanced down and waved with two fingers.

Riley laid his pistol in his lap and cupped his hands over his mouth as the chopper flew over the building. "Get 'em, boss!" he shouted.

"Was that Riley?" Horn yelled.

"Looks like he was with Meg and a couple soldiers," Beckham said. He prayed Kate and the other inhabitants of the island were safe. This time, at least, they would have been able to follow evacuation protocols. Everyone should be on their way to Building 5 to hunker down.

"Get ready on that gun, Horn," Jensen said.

Beckham checked on Red and his family huddled in the back of the chopper. They looked like they had been to hell and back. Then again, according to Red they had been. Beckham hated to drag them back into a war zone, but he had no choice.

The helicopter flew over a canopy of trees. Beckham spotted the towers and saw the flashes at the fences and the tracers spitting from the boxes. All of the rounds were aimed at the beach where a horde of Variants was advancing.

Not a horde, but an army!

"Holy fucking shit!" Horn yelled. "There's got to be a couple hundred of them." His tattooed forearms bulged as he held the M240.

"Those fences should hold them, right?" Valentine asked.

Beckham gripped his rifle so tightly his knuckles popped. Variants were trapped in the razor wire at the top of the first line of electric fencing, their flesh tearing and ripping as they struggled. Others crashed into it, earning themselves shocks that sent them flying backward. Even from the sky, Beckham could see many of the sinewy creatures were starving.

Starving meant desperate.

They flung their bony bodies against the defenses again and again. The more intelligent Variants leaped onto the pile of dead for a shot to clear the top of the razor wire, but none had made it yet. Beckham wasn't sure if they were coordinating their efforts to topple the fences or if they were simply crazed with hunger. Either way, they were slowly succeeding. The first fence leaned at an angle under the weight of the dead creatures. More were already scrambling up the incline.

He flinched as the first Variant made it over the top and charged the second line of electric fencing. Beckham snapped into motion. He raised his rifle and waited for the order that came a second later.

"Chow, Valentine, concentrate your fire on the fences. Beckham and I will swap when you reload. Horn, focus your fire on the Variants coming from the water," Jensen said.

The chopper shot over Tower 9 and the pilots maneuvered in a slow circle above the water. This gave Horn an opportunity to unleash everything he had on the mass of diseased flesh. He raked the gun back and forth, spraying a line of projectiles at the creatures emerging from the water. The crack of M4s joined in as Chow and Valentine entered the fight.

Beckham anxiously waited for his turn to shoot, using the time to monitor the battle. He spied Fitz shooting madly over the side of Tower 9. Below the box, he saw movement. It was Apollo, howling and pacing at the base of the tower.

If the Variants got over those fences, the dog wouldn't stand a chance. That wasn't going to happen. He wasn't going to let them get their claws into Fitz or Apollo. He thought of Kate, of Horn's girls, of Riley and Meg—even nerdy Ellis and cool-eyed Smith. Nobody he cared about would be at the mercy of those things, not if Beckham could do anything to stop it.

"Changing!" Chow yelled. He moved to the side and Beckham bladed his body to squeeze through. Finding a target wasn't a problem. The entire beach was crawling with them. The monsters had shown intelligence before, but now most of them just seemed suicidal. It didn't make sense. He didn't see any one creature leading the battle. Had this group not evolved like the rest of the Variants he'd seen? Or had their hunger made their minds revert to a more primitive stage? He didn't have time to speculate.

Beckham fired without restraint, emptying his magazine into a dozen of the monsters that had leaped over the first fence. Another dozen were attacking the second barrier. They used the fresh corpses Beckham had just taken down as springboards to leap into the razor wire. That was the last line of defense before they had free rein over the island.

"Don't let them bring down the first fence!" Beckham shouted. If they did, the second would quickly follow, and then there was no way they could stop the horde from reaching the buildings.

He stepped back to change his magazine, letting Chow back up front. Echo 1 and 3 were circling farther up the northwestern shoreline near Tower 8. The gunners were unloading on the creatures with double the firepower— and from the looks of it, they were actually winning.

Beckham's team, on the other hand, was fighting for every inch of sand. The first fence was leaning at an even steeper angle now, and whatever electricity it was producing seemed to do little to deter the tidal wave of creatures sweeping over it.

"Horn, redirect your fire on the first fence!" Jensen shouted.

Fitz had killed so many Variants that the corpses were three deep at the foot of the fence. The mountain of dead had created a ladder over the first electric fence.

It grew with every crack from Fitz's MK11.

Horn swept the M240 back and forth, grunting as he doubled his efforts to stop the relentless charge of starving monsters. Beckham switched places with Chow and squeezed off automatic bursts. The team had thinned the army down to a hundred, but still they came, talons ready and crazed eyes focused, determined to feed.

The monsters were freely climbing the chains of the first fence now, the electricity severed. Beckham took out three of the climbers with carefully aimed shots. They slumped against the metal as the fence finally came crashing down.

His heart skipped as the first Variants leaped over the fallen fence, vanishing in a cloud of sand and dirt. They emerged a second later and crashed into the second fence twenty strong. A tall, lean Variant with ropy back muscles made it clean over the top in a leap that would have won a gold medal in the Olympics. Beckham killed it with a shot to the head before it had a chance to land on the other side.

Apollo charged the barrier from the other side, barking ferociously at the intruders. The dog stood its ground, snarling at the monsters as they crashed into the last barrier.

"Get back, boy," Beckham whispered. He centered his rifle on the ground ten feet away from Apollo and squeezed off a shot. Dirt exploded into the air, and the dog took off in a mad dash for the Humvees where the other fire teams had already retreated.

"Do NOT let them take down the second fence!" Beckham roared over the comm. He stepped back to change his magazine, one eye on the final barrier as it too began to lean.

Dread filled him as he watched helplessly—this time he wasn't sure if they could stop the Variants. The sheer power of their numbers was too much to repel. They simply couldn't kill the monsters fast enough.

"Keep firing!" he shouted. "Don't let them take down that fence!"

Everyone on the island was counting on them now, in this moment. They either held the Variants here or Beckham lost everyone he loved. He wedged his way between Chow and Horn, firing with his M9. Bullet casings pinged off the floor of the chopper.

Everything was happening in slow motion. Beckham's senses had amplified like the Variants below him. He could see the rain drizzling from the sky, he could see body parts rolling across the sand, and he could see the fence as it leaned another inch. He heard Horn's labored breathing and Bo's sobs as Red tried to calm the boy. There was something else too. Another noise growing in the distance. A faint, mechanical whine.

He looked to the northwest as Echo 1 and Echo 3 swept across the sky, their M240s already dumping on the beach.

"Yeah!" Chow shouted.

Horn continued unloading his own heavy machine gun. The combined fire of 7.62 mm rounds sent a fountain of sand and flesh into the air. The beach was washed with crimson as the trio of Black Hawks circled and rained fire from the sky.

Beckham finished off his magazine, pulled it out, and then slammed a fresh one home. There was so much adrenaline swirling through his veins it seemed like he could feel his blood vessels enlarging.

The beach had transformed into a war zone. Injured Variants crawled over the dead, dragging stumps where their legs had been, while others staggered through the smoke, holding gushing wounds.

Fitz continued picking them off from the tower, one at a time, his rate of fire unwavering. The marine wouldn't stop until every single Variant had taken its last breath.

A few minutes later, the chaos subsided. The cry of the M240s faded as the gunners let up. The beach calmed, the only movement the twitch of dying monsters. Fitz fired off a final shot, taking out a female Variant still dragging her ruined body across the sand.

And then there was silence.

Beckham took in a long breath tinged with smoke and the stench of burned flesh. He felt the adrenaline empty out of him as realization set in—they had won the day, but they had lost a line of defense. The first fence was down, and it was going to be a bitch to clear the beach and put it back up.

Collapsing on the floor, Beckham turned to Red and his family and said, "Welcome to Plum Island."

17

The white walls of the space suit room pressed in on Kate. She sat on a stool across from Ellis and Sergeant Lombardi. All three of them were staring at the secure glass door leading into the hallway.

That's where the Variants would come from if they breached the fences. Like her old lab at the CDC building in Atlanta, the doors were designed to stop anything short of a grenade. But Kate wasn't worried about the reinforced glass—she was worried about the ceiling. If the monsters made it into the building, they would use the ventilation system. The filtered vents were meant to prevent microscopic monsters from entering, not Variants. If they breached the system, the only thing to stop them was Lombardi's rifle.

Kate shivered as she sat there. The space suit room was their designated emergency location, but she hardly felt safe here. Fear prickled through her body as she waited for the fourth time in a month for the monsters to come. She resisted the urge to cover her ears against the electronic whine of sirens echoing in the small room. Instead she eyed the rifle Lombardi aimed at the door. It was the same model she had used to kill Patient 12 in Building 4. If she had to, she could fire it again.

A flashback to that night rolled across her mind. She could still hear the scratching of the creature's claws as it skittered across the ceiling and the popping of its joints before she had killed it with a squeeze of the rifle's trigger.

The crackle of Lombardi's radio pulled her from the memory. She shivered again and wrapped her arms across her chest.

"What are they saying?" Ellis shouted over the alarms.

Lombardi brought the radio to his ear and then shook his head. "Nothing new."

Kate strained to hear the sound of distant gunshots. Before, it had been a constant stream, but now it was intermittent. That meant they had stopped the Variants at the beach...or else they had been overrun.

Either way, they would know soon.

The red glow of emergency lights danced across the hallway on the other side of the glass like a strobe light from hell. Kate froze when she saw a flash of motion at the far end of the corridor.

Lombardi had seen it too. While she backed away, he took a step closer and said, "Get behind me."

Kate moved with Ellis to the other end of the small space. They both crouched on the floor, trying to keep still and quiet. Two figures were rushing down the hallway outside the door, their bodies bending and distorting in the bath of red light. Kate wanted to close her eyes, but she couldn't pull her gaze away from the apparitions running down the hallway. Her heart skipped when she saw a flicker of pale skin.

Lombardi locked his shoulders and took a guarded step away from the door as the sirens suddenly stopped. The emergency lights clicked off, and the banks of white LEDs spread a carpet of white over two middle-aged Medical Corps soldiers.

Lombardi slowly lowered his rifle. "Corporal Cooper, Corporal Berg," he said with a sigh. "Jesus, you guys scared the shit out of me."

The soldiers stepped up to the door directly under the LEDs. They were Wood's men—that was obvious by their black fatigues. Both were built like linebackers, with broad shoulders and slim waists. They had matching black mustaches and the same short crew cuts under their helmets. If it weren't for Cooper's darker skin, Kate would have assumed they were twins.

Berg punched the comm link and said, "Sorry for the scare, Lombardi. My radio is busted or I would have told you I was coming." He glanced back at Kate and Ellis. "Doctors, the base is clear. Command has lifted the lockdown," he said. "They stopped the Variant assault on the beach."

Lombardi gave a thumbs-up to the soldiers and then faced Kate and Ellis. "All clear to get back into the lab."

Kate wrapped her arms across her chest. "Is Beckham back?"

Lombardi plucked the radio from his fatigues. "Command, Lombardi requesting a status update on Echo Two."

The response took a few moments. Enough time for Kate to consider the worst. She moved to the observation window as they waited and looked out over the BSL4 lab.

Lombardi turned the radio volume up so they could all hear Corporal Hook's reply. "Lombardi, Command. Echo Two is back safe and sound. They found three survivors in Niantic."

"More survivors?" Ellis asked. "After all this time?"

"Sounds like it," Lombardi replied. "I better get to my post. Corporal Berg and Corporal Cooper will escort you to your quarters."

"We're not going anywhere," Kate said. She checked

her watch. It had been six hours since they injected the mice with the adjuvant solution of peptide sequences. Their immune systems would be kicking in now. She tried her best to forget the attack on the island. She was exhausted, but there was work to do.

Ellis ran a hand through his slicked-back hair and joined her. "You thinking what I'm thinking?"

"Suit up," Kate said.

Ellis strolled over to his space suit. He spoke as he dressed. "The Variants are growing more desperate, Kate," he said. "If they attacked the beach, that means they're starving. Like any animal, they'll get more and more erratic and vicious."

"I know, Ellis. I know."

She pulled her key card and waved it over the security panel to their lab. Cooper and Berg hung back in the hallway, watching from a distance.

"What's with the twins?" Kate asked. "Since when do we warrant armed guards outside the lab?"

Ellis glanced over his shoulder as they entered. "No idea, but looks like they're sticking around."

Kate wasn't going to complain about extra security as long as they stayed out of her hair.

"Let's check the mice," she said. She hurried over to the cages. Most of the creatures were sleeping or hiding. She stuck her hands in both sides of one of the cages and used the internal gloves to grab a mouse. It struggled in her grip, twisting and squirming to get free. As it wiggled, she felt something unusual along its chest. She turned the mouse to see its stomach and spotted a tiny bump in its flesh.

"Shit," Kate whispered.

"What?" Ellis furrowed his brow.

"This one's growing a tumor."

"Damn. That could really mess up its immune

system, so I guess it can't be one of our antibody donors anymore."

"Right, if it has cancer, it isn't much use to us." Kate studied the tiny bump. She knew that tumors— especially mammary gland tumors like this one appeared to be—were common enough in rats and mice, afflicting almost two-thirds of those that weren't spayed. "We can't afford to lose any more if we want to start producing a mass supply of antibodies soon."

"Speaking of that, we need to figure out what we're attaching our antibodies to. I wish we could find something to use on the Variants that we already have in our stockpiles of drugs," Ellis said. "That way we wouldn't have to waste time manufacturing something new to knock out the Variants' stem cells."

A sudden epiphany struck Kate. "What did you say?"

"It would cut down on the manufacturing—"

"No, about the stockpiles."

"Oh, I was just thinking out loud," he said airily.

"I think you might be onto something though."

Ellis finished keying his credentials into his computer and glanced up.

"Maybe we do already have something that we could use," Kate said, looking back at the sick mouse with its budding tumor. "What about cancer drugs?"

"What about 'em?"

"If we could get our hands on enough chemotherapeutics like paclitaxel or docetaxel, we could encapsulate the antibodies in the drugs. Since the antibodies attach to the Superman proteins in the Variants, it would deliver the drugs straight to the cells responsible for the Variant's fast healing. You know how chemotherapeutics knock out rapidly dividing cells naturally, right?"

"Of course," Ellis said. "One of the side effects of chemotherapy is a weakened immune system." His eyes seemed to widen with realization. "Hell, high-dose che-motherapy destroys bone marrow stem cells—hence bone marrow transplants."

"Exactly. The Variant stem cells would gobble up the drugs attached via the protein-antibody linkage and die."

Putting his hands on his hips, Ellis said, "You're a fucking genius, Kate."

She smiled at that. If her idea worked, they'd be able to deliver the weapon much faster than she'd hoped.

"Let's start isolating the lymphocytes in these mice. We can fuse the white blood cells with a cancer cell line," Kate said. "Once we do that, we can use the hybrid cell line to start producing antibodies to help deliver the chemotherapeutics."

"Wait," Ellis said, holding up a glove. "We're going to need a huge amount of these drugs. Who's going to get them? And from where?"

The smile on Kate's face vanished. She had gotten so far ahead of herself that she had neglected the simple question of logistics.

When the answer came to her, she closed her eyes and heaved a sigh. The only way to collect enough drugs to build a weapon would be salvage missions—and Beck-ham and his team would be the obvious choice for the job. Her plan would send them and hundreds of other soldiers into harm's way again.

Beckham heard Kate come in around two in the morn-ing. Apollo let out a growl as she quietly opened the door.

"You okay?" Beckham asked groggily.

She didn't say a word as she stripped off her shirt and changed out of her pants into a pair of shorts. Beckham felt his blood pump through his veins. His sex drive had been almost nonexistent over the past few days, his mind elsewhere, but seeing Kate's curves in the shadows ignited his passion. She slipped into bed next to him.

"Are *you* okay?" she whispered.

"Fine. Everything is just fine," he said with confidence. Without thinking, he planted his lips on hers and rolled her onto her back with just enough force that she squeaked in surprise.

"You read my fucking mind," Kate said. She sat up, pulled off her sports bra, and started working on his T-shirt. Beckham felt the stitches on his shoulder stretch as she finally yanked his shirt over his head. But he didn't care; a few moments of pain were worth the pleasure both of them so badly needed. He gently pushed her back onto the bed and spread her legs with his. Leaning in, he kissed his way down her neck, over her breasts, and down to her stomach.

"I want you," Kate said. She added with a growl, "*Now.*"

Beckham grabbed her shorts and yanked them off. She pulled his own boxers down around his butt and he squirmed out of them. He had to sit up to finally pull them off. When they were free of his feet, he threw them onto the floor and climbed over Kate, using his fists to prop his body up. She ran her fingernails down his back.

A low whine came from the floor, where Beckham's shorts had fallen on Apollo. The dog shook them off and wagged his tail.

Kate and Beckham both laughed, and he pushed himself off the bed and led Apollo to the door. He opened it a crack to let the dog out and pointed at the hallway.

"Sit," was all he said before closing the door.

Beckham turned and saw the moonlight streaming through the shades, bathing Kate's naked body in its glow. He froze, studying every inch of her skin. Every memory and worry that haunted him vanished. Her beauty awakened something inside him that he had never felt before in his life. It wasn't just her physical perfection either—it was her relentless drive, her courage, and her brilliance in the face of the apocalypse. He promised himself he would do anything to ensure they could have a life together. He would fight the Variants with his bare hands if he had to, just to keep her safe.

Kate and Beckham had made love until they were spent, twice last night and once again this morning. She lay in his arms after the last time, feeling blissfully exhausted. She felt something else too—something a lot like love.

The emotion was tinged with guilt because she was alive to enjoy it while so many others had died. Her brother, Javier. Her mentor, Michael. She still didn't know the fate of her parents, but she had to assume they too had perished. Any happiness seemed wrong in the light of so much death.

After Kate had dressed, she brewed coffee in the tiny machine next to the sink. She poured two cups and took a seat on the bed to wait for Beckham to finish his sit-ups. The man was disciplined and relentless.

"Almost done," Beckham said. He grunted, his abs clenching, and Kate could see every muscle in his stomach.

Apollo rested at his feet, clearly waiting anxiously for a walk. He glanced up every few seconds.

When Beckham finished his workout, he wiped his forehead with a towel and then threw it over his shoulder. He pushed himself to his feet and sat next to Kate on the bed.

"Here," Kate said.

"Thanks," Beckham said, taking the cup of coffee from her.

Kate sipped the steaming liquid in silence, enjoying the minute of solitude with Beckham before they started another day. Birds chirped from the branches of a tree just outside the window. It felt oddly normal, like any given morning from before the outbreak.

"Never thought I would enjoy a mug of joe so much," Beckham said. He patted Apollo on his head and then walked to the window. Using two fingers, he parted the shades and looked outside.

"Going to be nice out. Don't see a single cloud in the sky."

"Too bad I won't see any of it," Kate said. "I'll be in the lab."

Beckham closed the shades. "I bet it's getting claustrophobic in there."

"I'm used to it." Kate finished the rest of her coffee. She was still working up the guts to tell him how she felt, but the L-word seemed to be caught in her throat. She wanted so badly to tell him while they still had the chance. She had just gathered up the courage to say it when a knock rattled the door.

"Kate, it's Ellis. You in there?"

Beckham walked to the door and opened it. Ellis blushed when he saw the shirtless soldier and spoke over Beckham's shoulder.

"Kate, Colonel Wood is en route. He wants a status update in two hours," Ellis said.

"Great," Kate huffed. "I'll meet you in the lab in a few minutes."

Beckham closed the door and threw on his shirt. "I have a briefing. I should get going too."

Kate reached for him and then hesitated, her lips hovering a fraction of an inch from his. She didn't care that

Beckham's breath smelled like coffee and that he badly needed a shower. She closed the distance between them, pressing her body against his.

"Reed," she whispered. "I . . . I wanted to tell you—"

He grabbed her waist and lifted her into the air, and she instinctively wrapped her legs around his waist. They kissed again, deeper and more urgent.

Reluctantly, she wriggled out of his arms and pulled her shirt back down. They didn't have time for round four, as much as she wanted it.

"You let me know if Colonel Wood gives you any problems, Kate. Or his men," Beckham said. "Okay?"

His strength made her want him even worse. She nodded, kissed him quickly one last time, and then hurried off to the lab.

Four weeks. That's how long Riley had been in a wheelchair. Looking out over the beach, Riley wished more than anything that he could get up and run. He desperately missed the ten-milers with the rest of Team Ghost in the heat of the summer. He could almost feel the sweat dripping down his body, saturating his clothes. He had almost always been on point back then, setting the pace for the other men grunting behind him as they struggled with their rucksacks.

Now he was stuck on the sidelines, unable to help with even cleanup duty the morning after the massacre on the beach. He glanced over at what was left of his team. Beckham stood with his arms crossed, Apollo sitting at his feet. Horn and Chow rested against the Humvee they'd used to get to the beach. Fitz was there too, taking in the destruction he'd helped inflict the night before. Meg sat in the open doorway of the truck, staring out over the bloodstained sand in disbelief. She'd asked Riley if she could come, but now he wasn't so sure she was glad to be here.

It seemed surreal, even to Riley. He still hadn't fully grasped the idea that the world had ended even though he had accepted the fact his family was dead.

The cough of a diesel engine broke out as a Medical Corps soldier fired up a bulldozer and began clearing the Variant bodies from the beach. A crew of Wood's men combed the beach in CBRN suits, picking up chunks of gore and putting them into trash bags. A second crew worked on securing a new fence. From the look of things, they had been at it all morning.

"Your girls doing okay, Big Horn?" Riley asked.

Horn took a drag on a cigarette and flicked the ash. "Yeah, man. They're actually doing pretty good, considering. Glad there are other kids here. I'm hoping they can help Bo."

"Bo?" Riley asked.

Horn crushed the spent smoke under his boot and said, "Kid we rescued from Niantic last night. Sounds like they've been through hell, but so have Tasha and Jenny. Helps kids deal when they have someone they can relate to."

Riley nodded like he understood, when in reality he had no fucking idea what it would be like for a kid growing up in this world. Frankly, he was having a hard time keeping it together himself, and he was trained for this shit.

"Those Wood's men?" Horn asked.

"Yeah," Chow said. "Saw them take off for the beach first thing this morning. Must be hot as fuck working in those CBRN suits."

"They're good at their jobs," Beckham said. "I'll give 'em that. Looks like they're going to have that fence back up by sundown."

Fitz shook his head. Beckham the unwavering optimist—it's what made him the best leader Riley had ever served under. Earning praise from Beckham had always motivated Riley to push himself to his limits. Now he felt worse than worthless. He couldn't do anything to help his brothers. Part of him wished they would just cut his legs off and give him blades like Fitz.

Riley flinched when he felt a hand on his shoulder. He glanced up to see Meg looking down at him, using his shoulder to balance herself. She had her hair pulled back in a ponytail that whipped in the wind. The bruises on her face were starting to fade, and he could see her freckles now.

"Don't worry. You'll be back on your feet in no time," she said.

"You must be a mind reader."

"Nah, you just look like you're warming the bench at a football game."

Riley let out a sad laugh. "Yeah, that about describes it."

"How long till you're out of the chair?"

"Doctor Hill said six to eight weeks, but with the compound fractures I'm looking at up to a year of rehab after the casts come off," Riley said, glancing down. "Doc said I might not ever run again." The words slipped out before Riley could stop them. He hadn't wanted the other operators to know for fear they would see him as a burden.

"We all know that isn't true," Chow said. "You're too stubborn."

"Clearly that idiot doctor doesn't know who he's talking to," Horn said laughing.

"Don't worry, Kid. You'll be outrunning all of us again in no time," Beckham added.

Riley fought to hold back tears of relief. The support of his brothers meant everything to him, and he cursed himself for doubting their loyalty.

"What about you?" Riley said, examining Meg's bandages.

"Just depends on how fast I heal. Doctor Hill told me that it varies." She pulled her hand off his shoulder and used it to shield her eyes from the sun as the mechanical thrum of a chopper cut over the noise of the bulldozer on the beach.

Riley turned to watch a long black Chinook approach. Two Black Hawks trailed the beast. They were still a half mile out but Riley could see the troop holds were packed with soldiers.

"Here comes the cavalry," Beckham said. There was a dark edge to his voice. Riley understood what it meant. Beckham didn't trust Wood, and that meant Riley didn't trust him either. Maybe there was something he could do to help Team Ghost after all. If Wood and his men were a threat, Riley was going to find out more about him. He massaged the handle of his M9 as the choppers descended over the island.

18

Kate hustled to prepare for Colonel Wood's arrival. Ellis was already busy isolating blood samples. By midmorning, the mice were producing limited antibodies. Her job was to see if the antibodies they got from those samples would attach to the Superman protein. That required a simple test with the Variant bone marrow biopsy they had already extracted.

Using a transfer pipette, she dropped a sample of antibodies suspended in a saline solution into a plastic tube. Then she used another pipette to add a fluorescent molecule to the mix. Since the antibodies were much too small to see using a light microscope, the fluorescent molecules would allow her to visualize them using a special filter under the scope.

Now came the real test.

She transferred the antibodies with their fluorescent cargo to a plastic dish filled with purified bone marrow cells from the Variant they'd biopsied. Each of those cells contained the Superman protein. If her antibodies attached to the cell, then she would be able to see the cell light up with the fluorescent molecules bound to the antibodies.

Kate held in a breath as she moved the plastic dish

under the scope. With the twist of a knob, the fluorescent filter clicked into place. Sure enough, the Variant cells lit up like they were on fire. The antibodies were attaching directly to the Superman protein, just as they'd predicted.

"It works, Ellis!" Kate said, pumping her fist in victory.

"Excellent," Ellis said. "But the next part is where things get dicey."

That was an understatement. What came next was the most important test, and the result would determine whether her theory was right. She felt confident the antibodies would enable the direct delivery of the drugs into the Variant cells. That, however, required injecting a live specimen with the antibody-drug conjugate.

If it successfully shut down the Variant's immune system, they could commit to massive production using their antibody replication facility. In those large drums, they would fuse lymphocytes with a cancer cell line. Combining these two cell lines created a new line— hybridoma cells. In biology, they were the closest thing to immortal cells, replicating forever, theoretically reproducing into infinity given a viable platform. Each of those cells would churn out the antibodies they needed for targeted drug delivery.

Even if Kate and Ellis succeeded, they still didn't have a solid plan for deployment of the weapon on a worldwide level. But that was General Kennor's headache. Kate's job was to create the weapon; Kennor's was to deliver it.

Kate was so lost in her work she almost didn't hear the chirp from the lab's comm link. When she looked up, she saw a half dozen men staring at her from the other side of the observation window.

"They're here," she said.

Ellis finished his task and set a vial containing blood cultures back into a housing tray. Major Smith and Lieutenant Colonel Jensen were at the back of the room beyond the glass, standing behind Colonel Wood and the twin corporals who had watched over Kate and Ellis's work the night before.

"Good morning, Doctors. I'm told you have an update for me," Wood said.

Kate smiled, though the expression felt false when directed at Wood. She launched into a brief report on her and Ellis's findings, assuring them that they were close to a breakthrough.

Kate watched Wood's reactions. His pockmarked face remained stiff, his jaw set, and his blue eyes were unnervingly still. His mannerisms reminded her a lot of Colonel Gibson.

"Superman protein?" Wood finally asked, sounding less than amused.

Ellis jumped in. "Called so because it speeds the Variants' healing capabilities. We also think we've found their Kryptonite, so to speak."

"Which would be?"

"Chemotherapeutics. Aka cancer drugs," Ellis continued after a pause. "We believe that we can use the antibodies we're producing for the targeted delivery of generic chemotherapeutics like paclitaxel—"

Wood raised a hand, cutting Ellis off midsentence. "You think you can use cancer drugs to kill the Variants?" The hint of a scowl formed on his scarred cheeks.

"Yes, Colonel," Kate said. "The chemotherapeutics normally destroy rapidly reproducing cells like cancer. An unintended side effect can be the destruction of immune and bone marrow cells, since these also proliferate at a high rate. The Variants survive and thrive because of their overactive stem cells and immune cells.

So if we can take those cells out, we believe we will shut down their immune systems and the Variants will die."

"Cut the science jargon and explain this in a way that everyone in this room can understand," Wood said.

Kate nodded, but inside she was fuming. "Think of the Superman protein as the exhaust on one of your fighter jets. The antibody we have designed is the heat-seeking sensor of your antiaircraft missile. The payload of that missile is the chemotherapeutics, and they will blow the damn plane out of the air. If we're right, the drugs will destroy the targeted cells."

"Sounds like a long shot," Wood replied.

"The good news is that we can save more lives by using drugs we already have instead of creating and manufacturing something new. Plus, there are enough chemotherapeutics stockpiled in this country to deploy the weapon to the whole world once we determine how to deliver it," Kate said. After a moment, she added, "Sir."

"Don't worry about deployment," Wood said. "That's General Kennor's arena. I'm sure he already has a plan."

"I was hoping he would, sir."

Wood nodded. "How long until you know if it works on a live specimen?"

"Twelve hours," Kate replied. "Maybe more, maybe less. Hard to say."

"I have a call with General Kennor at 2100, but I want to be present for these tests," Wood said. "I also expect you to be available for that call, Doctors."

Kate started to protest that she didn't have time to waste in a meeting, but Wood cut her off. "That's an order, not a request."

"We'll be there," Ellis said.

The colonel turned to leave but hesitated. "How many of these drugs do you think you'll need?"

"A lot, sir," Kate said. "And we'll have to coordinate with all remaining facilities to fuse the antibodies to the drug line before deploying the final weapon."

Wood frowned. "Jensen, Smith, prepare the men. I want them ready to go in a moment's notice. I'll inform Central Command and plan an operation to secure the drugs. Dismissed."

Kate's heart sank as everyone but Cooper and Berg cleared the room. She was thinking about Beckham and the other soldiers under Jensen's command being sent on another dangerous mission. She'd known that soldiers would have to raid facilities across the country to collect the drugs she needed to complete her weapon, but she had prayed those stationed at Plum Island might sit this one out.

She returned to her station with a heavy heart. She still had to encapsulate the chemotherapeutics in a protective polymer coating through microemulsion. Then she could chemically cross-link the antibodies to the encapsulated drugs and add the antibody-drug conjugates to a saline solution for a live test. There was still a lot of work to do—hopes and prayers alone weren't going to save the human race.

Lieutenant Colonel Jensen and Major Smith followed a group led by Colonel Wood through Building 4. Jensen still didn't have a read on Corporal Cooper or Corporal Berg, but both men seemed to be extremely loyal to Wood.

Jensen had led his own men down these very halls just weeks before to study the Variant specimens. No one stopped to examine the prisoners they kept in the dark cells this time. Jensen suspected Wood was used to similar conditions. Having been one of Gibson's cronies since Vietnam, Wood had likely toured countless top-secret prisons—ones that didn't follow any laws set forth by the Geneva convention.

The team marched down the corridor, unfaltering even at the hellish sound of a Variant's squawking. Jensen slowed to watch the monster skitter up the wall inside the cell. It hung in the corner, snarling and shrieking at him from the shadows. The sounds, combined with the pounding of Jensen and Smith's boots, attracted the attention of two figures at the end of the narrow corridor.

Drs. Lovato and Ellis were waiting outside the observation window that looked into the main isolation room. Through the glass, Jensen could see a female Variant already strapped to the metal gurney. A wave of déjà vu washed over him as he remembered the young female Variant who had died on that same table weeks before when his team had injected her with Kate's first bio-weapon, VariantX9H9.

"We're ready," Kate said. "This is Patient Three."

Wood stepped up to the window for a better look.

"Sergeant Lombardi will inject the specimen with the drug-loaded antibodies," Kate continued.

Wood folded his hands behind his back and leaned closer to the window. "Well, let's get on with it."

Kate nodded and hit the comm button under the window. "We're all set, Sergeant. Please proceed when you are ready."

Lombardi entered the isolation room, sporting the riot gear that all of the medical staff now used. The naked female Variant twisted on the table and arched her back at the sound of the door closing.

This was the Variant that had lost an eyeball, and the socket had developed a leathery layer of skin in a matter of days. The bandages that had covered its left arm and right leg had been removed, revealing thick scar tissue. Their healing ability was truly remarkable. It also made them damn hard to kill—something that Jensen found more frightening than impressive.

As soon as Lombardi approached, the Variant jerked its bald skull in his direction, homing in with the reptilian pupil of its remaining eye. It squirmed against its restraints, wormy blue veins bulging over its stretched flesh.

Patient 3 let out a high-pitched howl that intensified until it was so loud that several of the soldiers in front of Jensen started to fidget. Jensen reached into his pocket for his chew and wedged a piece between his gums and lip.

"It should take at least a few hours to see any results, but the Variants show a strong resistance to infection. That's why we're using the chemotherapeutics. The antibodies enable the targeted delivery of the drugs straight to the Variant's bone marrow stem cells, which should drastically reduce their immune and healing capabilities."

"In English, Doctor Lovato," Wood said, sounding bored.

"They'll die," Kate said. "Fast, I hope."

Wood seemed more interested in the creature's behavior than the doctor's explanation. He stepped closer to the glass. "You ever seen one of these things talk?"

Kate raised a brow. "Talk?"

"Yes, Doctor. Talk."

Shaking her head, Kate said, "Soldiers in the field have reported some of the Variants exhibiting traits that imply higher intelligence. And there was the case of Lieutenant Brett, a marine injected with VX-99 back in Vietnam who survived in the jungle for over a decade."

"Of course," Wood replied smoothly.

Kate froze, her features tensing as she glared at the colonel. "You're familiar with Brett?"

"Doctor, I'm here to protect our national security and save our country and its people. Do you really think there's *anything* about the current threat that I don't know?"

The colonel's voice was cutting, but his words sounded rote, like something he had memorized. Jensen had heard it all before. It was the same rhetoric powerful men throughout history had used: "It's just my job to know." Not very different from the words Colonel Gibson had spoken himself, in fact.

The Variant screeched as Lombardi inserted a needle into its arm, but Wood continued talking. "I'm here to see to it that the government uses your weapon properly, and also to ensure it doesn't fall into the wrong hands. Most important, I'm here to make sure this wasn't all for nothing."

"Wrong hands, sir?" Kate asked.

Wood looked away from the glass, suddenly uninterested in the test. "Yes, Doctor. And before you ask, *I* decide whose hands are the right ones."

Kate's face turned red, but she held her tongue. *Smart woman*, Jensen thought. Like Beckham and the others on Jensen's side, she understood the need for keeping a low profile while they all bided their time.

"Let me know the moment you get the results of your test." Wood jerked his chin toward the exit. "Let's go."

Jensen exchanged a glance with Kate on his way out. He could only think of one person worse than Wood to control her weapon, and that man was already buried in an unmarked grave on the beach.

Apollo darted after the stick Beckham had tossed onto the lawn outside Building 1. Fitz snatched it up and tossed it to Riley, who wheeled down the path. Riley reached down to get it, but Apollo beat him there. Riley bent down to wrestle the stick away when the dog suddenly backed up.

"Crap!" Riley said, losing his balance and toppling over.

Horn's daughters giggled from the landing of Building 1, but their father bolted down the steps. Beckham heard Meg gently chide the girls for laughing as he rushed to Riley's side.

"You okay, Kid?" Beckham asked.

Riley lay on his back, looking up at the sky, surrounded by his friends. "Yeah, I'm okay. Everything but my pride, that is."

"This coming from a guy who danced onstage at the Bing in his underwear," Horn said with a laugh.

"What's the Bing?" Fitz asked.

A grin broke across Riley's face, and Beckham realized then the kid was fine. The only thing bruised was his ego.

"The Bing is a strip club in the Florida Keys, and one of the best places on earth," Riley said. He reached up and Horn grabbed him under both arms. Beckham picked up his legs, and together they hoisted him into his chair.

The front door to Building 1 creaked open. Beckham turned to see Colonel Wood, Major Smith, Lieutenant Colonel Jensen, and four other men step onto the landing. Meg moved to the side to make room, herding Tasha and Jenny out of the way.

"Come here, girls!" Horn shouted.

They ran to their father, and he wrapped his thick arms around them. Wood stopped on the front step and scanned the lawn. Families were camped on the lush green grass. Red, Donna, and Bo were enjoying a picnic of MREs under a tree not too far from Beckham and his men.

Wood scowled and yelled, "Everyone, this is not a park! This is a military installation! You're supposed to be in your designated areas!"

Beckham swallowed hard, preparing for a confrontation. Wood loped down the stairs and onto the pathway in front of Team Ghost.

"Master Sergeant, I expected more from you and your men," Wood said.

Beckham bit back a retort. After a brief pause, he replied, "Sir, we're waiting for your orders and I thought everyone could use some fresh air after being cooped up all day."

"You will have orders sooner than you think," Wood said dryly. He snorted and continued down the path, walking fast and leaving Beckham to contemplate the words.

Team Ghost stepped up to flank Beckham. "I'm really starting to dislike that guy," Chow said.

Beckham let out a low whistle and motioned for Apollo and his men to follow. "You heard the colonel, everyone. Let's get inside. Sounds like we've got another mission to prep for."

19

Kate rushed into the lab and took a seat at her station. She keyed in her credentials and then moused over to a video with the USAMRIID symbol.

Ellis pulled up a stool as the black-and-white video popped onto the screen. "What are you doing?"

"Research."

Lieutenant Brett's naked body came into focus a second later, his arms and legs stretched into an X by chains attached to the ceiling and floor. Kate clicked the fast-forward button and paused the video as the camera angled toward the three uniformed men who were studying the mutated prisoner.

"Can we zoom in?" Kate asked.

Ellis motioned for her to scoot over as he dragged his chair across the floor. "This is one hell of an old video, but let me try something."

He punched at the keys and zoomed in on the grainy feed. Lieutenant Brett was looking up at the camera, his eyes crazed and bloodshot.

"Fast-forward a bit," Kate said. She turned up the speakers and listened to the rattling of chains as Brett thrashed against his restraints.

"Lieutenant Trevor Brett," Colonel Gibson said in the video. "Can you hear us?"

"Keep going," Kate said. The video sped up to such a high speed that it looked like Brett's body was being warped. He jerked violently against the chains. Then a second voice crackled over the audio so fast she couldn't make it out.

"Go back," she said.

"What are we looking for exactly?"

"Focus on that man next to Gibson," Kate said, pointing.

"Calm down, Lieutenant," the man said. His bored, flat voice was terribly familiar.

"This guy?" Ellis asked as he zoomed in further. "Oh shit," Ellis said as Kate's suspicions were confirmed.

"Shit is about right," Kate said. The footage was grainy and pixilated, but there was no mistaking the hardened, pockmarked features of Colonel Zach Wood. He had been there with Gibson from the very beginning of the secret VX-99 project.

The realization sent a chill through Kate. Somehow Wood had slipped under the radar, his connection to VX-99 hidden until now.

"We have to tell someone," Ellis said.

"And say what? This is the only evidence we have of him being associated with the VX-99 program. We can't prove he was ever at Building Eight or even knew about the development of the hemorrhage virus."

Ellis looked like he was about to protest but then dropped his gaze toward the floor. "How can we trust a man like Wood?"

"We can't," Kate said. "But we also can't say anything right now."

"So what do we do?"

"We keep working."

"What if we sent this to General Kennor?"

"I have a feeling Kennor already knows."

"Jesus, Kate. Do you know what this means? Kennor's like the emperor and Wood is his Darth Vader," Ellis said.

She couldn't help but laugh at Ellis's Star Wars metaphor. She hadn't felt much like laughing for the last month.

Ellis cracked a smile that vanished a moment later, his eyes locking on the observation window behind them. The chirp of the wall comm alerted her to the two Medical Corps soldiers, outfitted in all black, standing on the other side of the window. Berg and Cooper had returned, and while the glass separating the rooms was thick, she feared they'd overhead her conversation with Ellis.

One of them—Kate didn't know or care if it was Berg or Cooper—announced that they were there to supervise all of the lab activity from here on out. Kate felt her heart kick. The twins had already been monitoring her work, but their statement sounded almost like a threat.

"We're heading next door in a few minutes to observe Patient Three," Kate said.

"We'll escort you there."

Kate nodded and turned to face Ellis, keeping her back to the soldiers. "Say nothing," she mouthed.

"Ready to go?" Ellis asked brightly. "Got a lot of work to do."

Good, he understood.

They quickly changed out of their suits and followed the corporals. Kate glanced at her watch as they walked through the hallways of Building 1. It was already eight o'clock. That meant they had only an hour to spare before their call with General Kennor.

Cool night air washed over the lobby as Cooper pushed open the front doors. Kate scanned the base for any sign of Beckham or his men as they continued across campus. Besides the heavy machine-gun nest in the center of the lawn, the grass was empty. Two bands of Wood's men patrolled the walkways.

Wood's men were everywhere, monitoring everything. Kate cursed herself for not being more careful in the lab. She'd been sloppy today, and the truth she'd uncovered was as dangerous as any Variant. If she wasn't so valuable, she would probably have already been shunted off the island—or worse.

Now she had two of Wood's henchmen flanking her. She eyed their scoped guns, trying her best to remain calm. The only relief was the sight of Sergeant Lombardi waiting for them at the steps of Building 4—although she wasn't sure she could trust him.

"I was just about to radio you," Lombardi said. "There's been a development."

Kate didn't bother asking what development. A high-pitched shriek reverberated through the atrium as soon as Lombardi opened the doors. He halted and glanced over his shoulder.

"Steel yourself, this ain't pretty," he said before heading inside.

When they arrived at the main isolation chamber, Kate nearly tripped over her own feet. The Variant strapped to the metal gurney hardly looked like the creature she remembered from earlier. She took a step closer to the glass, her eyes falling on open sores peppering the creature's jaundiced skin. Swollen veins snaked across its body like rivers and were surrounded by lakes of rosy rashes.

These were advanced symptoms of immune system shutdown. The chemotherapeutics were working faster than Kate had ever imagined.

"Jesus Christ," Cooper said. He picked at his mustache nervously. "What the hell is wrong with it?"

Patient 3 let out another shriek and flexed every lean muscle in its body, straightening like a board. Vomit dripped down the sides of the creature's mouth. It choked and coughed out a spray of pinkish blood.

Kate cupped her hand over her mouth as she watched.

"What's happening to it?" Lombardi asked.

"Multi-organ failure," Ellis said.

The sergeant jerked backward as the Variant suddenly broke through the restraints covering its chest. Like a snake, it slithered out from under the torn straps and dropped to the floor.

Lombardi cursed. He reached for his sidearm and hurried over to the door.

"No!" Kate shouted. "We can't risk that thing getting out. Besides, I don't think it's going to last much longer."

The other two soldiers fell into line behind Lombardi, their rifles aimed at the glass. The Variant jumped to a crouch and scratched at the sores on its belly. Its talons drew fresh blood. Instead of coagulating in seconds, the blood flowed in a steady stream and began pooling on the floor. The monster puckered its sucker-shaped lips and let out a raspy screech. It went back to tearing at the rashes, but the monster's one remaining eye kept searching the room around it.

Hunting. Always hunting.

Patient 3 stared at the glass. Before Kate could react, it dropped to all fours and used its back legs to spring forward. It threw itself against the glass, sucker mouth sticking to the window. Kate crouched down for a better view of its wounds. Nearly every inch of its yellowing skin was covered in open sores or rashes.

The new weapon worked.

The Variant suddenly stopped trying to chew through the glass and tilted its head to the side. Kate realized it wasn't looking through the glass but rather at its own reflection.

Letting out a melancholy whimper, the Variant slid

down the window and collapsed to the floor, leaving a streak of blood behind. It lay on its stomach and continued to gaze at its reflection. Despite the monster's awful transformation, Kate recognized the flicker of sadness in its yellow eye.

Kate and the others watched for several more minutes as Patient 3 took in shallow, raspy breaths. They came in increasingly shorter intervals, slower and weaker, until it gasped one last time.

The Variant's eye met Kate's, and then the final spark of life left its grotesque body. Kate pulled her hand away from her mouth and placed it on her chest, her heart pounding. It had worked better and faster than she had imagined, but unlike VariantX9H9, this weapon would kill every last one of the creatures.

General Kennor sipped a cup of lukewarm coffee on his way through the narrow concrete tunnels leading to the command center. Pedestrians flowed in both directions. Everyone moved with urgency, as though whatever task they were focused on was the most important in the world. In Kennor's case, his task *was* the most important.

Minutes earlier, he'd been informed that the scientists had made a breakthrough on Plum Island. Whatever decision he made in the coming hours would determine the direction of the war—and the fate of the country.

"Sir," a pair of guards said in unison as Kennor approached the massive steel doors leading to the command center. Kennor gulped the last of his coffee as the doors screeched open.

He crumpled the Styrofoam cup and tossed it into a wastebasket as he entered the dimly lit room. The three monitors mounted on the front wall emitted a ghostly green glow. Five officers huddled around them and watched a live feed beaming in from the drones they'd sent to survey several abandoned cities.

As Kennor worked his way through the stations, the officers on duty stood at attention until he passed. He paid them little notice. When he got to the monitors, he said, "Which cities are we looking at?"

"L.A., Chicago, and New York, sir," said a woman with short black hair. She looked like she had just graduated from high school. Kennor was accustomed to working with men and women who had experience under their belts, not kids with pimples. It was yet another example of how strained their resources had become.

Kennor watched the screens for a moment. They showed only destruction and death. With a shake of his head, he continued to the conference room, where he was relieved to see his confidants. Colonel Harris, Lieutenant Colonel Kramer, and General Johnson stood as he entered.

He took a seat and looked to Harris first. "Colonel, let's get started."

"Yes, sir," Harris said. He switched on the wall-mounted monitor and then pressed the conference call button on the phone in the middle of the table.

"Colonel Wood, can you hear me?" Harris asked. "Are Doctor Lovato and Doctor Ellis with you?"

"Roger that," Wood said. "I'll let them explain what you are about to see."

A female voice crackled over the speakers. "General, this is Doctor Lovato. We're sending you a video of Patient Three here on Plum Island."

Harris clicked the remote again and the video flickered to life. It showed a Variant lying on a metal gurney.

"The Variant you see was injected with our new weapon. The reaction happened quickly, over a span of seven hours," Dr. Lovato said.

Kennor pulled his glasses from his chest pocket for a better look. The monster was covered in rashes and open sores that stood out brightly against its skin. Vomit trickled from its swollen lips. He leaned in closer and flinched when Patient 3 broke free of its restraints and leaped to the window. A few minutes later, it was dead.

Dr. Lovato briefly explained the medical science behind her latest breakthrough. Kennor understood less than half of it, but he did grasp one thing: The weapon worked.

"Doctor Lovato, this is General Kennor. I have a few questions. First and foremost, will this weapon affect humans?"

"Not like this. The antibodies attach to proteins only expressed in Variants. The chemotherapeutics will have minimal if any side effects on normal humans."

"You're sure of this?"

There was a slight pause before she said, "We haven't had a chance to test it on humans yet. However, since normal humans don't have the Superman protein, the drugs should mostly pass through their bloodstream, although some might be passively absorbed."

Kennor folded his hands together and examined his staff. "What does that mean, exactly?"

Her reply came across muffled, but Kennor heard every word. "It means it *might* weaken the immune systems of humans who come into contact with the weapon, but it shouldn't cause more sustained and permanent damage like in the Variants."

"This is the best you can come up with, Doctor?" Kennor asked. "Are you even sure it will kill all of the Variants? What if this—what did you call it? Spider-Man protein?—turns out to be a bust?"

"It's the Superman protein, sir, and so far we have only tested Patient Three. Until we try it on a larger population, I can't be one hundred percent sure," Dr. Lovato replied. "If you had waited until we had conclusive findings before demanding a report—"

Harris pulled the phone closer to him. "Doctor, this is Colonel Harris. Your last bioweapon turned approximately ten percent of those infected with the hemorrhage virus into something even worse. We can't afford to make the same mistake again."

"I know, Colonel. I'm willing to test this on myself, if I have to."

"We've run out of time for tests, Doctor," Kennor said. He let out a frustrated sigh. "Now is the time for action. We have no other option at this point but to use what you've designed. The other labs have failed to come up with anything."

"General, there's still an issue," she said. "We have no way to deploy this weapon on a worldwide scale. Jets won't do the trick this time. We need something that covers every inch of soil, every—"

"I know just the thing," Kennor said. He glanced over at General Johnson. His old friend nodded as if he could read his mind.

"Doctor, I'm going to have General Johnson read you in on a project the government has been working on since 'Nam," Kennor said.

Johnson pulled the conference phone across the table and said, "From 1967 through 1972, the US military worked on a project called Operation Popeye. Essentially, this was a weather warfare operation that was supposed to extend the monsoon season over enemy territory. By seeding the clouds with silver and lead iodide, we were able to flood much of the Ho Chi Minh Trail. It was largely successful, but the project was done in secret because Secretary of State Henry Kissinger sponsored the program without the consent of Congress. Since then, the legality of such operations has been hazy at best. Unfortunately, weather modification for military purposes falls under the provenance of the Environmental Modification Convention." Johnson paused and ran a hand over his bald head as he looked at Kennor to take over.

"The United States was also running a project called Stormfury at this time, with the goal of weakening tropical cyclones," Kennor said. "To make a long story short, we have been working on cloud seeding projects for the past fifty years. In 2014, our boys designed a system to distribute payloads into the atmosphere using long-range missiles. They called it Project Earthfall. The goal was to manipulate weather over countries like Iran and North Korea. These facilities are sited at strategic locations scattered across the globe, mostly military bases in Allied territories. We would have used them to distribute VariantX9H9 but decided to go with aircraft due to unpredictable weather patterns. Now Earthfall is our best shot."

There was a moment of silence before Dr. Lovato cleared her throat and said, "These drugs are sensitive. If we're talking missiles, the intense pressure and heat of a detonation could destroy the capsules."

"That shouldn't be a problem," Kennor said. "The missiles are designed to deploy without destroying their payloads."

"Then I suppose it could work," she said. "Initially, I was considering something airborne like VariantX9H9, but the lungs have all sorts of barriers. In this case, rainwater from the seeding project could reach places an airborne weapon couldn't. If we use adjuvants that promote skin absorption, then it could work very well indeed. The water will find its way into the sewers and other hard-to-reach places where the Variants are nesting."

"Excellent," Kennor said. "If that's all—"

"General, before we can even think about using Project Earthfall, we need to collect as many of the chemotherapeutics as we can get our hands on," Dr. Lovato said. "Then we need multiple bioreactors to culture billions if not trillions of hybridoma cells. That will take time."

"We are out of time," Kennor snapped. "Thanks in no small part to the failure of your first bioweapon."

He could almost hear the doctor squirming on the other end of the line. "Sir, I'll need at least a week to establish the cell line. Then another week to expand the cell line in order to begin antibody production."

Wood's dry voice emerged over the speakers. "I've already begun coordinating the project in our other facilities."

"I also want you in charge of coordinating the effort to collect the chemotherapeutics," Kennor replied. "In the meantime, Doctor Lovato will continue the drug tests. Make sure your weapon won't kill humans."

"Understood," she replied.

"Have you named this weapon?"

Two seconds passed before she replied, "Doctor Ellis did the honors. How does Kryptonite sound?"

"It sounds ridiculous," Kennor said. "Keep me updated. And good luck."

"Thank you, sir," she said. Even over the comm, the sarcastic tone of her voice was apparent.

Kennor ended the call and stood, looking at his staff. Harris, Kramer, and Johnson all wore the same unsure looks.

"Give science a second chance, right?" Kennor said on his way out.

20

Pinpricks of starlight decorated the sky over Plum Island. Beckham watched a single cloud creep across the sky as he walked. He'd hoped to talk to Kate before the briefing but hadn't seen her since she'd left for the lab earlier that morning. Since the service on the beach, she'd been good about checking in with him throughout the day. Today was different. Something was wrong, he could feel it—and his gut told him it had to do with General Kennor and Colonel Wood.

Beckham ran up the stairs to Building 2's mess hall, pulled open the door, and squinted into the bright glow of the LEDs. He worked his way down aisles of empty metal tables, the scent of stew from supper still fresh in the air.

Two weeks earlier, the room had been packed with more than one hundred men and women from every branch of the military. Now there were only a handful of marines, Rangers, and Medical Corps soldiers sitting at the tables. Team Ghost was together at one of them, surrounded by Wood's men. Riley had positioned his wheelchair at the end of the table. He patted the bench next to him as Beckham approached.

"Good to see you here, Kid," Beckham said.

"Think there's a way you guys could bring me with you this time?" Riley asked.

Horn chuckled. "Maybe we could put treads on those wheels and turn you into a tank."

"Whatever, man," Riley said with a scowl.

"No, seriously," Horn said. "We'll get you a mounted gun turret too."

"I already got a mounted turret," Riley said with a grin. "The ladies love it."

Their banter drew the stares of the Medical Corps soldiers. Beckham tensed—now wasn't the time for jokes. Even Jinx would have known better, and Horn should have as well. Beckham nudged the big man in the arm, and Horn fell silent.

They sat in silence as they waited for the mission briefing. The other soldiers watched the double doors at the front of the room patiently. In the past, his men and many of those he'd joined on countermissions would have displayed pre-mission jitters. Some would remain still and focused. Others would tap a foot anxiously or crack their knuckles.

This time he didn't see any of that behavior. The men packed around the tables were exhausted, their gazes those of soldiers fighting a war that seemed all but hopeless. There was no question that the mission Wood was about to announce was going to be tough—they all knew that next time they gathered in this room, there would be even fewer of them.

The large hand on the wall clock hit 2200 and the doors swung open a second later. Wood, Jensen, Smith, and a handful of soldiers strode into the mess hall. Beckham and everyone else snapped to attention.

"Good evening," Wood said in his dry tone. "I will make this briefing as quick as possible, as we are about to embark on what I believe is one of the most important missions of this war. A mission that could change the tide."

Beckham tensed his jaw. The tide was supposed to have changed with Operation Reaper and then Operation Liberty. In the end, both had just added to the growing pile of dead.

"Major Smith, get things set up," Wood said.

"Yes, sir," Smith replied. He began spreading maps across a table. Beckham worked his way to the front of the room and scanned the maps to see where they were headed.

"Doctor Lovato and Doctor Ellis have created a new bioweapon code-named Kryptonite. I won't get into the science, but I've seen it in action. The weapon works, and works fast," Smith said. "But before we can deploy this weapon, we need to collect chemotherapeutics." At several blank looks, he clarified, "Cancer drugs."

Concerned whispers broke out around Beckham. He trusted Kate, but cancer drugs? Kryptonite? Beckham shook the questions away. He was a Delta Force operator, not a scientist. His job wasn't to question Kate—his job was to protect her.

"Yes, I know how it sounds," Wood said. "But I'm told it's our best shot at stopping the Variants. At 0800, we will embark on the first stage of Operation Extinction. The second stage, deployment of the weapon, won't come until much later. For now, the mission is simple: Every available unit will be sent to medical facilities and other locations to collect as many chemotherapeutics as we can locate. Teams from Plum Island are being assigned a special mission. I'll let Lieutenant Colonel Jensen fill you in on that in a moment."

Wood paused and traced a finger over his chin as if he was deep in thought. "I suppose you're all wondering why this two-part mission is called Operation

Extinction." Narrowing his cold blue eyes, he said, "I'm going to share something with you that is not to leave this room. This morning, I received casualty projections from Command. There are approximately seven million human beings left worldwide. If the Variants continue killing and feeding at the rate they are now, then in a week human survivors will number just one million. In two weeks they will number in the hundreds of thousands, and in a month we will be down to tens of thousands or less."

"No fucking way," a Latino marine whispered. "I don't believe it."

Wood looked for the man and then worked his way around the table. He stopped inches from the man's face, towering over the shorter soldier.

"You don't believe me?" Wood snarled. "What part of 'extinction' don't you understand, son?"

The marine took a step backward, shaking his head. "Sir, I . . ."

Wood continued to the next soldier and leaned in until their eyes were level. "What about you?" he shouted.

"Sir, it's hard to imagine, sir!" the man yelled back.

Beckham felt his fingers curling into a fist. In his career he'd seen men and women exert their dominance over other soldiers in a lot of ways, but one way he'd never understood was intimidation. Beckham always led by example, not by fear.

Wood sneered. He strolled through the crowd and stopped in front of Fitz. "How about you, Marine?"

Fitz ran a hand through his strawberry hair and nodded. "Sir, I absolutely believe it—and that's why I'd like to volunteer for this mission."

Wood glanced at Fitz's blades and shook his head. "Sorry, son, but we need you here on the towers."

Fitz's cheeks flared red as Wood walked back to the front of the table. Beckham was hoping Wood would have changed his mind about Fitz after his valiant defense of the beach the other night, but instead of seeing talent and courage, the colonel had only seen a man with a disability.

Wood palmed the table and bowed his head slightly before glancing back up at the soldiers. "Make no mistake, gentlemen. We have entered the age of extinction. It will be up to men like us to protect our species from vanishing. I promise you one thing...I will do what I can to ensure that our great nation survives."

Just like Colonel Gibson promised, Beckham thought ruefully. Career brass like Wood talked a big game, but in the end it wouldn't be his ass in the field defending their country.

"I'm needed at Central Command now," Wood said. He took a moment to scan the soldiers one last time and then turned to his staff. "Until I return, Lieutenant Colonel Jensen will be in charge. I'm sure he can answer any questions as he distributes individual assignments. Good luck," he said on his way out.

The doors to the mess hall slammed shut. For a moment, no one said a word. Then Jensen took Wood's place at the front of the table.

"Gentlemen," he said. Though his voice was calm, his demeanor told Beckham he still carried the weight of the *Truxtun* on his shoulders—not to mention the subsequent loss of his command. Even Wood's parting words hadn't cheered the man up. Of course, Wood hadn't made the temporary transfer of command official, and Beckham suspected the men he'd left behind would remain loyal to Wood, even if Jensen wore a higher rank than they did.

Jensen's hands shook as he grabbed the closest map

and flattened it out on the table. But when he glanced up, his eyes had hardened back into the commander Beckham had come to know over the past several weeks.

"Listen up, everyone. We will be dispatching three fire teams from Plum Island. Sergeant Mikesell will take Alpha squad, and Sergeant Valentine will take Bravo."

Beckham looked for the Medical Corps soldiers. They were standing next to each other at the far end of the table. Unlike Valentine, Mikesell was a bulky man with fat covering old muscle. He didn't look like he'd be much good in a fight.

"Master Sergeant Beckham will take Charlie team," Jensen continued. "Our target location is the Raven Rock Mountain Complex in Pennsylvania. As many of you know, it was the backup site for the Pentagon and the alternate joint command before the hemorrhage virus hit. When shit hits the fan, that's where they send the big boys. Vice President Cheney favored this location when he was in office. It was amongst the most secure facilities in the world, but apparently it wasn't secure enough. Central Command lost contact with the complex several days ago."

Jensen waited a beat for the information to sink in and continued once the murmurs had died down. "Final radio transmissions paint a dreary picture. The Variants infiltrated the tunnel system and killed everyone, as far as we know. While the mission is to primarily retrieve caches of chemotherapeutics from a FEMA warehouse located inside the complex, we are also being ordered to look for any survivors. There were some very important people at Raven Rock when it went off-line."

Smith pulled a pen from his chest pocket and drew a circle on a map of the complex. "There are several entrances to Raven Rock. Alpha will scout for survivors through portals A and B." He marked another location and said, "This is the approximate location for the underground FEMA facility. Bravo and Charlie will locate the warehouse and secure the caches."

"Pretty simple," Jensen said. "But for those of you who have been out there, you know shit ain't ever simple anymore. Expect heavy resistance inside the complex."

Smith waited a few seconds for Jensen's words to sink in and then said, "Any questions?"

"Do we have reason to believe anyone is alive?" Chow asked.

"Our intel is limited at this point," Jensen replied. "I've been told Central Command already ran an evac mission that failed. Their team never made it out. Chances are slim, if you ask me."

Beckham glanced over at Mikesell. Beads of sweat ran down his forehead. There was no doubt that his was the toughest mission of the three.

"Anything else?" Jensen asked, waiting. "If not, then find your team leaders for further instructions. Good luck, men."

Beckham squirmed through the crowd to find Horn. "Big Horn ..." he began to say.

"Don't even say it, boss. I'm coming with you. Besides, if I don't go, my girls are going to join their mother in less than a month anyway, right?"

Even though he wanted to shake his head, Beckham found himself nodding. When he went to pat Horn's shoulder, he had to pause and uncurl his fingers. He'd kept his hand balled into a fist during the whole briefing.

Kate did her best to ignore Corporal Cooper and Corporal Berg. The men shadowed her and Ellis even after they finally left the lab. It was after ten o'clock when

Kate and Ellis finally got back to their quarters. The twins stood guard in the hallway.

"We'll be right here if you need anything," Berg said.

Kate nodded and hurried away. She was anxious to get back to her room, where she hoped Beckham would be waiting.

"Good night, Ellis," Kate called.

"Night, Kate," Ellis said. He opened his door, gave her a sad look, and then shut it softly behind him.

Kate stopped to use the bathroom before she continued to her room.

"Reed?" she said, gently knocking on the door. She pushed it open and smiled when Apollo greeted her, tail wagging.

"Jesus, Kate, where have you been?" Beckham said, standing. Moonlight bled through the shades, accentuating the muscles in his tight-fitting T-shirt, and without thinking Kate rushed over and wrapped her arms around him.

"Whoa," Beckham said, stumbling back a step. "Don't forget about my shoulder."

"I'm sorry, Reed," Kate said.

"It's fine. Hardly hurts at all now."

"No, I mean I'm sorry for what I've done."

Beckham rolled his head back and searched her eyes in the glow of the moonlight. "What you've done?"

Kate bowed her head. "The experiments...the Superman protein. If it wasn't for me, you wouldn't...I'm so sorry...I just..." The words were tumbling out of her, disorganized and rushed.

"Slow down, Kate," Beckham said. "Breathe."

Taking in several deep breaths, Kate focused her thoughts. "You're going out there to get the drugs, aren't you?"

Beckham seemed to consider her words for a moment

and then nodded. "Tomorrow morning. I'm leading a strike team with Horn, Chow, and Lombardi to Raven Rock."

Kate was too tired to protest. And even if she did, it wouldn't matter. She knew him well enough to know that he would never leave his men or back down from a mission. "I understand," was all she managed to say.

Beckham studied her and said, "You're okay with this?"

"What can I do? My work ended up killing billions and creating monsters. And now you're going back into harm's way. Because of me."

"Chances are I'd be going out there anyway, Kate. Besides, if your drug works, we could end this."

Kate felt a tear welling in her eye. She wiped it away with her sleeve. This was not the time to be weak; this was the time to pull on whatever strength she had left and tell Beckham what she'd learned from the tape.

"Colonel Wood is connected to Colonel Gibson," Kate whispered.

Beckham ran a hand over his closely trimmed hairline. "That's a pretty serious allegation, but honestly, it's one I'd already considered myself."

"Remember the video of Lieutenant Brett? The one where Colonel Gibson is shown interrogating the marine?"

"Yeah..."

"Wood was there."

Beckham's hand stopped on his scalp, and he narrowed his eyes. "You're certain?"

"Yes."

Beckham cursed. "Jensen told me Wood couldn't be trusted, but if the man has ties to Building Eight..."

"What do we do?"

"I'd try to get a message through to General Kennor, but chances are he already knows."

"I told Ellis the same thing."

Beckham shook his head. "Your weapon won't affect humans, right?"

"It could have a few side effects, but not anything serious. Why?"

"One of the most important things I've learned in my career is knowing when to strike. Now is not that time. I say we wait. We complete Operation Extinction, deploy your weapon, and destroy the Variants. Then we can deal with Wood and Kennor."

Kate took a seat on the bed and took a few minutes to think. He was right—now wasn't the time to pursue what many would consider a conspiracy theory. Even if they could do anything about it, Wood and Kennor had a damn army to protect them. Who would believe Kate? Even if she could convince people that Wood was involved in the VX-99 project, what good would it do to bring that information out now?

What mattered right now was saving humanity. They could deal with the men who had helped destroy it later.

Forcing a smile, she patted the bed. Apollo brushed up against her leg and she reached down to stroke his fur coat.

"I was gesturing for Reed, not you," Kate chuckled.

Beckham plopped down next to her and said, "What do you think, boy?"

Kate placed her hand on Beckham's thigh and leaned in to whisper in his ear, "Apollo thinks it's time to go in the hall so we can have some privacy."

Beckham snapped his fingers and led the dog to the door. Lying back on the bed, Kate closed her eyes, a moment of fear passing over her. At first she wasn't sure what had sparked it, but when Beckham hurried back over to her, she realized it was the same fear she'd had before every one of his missions—the fear that this would be their last night together.

A crimson bubble with veins of purple crested the horizon as the sun rose over the water. Beckham and his fire team fought the cool morning wind that whipped across the island. They had left the armory equipped with enough firepower to take on an army of Variants.

Horn carried an M249 SAW. Chow and Beckham had both picked up M4s. Lombardi opted for an AA12 shotgun with a drum magazine that held thirty-two shells. An unusual choice, but it would certainly stop any Variants they encountered at Raven Rock. Their vests were stuffed with as many magazines as they could carry, but this time they weren't equipped with suppressors. Beckham had ordered his men to not carry them after the *Truxtun*. The reduced sound was easily detectable by Variants and Beckham wanted to be able to hear gunfire inside the facility from a distance.

The short walk from the armory to the tarmac provided Beckham with enough time to get a read on his men. Despite the fact he was leaving his girls, Horn's freckled face showed no sign of apprehension. He smoked a cigarette as he walked, his gun slung casually across his back.

Chow wore a hardened look that told Beckham he was still harboring anger for Jinx's death. He'd hidden it on the *Truxtun*, but Beckham was worried Chow couldn't hold it in forever.

Beckham looked at Lombardi next and said, "Have you faced the Variants in the field?"

"Does dealing with them here on the island count?"

Horn laughed. "Nope."

Lombardi nervously scratched his beak of a nose. Beckham made a note to keep him off point when they reached the objective. Dealing with Variants chained to the ground in holding cells was very different from dealing with them out in the wild.

Ahead, civilians and soldiers were gathering at the concrete barriers on the edge of the tarmac. The sight of Kate, Meg, Riley, Fitz, and Horn's girls sent a combination of pride and fear through Beckham. There were other familiar faces that stuck out in the crowd. Red and Donna stood there with Bo. The boy caught Beckham's gaze and raised a hand into the air.

Beckham walked over to them and slung his rifle over his shoulder. "How are you guys doing?"

"Can't complain," Red replied. "Got a warm bed and enough food. We have you to thank for that."

Donna smiled and pulled Bo closer to her. "Did you want to tell Master Sergeant Beckham something?"

Bo tucked his head against her stomach and then twisted his face slightly so that one eye was on Beckham. He grinned and said, "Thank you, Mr. Master Sergeant."

"Welcome, kid," Beckham said. He exchanged a nod with Red and continued toward Kate and the others.

Tasha and Jenny rushed over to Horn. Jenny wrapped her arms around his right leg and said, "Don't go, Daddy!"

Beckham's heart melted at the sight. "Don't worry. I'll take care of him."

"Promise?" Tasha said.

"Promise." Beckham gave her a hug and then walked over to the group of Fitz, Riley, and Meg, saving Kate for last.

"Fitz, Kid, you guys look after everyone while we're gone, okay?"

"Will do, boss," Riley said.

Fitz nodded. "Wish I was coming."

"So do I," Riley said, his eyes downcast.

Beckham considered his next words carefully. "Protecting these people is just as important," he said. "If the Variants attack the island again, we need both of you to hold them off."

"Don't forget about me," Meg said. She gestured toward the handle of a knife tucked into her waistband and winked at Beckham.

"That's not the same one I loaned you in New York, is it?"

"Nope. Riley gave it to me," Meg said.

A shit-eating grin streaked across Riley's face, and Beckham couldn't hold back a chuckle. The kid had always loved women, and he'd made it no secret that he was attracted to Meg. From what little Beckham knew about her, giving her a knife was better than a bouquet of flowers.

The sad whine of a dog sounded over the chatter from the crowd. Apollo sat at Kate's feet. Like Fitz and Riley, the dog would protect her to the end. Beckham continued over to them and locked eyes with Kate.

"Try not to worry," he said.

She folded her arms across her chest and frowned. "You know that's not going to happen."

"I'm coming home," Beckham said. "I promise you." He planted a soft kiss on her lips and then gave Apollo a quick rub on the head.

"Be careful," Kate said.

Beckham nodded and kissed her again. The blades of the Black Hawks were already whipping through the air behind him, and he forced himself to pull away.

"Let's go," Beckham said. He began to lead his team to the birds but had to stop when Apollo darted after them.

"You have to stay here, boy," Beckham said.

Apollo whined and sat down, his tail thumping forlornly. Beckham waved his men on, and they continued across the tarmac toward Jensen and Smith.

"Good luck," Jensen said. He reached out to shake Beckham's hand and added, "You know I'd come with you if I could."

"I know, sir."

Jensen's lips spread into a grin beneath his mustache. "If you find any chew in the warehouse, snag a few cans."

"Will do, sir," Beckham said. He rushed over to the chopper, keeping low, and climbed inside. Horn and Chow followed, flanking him on both sides in the doorway. The crowd watched from the edge of the tarmac as the pilots performed their final checks.

Wood was already back at Central Command, leaving his men to watch the island while Beckham and the rest of the teams went on the mission. Beckham could just imagine Wood toadying up to Kennor, both of them hiding out in the bunker at Offutt. He didn't know the details, but he felt in his gut that Wood had been involved in creating the monsters they now faced. They'd made hell on earth, but it was Beckham and his men who had to deal with the fallout.

As the chopper ascended into the air, he kept his gaze on the crowd, knowing in his heart that once everyone he loved was safe, he would get his revenge for humanity.

21

General Kennor studied the picture of his grandkids. For the first four days after he'd arrived at Offutt Air Force Base, he hadn't been able to bring himself to look at their innocent faces. Every time he did, he imagined them being torn to shreds by the Variants.

That's why he'd put Colonel Wood in charge of all science operations. No one knew VX-99 better than him—at least, no one living. If anyone could defeat the Variants, it was Wood.

At first, when General Johnson had informed Kennor of Wood's connection to Gibson, he had considered tossing Wood into a prison cell and throwing away the key. But Kennor was a practical man and saw the situation for what it was—an opportunity. Wood understood the details of VX-99, and his country needed that knowledge.

A rap on the door startled Kennor. He put the picture down and said, "It's open."

Wood himself opened the door and strode inside. "General," he said, throwing up an impeccable salute.

"Colonel," Kennor replied. He raised a return salute and then gestured to the chair in front of his desk.

Wood straightened his uniform and slid into the

chair. "Plans are in motion, sir. We have over one hundred strike teams from multiple bases participating in Operation Extinction."

"Excellent news. How is the plan for stage two coming along?"

"Very good, sir. Once we collect the drugs, we'll ship them to four locations including Plum Island. All of the antibody reactors are on standby."

Wood continued speaking, occasionally stroking the fingers of one hand down his pockmarked cheek, but Kennor was hardly listening. He was thinking of his daughter, his son-in-law, and their kids. Men like Wood were the reason they were gone, yet Wood had also put the pieces in place to avenge their tragic deaths.

It wasn't ethical. It wasn't moral. And it wasn't right by any stretch of the imagination. Yet history proved that wars were both started and ended by men who didn't deserve to breathe free air. Wood was one of those men—and Kennor had become one too. He knew he was no better than Gibson or Wood, but in the end, morality meant nothing if there wasn't anyone left to judge.

Kennor heard a less than gentle knock on the door and emerged from his thoughts to see Colonel Harris standing in the doorway. His lips were pressed into a thin line so tight they were almost as white as his hair.

"I thought I said no interruptions," Kennor said.

"You did, General, but we have a problem."

Kennor folded his arms across his chest. "What kind of problem?"

For the briefest moment, Harris paused. "The Variants, General. They've found us."

Beckham grabbed a handhold and looked out through the open door. The bright morning sun glimmered off the skyscrapers of Baltimore. The reflection of their bird hopped from building to building. They followed Echo 1 over the city with Echo 3 close behind, their troop holds all packed full of weary soldiers.

"Remind me why they don't just send us to a hospital for the drugs?" Horn asked over the comm.

Beckham pointed to a crater a half mile away. The burned-out husk of a building protruded out of the center. "That's why."

"There aren't many hospitals left," Chow said. "And for the first time in this entire war, Central Command is thinking with their heads. The FEMA warehouse will have stockpiles of everything from tampons to cancer drugs."

"I thought the warehouses were just a myth," Horn said.

"Apparently not," Beckham said. "Hopefully the fact that they're 'secret' means they haven't been raided and hostiles are at a minimum."

Lombardi worked his way to the door. "Wouldn't count on that."

"You know something we don't?" Beckham asked. He twisted away from the view to look Lombardi in the eye.

The sergeant shook his head. "Besides what Lieutenant Colonel Jensen already said? Not really. I just know that Site R had a permanent staff of three hundred and fifty with room for another two thousand. I'm glad I didn't get assigned to Alpha. Mikesell and his team are probably walking into a slaughterhouse."

Beckham's earpiece crackled as one of the pilots said, "ETA fifteen minutes."

The chopper flew over woodland and pasture, leaving

civilization behind. The view wasn't very different from the one he remembered vividly from April, when Team Ghost had taken an Osprey from Fort Bragg to Edwards Air Force Base. The leaves had just begun to come in, and a herd of horses had been galloping through a field of lush green grass, just like the one below them now.

Spring was Beckham's favorite time of year because it signaled new life. But despite the vibrant colors, there was no sign of life below. No horses, no deer or rabbits. Not live ones anyway. The bloody carcasses of a herd of cows dotted one field. He turned from the gruesome sight. At first he'd wondered how animals were surviving the apocalypse. Now he knew that they weren't. The Variants had eaten most of them.

"Eyes on Raven Rock," one of the pilots said. Beckham scanned the horizon and saw a cluster of red-and-white radio towers. A multilayered fence surrounded the main building and several adjacent structures.

"Make a pass," Beckham said into the comm.

They circled the area for several minutes, allowing Beckham to sync his mental map with the one he held in his hand. He could see the access roads that connected a series of concrete portals leading into the hills. There were four in total, marked A through D. According to the map, Beckham was looking for portals C and D. The inner road would take his team south, past a ventilation control room, a domestic reservoir, and even a bowling alley. From there the underground passages curved to the west and connected with portals A and B. In the middle there were two power plants, a second industrial reservoir, and five buildings that included living quarters and the Presidential Command Center.

The complex was essentially an underground city. The thirty-ton blast doors were built to withstand a nuclear attack. Unfortunately, the engineers hadn't planned on stopping a weapon like the hemorrhage virus, or the monsters it created.

A red circle on the map marked the approximate location of the FEMA facility Beckham was looking for. It was next to the domestic reservoir. He flicked the map with a gloved finger and slipped it back into his vest as Echo 1 veered off toward their landing site. They set down next to a security building while Echo 2 and 3 continued on another pass.

Beckham scanned the access roads for a second time. There was a mixture of abandoned civilian and military vehicles clogging the pavement. Most of them were parked near portal C. He flipped his mini-mic to his lips. "Bravo One, Charlie One. You copy? Over."

"Valentine," came the reply. Beckham wouldn't waste his time reminding the man he was Beckham's subordinate, but he'd be damned if he'd call the guy by name.

"Your team takes portal C, we'll take D. We'll meet at the domestic reservoir," Beckham said. "And maintain radio discipline once we're inside."

"Roger that," Valentine said.

Beckham stifled another urge to give Valentine a dressing-down. Wood's man would either help or hinder on this mission, but Beckham was betting on the latter. And if he got in the way of doing what was right, or worse... Beckham shook the thought aside and searched the area for a potential LZ, focusing on an empty stretch of road.

"Put us down in between that Humvee and the semi," he said over the comm.

The clatter from the final pre-combat gear and weapons checks echoed through the troop hold. Beckham slammed a magazine into his M4 and then performed the most important final preparation by patting the pocket containing the picture of his mom.

"Hope she's watching over us," Horn said as he joined Beckham at the open door. "Hope she's watching over my girls at Plum Island too."

"She is, Big Horn," Beckham said. He watched the concrete rise to meet them as the pilots descended over the road. A moment later, the wheels connected with a jolt and Beckham shouted, "Go, go, go!"

Boots pounded the pavement as Beckham took point and raced toward a green fence. Through the chain links, he could see a massive tunnel cut into the hills. When he reached the gate, Echo 2 pulled overhead and vanished over the wooded bluff above the entrance.

Beckham turned to check on Valentine and his men at the other portal. The sergeant had already breached the gate and his team was running through.

The decision to split up wasn't an easy one for Beckham. A major problem with Operation Extinction was intel, or lack thereof. That and the fact the medical infrastructure had been all but destroyed by the firebombing of the cities during the initial outbreak. It was yet another reason he was questioning the mission. Coming to Raven Rock seemed more like a rescue op for any surviving political dignitaries or military brass. Beckham was all about saving more souls, but he hated feeling like cannon fodder. If that turned out to be the case, he'd have something to say to Wood—if he made it back at all.

"Looks secure," Lombardi said. "No sign of forced entry."

Chow pulled a string of bloody goo hanging between links and held it up under the sun. "No sign, huh?" he said with a raised brow. "Looks like someone or something opted for an alternative route." He wiped the blood on his flak jacket and pointed at the barbwire lining the top of the fence. Several pieces had been torn away and hung loosely over the side. Dried blood stained the metal.

Beckham banished any remaining hope for a simple mission.

"Let's go," he said, motioning toward the gate. Lombardi pulled a bolt cutter from his rucksack and snapped through the locks.

"What about a vehicle?" Horn asked.

"Don't want anyone to hear us coming," Beckham said. "We proceed on foot until we clear the facility. Horn, you're on point. The rest of you fall into line and keep combat intervals. If we find Variants, remember your field of fire. Nobody pull any cowboy shit."

He flashed a hand signal, and Chow pulled the gate back. Horn burst through with his M249 leveled at the lip of the tunnel. As they ran, Beckham mentally identified the escape routes he'd noted earlier on the map.

Ahead, Horn melted into the shadows. Beckham followed close behind, checking the walls, ceiling, and ground for any sign of struggle. He'd half expected to discover a battlefield inside with empty bullet casings and corpses. Besides a few streaks of blood, there wasn't anything but concrete and rock.

Horn stopped a hundred feet from a gate blocking their entrance into the inner roadways. Weak rays of sunlight leaking into the tunnel confirmed what Beckham already knew: The gate leading inside the mountain was already open.

"Radio discipline from here on out," Beckham whispered. He pointed to his eyes, then to Horn, and then to the open gate.

Horn acknowledged with a nod, shouldered his M249, and marched ahead, heel to toe, just like old times. And, just like old times, Beckham followed him into the darkness.

"You can't, Kate," Ellis was saying. "You're too important."

Kate steadied her breathing as she held a syringe of Kryptonite under a bank of lights in the small lab room and stared at her new weapon. She felt no sense of awe at creating something so powerful. In fact, she could hardly concentrate on her new creation at all.

She was focused on the fact that her period was a week late.

Kate wanted to tell Ellis, but she couldn't. Not yet—not until she knew for sure. At first she hadn't given it much thought, attributing her irregular cycle to the stress. But the more she thought about injecting herself with the Kryptonite, the more she wondered if it was the right move. If she was pregnant, it might cause serious complications.

After several moments of silence, she lowered the syringe and faced Ellis. He was running a hand through his slicked-back hair.

"Beckham is out there with the other soldiers, collecting chemotherapeutics that we hope will end this nightmare. We need to ensure it doesn't have any major side effects on the surviving population," Kate said.

Ellis held out his hand and let out an exasperated sigh. "Let me, then. You have Beckham, and Horn's girls have really taken a liking to you. I don't have anyone. If something goes wrong—"

"Don't say that," Kate said. "You have me."

He screwed his lips to the side and used two fingers to gesture for the syringe. "I'm still a better option. Besides, if we're correct, nothing's going to happen. Right?"

Kate nodded without hesitation. She was confident the drugs would have minimal side effects on humans, but they still had to be sure before they deployed it on a massive level.

"Let me help at least," Kate said. She sat Ellis down in

a chair and grabbed his left arm to search for a suitable vein in the crook of his elbow.

Ellis closed his eyes and said, "Make it fast."

"What kind of doctor hates needles?"

"I don't mind 'em as long as they aren't going inside of *me*."

Without warning, Kate inserted the tip of the needle into a plump vein and pushed in the cocktail. She quickly pulled it out again and put a cotton swab over the pinprick of blood forming on the surface of his skin.

"All done," she said with a warm smile.

Ellis placed a finger over the swab. "Thanks. What's next on the agenda?"

"I'd like to see how Patients One and Two are doing."

"But we just injected them a few hours ago."

Kate disposed of the needle and washed her hands. She pulled her hair back into a ponytail and said, "I need something to keep my mind off Operation Extinction."

"Fine," Ellis said. He opened the door to the lab and walked into the hallway, where Cooper and Berg were waiting.

"We're heading to Building Four," Kate said.

"Follow us, Doctor."

Kate spoke to Ellis openly as she walked. Her fear of Wood's men was still there, but she figured the best course of action was to continue acting as if nothing was wrong.

"I want to make sure we have the bioreactors online and ready to go as soon as possible," Kate said. "We can't speed up cell growth once we start the batches, but we can ensure we're producing as many as possible by coordinating multiple batches. Colonel Wood has already lined up three other locations."

"That's a good start," Ellis said. "But we're going to need more than four. What about other countries?"

"Wood said to leave that up to his science division," Kate said. She recalled the conference call from the night before. The colonel had answered Kennor a little too quickly and smoothly about coordinating the production of Kryptonite. She had been so caught up in the moment that she hadn't thought twice about it.

Until now.

The midmorning sun beat down on them when they got outside. Kate felt a trickle of sweat forming on her forehead. She dragged a sleeve across her brow and tried to think. If the first stage of Operation Extinction was successful, they could start the bioreactors immediately. They needed two weeks to expand the cell line and produce enough for deployment. But in two weeks, the human population would have dwindled dramatically worldwide. The thought made Kate stop in her tracks.

"You okay, Kate?" Ellis asked. "You look like you just saw a ghost."

"I did," Kate said. "Billions of them."

Fitz spat from the side of Tower 3. He watched the glob plummet and then whip away in the breeze. For the past three hours he had been on sentry duty, watching Apollo chase seagulls on the beach.

He brought the scope of his MK11 to his eye and glassed the post, stopping on Building 4. Kate and Ellis stood at the bottom of the steps with two Medical Corps soldiers dressed in all black. Fitz centered his crosshairs on the guards. Both had the same emotionless expressions and, weirdly enough, the same mustaches.

Why the fuck would Wood's men be trailing Kate and Ellis? There was plenty of security on the island, but it still seemed like a waste to assign two soldiers to guard Kate and Ellis. Unless that wasn't their primary mission.

Fitz made a mental note to keep an eye on them. He was bored as all hell anyway, and doing some recon wouldn't hurt anything.

A yelp pulled Fitz's attention to the grass below his tower. Apollo glanced up, and Fitz noticed a ball of fur struggling in his teeth.

"Bad!" Fitz said. "Drop it."

The dog spat out a live bunny, which darted away the moment its feet hit the ground, vanishing into a bush. Apollo wagged his tail as Fitz pulled a piece of a granola bar from his pocket and tossed it down to him.

Fitz chuckled and maneuvered his rifle back to Building 4. Kate's group had gone inside, but there were several others on the sidewalk. Riley wheeled his chair down the path with Meg hopping behind him. Fitz couldn't help but smile. The two made a cute pair. He wished he had someone to share the final days of mankind with, but he was happy Riley and Meg had each other.

Grabbing the bipod of his rifle, Fitz then repositioned the sight and zoomed in on the beach. He didn't have time for romance anyway—he had a promise to uphold. His job was to protect the island and his friends on it.

22

Beckham followed the glow of strategically placed ceiling lights as he and Horn delved farther into the complex. A breeze coming from vents on both sides of the tunnel brushed against Charlie team as they moved. The air was cold and stank of mildew, but it meant the ventilation system was still working. Beckham was no longer worried about suffocating or not being able to see—he was worried about what they would find as they got deeper into the complex.

Beckham sidestepped around a puddle and saw a sign that read VENTILATION CONTROL ROOM with an arrow pointing to a tunnel on their left. He could just see the last of Valentine's men disappear down that passage and hear the distant tromp of their boots on the concrete.

"Which way?" Horn asked.

Beckham flashed a hand signal to the south. They continued past the tunnel Valentine had taken, passing doors on both sides of the narrow corridor. He noted the marks of tire treads on the ground and scrapes along the walls, as though vehicles had squeezed through side by side. His heart hammered as they moved deeper into the mountain, part of him expecting to see Variants come clambering across the walls. There was no question they were inside the complex—but where?

"We're going to carry those drugs all this way?" Horn whispered.

"Was hoping we'd find a vehicle inside after we cleared the complex," Beckham replied. He hustled to catch up with Horn. Another sign and arrow indicated they were close to the domestic reservoir. The FEMA warehouse wouldn't be far.

A draft that smelled of rotting fruit hit Beckham's nostrils halfway down the corridor. He halted and balled his hand into a fist. There were two more doors along the wall up ahead, and one of them was open a few inches.

Pointing first at his eyes, Beckham then pointed to Chow and after that to the open door. Beckham made his way over to the wall in a half crouch. The smell was coming from inside the room. He waited several seconds, listening for anything moving inside.

"You take high. I'm low," Beckham said. "Sweep right to left. I'll go left to right."

Chow nodded and stepped forward, putting his foot against the rusted bottom of the open door.

"Execute," Beckham said.

Chow pushed the door open with his left hand and burst inside. Beckham followed close behind, arching his M4 across what looked like some sort of utility room. Dozens of boxy machines, each six feet tall, were situated throughout the space, blocking Beckham's view and dividing the area like a maze.

Beckham gritted his teeth and sidestepped around the nearest machine with his rifle trained down the first aisle. Chow started down the right side and disappeared from Beckham's peripheral vision.

The left side was clear, but as Beckham continued, the potent smell intensified. He halted when he saw four mangled corpses at the end of the room. Bones glistening with blood protruded from the sacks of flesh.

"Found something," Beckham whispered over the comm. He felt a presence to his right a moment later. Chow stood there with a sleeve over his nose, his gaze locked on the twisted corpses.

"Better check it out," Beckham said. He pulled his shemagh over his face and then led with his rifle. The bodies were so badly disfigured it took Beckham a moment to realize they weren't human.

Chow swiped a sweaty strand of black hair from his face, shook his head, and whispered, "If the Variants are eating each other..."

"Then they must have already eaten their way through any survivors," Beckham replied.

Their comms flared as they retreated from the room. Valentine's voice surged over the channel. "Charlie One, Bravo One, eyes on the objective. It's in a tunnel just to the left of the reservoir. You better get over here. Place is fucking huge."

Beckham pulled the scarf down and looked away from the gore. "Copy that, Bravo One," Beckham said. "We'll be right there."

Kennor snatched the picture of his grandkids off his desk and stuffed it into his pack.

"Hurry, sir!" Harris said, his voice just shy of a shout.

Wood was already gone. He had taken off with several of his men a few minutes earlier and they were on their way to the tarmac.

I'm too old for this shit, Kennor thought as he followed Harris into the command center. The room was packed with his staff. Most of them shouted into headsets as they stared at the wall-mounted monitors where a security feed played in real time on the screens.

"My God," Kennor said. He gripped his bag tighter when he saw what they were watching. The display on the left showed a battle inside one of the hallways. A trio of marines fired at a pack of Variants pouring through the doors. Fire erupted from their rifles as they emptied their magazines into the mass of infected monsters.

Several of the beasts flopped to the floor, but the majority of the pack surged forward, consuming the marines. A female Variant took to the walls. It dashed over the concrete on all fours. Its naked flesh came into focus as it crawled closer, like a subject under a microscope. The bulging veins crisscrossing its skin seemed to pulsate under the banks of LEDs. It slowed as it approached the camera, tilting its head and narrowing its yellow eyes at the lens. Its lips opened, revealing a black void, and it released a roar that only the dying marines in the tunnel would hear before it trampled the wall-mounted camera. The feed went black, and Kennor let out a breath he hadn't realized he was holding in.

"How the fuck did they get in!" he shouted.

"Through the utility tunnels," Harris said.

"Can we hold them?"

"I don't know," Harris said. His voice was shaky. "Sir, we have to go. *Now*."

Kennor glared at the colonel. Harris's features were pinched by fear. After all these years, he had never realized how weak Harris really was. The colonel wanted to run from the Variants, but Kennor had already retreated once. He'd left the cities, but there was no way in hell he would abandon Central Command. He wouldn't let it fall to the monsters, not without a fight.

"I'm staying," Kennor said. He dropped his bag on a chair and pulled his M1911 from the holster on his hip. The gun had been in his family since World War II. His father had carried it from France to Germany. It had killed Nazis, and now it was going to kill Variants.

Kennor worked his way through the stations, getting sitreps from men and woman young enough to be his children. They all reported the same thing: Blockade after blockade was falling to the Variants.

Even as the other bases across the country fell, Kennor had still thought they were safe here. He'd been wrong—again.

"Get a message through to Cheyenne Mountain," Kennor said. "Inform President Mitchell we're being overrun." He hadn't spoken to the president in several days, and he was the last man Kennor wanted to talk to now. He'd spend his final moments with soldiers, not talking to weak politicians.

Harris hesitated and then hurried away. "Right away, sir."

"Somebody show me a feed of the evacuation!" Kennor shouted.

"Over here, sir," Corporal Van said from his computer station. He was the same man who had informed Kennor when Raven Rock had fallen to the Variants. Now he was about to show him the evac of their own bunker.

Kennor hurried over to Van's station, his eyes roving from monitor to monitor as he crossed the room.

"Who's made it out so far?"

Van looked up with rueful eyes. "General Johnson and Lieutenant Colonel Kramer are in the air, sir."

"That's it?"

"From your executive team, yes, sir," he replied. "Colonel Wood and his men are on their way through the escape tunnels now."

"Anyone else?"

"Congressman Hauber, Senator Long, and a few civilians, sir," Van said. He cupped his hand over his headset and looked away.

Kennor turned back to the last remaining feed at the front of the room. The Variants were heading deeper into the base.

"How the fuck are they getting through the blast doors?" Kennor asked.

"They aren't," Harris said. "They're using the ventilation and sewer systems."

"Jesus," Kennor said. He pulled the magazine out of his M1911 and checked the bullets. It was an old habit. He already knew the mag was full. He jammed it back into the gun and pulled back the slide to chamber a round.

"Listen up, everyone!" Kennor shouted. "Grab a gun and prepare to fight. If the Variants break through the outer defenses, they will find us—and when they do, we fight to the end. *Every last one of us.* You got that?"

A flurry of youthful voices rang out from every direction. All of them were yelling the same thing: "Yes, sir!"

Outside the doorway of the FEMA warehouse, Valentine flashed a toothy grin. His team was already loading boxes marked FRAGILE into the back of a Ford Super Duty truck.

"Looks like Bravo hit the jackpot," Horn said.

Beckham squeezed past Valentine to stare into a room carved out of rock with a ceiling twenty feet high. The space stretched as far back as he could see. There were thousands and thousands of shelves piled high with boxes that had the FEMA symbol on them. Arrows painted on the floor and signs hanging from the shelves showed an organized and impressive facility. It was like a grocery store without the employees.

Horn let out a low whistle and strolled into the cavern. His wide eyes had fixated on a sign that read LIQUOR.

Beckham remembered Jensen's request and tapped Horn on the shoulder. "Only if you find a case of chew for the lieutenant colonel too."

Horn huffed and let his grin fade. "Now ain't the time to be thinkin' about drinkin', right, boss?"

"Right. Let's start loading the truck," Beckham said. He checked his mission clock. They'd been inside for twenty-two minutes and he hadn't heard jack shit from Mikesell.

Beckham flicked his mini-mic to his lips and opened a channel to all three of the strike teams. "Alpha One, Charlie One. Do you copy? Over."

Static crackled in his earpiece. He waited a few seconds and then tried again. "Alpha One, do you *copy*? Over."

"Already tried three times," Valentine said. "Headsets are useless down here. Too much rock."

"Shit," Beckham muttered. He paused to think as the other men loaded the truck. In some ways, fighting wasn't all that different from a game of high-stakes poker. Going into a mission without having a plan for insertion and escape was like playing a bad hand of cards with shit odds of winning. Now Beckham was deep underground, surrounded by rock and dirt, with no way of contacting Alpha team.

Beckham jerked his chin toward the Ford. "Is that the only truck you guys found?"

"The only one we saw," Valentine replied.

Beckham checked the other end of the tunnel. There had to be other vehicles somewhere inside. He cursed under his breath and smacked the bed of the pickup truck. "Let's get her loaded up and out of here."

Chow slid a box into the bed of the truck. "Going to need to make two, maybe three trips. There's a ton more boxes."

Beckham looked over his shoulder at the man Valentine had posted on sentry duty.

"Jesus," Beckham said, shaking his head. Posting only one lookout was a rookie mistake that could cost them their lives and the mission.

"Valentine, hurry this shit up. I'll hold security with Chow to the south. Get two of your men to set up position to the north where you came in. I want everybody else loading boxes," Beckham said.

Valentine acknowledged with a grunt.

Beckham whirled away before he lost his temper and gave the junior NCO more of a dressing-down in front of the other men. He scanned the hallway leading toward the middle of the complex for a second time. There wasn't much cover besides a forklift and a pile of crates. Not the greatest place to make a stand. Then again, Beckham wouldn't want to make a stand anywhere in this maze.

He followed Chow to a pile of boxes. Halfway down the corridor, he saw a sign that read DOMESTIC RESERVOIR. The passage curved to the right where there was a second sign for the East Power Plant.

"Wish Jinx were here to see this place," Chow said in a low voice. "He always had a hard-on for bunkers. Used to say that when shit hit the fan, he was going back to the one on his parents' farm. Apparently his dad was a paranoid son of a bitch. He built the bunker thinking the Soviets were going to nuke us."

Beckham kept his rifle shouldered with an ear in Chow's direction, listening to his whispers. Something about the old stories helped him relax.

"Remember that time Panda and Riley got into it at the Bing?" Chow said with a half grin. "Riley said Panda was hogging the dancers that night. But it really boiled down to the fact they both wanted the one with the big-ass booty. Do you remember that chick's name?"

"Tank."

Chow chuckled. "Yeah, that's the one."

"Same night that Riley danced in his underwear onstage."

It had also been the last night out Team Ghost had ever enjoyed together. Beckham blinked away the memories and scoped the passage.

"Keep sharp," he said.

"Sorry," Chow replied. He gently smacked the side of his helmet and centered his gun on the hallway.

Beckham flung a glance over his shoulder. The pickup was almost loaded. He pushed the mini-mic back to his lips to try Horn on the comm. He wasn't far, but Beckham didn't want to leave his post.

"Charlie Two, you copy? Over," Beckham said.

"Roger, boss."

"Take Charlie Four with you on the first load, leave the pickup, and return with another vehicle. There were plenty outside."

"Copy that," Horn said. He emerged from the warehouse a moment later, his tattooed arms flexing under the weight of three boxes. After laying them into the bed of the truck, he popped a thumbs-up and climbed into the cab. Lombardi jumped in the passenger side.

The diesel engine coughed to life, and the sound filled the tunnel. Despite the reassuring noise, Beckham felt uneasy. The narrow tunnels carried sound like a gong in a temple.

Horn maneuvered the truck around a forklift and then pulled away. Valentine's team continued stacking boxes outside the entrance to the cavern. Things were going smoothly.

Too smoothly.

That meant shit was about to happen. Beckham could feel it in his bones. As he turned back to the south and raised his rifle, the pain from the stitches lanced down his arm.

For fifteen minutes, Beckham and Chow waited there in silence. Beckham endured the burn of his injury as he stood with his shoulders squared. By the time Horn returned with a new truck, Beckham's M4 was trembling in his hands and perspiration was cascading down his forehead.

"Crates are secure," Valentine said. He set a final box at the entrance to the warehouse as Horn sped down the corridor in an early nineties Dodge Ram coated with rust. The clanking of the metal chassis sent Beckham's heart beating out of control. It was way too fucking loud. He strained to listen over the noise of the truck and pivoted back to the south. Chow was sweeping his rifle over the shadows, waiting, watching.

Horn parked the Ram outside the warehouse and shut off the engine. A sharp popping instantly followed. At first Beckham thought it was the muffler, but the second crack confirmed this wasn't the mechanical failure of the Ram—it was gunfire. A flurry of the cracks rang out in the distance. Beckham's heart rate escalated with every shot.

Chow looked around wildly. "Where's it coming from?"

"Load the truck!" Beckham shouted. "Lombardi, on me. Horn, you too." They formed a human wall, their weapons angled to the south, where the majority of the shots seemed to be reverberating from.

He had a decision to make: provide support to Alpha or retreat with the drugs? Without having any way of contacting Mikesell, he couldn't know how bad things were or if they could even help.

Beckham looked from the southern tunnel to the truck. Once it was loaded, he felt the burn of eyes on him.

With a heavy heart, he made his decision. The drugs were the most important part of the mission. Mikesell and Alpha were on their own.

"Move out," Beckham said.

"Wait!" Chow said. "What's that?" He trained his weapon on a vehicle zipping down the tunnel to the south. Beams from its headlights caught Beckham in the face. He shielded his eyes as a Humvee came screeching to a stop a few hundred feet away.

Beckham raised his gun and zoomed in on the bloody face of a Medical Corps soldier in black fatigues who stumbled out of the truck. Weaponless, the man waved his arms frantically and screamed for help.

The Dodge Ram crackled to life behind them, and Beckham glanced over his shoulder to see Valentine in the driver's seat. The rest of his men were piling into the truck.

"Let's go!" Valentine shouted.

Beckham turned back to the Humvee. The soldier from Mikesell's team collapsed in front of the truck and then pushed himself to his feet again, screaming, "We need help! We found survivors, but the Variants are everywhere!"

Beckham closed his eyes for a brief second, his mind shifting from thoughts of Kate to everyone else on Plum Island. They needed him there, but so did the survivors trapped down here. He wasn't going to leave soldiers or civilians behind. Not if he could help. He couldn't abandon anyone.

"I'll go. You guys get the fuck out of here," Beckham said.

"Like hell," Chow said.

"Not leaving you, boss," Horn said with a snort.

Lombardi looked at the staggering soldier and then back at Beckham. "I'm with you."

Beckham turned to the loaded truck. "Valentine, get the drugs to the choppers! Tell Echo Two and Echo Three to stand by for our extraction!"

Valentine held his gaze for the briefest of seconds and then nodded. The wheels of the Ram screamed, masking distant gunfire as Valentine peeled away. By the time Beckham turned back to the tunnel, his team was already running for the Humvee.

Ellis sat on the stoop of Building 1, his head in his hands.

"How are you feeling?" Kate asked, taking a seat next to him.

"Did I ever tell you I'm a hypochondriac?"

Kate smiled. "It's remarkable you became a doctor in this field, you know that? You're afraid of needles *and* diseases."

Ellis cracked a half grin. "That's what my mom said!" His smile disappeared when he grabbed his stomach. "Feeling a bit sick, not going to lie."

Kate checked her watch. It had been a little over an hour since she had injected Ellis with Kryptonite. Nausea was the one side effect she had planned for. She was feeling some of that herself, but mostly because she was worried sick. Beckham and the others would have landed at Raven Rock now. Operation Extinction was well under way.

"Do you feel anything else?" Kate asked.

Ellis shook his head. "Nope, just sick to my stomach."

"Hey, Doc!" came a voice.

Kate raised a hand to shield her eyes from the sun. Riley and Meg were making their way down the pathway. "Good job, Meg. You're doing great," Riley said as she hopped along on her crutches, keeping pace with him. Kate felt a mixture of sadness and happiness at the sight. While she was pleased to see her two new friends, it made her miss Beckham even more.

Riley stopped, locked his wheels at the bottom of the steps, and waved Kate and Ellis down the steps.

"Everything going okay?" Riley asked. "Those Medical Corps soldiers giving you any problems? I've had my eye on them."

Kate flung a quick glance over her shoulder. Cooper and Berg were chatting inside the lobby of Building 1. She could see their smug faces through the windows.

"Everything's fine for now," she said.

"You'd let me know if they gave you any trouble, right, Kate?" Riley said.

She nodded and changed the subject. "You hear any updates about Operation Extinction yet?"

"You mean about Beckham?" Riley said, grinning. He shook his head. "Nah. Probably won't hear shit for a while." He shifted his gaze to Ellis. "What's wrong with you, Doc?"

"Nothing. I'm fine," Ellis said. He grimaced as his gut made a complicated sound that Kate could hear from where she stood.

"We better get you some anti-nausea meds," Kate said. "Come on."

"Wait," Meg said. She hopped closer to the stairs and searched Kate's eyes. "The weapon you made…is it really going to work?"

Kate reached down to help Ellis up and said, "We sure hope so."

"Me too," Meg said, turning to face in the direction of New York. "I want to believe I can go home someday."

23

The metal doors rattled so hard Kennor almost dropped his M1911. He steadied the gun and kept it aimed at the entrance. The Variants pounded on the other side relentlessly. They had murdered and eaten their way through the entire base, and it was only a matter of time before they found a way inside the command center.

Harris stood his ground a few feet away. He cupped his hands over his headset, still listening for intel down to the very last second.

"Sir," Harris said. "I've got Colonel Wood on the line. He wants to talk to you."

Kennor nodded and reached for Harris's headset. He used his knife hand to hold his pistol and grabbed the headset with his other.

The emergency alarms screamed from every corner of the room, the electronic whine making it nearly impossible to think. Never in his career had he felt fear so intense. He'd given the orders that had sent countless others to their deaths, and before that he'd led men into battle—but even those bullet-riddled memories paled against the prospect of being torn apart by a horde of goddamn monsters.

"Go ahead, Wood," Kennor said after a deep breath.

"General, why aren't you on a bird?" Wood asked. His voice sounded distant over the headset, but Kennor could still make out his dry tone. It was almost as obnoxious as the emergency alarms.

"I decided to stay with my staff," Kennor said.

"Honorable, sir," Wood said, somehow making the word into an insult.

"Promise me you'll finish Operation Extinction, Wood."

"Colonel Gibson and I made a commitment to our nation that we would come up with a weapon to wipe our enemies off the face of the earth. I'm not going to give up now."

The door shook violently as a Variant rammed the other side. The thud echoed over the screeching sirens. Kennor gripped his gun tighter in his hand, his fingers slimy with sweat.

"Unleashing the hemorrhage virus wasn't exactly my idea of 'destroying our enemies,'" Wood said. "But in the end, I think it shall work out rather nicely. I plan on using Earthfall over the United States and selected territories. I'll probably save Puerto Rico. I always did like San Juan. In a few weeks, we'll take back our country and we'll never have to worry about enemies overseas…" His voice disappeared in a flurry of white noise.

"Colonel…Colonel!" Kennor shouted, his gut tightening.

"I'm here," Wood said a moment later.

"What about our allies? What about the British or the French? We can't abandon them!" Kennor shouted.

Wood sighed, his breath crackling across the line. "You used to remind me a lot of Secretary of Defense McNamara. Remember him? The architect of the Vietnam War? He put our national security first. Took the fight abroad. But you? You're a disappointment, sir."

"You son of a bitch, I should have known not to trust you," Kennor said. "You can't do this, Wood. You can't abandon our allies."

Wood let out a laugh. "What allies? We're on our own now, General."

The feed cut out. Kennor ripped the headset off and tossed it to Harris. "Get General Johnson and Lieutenant Colonel Kramer on the horn. NOW! Tell them they have—"

The sirens abruptly shut off and darkness washed over the room. Emergency lights flickered on, bathing the command center in a malicious red. The pounding on the door stopped too, and a rattling broke out overhead.

Kennor spun, the aim of his M1911 darting across the ceiling from panel to panel. Everyone in the room fell quiet.

"When they come, watch your covering fire," Kennor said.

Vicious scratching reverberated through the ductwork as the Variants clawed at the metal. Kennor shivered at the sounds, his breathing coming out in gasps. The marines at the door took up position behind Harris, and Kennor worked his way through the stations to meet them. The other officers formed a perimeter, holding their sidearms. Corporal Van was the only one still at his desk. He was staring at the tile above his station.

Kennor waved at him but froze when he saw dust raining from the ceiling. The flakes fluttered through the glow of the red light. Van turned and locked eyes with Kennor just as the panels overhead gave way.

Before Kennor could fire a shot, a Variant dropped from the ceiling. Van let out a nasally scream as the monster sank claws into his back and forced him to the ground. The scream abruptly ended when the Variant slashed Van's jugular vein and clamped its bulging lips around the gushing faucet.

Kennor ended Van's suffering with a shot to his head. He squeezed off two more into the Variant's back just as all hell broke loose. Ceiling panels all over the command center broke and plummeted to the ground. Variants poured from above.

Muzzle flashes illuminated the pale, veiny bodies of a dozen naked monsters. They darted across the room the moment they hit the ground.

Kennor focused on the creature still perched on Van's broken body. It pulled its lips away, clawed at its own back where it had been shot, and let out a guttural roar. He squeezed off a shot that hit the monster right between its yellow eyes, then whirled to find another target.

A crack sounded and in the split second it took for his mind to process the noise, he realized it wasn't a gunshot. Nails stung his back and the weight of a beast sent him crashing to the floor. His face smashed onto the ground with such force he could feel his front teeth knocked loose. He struggled to get up, but everything below his belt felt numb.

Kennor watched helplessly as his staff vanished one by one, the Variants pulling them into the darkness. He heard the popping of joints and scratching of claws before he saw the monster prowling toward him with its back arched in a catlike stance. With no small amount of effort, he rolled his head to the side just as the Variant leaped and sank its claws into his paralyzed legs.

There was no physical pain, only the mental anguish of his failure. General Richard Kennor, the Pit Bull of the American Military, had failed to save Central Command and failed to save his beloved country. From Reaper to Liberty and now Extinction—he had made all the wrong choices, and now he would pay for it. It was the last thought that crossed his mind as his vision went dark and the Variants dragged him away.

Beckham grabbed the injured soldier under an arm. "Where is Alpha?"

He pointed to the south and said, "Just outside the industrial reservoir. We found survivors hunkered down in the Presidential Command Center. We were evacuating them when w-we"—he stuttered, his long chin wobbling—"we woke the nest."

Beckham looked over at Chow. He knew what they were heading into. If there was a nest inside, then the chances of any of them making it out alive were slim.

"When we couldn't raise you on the radio, Sergeant Mikesell ordered me to come find you guys. I picked up the Humvee along the way," the soldier continued.

"How bad are you hurt?" Chow asked.

"I'll be fine," he said. He grimaced and pulled his hand away from a slash on his chest.

"What's your name, soldier?" Beckham asked.

"Sawyer," he said, still looking down at his red-stained hand.

"You did the right thing, Sawyer. Just hang in there."

The pop of gunfire echoed through the tunnel. It meant there were still soldiers fighting, and it snapped Beckham into motion.

"Horn, help Sawyer. Let's move," Beckham said. "I'll drive."

He climbed inside the Humvee and waited for the others to pile in. There was a turret with an M240 and a spotlight on top of the truck. It was a good old-fashioned M1 that looked like it had been used for patrols. No bells and whistles, just a diesel engine and a drivetrain that could handle virtually any terrain on the planet.

Beckham put the truck in gear and stomped on the pedal. With stealth out the window, he didn't care who heard them coming. He gripped the wheel tightly and sped down the tunnel, navigating around the crates and boxes that littered the road.

"How many are there?" Beckham asked.

"We found six survivors," Sawyer replied. "A scientist, a—"

"How many Variants?" Beckham said, his voice raised. He watched Sawyer's reaction in the rearview mirror.

The soldier shook his head. "I don't know. A hundred, maybe."

Beckham caught Horn's gaze in the rearview mirror as Horn pulled his skull mask over his face. When it was in position, he hefted his M249 out the open window.

"Mikesell, do you copy?" Beckham said into the comm. "Mikesell, where the fuck are you?"

A few words weakened by static made it through. "In…West Power…"

Beckham didn't need to look at the map still tucked into his vest to know where he was going. Pushing the pedal harder, he accelerated through an open stretch of tunnel.

"Get ready," Beckham said. "We'll pick up the survivors and evacuate through portal A or B. Whichever is clear."

"What if neither are clear?" Lombardi asked.

Beckham kept his eyes on the road. "Then we fight our way out."

They still had some outs, but Beckham didn't like the hand he'd been dealt. Five men against an army? It didn't matter how many bullets they had. The odds of making it out alive were dismal.

At the far end of the tunnel, he saw a flurry of movement. He flicked on the brights that cut through the shadowy passage and illuminated a sea of swarming Variants. They covered every square inch of concrete: the ground, the walls, and even the ceiling.

"Holy shit," Beckham whispered.

"There," Sawyer yelled. "That's the plant."

Beckham eased off the gas as they approached. He used the stolen minute to think of a plan. Sawyer had been wrong—there were more than one hundred.

As the Humvee coasted toward them, the Variants turned and centered their gaze on the truck. The Variants on the edges of the group scampered on all fours, some of them clawing and pushing their way through the throng.

"Boss, you got a plan?" Horn shouted.

"I'm working on one."

The Variants caught in the rays of the vehicle's lights broke off from the pack, squawking and leaping out of the way. Beckham had almost forgotten how much they hated light.

"Horn, get on the gun and turn on that spotlight!" Beckham shouted. "Everyone else, train your fire on the mob when I give the order." He pushed the mini-mic back to his lips and said, "Mikesell, we're almost there. I'll get as close to the doors as possible. Be ready to roll."

"Roger," Mikesell replied.

Horn pulled himself into the turret and a beam of light hit the swelling army a moment later as the Humvee rolled to a stop.

"Open fire!" Beckham shouted.

Streaks of red lanced through the tunnel. The focused gunfire punched a hole through the swarm and sent body parts flying in all directions. A macabre chorus of angry shrieks followed.

The team certainly had the monsters' attention now. Beckham leaned out the driver's-side window and fired his M4. The crack of gunfire was deafening. He could hardly hear the primal screeches of the creatures as the rounds cut them down.

The spotlight seemed to deter the Variants even more than the 7.62 mm rounds Horn was unloading into the horde. A dozen of the monsters attempted to gallop toward the Humvee, but they only made it fifty feet before they vanished in sprays of gunfire.

Beckham pulled himself back into the truck and waited for an opportunity to break through the army. The mob was dispersing now, retreating from the lights and rounds. He seized his moment and sped toward the power plant.

"Get ready, Mikesell!" Beckham yelled into the comm. They passed a series of doors that led to the living quarters, Presidential Command Center, and all of the other offices.

Beckham kept his foot on the pedal as they hit the minefield of bodies. Skulls, femurs, and rib cages snapped under the weight of the tires. The shocks jerked up and down as they ran over fresh corpses. A Variant missing its legs dragged itself across the pavement and reached up to shield its eyes from the beams of the Humvee. Beckham flinched as the bumper sent its body spinning into a wall. It impacted with a crack that echoed through the passage.

Most of the remaining Variants continued their retreat. Those that stayed behind were mowed down by Horn's unwavering barrage of gunfire. He was a genius on the M240, raking it back and forth with precision.

Beckham let up on the gas and pulled right up to the front door of the power plant.

"We're here!" he shouted. "Keep them off us, Big Horn."

The door to the plant swung open. Mikesell emerged and hurried toward the truck. There was a small group of civilians huddling in the shadows cast by the mechanical equipment behind him.

Mikesell stopped suddenly, staring with wide eyes at the Humvee. Beckham caught motion in the rearview mirror. A slow moment of confusion passed before he realized Mikesell wasn't staring *at* the truck but *behind* it. The monsters were streaming in through the doors they had passed earlier.

"Horn! Behind us!" Beckham shouted.

The spotlight rotated to their rear, and Beckham watched in horror as the army of Variants that had been retreating now turned and broke into a crazed run toward the truck. They were trapped on both sides. That left Beckham with only one option. There was no way they could hold off both waves of creatures.

"Everyone out!" he shouted.

"Boss, I can—" Horn began to say.

"Get out of the fucking truck!"

Beckham opened the driver's door and waved Mikesell back inside the power plant. He hurried to the backseat and helped Horn pull Sawyer out. When everyone was inside the plant, Horn slammed the door.

They were stranded, trapped underground for the second time since the sewers of New York. And this time, Beckham didn't think they'd ever see daylight again.

Kate looked through the window in the door to Holding Cell 2. *I did what you said, Michael,* she thought, remembering her mentor's final words back in Atlanta. *I created a weapon to kill every last one of the monsters.*

The Variant lying chained to the floor was nearly

dead. Rashes and open sores decorated its skin like polka dots. A skirt of pink vomit had puddled on the concrete where it had thrown up what looked a lot like stomach lining. The creature was nearing the final stages, and in a few minutes it would join the other two Variants that had already died. Plum Island would be monster-free.

Ellis nudged Kate softly. "Ever wonder who these things were before the outbreak?" Ellis asked.

"I have tried very hard not to think that way."

"Me too." He put a hand on her shoulder. "I think we did it, Kate. I'm feeling pretty good. The Variants are dying. All we have to do now is—"

The door to the hallway burst open, and Cooper and Berg rushed inside.

"Doctors," Berg said, stopping to catch his breath.

Cooper continued down the hall, speaking as he walked. "Doctor Lovato, Doctor Ellis, we just got word from Colonel Wood that Central Command has fallen. General Kennor has been killed."

"What? How?" Kate spluttered. "Who's in charge now?"

"Not sure," Berg said. "Things are chaotic over the Net. All we know is that Colonel Wood is en route to the island. He should be here in a few minutes and will be able to provide a full report."

Kate's heart skipped a beat. If Wood was in charge now, she wasn't sure what would happen.

"There's something else," Cooper said. "Bravo team just reported in. They're on their way back to the island with a full supply of chemotherapeutics. Alpha and Charlie, however, are trapped inside Raven Rock Mountain Complex. Their status is unknown at this time."

The words hit Kate hard. She could taste the stomach acid churning in her gut. She couldn't lose Beckham now. Not when they were so close to . . .

To what?

The world was dying. Command was gone and no one seemed to know who was in charge. There were much bigger problems in the world than losing Beckham, but she couldn't bear the thought of fighting on without him.

The sound of heavy boots in the other hallway pulled Kate back to reality. Lieutenant Colonel Jensen and Major Smith rounded the corner and strode through the open doors to the holding cell corridor.

Jensen stopped to stare at the dying Variant and then faced the doctors. "Kate—Doctor Lovato," he said, correcting himself. "Colonel Wood has requested to see you both when he returns."

Patient 2 let out an abrupt screech that made Kate clutch her chest. She could feel her heart thumping so hard it felt as if it was going to burst from her rib cage and plop into her hand. And not just because of the monster dying on the other side of the glass. The world was crumbling around Plum Island, and Beckham was stuck out there, again, because of the weapon she had designed.

24

Beckham ran through a maze of mechanical equipment. The door to the facility rattled behind them as the Variants continued their unyielding assault. It sounded like a miner beating on a wall with a sledgehammer.

"Who knows this place?" Beckham shouted over the noise.

"Ted does," Mikesell said.

Beckham halted in front of a row of generators and scanned the survivors as Chow, Lombardi, and Horn set up a perimeter. Six faces covered in grime stared back at him. An African American woman in black trousers and a white dress shirt bearing a US flag pin caught Beckham's attention. Her gray hair was pulled back in a bun, and when she saw him looking at her, she stood straighter. Her brown eyes flared with something Beckham couldn't place. Was it confidence? Defiance? Strength? He could tell she was important, perhaps a politician or a high-level bureaucrat, but he didn't have time to find out right now.

"Which one of you is Ted?" he asked.

A middle-aged man wearing thick, black-rimmed glasses pushed his way to the front.

"Me," the man said. "I know this plant better than anyone."

"Good," Beckham said. "Because you're going to show us a way out."

Ted pulled his glasses off and rubbed his eyes before slipping them back on. He glanced at Beckham and then at the steel door the Variants were still hammering. "I ... I don't..."

Beckham snapped his fingers. "Ted, I need you to tell me how to get out of here."

Ted looked away from the rattling doors and said, "There's an access tunnel carved into the rock that leads to the reservoir. It's the only path that doesn't take us back out to the inner roadway, but it's also where those things built their nest."

"Hopefully they've all left the lair," Chow said.

Horn snorted and said, "You're telling us that the only way around them is through their nest?"

"Yes, that's the only way," Ted said.

"Show me," Beckham said. "Big Horn, I want you on rear guard. Everyone else, on me."

Ted waved the group deeper into the plant. Beckham shouldered his rifle and played the muzzle over the equipment as they ran.

"Stay close," Beckham said. "And keep quiet."

They passed through a roomful of generators and into another one packed with pumps, air handling units, and boilers.

"This way," Ted said. He crossed to a door with a sign that read DANGER. CONFINED SPACE. ENTER BY PERMIT ONLY. He pulled a ring of keys from his pocket and thumbed through them. He picked a key and was reaching toward the lock when Beckham stopped him. The Variants had already flanked them once, and Beckham wanted to be sure there wasn't anything on the other side of the door.

"Out of the way," Beckham said. He placed an ear against the metal and listened. The pounding and shrieks

of the Variants at the entrance to the plant made it difficult to hear anything else, but he heard nothing to indicate
the monsters were waiting on the other side of the door.

"Unlock it," Beckham ordered. He raised his M4 and
aimed it at the door as Ted inserted the key. The engineer glanced back at the group uncertainly.

Beckham nodded, and Ted opened the door.

"On me," Beckham said. He went first, arching his
rifle over the dimly lit corridor. Empty. Nothing but
damp rock the color of sand. A network of cables and
evenly spaced lights snaked across the ceiling.

"Move," Beckham said. He hugged the walls, using
the orange glow from the lights to guide him through
the narrow passage. Water dropped from cracks in the
rock and collected in puddles on the ground.

Beckham's heart rate increased with every step closer
to the lair. Memories of the nest where he'd found Meg
surfaced in his mind. He was moving on pure adrenaline, his actions controlled by experience and muscle
memory. There was nothing he could do but count on it
to keep him and his people alive.

He stopped at a crooked sign marking the reservoir.
It hung from a door coated in rust and grime at the
next corner. Standing and staring wasn't going to get
them home any faster. After a few seconds of silence, he
motioned Ted forward.

"Big Horn, get up here," Beckham said. If there were
Variants still in the nest, he wanted the M249 on point.

Horn grunted as he made his way through the civilians.
"What's the plan?" he asked when he reached Beckham.

"We stay frosty," Beckham whispered. He faced the
others and said, "Whatever's on the other side of this
door isn't going to be pretty. No matter what you see or
hear, you keep quiet, you keep calm, and you follow us.
Got it?"

There were several nods and a couple of whispers of acknowledgment.

"Open it, Ted."

This time the engineer hesitated even longer before inserting his key, unlocking the door, and pulling it open. The metal scraped over the rocky floor.

Beckham cringed and followed Horn onto a catwalk that looked over a cavern. Greenish-blue water shimmered under the walkway. The calm freshwater lake was deceiving; Beckham knew there was nothing peaceful about this place. He followed Horn to the railing to scope the cave.

"There," Horn whispered. He pointed to the west where a shelf had been carved into the rock.

Beckham clenched his jaw when he saw it had been transformed into a meat locker. Dozens of human bodies were plastered to the walls, the ceiling, and the floor. He focused on a man in fatigues, his arms and legs stretched into a T, crucified against the rock. Red ropes hung from the man's stomach and piled on the ground beneath his feet. Beckham zoomed in to see it was the man's intestines.

"Jesus," he whispered.

"Think of any of them are alive?" Horn asked.

"I'd bet on it," Beckham said. "The Variants prefer fresh meat."

Beckham searched for the monsters, sweeping from left to right, but he saw nothing besides their human prisoners.

"Looks clear," Horn said.

After a third sweep, Beckham nodded and turned back to the others. He couldn't save the poor souls across the cavern, but maybe he could still save those behind him. He waved them onto the catwalk.

Ted grabbed the railing and hurried over to Beckham. "We just take this all the way around to the entrance."

"Let's move, Big Horn," Beckham said.

He put a hand on Horn's shoulder and followed him across the walkway. No matter how quietly the operators were trained to move, they couldn't mask the sounds the civilians made. The clank of their footfalls echoed in the cavern. With each step Beckham expected a Variant to answer with a shriek. They made it about one hundred yards before a dull thud reverberated through the chamber.

"Hold," Beckham whispered. He paused to listen as a second hollow noise sounded.

"Where's it coming from?" Horn asked.

Beckham turned and focused on the rock tunnel leading back the way they came, to the power plant. The sounds of crashing mechanical equipment coupled with shattering of glass came from the entrance of the plant. The Variants had found a way inside.

"Run," Beckham said. "Everyone run, NOW!"

Horn was already moving, his boots pounding the catwalk. The civilians surged forward and Beckham focused on the entrance to the reservoir ahead. It was only a few minutes away, but as the shrieks grew louder, he wasn't sure they had enough time to get there.

The walkway shook violently, throwing Beckham off balance. He looked over his shoulder to see Variants streaming out of the tunnel and onto the catwalk. One of them tumbled over the railing and plummeted to the water below. There was a splash and the heavy crack of gunshots.

Lombardi had stopped to lay down covering fire. Blasts from his shotgun sent three more of the creatures spinning over the side and into the water, but others quickly took their place. The Variants pushed and clawed their way onto the platform. Within seconds the metal groaned under the weight of two dozen monsters.

Mikesell halted and then ran back to join Lombardi.

They fired side by side as the monsters advanced. A second soldier from Alpha fell into line behind them.

"Fall back!" Beckham screamed. He stood his ground as Ted raced past him. Chow rushed by, half dragging Sawyer. They staggered down the walkway, Chow's M4 clanking against the railing.

Lombardi and Mikesell continued to lay down covering fire as they backpedaled. The shots pierced the flesh of the Variants in front, splattering those in the back with blood from the exit wounds. The injured creatures dropped and vanished under the stampede of monsters. A few in front skittered up the wall to avoid the shots.

"Take out the climbers!" Beckham shouted as the final civilian passed him and ran after Horn and the others. He caught a glimpse of the well-dressed woman he'd noticed in the power plant. There was something about the way she carried herself that made her stand out as she passed. Beckham shouldered his rifle and pushed her from his thoughts. If he hesitated another moment, they were all as good as dead.

Steady, Reed. Steady.

He stilled his breathing, planted his boots, and fired at the monsters clambering over the walls. The rounds punched through lean muscle and bit into rock. Two of the creatures skidded down the cavern wall, clawing and squawking. They crashed to the catwalk, and the remaining Variants trampled the life from the injured creatures.

Lombardi fired on a second wave that had taken to the walls while Mikesell and his squad mate worked on the mob rushing toward them. Bullets thinned the front line, but the tidal wave pouring from the tunnel seemed endless. The catwalk whined and sagged beneath their weight.

"Get out of—" Beckham began to shout. He was cut off by a metallic snap as an entire section of the platform broke off. The Variants and the three Medical Corps soldiers plummeted into the water with it. The men screamed as they dropped into the lake with the shrieking monsters.

Beckham dropped to his knees at the edge of the walkway and peered over the side into the churning blue-green water.

Two of the men never resurfaced, but Mikesell thrashed over to the wall. He dragged his fingers frantically across the rock, trying to find purchase.

Beckham looked for something to throw down to him, but it was already too late. The sergeant let out a scream as the Variants pulled him under. Frothy red bubbles churned the water as the monsters tore him apart.

Beckham closed his eyes for a split second, muttering something that was halfway between a prayer and a curse. When he snapped them back open, he saw Lombardi had finally surfaced and was swimming away from a pack of Variants.

"Get to the other side!" Beckham shouted. The crack of gunfire rang out behind him as he rose to his feet. Chow had handed Sawyer off to Horn and was now firing at the Variants spilling from the tunnel directly to the walls. They didn't need a walkway to get to their prey.

"Got to move, man!" Chow yelled.

Beckham raised his rifle and fired as they retreated. Three of the creatures lost their grip and splashed into the water. After clearing several more from the walls, Beckham turned and bolted after Horn and the civilians.

He looked over the side of the railing as he ran. Lombardi was swimming like a madman, his strokes deep and fast, but the Variants were gaining. They used their legs to glide smoothly under the surface like frogs.

Lombardi flung a glance over his shoulder in between breaths and then stopped to tread water. He peered up at Beckham, his eyes wide and panicky—the terrified look of a man with no hope.

"No!" Beckham shouted as Lombardi vanished under the surface.

Chow tugged on Beckham's flak jacket. "Nothing we can do for him! Come on!"

Beckham resisted, his eyes still locked on the bubbling water.

"Now, goddamnit!" Chow shouted.

Beckham let Chow pull him away from the railing and they sprinted across the final stretch of walkway. The group was waiting at a pair of doors leading to the inner roadway.

"Where are the others?" Horn asked.

Beckham shook his head. There was no time to hesitate or explain. They had to continue to the roadway regardless of what was waiting for them outside.

"Let's go!" Beckham said. He shoved his way past the terrified civilians and waited impatiently while Ted fumbled with his keys. The engineer finally pulled the door open, and Horn hurried through first. The crack of his gun sounded as soon as he entered the tunnel.

Beckham could see the Variants to the east. Most of them were still forcing their way into the West Power Plant, which the team had escaped into earlier. The truck was still parked outside.

He whirled and looked to the west tunnel leading to portals A and B that Alpha team had used during insertion. That's where Beckham had planned to escape, but it was a long hike. They would never outrun the creatures unless he bought them some time.

He pulled his spent mag out and jammed another into his rifle. "Horn, on me! Chow, you go west with the others!" he yelled over Horn's gunfire. "I'm going for the truck!"

The civilians hesitated, and Beckham bellowed, "GO!"

In the next instant, Beckham was running toward the Humvee. He stopped every few feet to fire at the Variants closest to the truck. His internal processor kicked into overdrive. He nailed head shot after head shot, plastering the walls and floor with gore. Horn fired his SAW to the left of Beckham. They cleared a path to the truck and Beckham flung his rifle over his back and pulled his M9 as he approached the driver's side.

An emaciated male Variant perched on the hood, snarled at him, and focused its yellow eyes on Beckham's neck. Everything froze in that moment. It was as if his world had been placed under a microscope. He could detect the smallest details, from the drops of sweat on the monster's face to the blood on the tips of its brown jagged teeth. Beckham could even smell the rancid scent of rotting fruit radiating off the thing's filthy skin.

He strode forward and executed the Variant with a shot to the temple. Its limp body slid off the hood and onto the ground. Beckham stepped over it, opened the door, and jumped inside. Horn shredded three more of the Variants before he climbed into the backseat.

"Let's roll!" Horn shouted.

"Get in the turret," Beckham yelled back. He put the truck into reverse and stomped on the gas. The vehicle jerked backward, the tires crunching over corpses. A moment later, the reassuring bark of the M240 filled the cabin.

Beckham threw the Humvee into drive, and it lurched forward. He gripped the steering wheel tightly and sped after the group of civilians. The Variants grew smaller in the side mirrors as Beckham left them in a thin cloud of smoke from burning rubber.

He smacked the steering wheel. *We're going to make it. We're actually going to get out of here!*

But at what cost? Were the lives of Mikesell, Lombardi, and the soldiers whose names Beckham didn't even know worth it?

Beckham blinked and eased off the gas as they

approached the civilians. Chow had waved the group to the side of the tunnel.

"Get in!" Beckham yelled.

The survivors scrambled inside, and a moment later the Humvee was hauling ass down the tunnel. Beckham tried his comm as the first signs of natural light from portal A spilled across the road.

"Echo Two, Echo Three, Charlie Team Leader. Do you copy? Over."

The reply from one of the pilots was almost instantaneous. "Echo Two here. Good to hear your voice, Charlie One."

Beckham looked in the rearview mirror, counting the people piled into the truck. "Echo Two, we need extraction for ten people. Repeat, need extraction for ten."

Past the frightened civilians, Beckham saw the army of Variants galloping down the tunnel after them. His eyes flicked back to the road and the green fence in the distance. Flooring the gas pedal, Beckham drove like a man possessed, his focus on their salvation.

He squinted into the sunlight that only moments ago he'd thought he would never see again. Through the glare, he could see the sleek outline of two circling choppers. Although he'd lost another piece of himself inside Raven Rock, he'd helped secure the drugs and saved lives—and he was returning to Kate. They were going to live. They were going home.

Fitz watched a seagull soar across the golden horizon. He was so bored that he considered shooting it out of the sky. The highlight of his day had been pissing over the side of the tower. Operation Extinction had taken most of the soldiers into the field, forcing him to pull a twelve-hour shift with no one to relieve him for a latrine run. A bucket and a bagful of sand waited behind him, and he knew he'd be using them soon.

He sighed when he looked at his watch. Still another two hours before he would finally be relieved from his post.

"Apollo, how you doing down there, boy?" Fitz said. He looked over the side and saw the dog was sleeping on a patch of grass that looked so comfy it made Fitz tired.

"Don't worry, boy. Beckham will be back soon," Fitz whispered, more to himself than the dog. He had just hoisted his MK11 back to the other side of the tower for a sweep of the post when he heard a faint mechanical thumping on the wind. He raised his rifle and centered the crosshairs on a single Black Hawk.

Fitz quickly scanned the horizon, confirming his fears. The bird was alone.

He followed it to the tarmac, where a four-man fire team spilled out and began unloading boxes. He zoomed in on the faces of each soldier, confirming that it was Bravo team. No Beckham. No Horn or Chow.

He checked the boxes next, focusing his scope on the crates that were marked FRAGILE. At least they'd secured the objective, but where the hell were Alpha and Charlie?

He waited thirty minutes for the other birds to show up. Valentine's men continued unloading the chopper and carrying the crates to Building 1. The sun sank on the horizon, the warm golden glow losing the battle to the carpet of darkness spreading over the water. Fitz had to force himself to look away from the sky. He checked on Apollo again to kill the time. The dog wagged his tail and glanced up when Fitz called his name.

In some ways, Fitz was jealous of Apollo. He'd had seen a lot of death, but there was no way a dog could comprehend the extent of the devastation. Fitz was envious of that. Some days, he wished he was in the dark too. Today was one of them.

An hour passed and the industrial lights clicked on across the post. When Fitz was about to give up his search for the other two teams, he heard the faint whipping of chopper blades. The sniper in Tower 1 radioed two choppers in to Command, but Fitz was hardly listening. He felt a smile spread across his face and hustled to the opposite side of the box to glass the darkness. Two red dots were growing larger in the sky, beacons of hope in an ocean of black.

Fitz focused on the troop holds as the Black Hawks set down on the tarmac. Something was off about the birds. Their markings were unusual, and their doors were closed.

He centered his crosshairs on one of the aircraft as soldiers in black fatigues piled out. *Mikesell's men had all worn black,* Fitz thought. *But these don't look like the same guys.* Who were they? And where was Charlie team?

The soldiers huddled around a central figure as they jogged away from the crafts. The sight reminded him of Secret Service surrounding the president. Whoever this person was, they were a big deal.

Fitz zoomed in on the central figure's face. He tensed his fingers around the handle of the gun when he saw it was Colonel Wood. Why would his men be guarding him like he was the most important person left in the world?

Unless...

Fitz gritted his teeth and lowered his rifle. He was a grunt and therefore not worthy of the sitrep that would have informed him if Colonel Wood had suddenly been promoted up the chain of command. But he was smart enough to know that something had gone terribly wrong—and if Wood was running the show, things were about to get a whole hell of a lot worse.

25

A cold draft of air blew on Kate as she sat waiting at the war table in the command center. She shivered, wrapped her arms across her chest, and sank a few inches in her chair.

"It's going to be okay," Ellis said.

Kate wanted to believe him. God, she wanted to. Beckham had surprised her in the past. She'd thought he was dead so many times before and then—because of a miracle, luck, or divine intervention—he'd come home. Battered and bloody, but alive. This time, though, she wasn't just worried about her own happiness. If she was carrying his child, she couldn't bear the thought of raising it alone. Especially in this new world.

She sat there with her head lowered, feeling defeated. The chatter of voices sounded in the hallway outside the room. She wasn't listening to the discussion. Part of her didn't care anymore. After thirty minutes of waiting, the doors finally swung open and Colonel Wood entered the room. Ellis stood, but Kate remained in her chair.

Wood walked to the observation window as his team sat around the table. Jensen took a seat next to Kate.

"Beckham will be back," he said quietly. "He's a hard man to kill."

Kate simply nodded.

"Everyone knows by now that Central Command has fallen," Wood said from the window. "That's the bad news."

Wood turned and then slowly strolled over to the table. Raising a finger, he said, "But there's good news too. Early reports indicate that the first stage of Operation Extinction has been an overwhelming success. We have recovered payloads of chemotherapeutics from around the country." Wood turned to look at Kate. "Doctor Lovato, am I boring you? I presumed you would be pleased to learn that our men secured the drugs you asked for."

"Good news," Kate managed to reply. She looked ahead, afraid to say anything else that might make her look even weaker than she did now. Despite her despair, she had to remain strong. Humanity was still counting on her. It was a burden she no longer wanted, a burden she would gladly hand to anyone—anyone, that is, except the man who stood in front of her.

"I'm told you have an update on Kryptonite," Wood said.

"We do," Ellis replied when Kate didn't answer. "Patients One and Two succumbed to the drugs a few hours ago."

"Excellent," Wood said, sounding pleased for the first time since the briefing began. "How about the human testing?"

"I was injected this morning," Ellis replied, faking a grin. "And I'm still here."

Wood's eyes flicked to Kate again. "Do you have anything to add, Doctor Lovato?"

"The weapon will work, Colonel. All I need is time to produce the batches of antibodies and for you to help coordinate the production before it's deployed," Kate said.

"Confidence," Wood replied. "Nice to finally see that you have a backbone under that lab coat." He scratched his cheek and said, "As for the deployment. There's been a change—"

A rap on the door cut him off midsentence. Kate whirled to see Cooper and Berg enter the room.

"Sorry to interrupt, sir," Berg said. "But we just got word from Echo Two and Echo Three. They're en route to the island."

Wood looked at the men like they were stupid. "We're in the middle of a briefing here," he snarled.

"But, sir," Berg said, "Bravo and Charlie teams found survivors at Raven Rock. I'm told they have the secretary of state with them."

Kate's heart thumped hard. So hard she felt dizzy. She wanted to ask if Beckham was on one of the birds, but she knew he had to be. She couldn't accept the alternative.

Wood's blue eyes widened ever so slightly. He looked to the floor and then back to Berg. "Prepare your men. We'll meet Madam Secretary Ringgold on the tarmac."

"Why didn't you tell me you were the secretary of state?" Beckham asked the woman sitting opposite him.

Secretary Ringgold shivered in the cold wind and wrapped her arms across a white dress shirt caked with dried blood. Beckham focused on the US flag pin on her lapel. He'd known she was important, but he'd had no idea she was next in line to the presidency.

"I've never liked preferential treatment. Besides, what would you have done? Given me a bulletproof vest? Carried me over your shoulder?" she said.

Beckham felt his lips forming a smile, but he didn't let

them. It would have felt like a betrayal to Lombardi and everyone else they lost at Raven Rock. He reached inside his rucksack and pulled out a rain jacket.

"It's not a bulletproof vest, but it might help with the cold, ma'am," Beckham said. "Glad to have you with us."

"Thank you," she said with a warm, sincere smile.

"Plum Island, ETA ten minutes," one of the pilots said over the comm.

Beckham worked his way to the open door and took a seat next to Horn. His best friend sat at the edge of the troop hold, his M249 angled into the darkness. Chow was camped against the wall behind them, a toothpick flicking back and forth in his mouth.

None of them said a single word for the rest of the flight. Beckham listened to the whoosh of the blades and stared at the empty cities, wondering just how many people were left to save down there.

Kate and Ellis stopped by Building 1 to pick up Tasha and Jenny on their way to the tarmac. Word had traveled fast about the homecoming of Echo 2 and Echo 3. By the time they arrived, a crowd had gathered. Riley and Meg were there. Red and Donna were standing next to them with Bo perched on his father's shoulders. It looked like every civilian at the post had emerged from their quarters to see the troops return.

It should have been a happy occasion, but Wood's men patrolled the crowd and landing zone, their eyes hidden by the shadows their black helmets cast. She counted a half dozen of them, all carrying the same model of weapon. Berg and Cooper continued to tail Kate and Ellis; she was beginning to feel like a prisoner. Instead of snapping at them, she pushed her anger aside, focusing on how good it would feel to wrap her arms around Beckham.

"Miss Kate, do you know when my dad is gonna be home?" Tasha asked.

Riley wheeled over to them and gave Kate a meaningful look. Neither of them seemed to know what to say. Kate leaned down and brushed the hair out of Tasha's face.

"Come here," Kate said. She scooped Tasha up and carried her. Kate could feel the small girl's beating heart through her shirt.

"What's with all the firepower?" Meg asked. "Those two goons with the mustaches keep looking at your butt, by the way."

"Wood's men," Kate replied. "With Central Command gone, he's pretty high up on the ladder now."

Riley's hand shifted toward the pistol he had tucked into his pants. His boyish features took on a hard cast.

"There," Meg said. She kept her crutches tucked under her armpits and pointed at the incoming helicopters.

"Daddy," Jenny chirped.

Wood, Jensen, Smith, and Valentine pushed past the crowd. Berg and Cooper followed them onto the tarmac.

Kate put Tasha on the ground and said, "Stay here, okay?"

Ellis took Jenny's and Tasha's hands, and Kate ran after Wood and his men. Halfway across the tarmac she saw Fitz and Apollo walking down a path leading from the beach. He flung his rifle over his shoulder as he continued toward the buildings.

Kate caught up to the group and stood next to Jensen. He nodded at her and gave his mustache a quick, nervous swipe as the choppers descended. A gust of wind pummeled the group a second later. Kate shielded her eyes, watching the troop holds anxiously. Kate smiled when she finally saw Beckham. He raised a hand and dropped it as the wheels connected with asphalt.

Beckham, Chow, and Horn jumped out of the first bird and turned to help a middle-aged woman who Kate assumed was Secretary Ringgold. Five civilians and an injured soldier poured out of the other bird. Her heart skipped when she saw Lombardi was not amongst them.

The pilots shut the Black Hawks down a moment later. Kate couldn't hold herself back any longer. She raced forward, ducking under the slowing blades, and wrapped her arms around Beckham. He kissed her on the cheek and then pulled from her grasp.

"Later," he whispered. "I need to know what the hell is going on. I heard that Central..." His voice trailed off as Wood approached.

"Welcome to Plum Island, Secretary Ringgold," Wood said, reaching out a hand. He didn't even look at Beckham or the other soldiers. "I'm Colonel Wood. I'm in charge of this facility."

"Thank you, Colonel," Ringgold said, shaking his hand. "You have no idea how happy I am to be here."

Wood waved two more of his soldiers away from the barriers. The men came running across the pavement. "And we're happy to have you. I'll make sure you have escorts at all times. My men will personally ensure your safety."

"I'd like an update. I've been trapped inside that tomb for far too long," she said. "What's the status of Central Command? I heard it was attacked."

"The Variants overran Command earlier today. I was there. Not many of us made it out."

"My God..." she said.

"It was a real tragedy," Wood replied with a rueful nod. "But the good news is that the first stage of Operation Extinction has been an overwhelming success."

"Operation Extinction?"

Wood ran a finger over his chin. "The operation to take back the country from the Variants. Our very own team of medical geniuses has designed a weapon that will be deployed all across the United States in the coming weeks."

He acknowledged Kate with a wave. Kate wasn't sure she understood him correctly and said, "*Just* the United States?"

Wood frowned slightly. "That's right, Doctor. As I was saying earlier, there's been a change of plans. We'll be deploying the weapon over our nation and select territories. I'm sure you understand. It's a matter of resources and priorities."

Kate thought of her parents, who could still be alive in Italy. "No, I don't understand, Colonel."

Wood addressed Secretary Ringgold as if Kate hadn't spoken. "My men will escort you to Building One, where you will find a hot shower, a change of clothes, and a meal waiting for you."

"Thank you, Colonel," Ringgold replied. She glanced over at Kate, her keen eyes questioning, before two Medical Corps soldiers led her away.

Wood turned on Kate. "Doctor, if you ever undermine me like that again..."

Beckham took a step forward and Wood froze, his eyes flicking to the operator. He seemed to think better of threatening Kate with Beckham standing between them.

"Lieutenant Colonel Jensen," Wood said, "I want you to load a chopper with half of the drugs and prepare them for a flight."

"A flight to where?" Jensen asked.

"That's classified," Wood said.

"I'm not sure I understand, sir."

"Did I ask you to understand, or did I order you to load that chopper?"

"Sir," Jensen said, "Operation Extinction was to be a worldwide effort. Am I correct in that understanding, sir?"

Wood glared at Jensen. "Rest assured, Lieutenant Colonel. The weapon will be deployed according to priority over cities in the United States and then our more rural areas. Now load—"

"What about our allies, sir?" Beckham asked.

"Did you not hear me earlier? They're on their own," Wood snapped. "What's wrong with you people? You sound like General Kennor. Did you really think that we would send help to someplace like North Korea or Iraq? This is our chance to end all wars. We'll wait until the enemy nations are overrun and *then* deploy the weapon."

"There are people there," Jensen said. "*Innocent* people. They aren't our enemies. The Variants are. The wars we were fighting with each other ended the day the hemorrhage virus got out of the fucking lab."

"A lab you helped run, isn't that right?" Kate asked in a sharp voice.

Wood shot her a venomous glare. "Cooper, Berg, escort the doctor back to her quarters. If she tries to resist, take her to a holding cell instead."

"Lay a hand on her and it's the last thing you do," Beckham growled.

Jensen shook his head. "This is all wrong. We're supposed to be saving people, not serving our own interests. When did you forget that, Wood? When did you become a monster?"

"I'm giving you a direct order," Wood said, his blue eyes like ice chips. "Load those choppers or you will be arrested and dealt with accordingly."

Jensen didn't budge. He spat a wad of tobacco on the ground and folded his arms across his chest. "You don't get to decide who lives and who dies."

"Wrong," Wood said. In a swift motion, he drew his pistol and fired two shots into Jensen's chest.

"No!" Beckham shouted. He pulled the strap of his rifle from his back and swung the muzzle toward Wood as Jensen crashed to the ground.

Major Smith dropped to his knees, yelling, "Jesus Christ! You shot him! You fucking shot him!"

Horn and Chow centered their guns on Berg and Cooper. The Medical Corps soldiers seemed just as surprised but they recovered quickly and aimed their own weapons at the operators. Between Valentine, Wood, and the twins, Beckham and his men were outnumbered.

"You son of a fucking bitch," Beckham said. He shifted his gaze from Wood to Jensen. The lieutenant colonel was bleeding out, blood gushing from his chest as Smith tried to apply pressure on the wounds.

"I would think very carefully about what you're doing right now, son," Wood said.

"I'm not your *son*," Beckham snarled. "Step down, Wood. Step down before we take you down."

Kate cupped her hand over her mouth as Berg and Cooper circled in. Four more Medical Corps soldiers came running from the post.

"Beckham, lower your weapon," Valentine said. "You don't want to do this."

"You're on the wrong side," Beckham said. "And I will give no quarter when the bullets start flying."

Jensen choked on his own blood, his chest heaving as he took in raspy, gurgling breaths. Kate wasn't an expert, but it sounded like he had a collapsed lung. If they didn't help him in the next few minutes, there was no way he'd make it.

"Get him a medic!" Beckham shouted.

Major Smith raised fingers slimy with blood and reached for his radio.

"You will do no such thing," Wood said. "Smith, you've done admirable work here, but your loyalty to your former CO will earn you nothing but a court-martial. Make the right choice now, and I can promise you'll go far. With Central gone, we need men like you in the upper ranks."

Smith froze, his eyes dancing from Beckham to Wood. For a moment, Smith seemed to consider Wood's offer, but then he lifted the radio.

Before he could speak, Valentine and the other six Medical Corps soldiers closed in. Kate watched in horror as they pointed their weapons at Smith and Beckham. The sudden crack of a rifle shot made them all flinch.

Wood's face disappeared in a spray of bone, blood, and teeth.

Beckham gently pushed Kate to the ground and dropped to a knee as Wood's body slumped to the asphalt. He raised his gun and fired at Berg in a blink of an eye. The rounds pierced the man's neck, and he fell, clutching his wounds. Scarlet blood poured through his fingers like a waterfall.

Kate's world slowed to an agonizing pace as all hell broke loose. Two more distant cracks sounded, and two more of Wood's men fell limply to the pavement. Screams of panic broke out from the crowd as the civilians ran for cover.

Valentine was firing wildly, not caring where he aimed. Two shots snagged Horn, sending him flying backward. Chow let out a scream and fired a burst of rounds into Valentine's gut. The sergeant fell to his knees, clutching his stomach and staring at Chow incredulously.

"You shot Big Horn, you son of a bitch!" Chow yelled as he put a bullet in Valentine's skull.

Another crack sounded in the distance and Cooper dropped, leaving only two of Wood's henchmen. One of them had centered his gun on Beckham before he was knocked to the ground by a blur of black and tan fur.

Apollo ripped out the man's jugular and then turned on the final guard. Chow took the man out with a shot between the eyes before the dog could get to him.

In less than twenty seconds, it was over. Kate rose to her feet, trembling as she surveyed the damage. Wood and all seven of his men lay in puddles of their own blood. The only one still twitching was the man Apollo had attacked.

Chow fired a three-round burst into the fallen man's body armor, painting the asphalt red.

"*Medic!* I need a fucking medic!" Smith yelled over and over again into the radio. He pushed down on Jensen's chest. "Lovato, you're a doctor! Get over here and help him."

Kate wasn't a medical doctor and didn't know how to explain that unless they got him to an emergency room, he wasn't going to make it. She could build weapons to take a billion lives, but she couldn't do anything to save Jensen from bleeding out in front of her. She rushed to his side nonetheless and did the only thing she could—she grabbed his hand to comfort him.

Distantly, she heard Reed shouting her name. She turned to see him fall to his knees beside Horn. Chow was already there, hand on the big operator's wrist. Blood blossomed across Horn's right bicep, but he seemed more shocked than hurt.

"I'm fine," he grunted, struggling to stand back up. He patted his flak jacket and then pressed a hand over the wound on his arm. Beckham hustled over and knelt by Jensen's side. He squeezed next to Kate and took over compressions from Major Smith, who slumped back onto the asphalt, his uniform stained up to the elbows with his commanding officer's blood.

"Hang in there, sir. We're going to get you help," Beckham said.

"Beckham," Jensen choked.

"I'm here."

"You have to…" Jensen coughed, blood gurgling at his lips.

"Sir, just hang on," Beckham said. He glanced up and yelled, "Where the fuck is that medic?"

Jensen fumbled with his holster and pulled his Colt .45. He didn't have the strength to lift it, and his hand flopped back onto the ground. "I want…I want you to have this."

Beckham looked down at the gun, and after a second of hesitation, he took it.

"I told you…She's my girl," Jensen said. "Take her. Defend the island. And make sure…" He gasped, choking as blood filled his lungs. When he spoke again, his once-powerful voice was barely a whisper. "Make sure Kryptonite gets deployed worldwide. Do the right thing. I know you will."

"I will, sir. I promise you," Beckham said.

By the time Dr. Hill arrived, Jensen was already dead, his dark eyes staring blankly at the sky.

Beckham slowly closed Jensen's eyes and then stood. Apollo, his snout still bloody, pressed against Beckham's leg. The dog let out a low, melancholy whine as if he understood what they had all just lost.

Beckham wanted to scream. He wanted to take Jensen's gun and unload it into Wood's corpse, but even that wouldn't make him feel better. Jensen hadn't just been a friend; he had been one of the only good officers left. Now they were leaderless, and for the first time in his life, Beckham wasn't sure what to do.

The sound of raised voices pulled Beckham's attention to the concrete barriers where the rest of Wood's men had gathered. The remaining marines from Bragg were already disarming the Medical Corps soldiers. Riley had his pistol aimed at a man on the ground. Meg was by his side, her knife drawn and one of her crutches pushed down on the fallen soldier's neck. The only member of Beckham's team missing was Fitz.

He realized then it was Fitz who had saved their lives. Only he could have nailed those head shots. He saw Fitz rushing over to aid Riley and the other men who had been loyal to Jensen.

Beckham looked down at Jensen. "Doctor Hill, get us a stretcher. I don't want to leave him out here like this."

"My God," Hill said, looking at the other bodies. "What do we do with them?"

"For now, we leave Wood and his men here. I'll bury the bastard in an unmarked grave next to Gibson. They can spend the rest of eternity rotting together," Beckham said.

Hill nodded, radioed for a stretcher, and then ran toward the buildings with Smith. Beckham rose to his feet and looked for Kate. She was checking Horn's arm.

"Keep pressure on the wound," Kate said.

"I know the routine," Horn said. "I better get to my girls."

"I'll go too," Chow said.

The men took off at a trot, leaving Beckham alone with Kate. He grabbed her hand and pulled her toward him.

"I'm sorry," Kate said. "I'm so sorry, Reed."

Beckham shook his head and looked toward the

horizon. He'd gotten his revenge on Wood and his men, but it did nothing to relieve the pain of losing Jensen.

They stood there in silence, Kate's hand in his. Seconds turned into minutes as neither of them moved.

"What happens now?" Kate finally whispered.

Beckham stared into the dark sky, watching a cloud drift across an ocean of flickering stars. "We get Kryptonite ready and send it over every corner of the goddamn earth."

Kate rested her head on his shoulder. "And after that?"

"We keep fighting," he said. "And we never stop.

If you want to hear more about Nicholas Sansbury Smith's upcoming books, join his newsletter or follow him on social media. He just might keep you from the brink of extinction!

Newsletter: www.eepurl.com/bggNg9

Twitter: www.twitter.com/greatwaveink

Facebook: www.facebook.com /Nicholas-Sansbury-Smith-124009881117534

Website: www.nicholassansbury.com

For those who'd like to personally contact Nicholas, he would love to hear from you.

Greatwaveink@gmail.com

Acknowledgments

It's always hard for me to write this section for fear of leaving someone out. So many people had a hand in the creation of the Extinction Cycle and I know these stories would not be worth reading if I didn't have the overwhelming support of family, friends, and readers.

Before I thank those people, I wanted to give a bit of background on how the Extinction Cycle was conceived and the journey it has been on since I started writing. The story began more than five years ago, when I was still working as a planner for the state of Iowa and also during my time as a project officer for Iowa Homeland Security and Emergency Management. I had several duties throughout my tenure with the state, but my primary focus was protecting infrastructure and working on the state hazard mitigation plan. After several years of working in the disaster mitigation field, I learned of countless threats: from natural disasters to man-made weapons, and one of the most horrifying threats of all—a lab-created biological weapon.

Fast-forward to 2014, when my writing career started to take off. I was working on the Orbs series and brainstorming my next science fiction adventure. Back then, the genre was saturated with zombie books. I wanted to write something unique and different, a story that explained, scientifically, how a virus could turn men into monsters. During this time, the Ebola virus was raging through western Africa and several cases showed up in the continental United States for the first time.

After talking with my biomedical-engineer friend, Tony Melchiorri, an idea formed for a book that played on the risk the Ebola virus posed. That idea blossomed after I started researching chemical and biological weapons, many of which dated back to the Cold War. In March of 2014, I sat down to pen the first pages of *Extinction Horizon*, the first book in what would become the Extinction Cycle. Using real science and the terrifying premise of a government-made bioweapon I set out to tell my story.

The Extinction Cycle quickly found an audience. The first three novels came out in rapid succession and seemed to spark life back into the zombie craze. The audiobook, narrated by the award-winning Bronson Pinchot, climbed the charts, hitting the top spot on Audible. As I released books four and five, more readers discovered the Extinction Cycle—more than three hundred thousand to date. The German translation was recently released in November 2016 and Amazon's Kindle Worlds has opened the Extinction universe to other authors.

Even more exciting, two years after I published *Extinction Horizon*, Orbit decided to purchase and rerelease the series. The copy you are reading is the newly edited and polished version. I hope you've enjoyed it.

The Extinction Cycle wouldn't exist without the help of a small army of editors, beta readers, and the support of my family and friends. I also owe a great deal of gratitude to my initial editors, Aaron Sikes and Erin Elizabeth Long, as well as my good author-friend Tony

Melchiorri. The trio spent countless hours on the Extinction Cycle books. Without them these stories would not be what they are. Erin also helped edit *Orbs* and *Hell Divers*. She's been with me pretty much since day one, and I appreciate her more than she knows. So, thanks, Erin, Tony, and Aaron.

A special thanks goes to David Fugate, my agent, who provided valuable feedback on the early version of *Extinction Horizon* and the entire Extinction Cycle series. I'm grateful for his support and guidance.

Another special thanks goes to Blackstone Audio for their support of the audio version. Narrator Bronson Pinchot also played, and continues to play, a vital role in bringing the story to life.

I'm also extremely honored for the support I have received from the military community over the course of the series. I've heard from countless veterans, many of them wounded warriors who grew to love Corporal Joe Fitzpatrick and Team Ghost. I even heard from a few Delta Force operators. Many of these readers went on to serve as beta readers, and I'm forever grateful for their support and feedback.

They say a person is only as good as those that they surround themselves with. I've been fortunate to surround myself with talented people much smarter than myself. I've also had the support from excellent publishers like Blackstone and Orbit.

I would be remiss if I didn't also thank the people for whom I write: the readers. I've been blessed to have my work read in countries around the world by wonderful people. If you are reading this, know that I truly appreciate you for trying my stories.

To my family, friends, and everyone else who has supported me on this journey, I thank you.

extras

orbit

meet the author

Maria Diaz

NICHOLAS SANSBURY SMITH is the *USA Today* best-selling author of *Hell Divers*, the Orbs trilogy, and the Extinction Cycle. He worked for Iowa Homeland Security and Emergency Management in disaster mitigation before switching careers to focus on his one true passion: writing. When he isn't writing or daydreaming about the apocalypse, he enjoys running, biking, spending time with his family, and traveling the world. He is an Ironman triathlete and lives in Iowa with his fiancée, their dogs, and a houseful of books.

if you enjoyed

EXTINCTION AGE

look out for

EXTINCTION EVOLUTION

The Extinction Cycle

by

Nicholas Sansbury Smith

There's a storm on the horizon....

Central Command is gone, the military is fractured, and the surviving members of Team Ghost, led by Master Sergeant Reed Beckham, have been pushed to the breaking point.

Betrayed by the country they swore to defend and surrounded by enemies on all sides, Team Ghost has one mission left: protect Dr. Kate Lovato and Dr. Pat Ellis while they develop a weapon to defeat the Variants once and for all. But after a grisly discovery in Atlanta, Lovato and Ellis realize their weapon might not be able to stop the evolution of the monsters.

*Joined by unexpected allies and facing a new threat none
of them saw coming, the survivors are running out of
time to save the human race from extinction.*

The divine glow of a brilliant sunrise crept across Plum
Island. On the walkway outside Building 5, twelve
Medical Corps soldiers in black fatigues knelt with their
hands tied behind their backs. Master Sergeant Reed
Beckham walked the line and stopped to point the barrel
of Lieutenant Colonel Jensen's .45 at the bowed head of
the closest soldier.

Beckham didn't know the man's name—hell, he
didn't even know his rank—but he was one of the late
Colonel Wood's henchmen. It seemed only fitting Jensen's gun should kill them.

The soldier glanced up, his long chin wobbling.
"Please. Please don't shoot me. I was just following
orders."

Beckham resisted the urge to pistol-whip the man
right then and there. If he had a bullet for every soldier
who had used that line, he would have enough ammo
to kill every Variant left in New York. Beckham had
helped disarm more than one hundred Iraqi troops during the fall of Baghdad twelve years ago, and they'd all
used that same line. It didn't excuse them from sectarian
violence or killing Kurdish women and children.

These men were soldiers, but even soldiers had a
choice. The Nazis had a choice. The Taliban had a
choice. Osama bin Laden's men had a choice. When shit
hit the fan, there was always a choice. Beckham had broken orders in Niantic to save a stranded family, and he'd
done so again when he killed Colonel Wood's men the
night before.

"I say we drop them off in New York City and let the Variants have at 'em," Staff Sergeant Horn said with a snort. "Although that would be a waste of fuel." The Delta Force operator's right bicep was still dripping blood, but he didn't seem to notice the pain. His eyes blazed. Corporal Fitzpatrick and Staff Sergeant Chow flanked him, their rifles all aimed at the Medical Corps prisoners.

Major Smith was there too, his arms crossed, supervising the scene. With the state of the world, Smith had elected to give Beckham free rein to deal with Wood's soldiers however he saw fit. He hadn't done so without objecting, though, and his final words on the matter rang in Beckham's mind: "*It may be their funeral, but it'll be your conscience.*"

On the lawn behind Beckham stood a team of Army Rangers and marines. Fourteen battle-hardened men, all stationed at Plum Island since the early days of the outbreak. Staff Sergeant Riley sat in his wheelchair next to Meg Pratt, the firefighter they'd rescued from New York. She was propped up on crutches. It felt good to have a small army at his back, but the longer Beckham listened to the sound of the crowd, the more he realized how fucked things really were.

"Kill them," one of the marines barked.

"Shoot 'em!" yelled another.

Beckham was still fuming from Lieutenant Colonel Jensen's death the night before, but this wasn't right. His men were better than this. They weren't executioners. Civilization was gone, but Beckham wasn't going to let justice go with it.

"Get up," Beckham said. He motioned with the muzzle of Jensen's .45.

The Medical Corps soldier struggled to his feet. He squinted in the morning sun, his youthful features scrunching together. He couldn't be more than twenty years old.

"What's your name, son?" Beckham asked.

"Keith," he replied, his chin still wobbling. "Keith Sizemore. I'm sorry, Master Sergeant. I'm sorry about Colonel Wood. I didn't know..."

"Shut the hell up, Sizemore," one of the other prisoners said. Beckham strode over to the man, a sergeant named Gallagher according to his uniform. He was the highest-ranking soldier of the group.

Beckham grabbed him under the arm and jammed his .45 into the man's back. "On your feet, Sergeant."

"Tough guy with a gun," Gallagher said. "Once they find out what you did to Colonel Wood, you're all going to wish you were dead. They're going to send an army after you fucking traitors."

The door to Building 5 creaked open. Dr. Kate Lovato and Dr. Pat Ellis stepped out onto the landing. Kate gave Beckham a critical look and slowly shook her head. The simple act washed away whatever bloodlust was still swirling inside Beckham. He took in a breath and holstered his .45. Then he pulled his knife and cut the ties binding the sergeant's wrists.

"What the..." Gallagher said.

"No gun," Beckham said. He sheathed the blade and added, "No knife. Just me...and you."

Gallagher's cocky smile revealed a mouthful of crooked teeth. He massaged his wrists in turn, then balled his hands into fists. In two swift motions, he planted a boot and threw a punch that sailed past Beckham's right eye.

Beckham hardly had the chance to move out of the way. Gallagher grunted, regained his balance, and swung again. He was fast, but Beckham was more agile. He grabbed the sergeant's arm, twisted it, and shoved him. Gallagher crashed to the grass.

"Take him, boss!" Riley shouted.

"Son of a bitch!" Gallagher yelled. He spat, wiped his lips with a sleeve, and pushed himself to his feet. As soon as he was standing, he launched another fist.

This time Beckham pivoted to the right, but Gallagher's fist still whizzed by his chin. By habit, Beckham stepped back, planted his left boot, stepped forward with his right, and used all the forward momentum to throw a punch that connected with the side of the sergeant's left cheek.

A bone-shattering crunch sounded over the shouts of the marines and Rangers. Blood exploded from Gallagher's mouth, a crooked tooth flying out in the mist. He spun and crashed face first to the ground.

Gallagher crawled a few feet before collapsing to his stomach. There was a moment of complete silence, broken only by the chirp of a bird in the distance.

"Anyone else still loyal to Colonel Wood?" Beckham asked.

Not a single one of the Medical Corps soldiers said a word.

"Good, because I'm going to make this really simple. You're either with us, or you're against us. This is the apocalypse. Things don't work the way they used to, but we all still have a choice. And I'm offering you all a very simple one—either join us, or my friend Big Horn will give you a ride to New York and you can fight the Variants on your own." After a pause to let the prisoners digest his words, he said, "Any questions?"

if you enjoyed

EXTINCTION AGE

look out for

THE REMAINING

by

D. J. Molles

In a steel-and-lead-encased bunker, a Special Forces soldier waits on his final orders.

On the surface a bacterium has turned 90 percent of the population into hyperaggressive predators.

Now Captain Lee Harden must leave the bunker and venture into the wasteland to rekindle a shattered America.

At 1215 hours he stopped running.

The last few miles were mentally excruciating, and several times he caught himself looking over at the computer. It was past the forty-eight-hour mark. He should be reading the mission packet. Every minute that went by he told himself to wait and give Frank a chance to call. At fifteen after, he realized if he waited any longer, he would be deliberately disobeying his standing orders.

He stepped off the treadmill and took another bottle of water from the fridge, then looped around the couch to his computer and sat down. In the time it had taken him to move to his desk, he had become painfully curious about what information the mission packet held.

He placed his thumb on the small black square on top of the box and, after a brief moment, heard the lock click open. He lifted the lid and looked inside. He had never opened his mission box before. This was a first.

The contents were underwhelming. Just a black thumb drive. He plugged it into his computer and let it load. The program it contained took the liberty of running itself. It was a program he had seen before when completing online training courses. It allowed the user to click through screens like a PowerPoint, but it was also narrated and contained bits of video.

The first thing he heard was Frank's voice.

For a moment he let himself believe Frank had called. He felt a moment of levity, then a flash of anger for being left in The Hole for so long without contact. But the voice was only a recording. Lee noted that Frank sounded relaxed. Not at all concerned. Just going through the motions.

It was at that moment that the knot returned to Lee's stomach.

"This is Colonel Frank Reid on behalf of the Office of the Secretary of Homeland Security in regard to Project Hometown and to all operatives therewith involved. Your mission has begun."

The screen displayed the seal of the Department of the Army, which faded to a map of the continental United States.

"What you will be dealing with topside is what our scientists are calling Febrile Urocanic Reactive Yersinia, or FURY for short. It is a mutated form of *Y. Pestis*, which was the cause of the bubonic plague and nearly every other European plague for the last four hundred years. Because it is a bacteria and not a virus, our experts are unsure of how it transmits from one person to the next; however, the plague has already shown an extreme propensity for contagion. Full Personal Protective Equipment is advised when in contact with infected or possibly infected individuals, and full decontamination afterward."

Four dots appeared on the map, one each in New York, Florida, Illinois, and California.

"We do not have a Patient Zero at this time. However, we can infer that the plague is from a source outside the country, due to the first cases in the United States being centered on our largest international airports in New York City, Chicago, Miami, and Los Angeles.

"From the research we have available at this time— June fourteenth—the prodromal stage symptoms of infection are fever, shaking or trembling, overt salivation, diarrhea, extreme hunger and thirst, rash on the torso or trunk of the body, projectile vomiting, some loss of fine motor skills, difficulty speaking, and sleeplessness. As the plague progresses into the illness stage, symptoms include complete loss of speech and understanding, pallor, hallucinations, loss of sensation, hyperaggression, uncontrollable screaming or yelling, and insatiable appetite—which we've seen result in the patient attempting to feed on their own limbs or on anyone within arm's reach.

"During the late illness stage, the patient will often go into a stupor, walk with an unsteady gait, and display slow reaction time. Respiratory rate declines, and in several cases, blindness has occurred. Not every patient will display all of these symptoms. In certain cases we have observed little to no aggression in the patient, except in cases of hallucinations; however, these are the exception and not the rule.

"The plague acts by infecting the cells of the body and quickly multiplying within the lymph nodes. The bacteria then causes the catabolic breakdown of urocanic acid and spreads to the brain and nervous system, causing hemorrhaging in the frontal cortex of the brain, which stimulates aggression, hunger, and thirst and suppresses the patient's instincts for self-preservation. It also affects cells of the thalamus and cerebral cortex that perceive pain, making patients unresponsive to painful stimuli. The bacterium appears to eat through brain tissue quite selectively, leaving primary biological functions intact, such as heart rate and respiration.

"Our main concerns with FURY, and the reason you are sitting in your bunker right now, are the incubation period and the fatality rate. As far as we have been able to determine, the bacteria will lie dormant for between twenty-four and forty-eight hours before symptoms even begin to show. In addition to that, we have failed to find a single instance of an infected patient actually dying from the plague. It appears that after the late illness stage, the patient's vital signs regulate themselves, and the fever will drop off, but the damage to the brain is done. This makes the likelihood of a wait-it-out strategy very limited in its chances for success. It does not look like the plague will burn itself out, but will likely go pandemic if initial attempts to contain it fail."

The red dots around the four largest airports began to trickle outward. Dots appeared at the locations of other, smaller international airports throughout the country and spread from there. The map looked like a piece of paper soaking through with blood.

"According to calculations, if initial attempts to contain the plague fail, the probability of containing all infected persons is essentially zero, as they are infected for up to two days without showing symptoms. During this asymptomatic time period, they are extremely contagious. We must assume that we will be unable to stop this threat before it affects the entire population."

Lee leaned forward in his chair and cupped his hands around his face. He found himself breathing heavily and his heart beating a step faster.

Probability of containment: zero.

"Operating as always under the assumption that we will be dealing with the Worst-Case Scenario, we set the survival rate at 9 percent, at least within the continental United States. In addition to the lives taken by FURY, there will be widespread rioting and looting, which will lead to more casualties. WCS, we are looking at a complete governmental collapse due to the plague. The power vacuum created by the fall of the institutional United States government will be huge, and there are many crazy people inside our borders who will be more than willing to take control and kill anyone who opposes, should they survive the plague. If WCS occurs, you will be fighting a war on several fronts. You will need to protect yourself and your group from infection, you will need to protect them also from the violent tendencies of those who have already been infected, and you will need to outmaneuver the warlords who will be popping up across the country.

"Tactically speaking, you will need to keep yourself on constant quarantine. No physical contact with anyone at any time. Immediately decontaminate if you are exposed to physical contact with anyone. Prepare your own food and do not share others' food or water. Wear PPE at all times when in the presence of others, particularly if you have reason to believe they are infected. There is no known cure at this time, so attempting aid to the infected will be a fruitless endeavor.

"Again, be aware that due to decreased mental functioning, some infected persons will be unable to speak, and most will not be able to reason. Do not attempt to speak with infected persons. If an infected person attacks you, attempt to gain distance. Use firearms to dispatch hostile infected persons and avoid hand-to-hand combat if at all possible. When engaging infected persons, you will find that due to brain impairment, they don't go down easily. We have many reports from police departments and municipal authorities around the country describing the infected individuals as overcoming apparently mortal bullet wounds and continuing to attack. Bring plenty of ammunition that packs a stopping punch.

"Also keep in mind that even though they have impaired mental functioning, the infected subjects are still human and still have some vestiges of basic predatory instinct. They can even prove to be clever, especially in the early stages of infection before it begins to affect their motor skills."

Lee's stomach soured. Was he being told to kill United States citizens because they were sick? Why not hospitalize them and attempt to find a cure? Yes, they were violent, but so were millions of mental patients around the country, and we didn't go around shooting them in the head.

"This concludes the brief for Project Hometown regarding Febrile Urocanic Reactive Yersinia. Gentlemen, you are all that is left of the United States government. Good luck."

Frank's voice was rote. Just reading a script that some scientists had put together.

At the time he'd recorded this message, just prior to Lee's restriction in his bunker, Frank clearly hadn't believed it himself. Just more nonsense from the Washington Worrywarts. They always believed the Worst-Case Scenario was right around the corner.

"Fuck..." Lee whispered. The screen once again faded to the seal of the United States Army. Lee stared at the screen. He sat motionless, except for the rapid pulsing of his carotid artery. In his mind, he had an image of himself taking out the thumb drive and throwing it against the wall, then stomping it into pieces. Losing control.

But instead, he leaned forward and removed the thumb drive from his computer, moving as though stuck in a tar pit. He placed the thumb drive back in the black box it had come from. He didn't close the lid. He wanted something to remind him that forty-eight hours had gone by, that he had already opened the mission packet and watched the briefing. A part of him hoped that perhaps he would wake up the next morning and find the box closed again. Then he would realize none of this had ever happened.

A fleeting, pathetic thought.

He stood up from his computer chair and looked at the sealed hatch to the outside world and the plaque that hung above it.

THE ONLY EASY DAY WAS YESTERDAY.

Thank you, Navy SEALs. One of his instructors had been a Navy SEAL, as the Coordinators received cross-instruction from several different Special Ops communities. They never received a Ranger tab, or a trident, or any other marker that designated them as Special Forces. But what they received was a vast knowledge of tactics and strategies and, most of all, a drive that never quit. Master Chief Reynolds had successfully beaten every ounce of quit out of the entire group of Coordinators and that was his favorite phrase: *The only easy day was yesterday.*

He thought about the other Coordinators stationed across the country. The last he'd seen any of them was in late January when they had their annual get-together to catch up and drink too much.

Standing orders included that they never communicate with one another while on restriction inside their bunkers. Lee had never tried, but as far as he could tell, there was nothing to stop him. He looked at the bottom of the computer screen and saw that the Internet connection appeared to still be in good working order. Surely one of the others could tell him that this was all a mistake and that Frank had contacted them and there was no violent insanity pandemic sweeping the nation.

He sat back down and opened his e-mail account and found that it appeared to be working fine. He typed in the e-mail address of his closest friend, Captain Abe Darabie. His message was short:

You hear anything from Frank?

He left out the fact that he had already passed the forty-eight-hour mark and had opened the mission packet. He considered the message for a moment. If this was all a big mistake, he would be written up for violating directives. If it wasn't a big mistake, who gave a shit about directives? And Lee had to know. He needed someone else to tell him this was real, because sitting by himself made it seem like he was just going crazy.

He clicked send. It almost solidified in his mind the concept that all of this was real. Almost. It was too big to just accept. He needed something more than a forty-eight-hour lapse in communication to make him believe that the United States of America had ceased to exist in a matter of three weeks. He waited at his computer for a long moment, then realized that Abe was probably not sitting at *his* computer, waiting for e-mails. He stood up and walked to the kitchen. He eyed the contents of his refrigerator, paying close attention to the case of Coors Light bottles. He decided now was as good a time as any to have a beer. After all, it was the Fourth of July.

As he twisted off the cap, he heard a tone from his computer.

He sprinted across the den area to his computer and sat in his chair, the beer forgotten. He put it down on the desk so hard it fizzed and overflowed, but he barely took notice.

Abe apparently had been waiting for e-mails.

Neg on coms with Frank. I'm at forty-eight hours... did you open your box?

Lee thought about it for a moment. There was no harm in admitting that he had. In fact, all the Coordinators probably had. He responded:

Yeah, I opened mine. Is this for real?

He clicked send, then waited. He took a nervous sip from his beer after the head had gone down. Cold drips fell from the bottle onto his bare chest. He ignored them. The reply came after about a minute.

I hope not... proly shouldn't be talking... just keep your head down and wait for them to cancel us... I'm sure they will.

Lee read the message three times. Abe's confidence that it would all blow over eased the jittery feeling in Lee's gut. Although they were equal rank, Abe had more time on and more combat experience than Lee. Though Lee had done time as a Ranger in Iraq in '03 and '04, Abe had served as a Delta operative for five years in Afghanistan before being looped into Project Hometown. Most of the Coordinators regarded him as their de facto leader.

Lee didn't respond to the message. He took his beer and left the computer.

Lee spent the remainder of the day watching a couple movies because he didn't know what else to do. He went through several beers and carefully lined the bottles in a row on the end table. At 1650 hours the second movie ended and he realized he was hungry.

It was the Fourth of July, so he opened another beer and decided to grill up two porterhouse steaks that he had defrosted in anticipation of being locked in The Hole on Independence Day. He couldn't grill them outside, so he cooked them in a pan. He cut the bone off one and gave it to Tango, who was waiting ever so patiently at Lee's side. Tango made quick work of twenty-two ounces of meat while Lee took his time enjoying it.

At 1815 hours Lee was on beer ten and, in a rush of alcohol-fueled energy, decided more push-ups, sit-ups, and pull-ups were in order. After these he felt better in general. He felt pumped up and ready.

At 2000 hours Lee attempted to log on to redtube .com but found the server was down. He cursed himself for not bringing adult DVDs with him.

At 2030 hours he was on beer twelve and staring at the computer, willing Frank to call and tell him it was over. He would look like shit, unshaven, half dressed, and obviously drunk, but who cared? He was in a damn bunker.

At 2100 hours he decided to switch to water to avoid a bad headache. He moved to the couch and decided to try his hand at the video game console he had purchased but never played. He fumbled with the controls for a few hours before passing out on the couch, the game still running. On the screen, his video game warrior stood stoically in one spot while he was assaulted from all angles by a horde of enemies.

Eventually, the warrior collapsed and died.